Llyfrgelloedd Caerdydd
www.caerdydd.gov.uk/llyfrgelloedd
Cardiff Libraries
www.cardiff.gov.uk/libraries

KU-050-827

ACC. No: 02470192

GIVE ME TOMORROW

Grocer's daughter Eveline Fenton's life changes forever when she's caught up in a suffragette march in the summer of 1909. She meets Constance Mornington, whose father is a wealthy Harley Street doctor, and despite their differing backgrounds they form a lifelong friendship. The girls do not conform to their parents' expectations – Connie is expected to marry well, but she falls in love with a lowly bank clerk and is forced to choose between him and her family, while Eveline is attracted to a gentleman she meets at a suffragette meeting – but is Laurence Jones-Fairbrook merely dallying with her affections?

GIVE ME TOMORROW

GIVE ME TOMORROW

by

Elizabeth Lord

Magna Large Print Books
Long Preston, North Yorkshire,
BD23 4ND, England.

British Library Cataloguing in Publication Data.

Lord, Elizabeth
    Give me tomorrow.

        A catalogue record of this book is
        available from the British Library

        ISBN   978-0-7505-2718-7

First published in Great Britain in 2006 by Piatkus Books Ltd.

Copyright © 2006 Elizabeth Lord

Cover illustration © Rod Ashford

The moral right of the author has been asserted

Published in Large Print 2007 by arrangement with
Piatkus Books Ltd.

All Rights reserved. No part of this publication may be reproduced,
stored in a retrieval system, or transmitted in any form or by any
means, electronic, mechanical, photocopying, recording or otherwise
without the prior permission of the Copyright owner.

Magna Large Print is an imprint of Library Magna Books Ltd.

Printed and bound in Great Britain by
T.J. (International) Ltd., Cornwall, PL28 8RW

All the characters in this book are fictitious and any resemblance to real persons, living or dead, is entirely coincidental.

To my good friend Beryl Meadows with thanks
for her valuable advice on the suffragette
movement and women's fight for their right
to vote during the early 1900s.

And to my two daughters who can now do so.

Chapter One

The buzz of Oxford Street's Saturday-afternoon shoppers had begun to be disrupted by the regular beat of a drum. Eveline Fenton glanced in the direction of voices raised in song, one strident voice, hollowed and amplified by a megaphone, repeating a familiar, rhythmic doggerel:

'Votes for women! Justice for women! Give women the right to vote!'

Heads turned. Some faces creased into expectant grins, others into frowns. Despite these women keeping to the kerb, traffic could be disrupted in which case the police would come down like a ton of bricks. A few truncheons would be raised, a few helmets knocked off, a few militants bundled kicking, flailing and screeching into a police wagon. One or two ladies' large hats would be trampled underfoot, carefully piled hair coming loose to hang in unsightly strands; perhaps even a sleeve or two would get ripped in the fray, womanhood being shown up – a good reason for leers and frowns according to popular opinion.

Once the wagon had driven off with its load to the lock-up, the rest would disperse to lick their wounds and plan another march, sure of eventual success in persuading a Liberal government to grant women the vote. When that would be was anyone's guess. Not this side of 1909, not for years, if ever. Even those massive rallies at the

11

Albert Hall and in Hyde Park last year had made no impact whatsoever on politicians. Still, one had to admire their tenacity.

Eveline certainly did, though until a moment ago her mind had been on a tea gown tastefully displayed in one of Selfridge's huge windows – white mousseline with silver lace and ribbons. She had been imagining how it would show off her dark brown hair and her slim figure with its eighteen-inch waist – the same in inches as she had in years. The gown was of course well beyond her pocket, costing all of four weeks of her pay, but she could still dream.

The American-style multiple store with its breathtaking displays, newly opened last Monday the fifteenth of March, was busy. So many ladies were pulling their menfolk to a halt to gape at the clothes that she'd had to squeeze sideways through them all for a better view, being jostled on all sides until, like everyone else, she was distracted by the drumbeat, the singing and the loud hailer.

They came on, a dozen women, striding out in single file, hugging the kerb – using the pavement could mean being arrested for obstruction, Heads up, they walked with a confident step, skirts swinging heavily about their boots muddy from the gutter still wet from last night's rain.

All held placards, several with the wording WSPU HAMMERSMITH BRANCH, displaying purple irises, hammers and horseshoes, others with the inscription DEEDS NOT WORDS. The large, well-made hats and several coats with astrakhan collars and cuffs proclaimed the wearers to be middle class with time on their hands. Working-class women with husbands and children had little opportunity to go on marches or even to stand on street corners selling Women's Social and Political Union newssheets.

Eveline didn't consider herself exactly working class, and certainly not poverty-stricken despite living in the poorer East End of London. True, she worked, as did her brother Len Junior, but Dad had a shop in Three Colts Lane, a general grocer's selling anything, from bootlaces, butter, tinned goods, dried goods like sugar, peas and rice, all loose in sacks, to candles, firelighters, gas mantles, and paraffin in kegs with taps for pouring it. Mum helped behind the counter while her other daughter May, who didn't work, was happy to be Mum's unpaid housekeeper. Making a modest living, two apart from Dad in a family of eight also bringing in wages, they didn't do badly, though not so that she could fritter money away on some fine dress in Selfridge's window.

Eveline watched the marching women as they came abreast of her. Dad was dead against them. 'Lot of blooming nonsensical females,' he called them, his walrus moustache bristling. 'Ain't got nothing better ter do but stirring up a lot of blooming trouble.'

He never swore at home, and respected female sensitivity, but still brooked no contradiction. He was the breadwinner working all hours God sent in his shop a few yards from Bethnal Green railway station and saw his family as having enough to do without bothering with politics and female dissension. A woman wouldn't know what to do

13

with a vote anyway, if she got one. That was what Eveline too had thought until last summer had helped to change her mind,

Eveline and her workmate, Ada Williams, had wandered off on that Saturday in June to watch a huge procession of suffragettes from every part of the country make their way to the Albert Hall. On the Embankment beside the Thames the parade had taken over two hours to pass in a continuous river of colour and music. She'd been so awed that the following Sunday she persuaded Ada to go with her to Hyde Park to see a similar rally.

In the bright warm sunshine it was a sight for sore eyes with seven separate processions marching into the park, carrying hundreds of coloured banners to the accompaniment of stirring music; nearly eight hundred women stood on twenty platforms and thousands of milling onlookers enjoyed it all, though Ada hadn't been all that impressed, apart from relishing the spectacle.

'All very well fer them what's got time to mess about,' she'd said, wrinkling her thin nose. 'But the likes of us 'ave got ter work for a living.'

'They are right though,' Eveline argued. 'Some women can't stand up for themselves, they need people with a voice.'

Ada had shrugged again. 'You try taking time off work to go off ter meetings. And fluttering yer pretty eyes at that leering old Mr Prentice won't 'elp.' Ada, plain as a stick, was always on about her being pretty. 'No boss is going ter give you 'alf a day off work just when you want. You'll be out on your ear fast as love against a wall, even if old Prentice do fancy yer.'

14

Her office manager would leer at her, if he got the chance would lean over her, hot hands on her shoulders, to see if her sums added up correctly. She'd tried pushing him away but it wasn't easy. He was her boss. If ruffled he could find an excuse to sack her.

'Where will yer votes fer women be then? And yer dad wouldn't 'alf 'ave something to say.'

Ada was right, but one speaker had made her think when she described women refused a say in their own destinies, downtrodden at home, poorly paid at work; they had no voice, nor, along with convicts and lunatics, were they allowed to vote – the first time she'd heard it stressed that way. Realising her own little worth, it had made her angry. It still made her angry whenever she thought of it but she'd put it aside in the flurry of becoming eighteen with lots of friends and things to do. Now, this afternoon, as this small column of women with their placards and their single drum drew abreast of her, the anger came flooding back.

Though it was not a particularly impressive procession, Eveline's spirits rose at the defiant clump of their feet striding out in step to their song, eyes unflinching before the derisive taunts of some male bystanders. As they passed something made her want to keep up with them for a little while at least. But moments later, without quite realising why, she had stepped off the pavement to fall in alongside the last person in the procession. Hazel eyes glanced at her from below an enormous hat and smiled. 'Thank you for joining us,' she said, taking Eveline's hand in such a friendly way that even if Eveline had intended to leave she couldn't

15

decently have done so now.

Fortunately no police interfered. One constable was walking alongside just in case of trouble from bystanders, but there was none, just one or two catcalls or the odd remark, 'Go back to your kitchen!' Often Eveline could hear ragged clapping, no one showing any real belligerence. The owner of the megaphone was now announcing: *'There is a meeting at Ambrose Hall – two thirty this afternoon! Come and listen to our brave and talented speaker Mrs Annie Kenney! All ladies welcome – men too!'*

The marchers were dressed for March weather, not like at the huge June rallies with white dresses and red sashes, or the green, white and purple of the suffragette's adopted colours. Warm coats and hats kept in place by veils were the order of the day for this little band.

Despite her own warm, half-length coat over an equally warm skirt, Eveline couldn't help feeling a little shabby beside her new companion's fashionable tweed coat with embroidered collar and cuffs. Against that large-crowned hat with its satin bows and silk roses perched sedately on a mass of hair like an enormous mushroom, hers struck her as small and drab even with its wide brim and brave ring of flowers and leaves.

The girl, just an inch taller than her own five foot five, had an arm now firmly linked through hers; it seemed that having secured a new recruit she had every intention of keeping her. Such familiarity should have put Eveline off, yet it didn't. The drum's steady beat and the singing brought a sense of exhilaration as the procession

16

turned off Oxford Street into a side road.

Converging on a stone building were streams of other women, some having marched there from different directions, others just coming along in small groups. There were even a few men. Surrounded on all sides as they reached the building, Eveline and her captor mounted the worn steps.

'I do so enjoy these meetings,' said the young woman, her arm still tucked through hers. 'I'm sure you will too. They're wonderfully interesting. I try not to miss any if possible.'

Eveline couldn't help but smile as she was led inside. This girl had never had to sit at a desk from eight in the morning until six at night, five days a week and half day on Saturday, adding up figures on a comptometer behind a glass partition above where the factory workers stood packing biscuits on a moving belt. They were allowed a half-hour midday break and five minutes mid-morning and mid-afternoon to visit the toilet. At least she as office staff could visit whenever she had to, though she still had to ask permission from Mr Prentice, the office manager. She could bet her Sunday best that this girl had no idea how the other half lived.

Entering with the crowds, Eveline wondered how this girl filled her day other than by attending her precious Women's Social and Political Union meetings and going on marches and rallies? It didn't matter. What mattered was to stay close to her and not to lose her or she would really feel like a fish out of water, not having intended to come here in the first place.

The meeting hall was large and windowless

17

though it was well lit. It smelled of dust, musty books and mildew and the stage curtains had aged to a streaked, nondescript brown and hung limp and uneven. The backdrop meant to depict some sort of garden scene was so faded as to be hardly distinguishable as such. On the stage were three chairs and a table. Two ladies still with their large hats balanced on their piled-up coiffures were arranging carafes of water and sheets of paper, giving the impression of lengthy speeches to come – lengthy and boring suspected Eveline. She chewed her lip. Why hadn't she pulled away from the girl at the very first, made her excuses and hurried away? Too late now.

The place, already three-quarters full, hummed with animated voices, news being swapped, recognition of acquaintances from other meetings. It made her feel isolated, her earlier enthusiasm dissipating. Her temporary companion was conducting her towards two vacant seats several rows from the front. She began exchanging greetings with a woman already seated next to them, whom she obviously knew. Feeling oddly neglected and forgotten, Eveline sat down, quietly preparing to keep herself to herself and suffer it until the blessed end gave her a chance of escape.

Her fair-haired companion turned to her, her voice animated. 'By the way, I'm Constance Mornington. I'm usually called Connie. Only my parents use my full name. They're awfully strait-laced.'

'My name's Eveline Fenton,' Eveline offered, relieved to be included in things again as Connie indicated the woman on her left.

18

'This is Martha Strickland. We often come up against each other at meetings.' So the woman, who looked to be in her thirties, wasn't a close friend after all.

Martha nodded politely, but no more than that, and it seemed to Eveline appropriate to at least help the introduction along in the hope of enticing a smile from those narrow, somewhat fierce features.

'I've never been to one of these meetings before,' she said in her best voice. 'So I don't know what to expect.'

'Oh, you'll enjoy it!' Connie broke in. 'Won't she, Mrs Strickland? It's so very uplifting and inspiring. When you hear what they have to say, you'll want to listen again and again. You might even want to become a member.'

That was probably why she'd befriended her, came the unbidden and vaguely uncharitable assumption as they stood up to let three more women move past them to several empty seats further along, before settling again.

'Some of these people are so courageous,' Connie went on, unpinning her hat, taking it off and reinserting the hatpins to lay it in her lap. Now that the fashion was for hats so huge as to obstruct the view of those behind, a lady was expected to remove hers in places like this. Those who didn't, especially in music halls, could bring a growl from any man behind her to 'take orf yer blooming 'at, lady – I can't see a blooming fing!' Not here, of course, where everyone was polite and orderly.

With others removing theirs Eveline followed

suit even though hers wasn't that big. There were quite a few plain hats, she was glad to notice, the owners what she would consider ordinary, like her. The knowledge instantly gave her a good feeling. Perhaps she would enjoy this after all.

'How long will it go on for?' she asked Connie. She didn't want to be too late home and have them asking questions.

'Oh, about an hour, perhaps just a little over,' Connie said quickly, her pretty face showing deep concern that her guest might get up and leave if she thought it was any longer.

'We have wonderful speakers,' she hurried on. 'And courageous. They have my greatest admiration. We are so lucky to have Mrs Kenney speaking to us today. Even the government has to admire women like her, despite condemning them, and despite what many politicians say about us – though there are some who are for us – and despite the way a lot of people sneer and call us sour spinsters and frustrated females.'

Again Eveline had to smile. No one could call this girl a frustrated female. Eveline guessed her to be a year or two older than herself, twenty perhaps. The large hazel eyes, glowing with a zest for life, the softly rounded features framed by an abundance of beautifully dressed hair were hardly those of a soured woman. Used to genteel living, she had the confident look of money, but she seemed happy to do battle for her lesser sisters.

There were other young people here, but the older women were no doubt those of means with husbands who indulged them to go off to their clubs and social meetings, including the suffragette movement. The older ones who didn't look quite so well off *were* probably spinsters or widows – difficult, if not out of the question, for a married working-class woman to have any pastime outside the home except for the pub with her man, who saw it as his wife's place to look after the home and him and his children.

Connie was still chatting away. 'It's been going for more than fifty years, you know, but the actual organised suffragette movement only really started this century. We're in the right. How can it be fair for any drunken labourer to have the franchise when respectable and upright women of property are left outside the polling booth?'

'I don't think it's fair, either,' Eveline obliged, but Connie hardly stopped for breath.

'There are lots of women compelled to pay taxes to the country yet still forbidden any opinion on how that tax is to be managed. You will hear in a moment how very wrong it truly is and how we must and will continue to fight by whatever means for the right of women to be given the vote.'

She sounded so fervent, as though quoting words drilled into her by an endless succession of speakers, that Eveline was almost tempted to ask if she had any opinion of her own. But it was best not to antagonise someone who had just be-friended you so generously, so she contented herself nodding or shaking her head where appropriate while surreptitiously taking stock of those around her. Everyone seemed to have the same intense expression as they talked among themselves or watched the goings-on on the stage.

People were still coming in. As the hall filled

rapidly, more chairs were being found and set up along the back. Connie had turned back to Mrs Strickland, leaving Eveline free to look about her, and she amused herself by picking out working women, factory girls taking advantage of half-day Saturdays; shop girls were not so lucky, having to work until eight or nine this evening.

She was surprised to see more men than she had expected. It was good to know that not all were against the effort of women to gain a say in their own country, an effort that had so far brought them only hardship and suffering.

Suddenly her roving gaze was brought up sharply by a young man seated two rows behind and three seats to her right, staring straight back at her quite openly, his eyes brilliant blue.

Her cheeks grown suddenly hot, Eveline looked quickly away, returning her attention to Connie.

'Next week,' Connie was saying, quite unaware Eveline's attention had strayed, 'there is a big demonstration planned outside Number Ten Downing Street. You might like to be there. You're not expected to be one of those who will chain themselves to the railings, of course, but we need all the support we can get.'

She seemed to take it that her companion would be only too eager to attend. 'It could become rough, my dear, and some are not up to that. But you'll be quite safe if you stay on the perimeter.'

With no wish to be hustled into joining without giving it any thought, Eveline said she'd need to think about it.

'On Saturday afternoons,' Connie continued, 'a group of us meet for a social gathering with tea and scones. We chat about this and that, not all politics, just general small talk. Perhaps you'd like to come along. It's in George Street, near Marble Arch. I'll give you the address as we leave.'

Eveline nodded obligingly, still sensing the young man's eyes upon her. She just had to make sure it wasn't merely imagination and under the pretext of patting her hair in place she stole a quick peek.

He seemed to be with a woman, at least that was what it looked like from here, the woman talking away to him although he appeared not to be paying much attention. Instead, to her intense alarm he was still regarding her as if his eyes had never left her and, as he met her glance, the corners of those wide, sensitive lips beneath a small moustache lifted in a faint smile of amusement. Confusion rippling through her, Eveline turned hastily back to face the front and concentrate on what was happening on the stage. How could she have been such a fool, turning round that second time? And to have him smile at her, so obviously aware of her subterfuge.

Now she felt angry. How dare he smile at her? She didn't know him. Who did he think he was? More to the point, who did he think she was to be looked at with such familiarity?

The answer to that made her feel all hot and cold. Had he taken her for a cutie, a bit of all right? Their eyes meeting not once but twice, she must have struck him as a bold hussy?

She turned quickly to her new companion and for something better to say, asked, 'What if there's not enough chairs – people are still coming in?'

'They will stand, my dear,' returned Connie. 'Mrs Kenney is such a popular speaker.'

Eveline had to force herself not to turn again to see whether *he* was still staring at her or had lost interest. It was hard to relinquish the image of that audacious invader of her peace of mind. All through the speeches she could almost feel those blue eyes penetrating the nape of her neck and she hardly heard a thing that was being said.

There were two speakers before the main one, each getting a huge round of applause, but Mrs Kenney's stirring, rallying speech that had included the announcement of a great pageant to be held in April had the audience rising to its feet as she came down from the stage and along the aisle, acknowledging this one and that as she left.

'Wasn't she rousing?' Connie said as they joined the crush slowly making its way out of the hall. 'I've every intention of going to that pageant next month. What about you?'

Eveline nodded absently. The young man with the brilliant blue eyes, the well-groomed dark hair and the trim moustache had joined those filing out, the woman she'd seen with him having threaded her arm through his.

'It's to be the Pageant of Women's Trades and Professions for the International Suffrage Alliance,' Connie quoted, laughing. 'I'm sure they could have chosen a shorter title but I suppose it encompasses everything. Mrs Kenney said it is to start at dusk. I think that's very clever because working women as well as trade and professional ladies will be able to be there. It can't be easy for working women.'

In the growing crush around the exit Connie said, 'I hope you can come. Mrs Kenney says the procession will be lit by hundreds of lanterns and there'll be at least ninety different occupations gathered at Eaton Square. It should be marvellous. I forgot to ask, what is your occupation?'

The direct question dragged Eveline's mind from the back view of a man's head that might have been that of the young man who'd smiled at her and with an effort of will she focused on Connie. 'I work in a biscuit factory.'

'Oh, you have a trade.'

'Not exactly.' Eveline experienced a strange fancy to shock this gently brought up young woman out of her high-minded if well-meaning vision of working women. 'It's where workers put biscuits in packets on a moving belt, hour after hour, day after day. It's not a trade. It's boring, mind-sapping work!'

She hadn't meant to be so curt and the look on Connie's face made her immediately regret her words. She relaxed her expression a little.

'I don't do that though I can see the factory people through a glass partition of what I suppose you can call an office. There are five of us, two typists, a secretary, the office manager and me – I do the adding up and things on a calculating machine. There's other offices but that's where I work – overlooking the factory.'

Connie beamed, the correction quickly dismissed. 'Then you're an office worker. Your banner will probably show that. Mrs Kenney said there are to be banners depicting every trade.'

A thought stopped her and she regarded Eveline

dubiously, realising she had been overlooking something. 'Do you think you'll join, then?'

'I don't know.' She hadn't really thought about it. The back of the head on which she'd been trying to keep her gaze was now almost lost in the crowd converging on the main exit. Soon he would put on his hat and become just another figure merging with all the others.

'My dear! After all you've heard?' There was accusation in Connie's tone. 'And you don't know?'

The hurt tone made Eveline turn back to her, full of contrition. 'I do want to, but I have to work. It makes it difficult to attend lots of meetings.'

'You don't have to attend every meeting. No one expects to give up her entire life for the cause – only those who have dedicated themselves to it and they are special, women like Mrs Pankhurst and her daughters, and Annie Kenney and Mrs Pethwick-Lawrence, and ... oh, the list is endless!'

They were being jostled between the double doors, people pressing on all sides. Moments later they were out into the chill of late afternoon, the still wintry sun going down. Eveline realised she was hungry and she needed to visit a toilet somewhere after sitting so long. She also realised she had lost sight of the young man who had smiled at her.

Chapter Two

By the time she'd got off the omnibus at the Salmon and Ball pub in Bethnal Green Road, Eveline had decided to say nothing to anyone, much less her family, about the suffragette meeting. Dad would go potty if he knew and most likely Mum would support him even though she normally ruled the roost in most things.

With her mind still on the way the young man at the meeting had looked at her, Eveline made her way homeward, past Gales Gardens, Pott Street police station and Corfield Street before turning into Wilmott Street. She certainly wouldn't say anything about him, which would mean letting on as to where she'd been. Not only that, Mum would start prying, forever eager to see her daughter settle on some nice lad and not be, as she saw it, left on the shelf. Mum's idea of being left on the shelf began at the age of eighteen. *'If you ain't going steady by twenty, you'll find yerself left on the shelf you mark my words.'*

Mum weighed up every lad she so much as glanced at. Visualising yet another admirer on the horizon, she'd start up an inquisition. 'What's his name? What sort of bloke is he? Do we know him?' The business of the suffragette meeting was bound to come out. Her face would give her away. It always did if she tried to fabricate. Dad would have a fit – his daughter in the company of *'them sort of shrieking females!'*

Confiding in friends of course, they'd see the funny side. *'Is that all yer've got to do, go orf to some stuffy old suffragette meeting?'* Even her best mate Ada Williams would chortle, her other friend, Daisy Cox, even more so.

There was her younger sister, May, sixteen and eager to lap up any hint of a romance, but she might blab to Mum about this suffragette thing.

Eveline pursed her lips, her mind still on the meeting as she passed the black-velvet-lined window of the undertaker's, the closed, rickety gates of the wood yard, the silent, frowning edifice of Wilmott Street School, and on to Finnis Street where her gran lived.

One person she might tell in confidence was Gran. Her second-floor flat, or letting as they were called, was at the far end of the street. Mum was her daughter. Gran and Grandpa Ansell had lived there ever since Waterlow Buildings were built. Though Grandpa had been dead four years now, his widow Victoria had refused to move to a smaller letting, even though smoke from the railway that ran just a hundred or so feet from her window billowed by at regular intervals, leaving sooty specks on windows and yellowing the curtains.

She continued to rattle around in two large bedrooms, living room and kitchen while Eveline's family's flat over Dad's shop housed eight: him and Mum, her and May and their four brothers, Len, Jimmy, Bobby and Alfred. It had been even more crowded before her married sister Tilly and brother Fred had left.

Glad to have someone to tell about her little

adventure, Eveline decided to pop in and see Gran. For all her seventy years, Gran was an open-minded, outgoing woman who didn't always see eye to eye with her daughter. She could keep secrets, especially from Mum.

Eveline quickened her step, striding out beneath her skirts, hurrying past the many stone entrances, the iron railings that shielded the basement lettings below their sloping patches of grey grass that battled with the dry, infertile soil and dusty dandelions, passing the ground-floor window where Bert Adams, his brother and widowed mother lived.

She'd seen Bert Adams on a couple of occasions in Bethnal Green free library and thought him quite attractive in a broad-faced sort of way, his faded flat cap with its frayed peak set at a jaunty angle. She had in fact felt a tug of interest until her friend Alice let drop that he had a bit of a roving eye for the girls. Whether that was true or not, she'd put him out of her mind.

She put on a quick spurt past the window, forced to sidestep a group of children playing an energetic and noisy game of tag, these cobbled streets their playground. Reaching her gran's entrance she hurried up the first half-flight of stone stairs, turning along the draughty, open-fronted landing with curved iron railings to stop anyone falling out, then up the next half-flight to Gran's landing, her ascent impeded by half a dozen boys boisterously stampeding past her downstairs to the street.

Eveline smiled as she stood back against the brown-and-green-painted concrete wall to let the tribe scoot by. She knew they were up to the game youngsters had played ever since these places had been built – tearing up the ten flights of stairs to the top of one block, scampering across the tarred, flat roof with its smoking chimney stacks, down the next block, along the street and up the next and so on, making as much noise as possible to upset the tenants, even knocking on doors as they whooped past. Another game was to tie string to the door knockers of the two opposite neighbours on one chosen landing, knock on one, then scamper off to wait for it to be opened, jerking the string on the door opposite to the fury of both occupants.

It was risky if the door to the roof over which they'd make their escape was locked. It meant retracing their steps to suffer a heavy hand from the irate tenants they were compelled to pass. And serve them right, Eveline thought as she continued upward.

Gran cautiously opened her door to her. 'Oh, it's you, love,' she said with relief. 'I could 'ear them noisy little buggers going past, up to their pranks again. Landlords don't do nothing, nor do the police. Come in, love. Nice of you to drop by like this.'

'I thought I would on my way home,' Eveline said, following her in.

There was a time when she had spoken the way both Gran and her parents did, but working in an office, if only a factory office, she'd been expected to speak as nicely as she could. The office manager, Mr Prentice, set standards for his few staff and would glower if she let the side down. 'I will not tolerate sloppy speech, young woman. So either you mind yourself, or...' The unfinished sentence left her in no doubt that termination of her apparently prestigious position could follow. Trying to speak nicely was now here to stay. She remembered Gran having a sister who had been in service as a young girl, speaking beautifully to the day she died, despite living all her married life in the East End.

'I'll make us a nice cuppa,' Gran was saying as she preceded her into the neat little living room. 'Brightened up my day, you 'ave, popping in.'

Gran spent her days cleaning her little domain, keeping it as neat as a new pin in spite of the bugs that crept up the waste chute to lurk behind the wallpaper and which she fought with the stamina of a soldier going into action. At seventy she still regularly and vigorously scrubbed her portion of the stone stairs, a weekly chore usually shared between the two tenants on each landing, and complained about the stink of stale cabbage, and worse, the one that emanated from the less clean letting on the floor above.

'Dirty lot,' she remarked. 'Don't deserve to live in nice 'omes like these what was built for decent people. They'd make a slum of a palace, and if you ask me, that's where the bugs come from – from them upstairs!'

'So what've you been doing with yourself today?' she asked now as she came back into the room after putting on the kettle in the kitchen.

Eveline took off her hat, reinserting the long hat-pins, and laid it beside her on Gran's old-fashioned couch. She took a deep breath. 'I went to look at that new Selfridge's store in Oxford Street. It's beautiful. Their window displays are enough to make your mouth water. And while I was there...'

She paused, seeing Gran's interest rise and hurried on before she could think better of it. 'I was looking in the window when some of those suffragettes came marching along.'

Quickly she described how brisk and unwavering they had looked, breaking off while her gran got up to go and attend the clamouring kettle, returning with the tea and a plate of biscuits. Handing her tea to her, Gran sat in her wooden armchair and prompted, 'Go on, love. You was saying?'

Quickly Eveline told how she'd fallen into step and, fearing to offend the young woman who had taken her arm, had ended at the hall listening to speeches given by some quite prominent speakers. Gran looked stern.

'You'd best not let your dad know where you was.'

'That's why I'm telling you,' Eveline said, sipping the hot, sweet tea.

Gran always used sugar, never condensed milk. She wasn't badly off for money, having married someone with a nice little grocer shop. She had never known hard work; in the past she had been able to afford someone to clean her house and even now sent her washing out, her hands still soft as a girl's.

It was Grandad who had put Dad in his shop when he and Mum first married. Grandad had been something of a gambler, horses mostly, but died before getting through all of his money as

32

gamblers can often do, sparing his wife the poverty she might have ended up with if he'd lived.

She settled further back into her chair. 'Is that it – the thing what's making you look so flushed?' she queried. 'You went to a meeting?'

'Yes, but...' Eveline let her words trail off. While Gran had been getting the tea she'd had time to think. Was she making a fool of herself about a young man she would probably never see again?

'Well?' came the prompt. 'Something else must 'ave 'appened to bring your colour up like that.'

Eveline made up her mind. 'There was a really handsome young man, sitting behind me. When I looked at him, he smiled. It was a lovely smile. But he had someone with him, a young lady, so I didn't look at him again.'

It now sounded very silly. She slowed her words. 'But I kept feeling him staring at me all through the speeches, but when we came out, I lost sight of him.'

She ended as breathless as though she'd been running and sat there staring mutely at Gran, half expecting to see some revelation or other written on that smooth forehead with its greying hair swept up into an old-fashioned topknot. One hand was toying speculatively with the jet brooch at the high neck of the black blouse. As a widow she still wore black, even after four years. Looking younger than her years she might be, but at seventy was no longer of an age to dress brightly.

'And now you've got yourself all of a lather over an 'andsome face you saw for only a few minutes or so,' she said slowly, then tutted. 'Well, it do 'appen. But don't worry, I won't tell your mother.'

'It's not that,' Eveline hastened. 'It's the suffragette bit. I don't want her and Dad to know anything about that. You know what I mean?'

'Oh, I do know all right, love.' Gran gave a titter as though seeing it as some cloak and dagger escapade. 'I won't say nothing about that either.'

She was obviously enjoying every minute of it. Encouraged, Eveline found herself asking what she should do about the Saturday meeting that had been mentioned.

Gran looked smug. 'It ain't for me to say, love. You'll 'ave to make up yer own mind about that. All I say is, women are people too and one of these days they'll 'ave to 'ave a say in their own country's future. Not me, I'm too old and your grandad was the salt of the earth, apart from 'is gambling, but he'd 'ave said I didn't want for nothing so why would I want to go kicking over the traces? Mind you, there's lots of women still don't 'ave much of a life. They need someone ready to stand up for them.'

Emboldened, Eveline told her about the planned demonstration outside Number Ten.

This, though, was met with a warning frown. 'Don't go getting yourself too mixed up in things like that, love. It's one thing going to little meetings, but causing a disturbance – you leave that to them what enjoy such things. I say, go to your meeting on Saturday – I won't say nothing to your mum, I promise. But I won't smile on any more than that.'

It was a warning that secrets only went so far. Eveline didn't pursue it or point out that if she joined she might be expected to take part in such things. She wasn't sure herself if this was what she wanted. Might a particular young man be at one of these meetings? Though why he would be she couldn't imagine. Anyway, she worked all week so any weekday suffragette activity would be out of the question.

Her umbrella held at a fighting slant against the onslaught of March going out more like a lion than a lamb, Eveline pushed along George Street.

Counting the house numbers of the fine edifices she passed, she now wanted only to find the right place and be out of this weather. As the week had progressed, she had found the prospect of this meeting less and less attractive until she wasn't looking forward to it at all.

A wild goose chase, that's what it was, a fool's errand. Of course the face she hoped to see wouldn't be there. But having come this far, it would be stupid to turn back, especially in this weather. Besides, she had promised Constance What's-Her-Name that she'd come.

All the way on the bus she had even felt a little sick for thinking about it, partly because if Constance wasn't there she would know no one, and partly because the vehicle kept slowing and stopping for passengers getting on and off, and being held up by other traffic. Horse-drawn vehicles, even in congested parts, had somehow always been kinder on the stomach.

Things had changed so fast in just six years. When she was twelve there had been hansom and hackney carriages and horse buses. Now the only horse-drawn vehicles were traders' carts and

35

CARDIFF
CAERDYDD

brewers' drays.

Anyone could see that the day of the horse was gone forever. Nowadays it was noisy and stank of petrol where once there had been only the clop of hooves and the shouts of drivers and it had smelled only of horses and their droppings. Though that too had stunk, it had been a natural stink.

Engine fumes were pervasive. So was the odour of wet clothing inside the bus. She had been glad to reach her stop and inhale the fresher air of the side streets. But the empty feeling inside her hadn't diminished. In fact the nearer she got, the worse it was becoming.

In such atrocious weather she could have been nice and warm at home crouched over a book before the kitchen range. It was the lure that she might see *him*. All week the word, *him*, had clogged her brain, taking up her every thought until Mum had lost her temper saying she wasn't pulling her weight with the household chores and leaving it all to May. At work Mr Prentice had towered over her accusing her of wool-gathering and pointing out that her totals were utterly incorrect.

The trouble with Mr Prentice was that she never knew how to take him. One moment he'd stand over her, criticising, the next he'd have one hand on her shoulder, rubbing it with a sort of kneading motion as he praised something she'd done, saying what a good worker she was, what a good girl, and this week saying that if she had any problems, she only had to bring them to him and he'd be happy to help her.

She didn't need his help. All she wanted was to

see that young man just once more and lay the small ghost he had awakened. Just once more and she would know how she really felt about him.

Finding the house number at last, Eveline hurried up the flight of six steps and folded her umbrella as she gained the shelter of the pillared doorway, jerked the bell pull, hearing it jangle on the other side of the wide door's stained-glass panels. The door was opened by a thin, middle-aged lady, whose expensive cream blouse and neat beige skirt caught Eveline's eye.

'Good afternoon, my dear,' she said in a cultured but wavering tone. 'Do come in, please. You are new, aren't you?'

'Yes, I am,' Eveline said, stepping inside.

'Well, you are very welcome. Do you know anyone here?'

'Er, Constance...' The name flooded back in a rush. 'Mornington.'

'Oh, yes. She has not arrived yet. She should be here soon. Now, the cloakroom is downstairs. Leave your outdoor things there, then come and join us.' Eveline could hear the drone of women's voices from a room further along the corridor.

'You'll soon get to know everyone.' The woman turned away to answer the door, laying an apologetic hand on her arm. 'Please excuse me, dear.'

Two ladies were coming up the narrow but well-lit curving stairs she had indicated. Deep in conversation, they glanced at Eveline, smiled as she stood back for them to pass, and went on with their conversation. They looked so elegantly dressed that she felt conscious of her showerproof coat and galoshes, all of which smelled faintly rubbery as she negotiated the awkwardly curved stairs, holding on to the shiny brass handrail.

The tiny cloakroom, set next to a kitchen and a storeroom, was full of women and she had to thread her way through to the row of pegs to hang up her things, dropping her wet, plain black umbrella into the stand along with several far more expensive ones. No one took the slightest notice of her, all chattering away to friends. She was grateful to disappear into one of the two toilets and be on her own for a moment or two.

She let the minutes stretch out in blessed peace, until suddenly the door handle turned as if of its own accord. A voice said, 'I think there's someone already in there, Emily.'

She recognised the voice of Constance – Connie, and tension turned to relief. Quickly adjusting her long petticoat and skirt, she tugged at the chain and opened the door, muttering an apology to the young lady in need of the place she had so selfishly occupied far too long. Connie's small, pretty face was alight with joy. 'Oh, you *did* manage to come after all. I'm so pleased!'

All at once she was part of this meeting, introduced to this one and that, glad to see that not all of the twenty or so ladies were as wealthy as she had expected, with not the tiniest hint of class distinction. In no time she began to feel at home. If this was what being a suffragette meant, women helping other women of all walks of life, then her fears had been unfounded. It was turning into a delightful afternoon as she chatted, told people where she came from, what her parents did, listened to various exploits – one woman had climbed the Alps, another had had a brush with a minor MP at a Christmas party when he'd insulted her to her face; she'd given as good as she'd got, proving herself to be the more intelligent.

'And all without raising my voice,' she said with quiet satisfaction. 'I left him utterly lost for words and blustering.'

A scheme was to be put before their branch committee for another militant attendance outside the House of Commons, everyone talking of the huge April rally of workers and professionals in Eaton Square.

'The next meeting here,' announced the lady in charge, 'will be graced by no less a person than Mrs Edith How-Martyn, who is our joint Honorary Secretary and, as you may know, one of the first and former members of the WSPU to serve time in Holloway three years ago after being arrested and charged for obstruction outside the House of Commons. She will tell us all about her experiences.'

'Will you be coming next week?' Connie asked as the meeting broke up after two hours of tea, cake and conversation.

Eveline nodded. She rather fancied hearing someone who had been imprisoned for her beliefs. But more, she had been disappointed to find no sign of the young man she'd sought, so perhaps next week he would appear.

'Oh, that's wonderful!' Connie cried. 'So you have decided to join us, become a suffragette. Everyone, listen...' Raising her voice, she swept out an arm to attract the room's attention, the other holding Eveline's hand. 'We have a new member. Isn't that splendid?'

Too late to wriggle out of it now as women and the three men here, supporters of the cause, came to congratulate her as Connie led her to the registration desk.

'I need your name and address, my dear,' the woman in charge of the register smiled up at her. 'So we can send you a news-sheet and literature.'

'Oh, no!' Eveline's face registered her horror. 'My family don't know.'

The woman was immediately sympathetic. 'I understand. I will make a note warning that you must not be sent any literature as yet. If you attend regularly you can pick it all up here.'

Reassured, Eveline bent and put her name to the form being handed to her, straightening up to see Connie's face glowing with triumph.

'Welcome,' she said, the first words she'd used when they'd first met, and just as warm. 'Don't worry, Eveline, everyone knows that we can't all be free to follow our hearts.'

Eveline was already having misgivings about what she had done, and now was hardly able to retract. 'My father mustn't ever know about this,' she said so that Connie would be left in no doubt that what she was doing was not to be taken lightly. It was all very well for people like Connie with money who could do what they liked. 'My father hates the suffragettes.'

'Mine too,' Connie said solemnly, the admission taking away Eveline's breath. 'He too knows nothing of what I am doing.'

Chapter Three

From the way Eveline Fenton had looked at her, Connie was sure she had no idea women of upper-middle-class families could be as suppressed by the head of the house as those of the lower classes. Intimidation wasn't the sole property of the poor; an otherwise respectable Harley Street physician such as her father could browbeat his wife, as could any common labourer. Not that he had ever struck her mother, but he had the ability to dominate and subdue her to silence with a single disapproving look.

She could open Eveline's eyes about her home life, though she preferred not to. Explaining how it was would have given her quite the wrong impression, for he was a good husband and father, more than adequately providing for his family, seeing to the education of his two daughters as well as his two sons and taking his responsibilities seriously and soberly. Yet his word was law by sheer virtue of doing these things.

On the train home, she felt Eveline had much to learn if she thought being wealthy and privileged was a bed of roses. Eveline had gone to great pains to let it be known that she wasn't particularly poor even though she came from the poorer East End, her father a shopkeeper.

Connie smiled. Tradespeople. Father looked on tradespeople as on the same level as servants. He'd never admit that suffragettes saw women as equal, certainly in their fight against political exclusion.

With the train puffing slowly into Perivale, Connie got up from her seat to be jostled by a man in a hurry to alight before anyone else stood up. Others were more considerate; one even lifted an apologetic hand to the brim of his bowler as his shoulder brushed hers, so she nodded acknowledgement of the young man's polite gesture. Oddly enough, it was exactly what her father would have done were he to accidentally brush against a woman, exuding politeness, charming her with his manner. At home he was a different man.

Home was a short walk from the station. The rain had stopped, the sky clearing, but it had become colder and she put on a spurt to be home all the quicker. Also she knew she was later returning home than intended.

Her mother was already in the hall, having heard the doorbell. As the housemaid, whose given name was Victoria but with Father thinking it too grand for a servant was called Agnes, admitted her, Connie noticed the anxious look on her mother's face.

'Where have you been, Constance?' Her voice was a whisper. 'You should have been home over an hour ago. Your father has been asking where you were. We know nothing of this friend you said you were seeing.'

'I told you, Mummy,' Connie said, taking off her hat and gloves and handing them with her coat to Agnes, who hurried away with them. 'An old school friend I'd arranged to meet for lunch

42

in town. A sort of reunion.'

Her mother's sceptical expression made her squirm, or perhaps it was her own guilt at lying. She was in fact running out of excuses to cover these suffragette meetings of hers. If she said it was a ladies' club, Father would be asking its name and checking whether it was suitable. Sometimes it was worse than being a prisoner.

Eighteen months since leaving Griggs's School for Young Ladies, to suddenly have this old school friend popping up, what other excuse could she have made than a reunion? Her parents knew all her friends and Father would contact any she named to corroborate her tale. It demonstrated the extent of the control he exercised over his daughters. At nineteen she was still answerable to him. Were she twenty-one, which would not be for eighteen months, not until June of next year, it would make little difference while under his roof. Her only hope of escape would be marriage but even then she'd probably only be swapping her father's domination for that of her husband. Things would have to change very drastically before any wife would ever see herself as her own mistress.

Of course, at first she would be glad to be under her husband's protection but in time he'd expect it and that would be a different matter. What if she became like her mother, the subdued wife hanging on her husband's every word – if she didn't kill him first. Anyway, as far as she was concerned, nineteen was too young to marry, even though her father already assumed that she and Simon Whitemore would eventually tie the knot.

Simon had been introduced to her by her father at her coming-out party last year, and he was now regarded as her chosen suitor. The son of a long-standing friend and colleague of her father and a medical man like himself, Connie had to admit he was quite handsome and sociable. She had liked him at first but lately found his serious nature quite boring. He was too much in the mould of her father for her liking and she could visualise herself ending up exactly like her mother if she didn't watch out.

She hadn't yet told Simon how she felt, wanting not to hurt his feelings. But now he'd begun talking seriously of marriage, his attentions becoming steadily more purposeful, and with her father's mind set on an engagement in the not-too-distant future, she saw herself fighting a losing battle if she didn't make a stand very soon.

'Where is Father?' she asked, hastily changing the subject before her mother's questioning gaze.

'In his study. He has had a busy surgery. He is asking why you are so late coming home. He wasn't happy with you meeting someone neither of us knows. It could have been simply anyone.'

'It wasn't *anyone*, Mummy, it was an old school friend.'

The lie made her squirm as she moved past her mother towards the drawing room. The trouble with lies was that they always needed expanding to make them plausible. 'We had so much to talk about that we quite forgot the time.'

She was about to add that the train was also delayed, but that would have had Father telephoning the railway station asking the reason why. She would have been found out in a trice. One lie too many was never advisable.

'Where did you go after lunch to have made you so late home?' her mother persisted, following her into the room.

Connie thought quickly. She was running out of excuses. 'We visited the British Museum.' There came a temptation to enthuse on the museum's treasures, but again that would be overdoing it. Mother was still frowning.

'How did you come to contact each other after so long a time?'

'I bumped into her in London several weeks ago. She wrote to suggest we meet for lunch.'

It was a silly mistake. The frown on her mother's elegantly narrow face deepened. 'Your father has seen nothing addressed to you.'

He read all mail that came into the house. Bentick, their butler, would bring the post and morning paper to the breakfast room. Father would open each envelope with a silver paper knife, putting aside bills that needed to be paid or that dealt with his practice. He would open any addressed to her mother, taking it as his right. The family would sit in silence, anyone daring to speak receiving a sharp, reprimanding glower. As children she, her sister Verity, or her two brothers, Denzil and Herbert, had been ordered to their room without breakfast before now. Meals too were eaten in silence unless he spoke, exacting a response. Mother seemed quite content, or perhaps was resigned to her correspondence being read, often aloud, usually invitations to social gatherings and such, or from

45

her only living relative, Aunt Mildred.

Whether Verity, having left her school for young ladies at Christmas, resented what little mail she did have being read out, she never let on, but Connie resented it deeply as an intrusion into her privacy. At nineteen, a woman now, why should she be subjected to such a demeaning practice? Little wonder she'd secretly become a suffragette. Her parents were a leftover from Victorian times; their ideas hadn't moved on, they remained as old-fashioned as their home, stuffy and over-stuffed. Things had changed. It was 1909, when old customs and old values were fast receding, except of course in this house.

Now she must concoct yet another fib, one spawning another. 'As Bentick crossed the hall with the post I saw a letter for me, so I took it.'

Her mother's expression changed to one of shock. 'How could you be so underhanded, Constance? Your father receives all the day's post.'

'Oh, Mummy!' Connie made for the sofa before the drawing-room's marble fireplace with its blazing fire. 'I didn't see it as any of his business. One would think I was having a clandestine meeting with a strange man.'

'I should hope not when you and Simon are practically engaged.'

'Simon and I are not yet engaged, practically or otherwise!'

Her mother turned away in exasperation to finger the leathery leaves of the large aspidistra in its blue pot on the window table before the drawn curtains; the ornate gas lamps had already been lit with evening closing in.

Connie couldn't resist a brief, self-satisfied smile. 'At any rate I feel I'm not ready for marriage yet.'

Her mother turned abruptly. 'Your father would be aggrieved to hear that. He has high hopes for you and Simon, who will himself one day be an eminent surgeon. You could do no better than marriage to Simon.'

'I'm still not ready and Father cannot honestly expect me do what I'm not ready to do.'

'*What* can I not expect you to do, my dear?' came a deep voice and both turned to see the tall, spare, bearded figure of Willoughby Mortimer Mornington framed in the doorway.

Connie stemmed the sudden anxiety that sprang up inside her. 'I was saying I can't be pressed to marry until I feel certain of what I am doing.'

She heard her mother give a little gasp. There was a long pause in which both women watched his slow approach. Connie stood up, holding herself very upright, almost as tall as he, in contrast to her mother, small and thin and uncertain of herself.

They watched as he crossed the room to the domed clock on the mantelshelf over the fireplace, reached into his fob pocket for his gold hunter to check the time against it and opened the glass front to move the clock's minute hand forward a fraction, returning the watch to his fob pocket. The heavy, gold Albert, looped across his dark waistcoat, glinted in the gaslight as he turned back to the two women.

'No one is pressing you to do anything, Constance,' he said slowly. 'But it must be said, you are of an age to begin thinking of marriage. You and Simon have known each other for almost a year and have become good friends and that friendship has lately grown far deeper?'

Connie took in a deep breath, her lips compressed. 'I don't know how he feels about me, Father, but my feelings for him remain cool.'

Within the well-trimmed, distinguished beard his lips quirked into a faint smile. 'Which is as it should be, my dear. A young lady should not reveal too great a response in that direction before marriage. It is for her fiancé to be understanding and to gently warm her heart to him.'

Perhaps that was what was wrong. If he were a little more passionate she might feel differently about him, but he was stuffy, correct to a fault. Maybe it was their schooling; hers had taken place at a school for young ladies, his at a public school for boys then an all-male university. Even now, at twenty-four, still engaged in medical training, he'd had scant dealings with women until they'd met. As for herself, she had no knowledge of what went on between man and woman. Little use asking Mother or even friends, they as innocent as she; it wasn't a thing to discuss in polite society.

She felt nothing when Simon kissed her, few as his kisses were. He, no doubt, took her reluctance to be a woman's natural fear of the unknown and perfectly normal. It was obvious from what he would say when she drew back.

'I understand, darling, not until we are married,' almost an exact echo of her father's words now.

But she didn't want to marry him. There had to be something more, something her senses told her had to happen when kissed by a man, a man she truly loved.

'I think very soon,' her father was saying, 'Simon will be requesting your hand in marriage, Constance, within the next week or so for sure. And I am sure your response will be a positive one, my dear.'

Connie returned his gaze silently, but her heart was saying that it would indeed be positive. It would be her last chance to make a stand. How could she marry a man who showed every prospect of becoming so like her father as the years went on, likeable though he was now? If Simon came pressing his suit, her answer had to be an emphatic no. In a way she felt sorry for him. It would be as traumatic for him as for her, and she couldn't help a shudder at the repercussions she knew her answer would bring. It was a big step she was taking.

She'd half expected him to broach the subject that very evening and was somewhat relieved when all he said as they returned home from a social evening with friends was that he loved her very dearly and eagerly looked forward to the time when he could prove it, tantamount to yet another hint at marriage. Except that as he kissed her on parting company he murmured that he might very well be having a word with her father in the near future, with her consent of course, to which she said nothing, not wishing to commit herself either way at that moment.

This Saturday she forgot all about him as her George Street meeting revolved excitedly around the earlier protest outside Number Ten Downing Street, the scuffles, the brave women who'd chained themselves to the railings outside and had had to be cut free with heavy wire cutters by the police.

Listening, Connie envied them their courage but was glad she hadn't been among them, though she should have been. She had courage enough to face arrest and she'd be in good company. But it would have meant her father finding out about her and that must not happen. The longer this was kept secret, the better.

'Were you there?' Eveline asked as they listened to the woman who gave a little speech about how she had been carried away off her feet by the police, the indignity of it, her arms pinioned to her sides as if she were a rag doll. But she hadn't fought them or cried out, allowing herself to be borne off. She had spent two days in police cells with the minimum of comforts and was sent back for another two days for refusing to pay the fine they imposed. She was, in fact, incensed that her brother had paid it for her, and was still angry.

Connie shook her head to Eveline's question, aware of her scrutiny. 'I would have been there but I was obliged to stay at home,' she said, acutely conscious of the flimsiness of the excuse.

Eveline fell silent as the speaker continued talking, but as they left she brought up the subject again. 'I wish I'd been there. I had to work. I'd have got the sack for skipping off. Bad enough being off when you're ill, they question you as if

50

you're a criminal. I kept thinking of you being there.'

'I wish I had been but it wasn't possible.' She spoke with a bitter ring to her tone as they stood outside the building before parting company.

Why did this girl persist in seeing her as being free because she didn't work? Her life had its prison bars too. If this girl could see how a dictatorial father could rule someone's life every bit as much as did her working day, watching and questioning, mapping her life out for her, she'd think differently.

'I'd like to join in with everything,' Eveline was saying. 'Even if you didn't go on the Downing Street protest, you're an old hand. I'm still new.'

Connie couldn't help herself. 'I want you to understand, Eveline, it's my father; he has no idea about all this. If he had he would take steps to see I never attend another meeting.'

Eveline regarded her with incredulity. 'What could he do?'

'What would your father do if he wanted to prevent you?' She waited, but Eveline had grown silent. 'As to my being an old hand, as you put it,' she went on. 'I joined the suffragette movement just after Christmas so I'm almost as new as you are. Too early for me to be of any great use to the sort of women who are ready to lay their heads on the block for their cause.'

Eveline did not speak for a while. Then she placed a hand on Connie's arm. 'I didn't realise. It looks like we're both in the same boat. I dread to think what my father would say if he found out.'

She gave a little giggle. 'Looks like we'll be holding each other up from now on.' And as Connie livened up she asked with a hopeful expression, 'But you will be at the Eaton Square rally, won't you? Because I don't want to be there on my own.'

'I shall be there,' Connie said with conviction. 'Come what may.' But for some reason the words brought Simon to mind and turned her thoughts to this evening.

He'd finally decided. He'd told her in the week that this Saturday evening he intended to call on her father to formally ask for her hand in marriage. She'd felt herself go cold but hadn't had the courage to express how she felt on the matter. A pity she hadn't done so, for now she had it all to do and at a most critical time too, there in front of her parents; for the life of her she could hardly imagine how she was going to face it.

On the train home it was all she could think of. With her face buried in a pamphlet she'd picked up at the meeting, she kept reading the same words over and over, hardly noticing the passing panorama or the other passengers in this crowded carriage, her view of the opposite seats blocked by people having to stand. She only looked up as Perivale crept into view, the train puffing and jerking to a stop amid a billowing of smelly coal smoke.

As she patiently waited for her turn to alight from the compartment, someone immediately behind her said quietly, 'Hello, there.'

She turned abruptly and found herself looking

into the clean-shaven face of the tall young man who'd touched his bowler hat to her last Saturday and whom she suddenly recalled with a pinking of her cheeks had been exceptionally good-looking. She felt her breath catch in her throat and a sudden racing of the heart as she became aware of a faint wafting of soap.

'Hello,' she returned, strangely shy. She was not by nature shy and this new feeling rather startled her. He had a most gorgeous smile and that too made her feel quite foolishly overwhelmed.

'I remember you getting off this same train last Saturday,' he was saying as they alighted on to the platform. 'You were rudely jostled and when I practically committed the same offence, I felt I needed to apologise.'

'You didn't jostle me,' she said somewhat stupidly. 'All you did was brush my arm. And you did tip your hat.'

'You remember!' His tone had a lightness to it that betrayed a natural sense of humour. 'So now I'm taking the opportunity to apologise in person.'

Connie smiled, keeping her gaze on the platform a little way ahead. 'There is no need, but it's very nice of you.'

They walked together to the exit, handing their tickets to the ticket collector, and came out of the station on to the street.

'I go this way,' he said. 'Just a short walk to where I live.'

'And I go this way.'

She was aware of a disappointed ring to her tone, but saw him brighten instantly. 'I could escort you to your home.'

'No.' She couldn't have that, not with this evening's ordeal looming. 'No, thank you. It's not far.'

'Then maybe I'll see you again?' His downcast expression made her smile up at him and he brightened again. 'I work in a City bank. After we close on Saturdays I usually have a bite to eat before catching this train home, so it could be I might bump into you again next week?'

'Perhaps,' she said, a little too quickly for her liking.

He was grinning but with pleasure, not ridicule. 'I'll look forward to that.'

She didn't dare say that she too would look forward to it. Even a nod might have indicated the same thing. So she just said, 'Goodbye then,' coming away strangely light of heart. Yes, she'd definitely be able to face the boring Simon and quite cheerfully say no to him.

She heard the jangle of the front doorbell, heard Bentick go to the door, his rather hollow voice saying, 'Good evening, Mr Whitemore,' Simon asking after her as he entered, Bentick replying, 'Miss Constance is in the drawing room, sir.'

Moments later he was being shown into the room, Connie looking up from the book she'd been affecting to read while her mother had fussed and fidgeted with ill-concealed excitement at the coming proposal.

The instant he appeared her mother all but leapt up from her chair and hurried over to him. 'She has been waiting for you, my dear Simon, so I will leave you both alone.' With that she was out of the door and gone.

Connie watched his confident approach, making room on the sofa for him to sit, but kept a tight hold on her book as if it might form a barrier to what he was about to say. Undaunted, he laid a cautious hand on the one that was free, taking time to ask if she was well, what had she been doing all day and confiding that he'd been as nervous as a kitten turned out of doors, waiting for this evening to arrive, finally and with some effort coming to the point.

'Constance, my darling,' he began hesitantly. 'You know, of course, why I have asked to see your father this evening?' She nodded, refusing to relinquish her grip on her book.

'I've looked forward to this for so long,' he went on. 'I think I've been almost fearful of it, but as you offered no objection last week when I said I intended to ask your father for your hand, the time seemed so right.'

She'd offered no objection? She had said nothing one way or the other and he'd automatically taken her silence as consent. What a fool not to have revealed her feeling to him there and then.

'And now, my darling, with your consent, I'll speak to him now.'

Connie came suddenly to life. 'No!'

The word seemed to leap from the very pit of her stomach before she could stop it. But it had been said. Now she could repeat it with conviction. 'No, Simon. I'm sorry.'

He blinked. 'What d'you mean, darling, no, you're sorry?'

She couldn't look at him, staring at the carpet. 'Exactly what I said, Simon. I've thought it over and I don't feel I can marry you.'

Tense, she waited for his reply but before he could do so, the door was carefully edged open and her mother's narrow, beaming face appeared around it. 'Is all going well, Simon dear? Have you asked her yet?'

Connie's reply was sharp and peevish at this interruption, at the same time relieved. 'Yes, Mother, he has asked–'

Her words were cut short as her mother hurried across to embrace her. She held up a hand to stop her. 'You haven't let me finish, Mother. I was about to say that I have said no to him.'

'What?'

'I have told Simon I do not want to marry him.'

There was a totally bewildered look on her mother's face. 'Why? What is the matter with you, child? Of course you do.'

'I'm sorry, Mummy.'

Simon had risen from the sofa. He stood there stiff-backed. 'I think Constance isn't ready for marriage yet. I may have taken her by surprise a little. It may be that she didn't completely understand what I was alluding to last week when I asked her consent to call on her father. I recall she didn't answer me at the time though I took it to mean...'

He broke off awkwardly. 'I probably misconstrued the signs.'

'Of course you didn't!' Isabel Mornington retorted, far more sharply than her usual soft-spoken tones, in command of herself for once. 'She is being silly, that is all. She will come to her senses in a moment. Constance?'

'I mean what I say,' Connie returned. 'I've come to the decision that I can't love Simon. It would be unkind of me to lead him on to thinking that I could.' She turned to him. 'I'm so sorry, Simon.'

His face had grown pale. 'Perhaps under the circumstances I had better leave,' he said stiffly.

Her mother's expression became alarmed. 'My dear, I am sure we can thrash this out. She will come to see sense. Please, Simon, you must stay!'

Connie was aware of him looking at her, his expression now set. 'I think not.' He seemed suddenly so strong that Connie almost felt admiration for him. 'It is best I leave. I would be most grateful, Mrs Mornington, if you would kindly convey my apologies to your husband? Goodbye, Constance.'

Turning on his heel with such dignity that Connie had to stop herself crying out to him, he left the room. She had never seen anyone look so hurt. She heard Bentick let him out to where his motorcar stood waiting, Bentick solemnly closing the door on his departure.

Chapter Four

Eveline was making her way to her lending library but her mind wasn't on books. On the twenty-seventh of this month, April, there would be this huge pageant. It was to be a very important affair and she'd be part of it, and to think she'd only been a suffragette for a couple of weeks. So much was happening – it was exciting. She hadn't dreamed that being a suffragette could be this enjoyable.

The pageant would be held in the evening so there was no need to worry about being absent from work or having her dad find out what she was up to. In time he would, but by then she'd have become so involved that there'd be little he could do. But until then it was best he didn't know.

Stemming her excitement, she entered the library leaving the last glimmer of daylight still glowing beyond the rooftops. She loved reading, romantic novelettes with amorous young females melting into the arms of smouldering men, usually against the wishes of their fathers and, after a stormy passage, eloping with their handsome and virile lovers to everlasting happiness, love conquering all. But she'd been unable to concentrate on this present book for thinking of the pageant and next Saturday's meeting.

Handing the book in at the desk, she made her way over to the shelf that held romantic fiction.

Scrutinising the rows of well-thumbed books that always smelled of mustiness and other people's homes, she skimmed over the titles. A fast reader, she'd read most of them. Authors never wrote quickly enough for her. What did they do all day when she could get through so many even with the interruptions from a family of eight and Mum wanting chores to be done?

The library was a haven where a person could be left alone to browse in peace and not have Mum crying out, 'Wasting time again with yer nose in a book the moment something wants doing round 'ere.'

Mum blamed her for being lazy while her sister May made six of her because she always found some excuse to get out of doing something.

'As soon as there's washing-up ter be done, it always seems you've got something else ter do, disappearing inter yer room. I know what yer up to there – reading, that's what, leaving yer sister ter do all the work.'

What was the point of arguing except to say sorry and promise to pull her weight in the house? But with Mum accusing her of laziness should she pick up a book during any spare moment at home, leaving her little time for reading, where else could she escape to?

There wasn't much here in the library this evening to choose from. Selecting a book at random, she was startled by a voice directly behind her.

'Ello there!'

She swung round to see Bert Adams, his broad, good-looking face creased in a wide smile.

'Ooh, you made me jump!' she burst out.

He didn't apologise.

'I see yer come in. I come 'ere a lot meself. I seen you in 'ere quite a few times. I was over by the reference books.'

He laughed as she wrinkled her nose.

'I'm 'oping ter be a surveyor one day, that's what I'm studying this sort of stuff for.'

He held out the tome for her to see. The black cover looked horribly uninteresting and as he thumbed through it for her benefit every page showed endless dull prints and diagrams.

'Weren't no chance of study at school,' he went on. ''Ad ter leave before I was due, 'cos we lorst me dad. Me mum needed me ter bring in a bit of money ter keep us – me, me bruvver and 'er. He's around eighteen months younger than me. He works too now, so it ain't too bad. We lorst me two sisters when they was kids. I'm a butcher's lad at the moment, the pork butcher's in Bethnal Green Road on the corner of Valance Road. I get tips fer delivering stuff so I can save up fer night school fees, 'cos I want ter get on.'

This was the first time he had ever spoken to her and yet it was as if he'd known her for years, hardly coming up for breath, while she stood, book in hand, smiling politely with no real interest in furthering the conversation even if she'd been given an opportunity.

He was, as her friend had said, quite handsome in that rugged way that could be attractive to girls. He wasn't much taller than her but she would say he was so well-muscled as to be thick-set. The grin that wrinkled his face seemed to

60

light up his whole features.

'Been a butcher's boy ever since I left school,' he went on. 'Ain't no future in it, but then I'm studying, ain't I? Six years since I left school. Ain't even been put be'ind the counter yet. He's got a son what does that and there ain't room fer the likes of me. So I still pedals me bike and do the deliveries. But one day, yer won't see me rear fer dust. Can't afford no college, so I'm studying off me own bat.'

She'd never seen such determination in a person's eyes. Admiration flowed through her. 'I hope you get what you want,' she ventured.

'I 'ope so too. I've seen you in Bethnal Green Road sometimes.'

Yes, she'd seen him too, glimpsed him in passing when she and Ada or Daisy joined in the evening parade of young hopefuls up and down the main road eyeing the lads similarly parading in twos, threes and fours. Many a couple would team up from these patrols. Daisy had, but only casually as yet. Whether it'd develop into something more permanent was another matter. Eveline had never seen any she fancied so far, being a bit too particular. But Daisy going off had left a hole, although her interest in suffragettes had helped to fill it.

'By the way, I'm Bert Adams, if yer don't know,' he supplied.

'Yes, I do know,' she said.

'And you're Ev Fenton.'

'Eveline,' she corrected. She'd always hated hearing it shortened.

He beamed, unperturbed. 'Eveline, sorry. Your dad's got that grocer shop in Three Colts Lane. Though I ain't never seen you in there.'

61

'I don't work there,' she explained. 'Only him and my mother, and my sister sometimes. They don't need any more behind the counter. I work at the biscuit factory.' Why was she telling him all this? 'In the office,' she added quickly in case he thought her a lowly factory worker.

She had run out of words and now noticed a small pimple on one cheek well on its way to erupting. In spite of him being quite good-looking some of her interest faded. Yet he was nice – and polite, unusual in lads from around these parts. She came to herself with a start.

'Well, I must be off. It was nice talking to you but I've got my book and I need to get home before it gets too dark.'

'I could walk yer.'

'No.' She moved away. 'It's all right. You go on with your studying.'

'Sure?'

'Yes, perfectly.'

'I'll see you in 'ere some other time then.'

'Yes, some other time.'

Hurrying off, she wondered why she'd said that. An open invitation if ever there was one. Now she'd have to avoid him. Fine to fancy someone's looks from a distance, but he had a pimple. The young man she'd seen at the suffragette meeting hadn't got pimples.

For Connie it had been a week she would never forget. Seven days starting with argument and threats and ending with brooding silences, her mother in despair, her father refusing to speak to her.

Trying to plead her case had fallen on deaf ears until finally she had retreated to her room where she had remained for the rest of the week, not coming down to breakfast or lunch though good manners demanded she appear at dinner. This though was eaten in deeper silence than usual; poor Verity, her younger sister, visibly ill at ease while her mother toyed with the food on her plate, announcing herself too devastated to eat, her father gazing straight ahead as he ate his meal at an agonising, steady pace, finally rising from the table to stalk from the room without a word to anyone.

At night, determined not to relent, she would lie awake hearing Verity going off to her room, her parents to theirs, Agnes raking out the fires downstairs, Bentick bolting the front door and locking windows, the silence that followed leaving her to continue an imaginary argument with absent parents, her head filled by their counter-arguments, none of it solving anything.

Now and again Verity would steal into her bedroom to give her support, and on Friday had burst out impulsively: 'I think Simon Whitemore a thorough bore. *I* wouldn't want him for a husband, well connected or not.'

'I wouldn't say he is that bad,' Connie said, defending the man in his absence. 'He's a good person, but I don't love him enough to marry him.'

Verity had taken the mild reprimand calmly to gaze at her sister in awe. 'Father is livid. I wish I had your courage to stand up to him.'

Connie had smiled at that. When something

was important enough to affect a person's entire future, some sort of stand had to be made exactly as many a woman was doing for the suffragette cause.

As Verity left, Connie's thoughts turned to those women, helping her to take her mind off her own troubles. Like Eveline Fenton she too had been only mildly interested at first but what they stood for had quickly taken over. Of course her father would eventually find out and it wouldn't merely be a matter of refusing a suitor; after all, another could easily be found for his beautiful daughter. Belief in a strong cause wasn't so easily put aside and she had a horrible premonition that one day it would reap dire consequences.

Now it was Saturday. She'd be going to her suffragette meeting. She awoke strangely lighter of heart and even came down to breakfast to suffer her father's steely disregard. After lunch, dressed for town, as she adjusted her oversized hat in the hall's ornate mirror while little Agnes stood with coat and gloves, her father's study door opened. Next minute he was in the hall, his face with its trim beard reflected behind her in the mirror.

'Where are you going, Constance?' It was the first time he'd spoken to her directly in days. She turned to face him.

'I am meeting my school friend, the girl I saw last week.'

'I'm afraid you do not leave this house, Constance, until you come to your senses,' he said as if addressing a child. The words would have been laughable had it not been so serious. 'You may send your friend a telegram informing her that you will not be meeting her.'

'I don't know her address,' Connie said, the lie stiff on her lips.

'Nevertheless...'

Sudden anger flooded over her. 'You can't stop me, Father!'

For a moment he looked stunned that she could speak to him in this manner but swiftly regained his composure.

'Leave this house, Constance, and you can take my word that this door will not be opened to you on your return.'

Hardly able to believe her courage, Connie glared back at him. 'Then so be it!'

He seemed to mellow a little. 'This *friend*, is it a man?' he asked, his tone slow and soft. Now she could at least tell a partial truth.

'No, Father. My friend's name is Eveline and we have been meeting each Saturday to have lunch together.'

There she left it. Best not to say more before it became too involved for her good. He must never know that this wasn't an old school chum but a fellow suffragette. She continued to stare him out while Agnes, holding her coat and gloves, gazed uncertainly from one to another.

For a moment longer he returned her steady gaze then, turning on his heel, refusing to be drawn into an undignified squabble in front of a member of his staff, strode back to his study, the door closing softly. But she knew there'd follow weeks of uncomfortable silence and little she could do about it.

This Saturday afternoon saw a larger than usual group attending at George Street, all talking about the preparations for the Tuesday evening pageant.

Eveline had difficulty finding any vacant pegs for her coat in the cloakroom with so many hanging there. She kept her hat on as quite a few did, more for convenience with all that removing and re-inserting of hatpins, large brims with their wealth of trimming knocking together as ladies gossiped.

There were two men present too. They stood out like sore thumbs amid the squash of females. The middle-aged one did appear interested, unlike the second, a much younger man looking utterly bored. Eveline recognised him instantly as the young man she'd seen at that first meeting. She saw too that the young woman he'd been with then was with him again.

It was silly, the dismay that went through her on seeing the woman – no doubt a steady lady friend, who had probably dragged him along with her judging by his reluctant expression. But even see-ing him here, from then on Eveline found herself unable to concentrate on anything else.

'Are you all right?' Connic asked as she came to sit beside her.

She forced a smile. 'I'm fine,' she said a little too exuberantly then sobered. 'You see that young man in the corner talking to that woman?' She waited for Connie to follow her discreetly directed gaze. 'He's the one who kept staring at me at the Ambrose Hall meeting.'

Connie was looking a little bemused and she realised that she hadn't so far mentioned him to her. She now needed to play it down. 'I expect he was probably looking at someone else but I wonder what he's doing here?'

'I suppose the same as we all are,' Connie said without too much interest. 'There are plenty of men sympathetic to our cause, thank the Lord.'

The lady chairman, Mrs Edith Duffield, was commanding attention from the small dais, her voice raised above the general chatter.

'Thank you! Thank you, everyone!'

Hush descended. The ladies standing about talking hurried to their own seats. The young man leaned back in his. The woman with him was sitting much too close to him and again Eveline experienced that deep sense of dejection.

'It is so very pleasing,' Mrs Duffield was saying, 'to see so many of you here. But of course it was expected, being such an important week in our calendar. I refer to the International Woman Suffrage Alliance holding its Quinquennial Congress in London and in the very same week the Pageant of Women's Trades and Professions. Let me tell you a little about that.'

She gazed around at fifty or more pairs of attentive eyes, their owners having squashed into a room designed to hold hardly more than forty, and it included a table for committee officers and speaker.

'There will be a good thousand of us from ninety different occupations gathered under the trees in Eaton Square. The procession as you know will be lit by lanterns as we move off down Sloane Street skirting Hyde Park and terminating at the Albert Hall. It will be a sight to behold.'

'We will make such a show,' cried one member,

totally carried away. 'We'll be a blaze of light with torches and lanterns and emblems, an endless column of light,' to which everyone agreed with enthusiasm.

The talk turned to the procession itself, Eveline finally dragging her gaze away from the back of her quarry's head as their chair lady continued.

'The procession is to proceed in five separate blocks, according to trade and profession. Each block will have a number. Block One will be for farmers, market gardeners and all others in that field. It will also include housewives, house-keepers, and trades such as sweet and jam makers, cigar and cigarette makers, and so on. I have lists of every trade here so that those of you who do plan to join us can come and take one to find out where you will be.'

'I expect I'll be in Block Four,' Eveline said to Connie as they went up for their list. 'I am more or less an office worker.'

It was a good one to be in, among the secre-taries, shorthand typists, indexers and printers, also including writers and journalists, actresses and singers and musicians. She, a mere calcu-lating machine operator, felt quite elevated to be among such distinguished people.

'I'm not sure where I shall be,' Connie said somewhat glumly. 'I don't have a trade and I don't work. I feel a little left out. I shan't be wanted.'

Eveline looked at her in surprised sympathy. Only a few weeks ago it had been she who'd felt like that, a stranger glad to be taken under someone's wing, that someone being Connie, for which she had felt eternally grateful. Now here was Connie admitting to feeling left out.

'Of course you'll be wanted. There must be something you do. Maybe you help with some charity work or other?' Connie shook her head. 'My mother does. She has lots of charities.'

'Couldn't you choose one of them and say you do those things too?'

Again Connie shook her head. 'I don't think this includes charity work.'

'Well, what do you do for a pastime?' Eveline urged helpfully.

Connie pursed her lips. 'I like to paint. I paint landscapes and...'

'Well there you are then!' Eveline felt suddenly in control. 'You could be in Block Two with the painters and sculptors and fashion designers and all those sort.'

Block Two would also have house decorators, florists, dressmakers, milliners, pottery painters, especially when Connie divulged that she had also turned her hand at a little pottery at a class she went to.

'There you are then,' Eveline said again. 'The other two blocks don't concern us – industrial workers and the nursing professions. I'd like to have an emblem of some sort like what's been described but not the secretary bird they suggested because I'm not really a secretary. I suppose I could draw a calculator machine but I'm not very good at drawing.'

'I'll design one for you,' Connie said, suddenly full of enthusiasm. 'I could paint a tape of calculations in red coming out of it. I'll make something for myself too – an artist's pallet and brush.'

69

As the meeting began to break up with everyone chattering at once, Eveline regarded her with envy. 'I wish I was as clever as you,' she said as they moved over to the refreshment table with the rest for more tea and cake to send them on their way. 'And I wish I had your freedom too.'

'Freedom!' The word burst from Connie's lips. 'If only you knew. What freedom I have is won at high cost.'

In short bursts she related the way she had defied her father over the man he had set his mind on her marrying.

'Why should I marry someone I don't really love, just to please him?' she went on vehemently. 'Simon and I got on to a certain extent but he was too much like my father, too full of his own importance for me to want to settle down as his wife.'

Words tumbled out, how she had spoken her mind before both sets of parents, Simon shocked, stunned rather than devastated, everyone shocked; the week of remonstration that followed. Connie lifted her chin defiantly.

'I've rather burned my bridges in that direction. It's only a matter of time before I burn a few more by telling my father that I'm a suffragette. He utterly disagrees with women having independence. I'm sure it stems from a fear of us becoming independent, able to do without them, especially men such as he of high standing. He's a doctor, you know. But I don't care if he does throw me out of the house; I am determined nothing is going to stop me continuing to be a suffragette.'

Eveline felt of the same mind but in a different

way. Her father might not go picking a husband for her but he'd air his opinions all right regarding what he called them shrieking suffragettes. Finding his daughter was one of them would really make him see red but though she couldn't imagine him throwing her out, how could he stop her? Lock her in her room forever?

She grinned at the notion but seconds later she was distracted by the sight of the young man she'd been eyeing throughout the meeting sauntering towards them at the refreshment table. In a sudden surge of anticipation she turned in his direction. Not looking at what she was doing, her sleeve caught the slice of Madeira cake on her plate, sweeping it off.

'Oh!'

She tried to catch it as it fell but succeeded only in giving it a whack so that it landed in several pieces at the young man's feet. Flustered and embarrassed, she made an ungainly lunge in her tight skirt to retrieve it, her elbow catching the plate she'd been holding. It landed on top of the already broken cake, splattering it even more. All eyes turned towards the disruption.

'Oh dear, I'm sorry!' she gasped in dismay.

She was vaguely aware of a reassuring hand on her arm, the slim fingers gently curling around it.

'Allow me,' he said in a low, easy tone. Before she could stop him he had bent and gathered up both plate and lumps of cake, depositing them in the hands of the lady dispensing teas who had hurried around the table to see what she could do.

'I'm sorry,' he said. 'I seemed to have been a

little clumsy.'

The older woman simpered before the fine blue eyes. 'Not at all, dear man. Accidents happen.'

'Thank you,' he said in the same low tone and turned back to Eveline, she by now blushing furiously. 'Are you all right?'

'Yes,' she managed. She was aware of Connie looking on. 'I'm fine, thank you. But it was my fault. You shouldn't have taken the blame.'

'It shouldn't matter,' he said. 'It's over now.' He was regarding her closely. 'I'm sure we've met somewhere.'

'Ambrose Hall, a few weeks ago,' Eveline blurted without thinking. It was too late to retract. She saw Connie regarding her with some amusement. 'A few weeks ago,' she repeated lamely. 'We didn't speak, though.'

'I remember,' he returned. 'I was sitting a little way behind you.'

He didn't need to say more. She was painfully aware from the look in his eyes that he recollected their glances meeting, and her turning a second time to look at him. The memory brought up her colour quite violently. What must he be thinking of her?

'I'm glad I've met you again,' he was saying. 'As there's no one here I can ask to introduce us, I will introduce myself if you have no objection.'

She gave a small shake of her head, still aware of Connie looking on, less amused now so she thought. Was she seeing her as an outrageous flirt?

'My name's Laurence Jones-Fairbrook. Larry,' he ended lightly.

'I'm Eveline Fenton,' she said in a small voice. Then, unable to help herself, she burst out, 'Is that young lady you're with your fiancée?'

The question instantly struck her as utterly rude, but he laughed, half turning to where his companion sat talking to another woman. 'My cousin,' he said lightly. 'She's a bit of a suffragette and when in town likes to pop in here, but insists I chaperone her, though why, I don't know. She's a capable enough person. Still, only right I oblige.'

Connie had put her cup of tea back on the table. She laid a discreet hand on Eveline's arm. 'I have to be off. I shall leave you two together. I'll see you on Tuesday evening at the pageant?'

Eveline's gaze was trained on Laurence's handsome, narrow face as if held there by a magnetic force, relief and delight all but overwhelming her. 'Yes, of course,' she murmured absently, aware that she was alone with this man, alone in the crowd of departing attendees.

'You'll be at the pageant?' he asked quietly. As she nodded he said, 'Then I shall make certain to be there too. My cousin will have gone home, but I shall look out for you, if I may. If you don't mind?'

She shook her head. 'Not at all.'

'Very well,' he said.

Going home, her heart pounding with excitement, she could hardly believe what had happened, that he was actually unattached, had spoken to her, had even spoken of seeing her again if only at the pageant.

Chapter Five

'And what're you looking so 'appy about?' Mum asked the moment Eveline showed her face that evening.

She couldn't help smirking. Happy? She was ecstatic but had hoped it wouldn't show. Even a dismissive shrug couldn't conceal her feelings.

'Yer look like yer've lost a penny and found a pound.' Mum loved changing idioms around to suit the occasion.

'I've had a nice afternoon, that's all,' she muttered as offhandedly as she could but knowing full well that wouldn't fool her mother for a minute, ever in hope of her finding a suitable young man.

'Meet someone nice, did yer?'

'Where's Dad?' Eveline evaded, hanging her coat on the peg behind the living-room door to be followed by her wide-brimmed hat. She would see if she could buy a new, more fashionable hat ready for the Tuesday pageant – dig into her modest savings for it.

'Still downstairs,' came the reply. 'Where else on Saturday evening? Yer sister's giving 'im an 'and down there while I do the dinner.' Mum was regarding her keenly. 'So who is it then what's made yer face all glowing?'

Eveline dropped on to one of the upright chairs in the family living-cum-dining room.

There were only two armchairs, one for Mum

74

and one for Dad and woe betide anyone who used them without permission. No room for a sofa what with the dining table large enough for a dozen people, the chest of drawers and the bed in one corner partially shielded from sight by the Chinese screen that had belonged to Gran, all taking up so much space. It was left for everyone else to use the six hard chairs and two stools, often drawn up to the table not only for meals but when the family was indulging in their various hobbies of an evening, elbows supported on its surface on which after every meal was done Mum would spread her maroon chenille table-cover.

Mum came to stand over her. She'd grown plumper with the years but at forty-one she was still as solid as she had ever been – a worker, helping her husband in his shop and doing her own chores, disdaining paid help though most in her position would at least have had someone to do the general housework. She did however relent about the laundry, sending it out to a woman who lived not far off, on the other side of the arches.

Mum would inspect every article that came back, her brown eyes in her rounded face sharply critical while she remarked without fail, 'I could of done this better meself,' but she never did nor changed her washerwoman.

'So, who is it?' she prompted Eveline, who responded with a resigned sigh. You couldn't keep anything from Mum for long.

'Just someone I met.'

'Nice, was he?'

'All right, I suppose.' To her relief the non-committal reply made her mother relent; suddenly she deemed immediate matters to be more pressing.

'Well, don't just sit there! There's things ter be done so make yerself useful. The table's still got ter be laid and the cabbage needs ter be strained and taters mashed.'

Mum moved past her towards the kitchen, pausing to look over her shoulder.

'Come on then, blooming Miss Lazybones. Sausages are nearly done. I just got ter make the gravy.'

To her, plain sausage and mash was common fare. Saturday called for them to be done in the oven with onions and Bisto gravy.

'Yer dad ought ter be closing up now and ready for 'is tea.'

She said it hopefully. If a customer banged on his door for a purchase they'd left until the last moment, even if he'd that minute locked up and drawn down the door blind, he'd open up for them: whether from goodwill or just to make that few extra pennies was never certain, though to pay rent on the shop and flat and feed a family every penny helped.

Tonight he'd closed on time, coming up the back stairs with the cash box under his arm, May following. Coming in he glanced at Eveline, grunted but said nothing. He didn't approve of what he called idle gadding.

Len Fenton was a man of few words but expected his authority to be respected. Stocky, having become slightly bow-legged as the years wore on, he looked the typical London Cockney. Uneducated though he was, he still had a good head for facts and figures, and although he rarely aired his opinions, when he did everyone knew immediately where they stood. His taciturnity would sometimes give Mum the impression that it was she who ruled this roost, then one word, one look from him would tell her that she didn't. All in all, things in this house went along smoothly enough. Only Eveline, being very much like him except that she talked more freely, was a thorn in his side more often than not.

To her relief Mum, involved in dishing up, eating, discussing the shop and the takings and the way money went out of the house, said no more about the someone her daughter had admitted to meeting.

The evening meal was a time for lively chatter. No one ate in silence. Her younger brothers, nine-year-old Jimmy and seven-year-old Bobby, were giving each other lip until Mum, who'd been ladling gravy on to little Alfie's plate – at not quite three he still needed help with his food – turned and tapped each squabbling boy sharply on the head with the gravy spoon. This left traces of gravy which they spread further into their hair as they vigorously rubbed away the sharp little pain from the contact of spoon on scalp.

Seventeen-year-old Len was talking football to Dad. Very athletic, he was playing in his club's Sunday match tomorrow and Dad was going there to cheer him on. May and Mum were discussing trivialities between mouthfuls of mash, cabbage and sausage but Eveline knew it was only a matter of time before Mum turned to her to hear more about this young man she'd met. It had to come – the way she kept glancing at her while talking with May.

'So what's 'is name, this bloke yer met?' she finally asked as May got up to clear away the empty plates.

Dad had gone to sit in his well-worn armchair by the fire to study football results in the *Evening Star*. He looked up enquiringly, but Eveline didn't return his look as she got up to help her industrious sister.

Mum's eyes followed her. 'Or didn't he say what 'is name was?'

She didn't like the way it was being made to look as if she had been casually picked up. She had to correct that.

'Of course he said.' May came in for the rest of the debris and Eveline busied herself gathering up the tablecloth ready to shake over the kitchen sink, keeping her eyes down.

There was no escaping her mother's probing. 'What was it then?

The name already felt at odds with the world she lived in. 'It's ... it's Laurence. Laurence Jones-Fairbrook.' Strange that she could remember it, she who never had a great memory for names. 'Larry,' she ended lamely.

'Good Lord!' her mum burst out. 'You don't 'alf pick 'em! You ain't goin' ter see that one no more, I can tell yer. Bloke with a stuck-up name like that – yer won't see 'im again.'

Yes, she would – in three days time, at the pageant. And she was going to buy a new hat on Monday evening so as to impress him.

'So, where did yer meet 'im?'

'Up West.'

'How? How did yer come by meeting a bloke with a name like that?'

It was getting harder by the minute. She ignored the throaty cough from her father signalling his interest as well. She ignored too the stare from May. May, not working but seen as the good daughter, the stay-at-home who seemed to prefer household chores to going out of an evening, May being held up time after time as an example to herself.

'I just met him, that's all,' she said a bit too sharply and hurried out to the kitchen with the tablecloth. Shaking it over the pots and pans lying in the sink she quickly folded it and thrust it in a kitchen drawer.

Even out here there was no peace. May's eyes were on stalks behind her round, steel-rimmed glasses. 'Yer can tell me,' she said.

'Nothing to tell,' Eveline retorted. 'I just met some bloke, that's all,' she said sharply and as Mum came into the kitchen, she made off to the toilet, to sit and think of Larry Jones-Fairbrook just for a few minutes, daring Mum's wrath at seeing her as again trying to escape the washing-up.

May watched her go as Mum began sprinkling soda into the hot water she'd poured into the basin from the kettle to start washing up with swift energy and much noise, while May wiped and put away in the kitchen cupboard.

Mum was right when she called Eveline a lazy little cow gadding about when she should be pulling her weight at home. It didn't worry her that Eveline didn't pull her weight – she enjoyed basking in Mum's approval of her as against her sister. She didn't go out a lot, not as much as Eveline, though when she got to her age it might be a different kettle of fish.

Having stayed at school right up to fourteen, she'd got a job straight away but ten months later had been laid off. She hadn't gone after another, happy being at home helping around the house while Mum was in the shop, and sometimes, like this afternoon, she'd work down there while Mum got dinner ready. Dad gave her a little salary and Mum gave her pocket money.

She was aware that Mum saw her as being cheaper than employing someone, but she didn't mind. Housework was better than getting up and going out to work and when she was in the shop she met lots of people. Everyone knew her. She lapped up remarks on how efficient she was and it kept her in Mum's good books, not like Eveline.

This evening there was something different about Eveline. She met lots of boys though none of them lasted. But this one, whoever he was, she was being unusually secretive about. May had never seen her glow like this before and she itched to find out more about it, but Eveline was being so cagey.

In the bed they shared she began tentatively to probe and this time it seemed Eveline couldn't keep whatever it was to herself any longer.

'I've met someone, someone really wonderful. But if I tell you where, you must promise you won't tell Mum and Dad. It's important. If you do, I'll lose him, and I will kill you. My whole life will be ruined.'

'I promise,' she said, and she meant it.

Sitting upright she gazed down at her sister. Whatever Eveline might think, she was no sneak. In fact keeping secrets was exciting, knowing something no one else knew.

It was a wonderful tale: the suffragette procession, this unusual friendship Eveline had struck up with this Constance person whose family were apparently upper middle class; now this young man who by the sound of it was also pretty well off. And why shouldn't a person like that fancy her sister, whose pretty features, dark brown hair that glowed so healthily and light brown eyes were enough to turn every young man's head in the land?

Ever the romantic, tending to live off other people's exciting lives, May felt suddenly important. Her sister's fate lay in her hands; she was now sworn to secrecy. If Dad knew where she was going he'd put a stop to it, make such a ruckus that Eveline's life wouldn't be worth living and she might never see this Larry again. Oddly enough it would be to her advantage, to the advantage of them all, if Eveline and this young man did become serious. Money would rub off on the rest of them. This was a secret to be kept all right.

Constance walked slowly through the platform barrier in Paddington Station. Her train was already there and breathing heavily like a contented old bull.

She was in no particular rush to get home. Her

81

Saturday afternoon meetings were a boon, an escape from a family that was growing ever more possessive, worse since her traumatic rejection of Simon. But she had no intention of being one of those demure and obedient daughters of the privileged who at eighteen came out, finished, polished, primed for marriage.

Already gossip had spread concerning her callous spurning of poor Simon Whitemore. How could she do such a thing? Her family wasn't speaking to her, her father even threatening to cast her out, Simon must be out of his mind with grief, and he such a catch, a most suitable suitor, she must be completely mad; so went the comments.

Some of her friends had already approached her, eager to know the facts. What could she tell them but what they had already made up their minds to? Others were pretending it hadn't happened, looked awkward in her presence as if there had been some tragedy. One way or the other she was the unwilling centre of attention and it was hateful.

She walked slowly along the platform going over last Saturday evening as she recalled Bentick and Agnes standing ready to clear the first course and serve the next – mute, deaf and expressionless as good staff ought to be. She'd been conscious of a sort of masochistic glee that behind those rigid countenances they took in the small drama.

If only she had known she wouldn't have been so smug. Perhaps a maid hadn't been such a loyal servant and that's how it had all got out. Father took care never to discuss family business at table, even though Bentick was trusted to the umpteenth degree. No, there'd been tittle-tattle from Agnes outside work.

Things like this could never happen to Eveline Fenton. She'd probably marry whomever she wanted. There came as well a small prickle of envy over the young man who'd come up to Eveline at the refreshment table, practically ignoring Constance. How could the daughter of a tradesman attract a person of such obvious means? Admittedly Eveline was pretty, vivacious, had a charming figure. But so had she. She however had the upbringing to know not to flutter her eyelids at any man...

Connie stopped sharply. What was she thinking?

Angered at having such uncharitable thoughts, she told herself she didn't envy the interest the man had shown in her friend but Eveline's self-assuredness. Nor should a suffragette harbour envy towards another but she could not help feeling just a little thwarted by this afternoon's events.

She thought again of Simon. Perhaps she should have thought twice before behaving as she had. She had upset everyone, and for what – to prove a point? After all, he was intensely good-looking in a stuffy sort of way, like her father, and it had got on her nerves. But engaged to him she would have been looked upon as someone of consequence, instead of suffering this sense of being left out when another drew a young man's eye. Perhaps if she were to apologise to her father, say she would accept Simon's offer of marriage if it wasn't too late, this sense of envy would disappear.

Moving on down the platform she found she'd walked its entire length, realising it only as a jet of steam released from the engine in a terrific shriek made her jump. Hastily she retraced her steps, in her confusion clambering into the last carriage to drop into the one vacant seat by the window looking out on to the platform; the other three window seats were already taken.

The minutes ticked by as she fought to catch her breath. The carriage began to fill, the door continually opening to let someone in, along with the smell of engine oil and coal smoke, before being pulled shut with a bang by its leather strap; ladies brushed by her in their long skirts and laden with parcels dangling on strings, men with exaggerated gentlemanly politeness sidled past, effortlessly hoisting their attaché cases on to the sagging net rack, one of them helping to put a lady's bulky parcel up for her.

Connie hardly noticed, her eyes gazing without really focusing on the stream of people going home either from work or shopping.

The train whistled, shook itself, making the carriage jerk noisily, and began to move, puffing and juddering, slowly and with effort to gather a little speed. Connie settled back and resigned herself to looking over some of the pamphlets she had picked up at the meeting, trying not to think too much.

A figure racing by her window made her glance up. Recognising the figure she felt her heart leap. He glanced in but noting the full carriage, he raced on, just managing to gain a little on the moving train. She expected to see him come to a stop, defeated. She too felt suddenly defeated, knowing she wouldn't see him at Perivale this Saturday. The train pulling out fast now, she saw the platform deserted but for a guard looking somewhat put out by some fool having jumping into a moving carriage.

It could only have been the next carriage along from hers. He couldn't have got any further. Why did she feel such excitement? For the rest of the journey, she was unable to digest one word of her pamphlets for thinking about him. In her mind's eye she could see him grabbing the carriage door handle, yanking the door open and making an agile leap into the moving carriage with someone maybe grabbing him to stop him falling back.

As she got out at Perivale her eyes began searching the carriage before hers, already emptying, but there was no sign of him. It couldn't have been him after all. Deflated, she made her way to the exit, giving up her ticket, her mind momentarily taken up by the first spattering of rain that had been threatening all afternoon. She had no umbrella.

Then she saw him. He was buying an evening paper from the newsboy by the entrance. Now elation turned to indecision. Should she say hello or just walk by? She had spoken to him only that once. She didn't know his name and it wasn't a young lady's place to make the first move, yet if she ignored him he would think her stand-offish and keep his distance from then on. She could of course pause to buy a newspaper...

Hurrying forward, purse at the ready, she came to stand beside him, selecting the *Evening Stand-*

ard, all she could think to pick up, very seldom buying a paper. To her joy he looked at her.

'Hello, again!' His voice held a cheery ring. 'I never thought to see you a third time. Do you catch the same train every Saturday?'

She normally didn't, but she'd come away early, not to get home quickly but to leave Eveline with that young man. Also at the back of her mind was the knowledge that this particular train had twice held her own quarry and could again. That hope of course had been realised.

'I have done so these last few weeks,' she said truthfully.

He handed a penny to the newsboy and then another. 'For the young lady's paper,' he said.

'Oh, no, please don't!' The action flustered her. 'Please, you mustn't!'

Her protest seemed to be ignored. 'So will you be on the same train, say next week?'

'I don't know. I hope ... I mean I might...'

She tailed off, anxious not to commit herself too much. 'Please, you must let me pay for my newspaper.'

He was smiling. 'I wouldn't dream of it,' he said lightly, folding his own paper under his arm.

She couldn't go on protesting but she had to say something. 'I ... I thought I saw you run by my carriage. Did you get in the next one?'

'Full. I had to dash on to the one after that. Made it only by the skin of my teeth in fact.'

That was why she hadn't seen him get out; her eyes had been trained only on the carriage in front of hers. 'Saturday-afternoon trains are always pretty full, people going home,' she said in an effort to make small talk. 'You said you worked in a bank?'

'That's right.' He was eyeing the leaden sky and began unfastening the long, black umbrella he carried. He was in a hurry to be away. Connie's heart sank.

'I'd best be on my way then,' she said inadequately. 'Before it really comes down.'

'Haven't you a brolly?'

'I didn't think it would rain.'

'Then, look – we'll use mine. I'll see you home, safe and dry.'

'Oh, no.' She had visions of her father seeing her with a strange man. 'It's all right, I'll try to get a taxi.'

He smiled. It was a gentle, kindly smile. 'Why waste money? Please – allow me to escort you. I'm sorry, I don't know your name.'

It was usual for a young lady of her standing to rely on a third party to make introductions, but that world was changing, and after all wasn't she a suffragette, working for women's rights, and not just to get the vote? So she should flout the old niceties. She would let him to walk her home.

'My name is Constance Mornington,' she offered without hesitation.

'George Towers,' he obliged and crooked an arm for her to take, which she did, aware of warmth even through her thin black leather glove.

It seemed the most natural thing walking beside him under the one umbrella. With her other hand she lifted her skirt clear of the now wet pavement; she told herself that holding his arm was merely to keep them both dry.

There was a wonderful sense of ease between them, even to the extent of laughing together as her large and cumbersome hat got in his way to be knocked slightly sideways so that she had to stop twice to readjust it.

Conversation too came quite naturally as though they had known each other for ages. By the time they'd gone the ten minutes to her home, she knew all about him.

He said he lived with his widowed mother in rented accommodation; that she was ailing with a heart condition, so that looking after her impeded any social life he might have had; that, and not a lot of money coming in.

'Only my wages,' he said. 'I'm merely a bank clerk. Had I not lost my father, who worked there and would have spoken up for me, I might have had promotion by now, but that's how things go. I could have done worse.'

He spoke with no bitterness, almost as if amused by the tricks fate could play on a person.

She in turn told him about her own life, managing to play down her family's high standing. She even had him laughing as she described her shocking rejection of the young man her father had wished her to become engaged to.

'I don't think he'll ever forgive me,' she giggled, hearing him chuckle. It seemed to matter little to him that her family were well off and he wasn't.

At the gate of the drive she broke away from him for all her determination to appear emancipated, fearing her family seeing her with this strange man. Thankfully her house was shielded from the road by trees.

'This is where I live,' she stated. 'I'll be fine from here.'

He grimaced up at the now steady rain. 'It's starting to come down a bit. The least I can do is to see you to your door.'

'No,' she said in alarm. 'It's a short step. I shall run.'

He hovered. 'Will I see you on the train next week? I could wait for you.'

'I don't know. I can't say.' But he was looking so hopeful and she wanted so much for him to meet her. Suddenly she knew that even if there were no meeting next week, she would go into London just to catch that particular train home. He'd said he would be waiting for her.

'Come to think of it, I expect I will be catching the same train.' This surely was being quite mad.

'Splendid!' he burst out. 'Then, same time, same place?'

'Yes. And thank you for the paper. You really shouldn't have. A lady shouldn't accept gifts from a man she has hardly–'

'A penny,' he broke in with a laugh. 'Hardly a gift.'

She found herself laughing with him but saying she must go. Moving off and forgetting to thank him for escorting her home through the rain, she hurried up the driveway, almost breathless with excitement. Somehow it did not matter that he obviously had very little money. All she knew was that she could hardly wait to see him again.

Chapter Six

Mum was being awkward. 'Always swanning off out, you are,' she flared at Eveline as May got up to clear away their tea. 'Bad enough Fridays and Saturdays but it's Tuesday. Yer've just come in from work an' look at yer, golloped down yer tea like you 'adn't two minutes ter spare. I s'pose yer off now ter put on yer glad rags. Can't even stop to 'elp yer sister. What's so special about tonight?'

Eveline smothered her frustration and turned back to at least offer them a token helping hand. Not to have done so would start an argument and delay her all the more. The pageant was her first ever rally, the last thing she wanted was to be late. Laurence had said he would be there waiting for her.

'I'm meeting someone,' she said, helping to gather up the dirty plates.

Her mother took them from her to regard her closely. 'Is it this new bloke you met?'

'I don't want him to think I've let him down.'

Her father glanced up from his paper. 'If he's orright, he'll wait.'

Mum ignored him. 'Serious then, is it?'

Was she thinking this might be the one and didn't want to spoil her daughter's chances? There was nothing to do here this evening but watch her darn Dad's socks, him with his face in his evening paper, May with hers in a penny magazine, Jimmy and Bobby at the table playing draughts. Little Alfie was already in bed. Len would be out with his mates. Even so, her mother had to have one last dig.

'I wouldn't mind, Ev, but yer don't do a thing around the place.'

At home she was called Ev. Having gone to the trouble of giving her a nice name, Mum and Dad spoiled it by shortening it to that horrid-sounding one.

'I do as much as I can,' she protested. 'But I work all the week. I'm not out every night.'

May caught her eye and smiled apologetically, but Mum wasn't done yet.

'It's practic'ly getting that way. There's me and yer dad slaving in the shop all day ter keep this family together and all you can think of is looking after yer own pleasure.'

Dad looked up. 'Yer Mum's right, gel. Yer should stay in more.'

He turned back to his paper, seldom interfering in what Mum said unless something concerned him personally.

True, he did work hard in his shop, on his feet all day. But once the shop closed, his paperwork done, all he wanted to do was put them up.

Dad's feet were the most noticeable thing about him, slightly splayed out. 'Quarter-to-three feet,' Mum called them; it gave him a somewhat flat-footed gait. Like a lot of East End Cockneys, he was wiry and pale, but he made up for it with a mane of tawny hair, which he plastered flat with brilliantine, hardly a strand of grey anywhere. His walrus moustache too was tawny, stained by the strong tea he drank.

It was from that moustache that he now noisily sucked the drains of his teacup as he settled back to his paper.

Looking over at him, Eveline briefly wondered how he and Mum had ever got together. She at forty-one still showed traces of the beauty she had once been and stood an inch or so taller than him. He'd probably been handsome once or Mum wouldn't have chosen him. She often said she had been a choosy one. Eveline herself was choosy and this time it seemed her choosiness might be paying off with the young man, Larry, saying he'd see her at the pageant. She just had to be there.

'I promise to help twice as much, but not to-night. I can't not meet him. He's taking me to the Albert Hall. We'll be with other people so we won't be alone. He's very polite and well brought up.'

Mum looked at her for a long time while May went off to the kitchen with her load. Mum was finally melting, thankfully forgetting to ask what was on at the Albert Hall.

'Well orright then. But don't be too late 'ome. And mind you stay with these other people,' she added with dark warning, but Eveline was already making for her bedroom to change into her best skirt and blouse, her coat and hat. When she reappeared, Mum followed her to the door.

'Remember ter stay with other people,' her voice trailed after her as Eveline hurried down the stairs to the side door by the shop. 'Yer don't know 'im enough yet ter be alone. That's of course if he meets yer. Remember, be 'ome by ten or yer dad'll 'ave somethink ter say. Ten o'clock, remember.'

'Ten thirty, Mum,' Eveline called up.

'Orright, but not a minute–'

Closing the street door behind her, Eveline didn't catch the rest.

It was a gusty evening, overcast skies bringing in the dusk all the quicker. Eveline craned her neck to see over the thousand or more women milling under the trees of Eaton Square to join their respective blocks before moving off. It was going to be hard finding Laurence Jones-Fairbrook in this crowd. That was if he'd really intended to be here. Mum's parting remark about that now left her uncertain. Perhaps he had been just flirting with her the other afternoon and having weighed her up had changed his mind.

After Connie left, he'd lingered on, asking where she lived, what she did. He'd volunteered nothing about himself and she'd not had the cheek to ask, but he hadn't seemed put off by what she told him about herself.

He had said he'd be at the pageant but he hadn't really struck her as being one of those men who sympathised with or even worked for the suffragettes' cause. Was it was only on a whim that he'd said he'd be here, adding that if they didn't find each other in the throng in Eaton Square he would probably look out for her when the rally reached the Royal Albert Hall.

Thinking of it, her excitement at this bustling crowd that had set her blood tingling slipped away. What a fool she was to imagine someone like him would be interested in someone like her. But he'd sounded so genuine.

'I'll be at the south steps or just inside,' he'd said jauntily. A little too jauntily it struck her now.

'Oh, there you are!'

She turned at the sound of Connie's voice, and in the light of a nearby lantern, hurriedly mustered a welcome smile to cover her disappointment.

'I hoped you'd come,' Connie went on. 'Isn't it wonderful?'

It was wonderful, thrilling, a sight never to be forgotten. Orderly, dignified, for a second Eveline thought of her father – if he could only see this he would never again view them as what he called frantic females and a thorough waste of time. But her mind wasn't on Dad or even the wonderful scene here in this brightly lit square, or even on Connie, but on Laurence Jones-Fairbrook.

A woman came up handing out sashes to each person according to the block she would be joining.

'I'll see you there,' called Connie as she donned her sash and went off to find her own group, leaving Eveline to find hers.

Eveline moved off too. There was still no sign of her quarry. Perhaps he had decided to make his own way to the Royal Albert Hall. Or perhaps he had changed his mind after all; he probably had better things to do. Trying not to feel despondent, she found her own group containing secretaries, office workers and the like, all making ready to move off.

Soon the pageant would string itself out into proper order, banners and emblems lit by lanterns hanging from decorated poles like a

94

blaze of stars in the dusk, each block headed by a young Church Brigade lad and flanked by policemen who, if they were expecting trouble, would be doomed to disappointment. This was to be a peaceful procession.

As her group finally began to move she experienced a deep twinge of excitement. She was one of them. A few weeks ago, she'd never have dreamed of being here. But here she was and her heart swelled with the pride she felt.

The procession was long. Connie's section would be well down Sloane Street, turning into Kensington Road to skirt Hyde Park and nearing its destination, by the time her own section really got started.

It wasn't a swift march. Orderly and dignified, they walked with a steady but purposeful step, every face, every banner, glowing under the gleam of their lanterns and street gas lamps. Good-humoured, some women even held conversation with the flanking police who so far bore them no ill will.

Newspaper photographers with their cumbersome cameras had gone ahead ready for the first of the marchers coming into view. Though the chill, breezy evening had kept away the hoped-for numbers of spectators, the press at least was here in force, which was far more important.

In fact the *Morning Leader* was later to report it as having been 'a superbly stage-managed spectacle which had the best Lord Mayor's Show anyone could remember worn to a frazzle' while the *Common Cause* happily compared it to a medieval trades-guild pageant, with its emblems historically correct and artistic. Even the nationals proved begrudgingly gracious.

As Eveline's group reached the Royal Albert Hall's impressive main entrance, her pride began to be overtaken by the hope of seeing Laurence standing waiting for her to appear. But there was no sign as each of the five divisions paused at each of the hall's entrances before filing in.

Inside, the vast, domed auditorium rang with voices all talking at once. From where her group had been stationed, Eveline looked over the moving sea of female humanity, trying hard to pick out two familiar faces, Connie's and that of the young man who had said he would meet her here. It was an impossible task.

'Isn't it just wonderful,' sighed one of the girls she'd been walking beside all the way here. 'It's so impressive. I've never been inside this place in all my life, and here I am!'

The girl had said she worked in an office in a bank, and Eveline had told her in return that she worked in the office of a factory for the company manager – a small lie but she might never see the girl again, so it didn't really matter.

Now she merely nodded, her eyes intent on surveying the vast, domed interior with its encircling balconies and its arena hung with bright banners. This was how it had probably looked last June as *The Times* had reported it. Then she had merely stood with Ada watching the spectacular procession go by along the Embankment on its way here too. Now she was part of it. But where was Connie? More to the point, where was Laurence Jones-Fairbrook?

A small army of working women was filing down the arena to the deep, thunderous music of the organ and cheers from the assembly to be received by the President of the International Suffrage Alliance. Mrs Carrie Chapman Catt's significant greeting, 'You are an Argument!' rang clear across the vast, glass-roofed amphitheatre, prompting a tide of cheers that completely drowned out Eveline's own voice.

There was more singing, and speeches emphasising the fact that the vote wasn't limited to any class but all wage-earning women including the housewife equally interested in securing the franchise. She discovered how women farmers paid heavy rates and taxes – she hadn't realised that women owned farms in their own right – and for the first time knew how belittling it must be, denied the vote yet seeing it given to men in your employ. With every voice raised against the indignity of women running their own businesses yet seeing themselves excluded, Eveline finally came away fired up to do her bit for the women of her country.

As the assembly slowly dispersed, she found Connie outside, the girl hurrying towards her through knots of women chatting together in the faint glow cast by street lamps over the evening's events.

'I saw you from a distance,' she gasped. 'But I couldn't get to you. Were you all right on your own?'

'Fine,' Eveline said, gazing about. There was still no sign of the young man who'd promised so faithfully to meet her. She had thought it faithfully at the time. 'I made some friends among the people I was with.'

Returning her gaze to Connie, she felt the girl's eyes had chilled a little, and hurried on, 'Nothing permanent, just talking and things.'

Why was she excusing herself? She hoped the girl wasn't turning out to be the jealous sort, claiming her attention the whole time. Surely she had friends in her well-to-do circles, just as she had in her ordinary ones, Ada, Daisy, lots of others and, she supposed, Bert Adams. They had chatted a couple of times since that first meeting at the library, so she could more or less count him a friend too. Though he wasn't a patch on Laurence Jones-Fairbrook. Where *was* Laurence Jones-Fairbrook?

People were still streaming out of the building. Then she saw him hurrying towards her. He was waving, almost frantically she would have said, his well-bred features animated, his lips parted in a wide grin beneath the trim moustache.

She felt Connie move back a little at his approach and was again conscious of a tinge of jealousy emanating from her. But she didn't care. With her heart having begun to pound like a drum, she didn't care.

'I was looking everywhere for you,' were his first words. 'I was a bit late getting here and managed to squeeze in as the first delegation made its way across the arena.'

'I'm glad you could make it,' she managed to gasp out. 'I even lost my friend in the squash.' She took Connie's arm and drew her forward. 'This is Connie Mornington. We met through the organisation. We've become really good friends.'

Connie was smiling, but for all Eveline's efforts he hardly glanced at her except to acknowledge the introduction, his eyes switching straight back to herself.

'So, where can I take you? Somewhere for coffee, you and me?'

It was a blatant indication that her friend wasn't included and she felt herself blush for Connie. But Connie was ready with her reply.

'I have to be getting along, Eveline. It's half past nine and I promised not to be too late home and I have a train journey ahead of me. Will I see you at the meeting next Saturday?'

'What meeting?' Laurence cut in.

'George Street,' said Eveline, embarrassed on her friend's behalf.

'Oh, yes,' he said, losing interest.

She turned to Connie. 'Wouldn't you like a cup of coffee before you leave?' The beverage sounded strange on her lips, she who only knew tea at home apart from that awful bottled Camp coffee.

Connie shook her head. 'My father will not be pleased if I get home too late. He thinks I have been to a recital with a friend.'

'Then it's just you and me,' Laurence said jauntily.

Something made Eveline leap. 'I don't think so, thank you very much. I must go with my friend to her station or she'll be walking all on her own.'

She saw him blink. In the pit of her stomach a weight settled, any chance she had with him fast receding. But no young woman should be walking on her own through the dark London streets. It hadn't occurred to her that once she left Connie, she herself would be the one on her own. But it was done now.

'It's quite all right,' Connie was saying. 'I'll take a taxi. There is a line of them waiting over there for fares. I shall be quite safe.'

Eveline hadn't thought of taxis. She always went by public transport, or else walked. She and Connie trod different paths.

'I'll see you next Saturday, Eveline,' Connie said abruptly and was off before she could stop her, feet tripping lightly beneath her skirt, one hand holding on to her huge hat that threatened to take off in the stiff, damp breeze despite its several long pins, the brightly coloured sash she'd been wearing fluttering from her other hand.

Eveline turned back to Laurence as her friend disappeared inside a taxi and it began to move off. She expected to see him shrug, to hear his nonchalant, 'Another time then.' But he was grinning at her, his narrow, clipped moustache twitching almost roguishly.

'So, how about that coffee?'

Eveline hesitated for a split second only. This was important. She'd never get another chance like this. If she did end up getting home later than promised, then so be it. At least he'd not suggested a stronger drink.

'That would be nice,' she said in an accent she hoped sounded as refined as his. The next minute she felt her hand being threaded through the crook of his elbow, and he was already hailing a taxi.

It was a wonderful end to a wonderful evening. In a small restaurant they drank real coffee she found quite palatable, poured from an elegant bone china coffee pot with milk from a matching jug, and sugar cubes in a bowl complete with silver sugar tongs. But she had refused supper, feeling too tensed up to eat. Trying to be on her best behaviour never went with eating. She might have made a mess of it, and that would be unthinkable.

She watched as he smoked a fragrant cigarette taken from a gold case. She declined the one offered her, never having smoked, but sat lapping up his words as he told her about himself.

'My folk are horsy people. My father breeds 'em – thoroughbreds, hunters. They enjoy point to point. Flat racing finds them well to the fore, and of course steeplechase. My father is a great betting man. He knows form like the back of his hand – makes a pile I believe.'

Eveline decided to say nothing about her grandfather as a betting man and continued to listen as Laurence went on. 'They enjoy socialising. My mother's quite a beauty, and a wonderful hostess. They've a large circle of friends, mostly horse people like themselves. I don't care much for the brutes myself, I much prefer town life.'

He had such a breezy and carefree air, and was so well-mannered. After the boys she knew, rough-tongued and cocksure, he was a breath of fresh air. Even the elegance of this small restaurant with its comforting tinkle of china and low hum of conversation was different to what she was used to.

Her heart going pit-a-pat, she prayed he'd ask

101

to see her again. But as he saw her to a taxi, giving its driver money in advance plus a sizeable tip, he said, 'I shan't see you home but you'll be safe enough in a taxi.'

Then as she made to get in, he grasped her waist and drew her to him, kissing her full on the mouth. Nothing tender about it, a hungry kiss and it frightened her. Taken by surprise she pulled away.

'I'm not that sort of girl!' she gasped, instantly feeling that she might have misinterpreted his actions. What she should have said was that she'd known him for too short a while for them to kiss but it was too late. His lips had grown tight as he leaned forward and jerked open the taxi door for her. The taxi driver was looking straight ahead. He'd seen this all before, and that alone made Eveline feel she was being taken by him to be *that sort of girl.*

For a moment or two Laurence stood looking at her, his hand on the open door. Perhaps he *had* been anticipating something more once inside the taxi but she would never know.

'I won't be at your meetings for a while,' he said, making her heart sink despite the fright he'd given her. 'My cousin will not be in London for quite some time and won't need me as a chaperone. I'm staying with my people for a week or two then off to Nice seeing a few friends there.'

A sudden grin took her off guard. It was as if those few moments before had never taken place. 'When I'm back in London I could take you to the south coast one Sunday. Have you been to Brighton?'

'No,' she said, awed but happy again, and deeply relieved. Despite all, her heart told her she did want to see him again. 'I've never even been to the seaside, ever.'

He was smiling. 'Then that's where we'll go.' This time his hand was gentle as he helped her into the taxi, standing back and closing the door.

It didn't matter if she was a bit late home. With all that had happened to her this evening she was ready to meet a scolding from her mother but it was her dad who was waiting up for her.

'What bloomin's time d'yer call this?' he bellowed, following her into the living room. She glanced at the clock on the mantelshelf, not daring to face him. She hated it when Dad got his dander up.

'I'm only a quarter of an hour late.'

'Quarter of an hour? *Three*-quarters of an hour!'

This time she felt justified in facing him. 'Mum said I could stay out until ten thirty.'

'I never 'eard 'er. Far as I know she said ten, and that's that!'

'At the door she said ten thirty,' Eveline insisted. She saw her father's moustache bristle as his mouth went tight. His pale amber eyes bulged.

'Don't talk back ter me, gell And don't lie ter me neither.'

'I'm not lying, Dad. Ask Mum.'

'Yer mum's in bed. Where all decent people should be.'

'But she did say–'

Her words were cut off by his raised hand. A slap to the back of the head could easily follow. It wasn't the hurt but the indignity; her hat would probably go flying off. But the hand yielded, though not his roar.

'As far as I'm concerned it was ten clock, so don't try coming it with me, yer saucy little minx! You ain't too old ter feel the weight of me 'and.'

A voice from the doorway broke in. 'Hi, what's all the bellowing about? Yer woke me up.'

Her mum stood there in flannel nightie and woollen dressing gown, faded brown hair hanging down almost to her waist. Somehow the loose hair made her look older rather than younger.

'What's all the blessed commotion?'

'This one thinks she can come in all hours then tell me lies,' blasted Leonard. 'Said you told 'er she could be 'ome 'alf past ten, not ten.'

'So I did,' came the reply and he wilted a little, then blustered on.

'Well, it would've been nice ter've been told! But I'm only the man around 'ere. When I said ten I meant ten. I won't 'ave me authority cocked a snook at.' He looked about ready to swear, something he rarely did in front of his womenfolk, but fell silent instead as Mum turned and went off back to bed.

Let off, Eveline went to bed too, ignoring her sister's enquiries as to how she'd enjoyed her suffragette rally, and pretended she had fallen asleep the moment her head hit the pillow.

In reality she lay awake for ages too excited to sleep for thinking of Laurence Jones-Fairbrook, his fine upbringing, his wealthy parents, his jaunty manner. She could even forgive him that moment of weakness that had alarmed her so.

104

Chapter Seven

It was well into summer and she had seen no sign of Larry, the name by which he'd said he preferred to be known. Well, what had she expected? Anyway, she had more or less got over the gloomy period of waiting.

Even so, still hoping, she had refused Bert Adams's guarded invite to go with him to see a picture show at the Hoxton. He'd not asked her again but she'd often notice him looking at her from across the bookshelves at the library, or in Bethnal Green Road some evenings with his mates, his eyes following as she passed by with her friends. He was good-looking but he could never match the refined Laurence Jones-Fairbrook even if that bit of her life looked to be over.

She did force herself to think of it as over and instead sank herself into her suffragette activities. Surprising how a thing starting out as a mere passing interest had taken hold. Listening to so many brave exploits, she began to feel that until she did something brave she would never truly be a suffragette. Her only fear was that the more she became involved, the greater the risk of her parents discovering what she was up to. Then the fat would truly be in the fire.

'One day we're going to get arrested and sent to prison,' she said to Connie as they came away from one of several demonstrations, this one comparatively mild, not causing enough disruption for the police to turn up. 'We've been lucky so far,' she went on darkly. 'But if it happens then our parents *will* find out.'

Connie's shrug looked almost complacent, as if it didn't matter to her any more. 'We knew it could happen when we joined,' she murmured.

The gesture irked slightly. Eveline wished she could feel as easy in her mind as wealthy Connie. Knowing she must soon do more than just join the odd rally or attend a few meetings had made her see that this was no game. If called upon she mustn't fail her friends and what they stood for, fought for, often suffered for. It was the prospect of her dad finding out that made a coward of her.

'Don't it worry you at all?' she snapped, grammar blown to the wind.

'So far we've been lucky not to have got into trouble,' Connie's change of tone took her by surprise. 'But one day it'll happen, and then...'

The sentence was left unfinished; she saw Connie was in fact far from complacent, as much in fear of her family's reaction as Eveline of hers once her secret was out. It was inevitable. Having money didn't buy security and peace of mind. One look at Connie's face told her that and she felt momentarily humbled.

They had narrowly missed arrest on a previous demonstration on June the nineteenth. They'd gone with a sizeable body of the WSPU to the House of Commons to distribute leaflets quoting part of the 1689 Bill of Rights on the right of any subject to petition the king's representative and render any attempt by the police to obstruct their passage illegal. It had all ended unsuccessfully and in confusion with a hundred and twenty-two women arrested.

At their first militant foray, she and Connie had only just avoided being caught, scurrying off as the police arrived. She'd felt a coward, a traitor. It plagued her for days after. At the next George Street meeting she was hardly able to look others in the eye even though no one blamed her. Connie said she felt exactly the same, but arrest would mean complications regarding her family. Although the cause was beginning to take precedence over fear of family reaction, they still dreaded that day even above the possibility of arrest.

After the skirmish, they had parted company, neither of them caring to join in an evening's spate of window breaking at the Treasury and Home Offices, later to hear that thirteen more women had been arrested.

Convicted, the thirteen were taken to Holloway where they had gone on hunger strike. After six days they were released. Eveline had to admire them. Six days voluntarily starving themselves! She who enjoyed every meal Mum put before her wondered where they found their courage, many being women of good breeding who usually ate far better than she ever did. She was aware that one day she too could expect to stand in court alongside those brave souls for a cause that mattered more to them than anything and on whose actions hung the right of women to be included with the voting masses.

'Perhaps going on hunger strike might not be as

bad as it sounds,' she said to Connie, thinking of the artist Marion Wallace Dunlop who had stencilled the extract from the 1689 Bill of Rights on the wall of St Stephen's Hall in the House of Commons and been given one month's imprisonment for refusing to pay her fine. Her demand that she be placed in the First Division as a political prisoner denied, she went on hunger strike.

'They released her after only four days,' Eveline went on. 'I suppose a person can put up with not eating for four days. It's a surer way of getting out of prison before your time's up.'

Connie was rueful. 'If they did let you starve yourself to death it's an even surer way of getting out before it's up.' Which made Eveline think.

Connie was aware she was being too melodramatic. There'd be such an outcry were a woman to be left to starve to death. But at the moment she was more worried about the repercussions should her family discover what she was doing.

Eveline had far less to lose, since her life was not bound to the rules of polite society. And Eveline had only one secret to conceal from her family. She had two, one that she was an active, militant suffragette, the second that she was keeping clandestine company with someone they would never accept, someone with hardly any money and no apparent prospects.

George was waiting anxiously at the ticket barrier as she threaded her way through crowds of summer holidaymakers and weekend trippers.

'I'm sorry,' she blurted. 'I am a bit late.'

'You're not late,' he said, taking her arm as they

showed their tickets at the barrier. 'I'm early.'

The cigarette smoke of a second-class carriage made her eyes sting a little; she preferred a first-class ladies-only compartment, even if not every time, because her father kept strict control of her allowance as though she were a child. As a result a second-class ticket often had to suffice. But this was how she had met George Towers, so she could thank her father for that. Sitting beside him, feeling the warmth from his shoulder as it pressed against hers in these cramped seats on a warm afternoon, she blessed that particular day she had dutifully conserved her allowance.

They talked the whole way home; there was no need to worry about others overhearing, the compartment was already buzzing with conversation, unlike the sedate silence of the first-class ladies-only. He spoke of his life, his ailing mother, his father's death several years ago, her need to be cared for. Connie listened, whatever he said suddenly vastly important.

'It means of course that I can't go out just whenever I wish,' he said. 'I pay a neighbour to come in if I need to. I try not to make it too often and get back as soon as I can. Expensive otherwise,' he laughed.

It didn't sound much fun but did indicate that he probably didn't have a girl in his life. It was rather proved to her as they got off the train.

'I hope you don't mind, but I'd very much like to take you for a meal next Saturday before catching the train. It means my getting home later but I'm sure my mother's neighbour will give eye to her for an extra hour or two.'

Connie's heart leaped with delight. Despite his regard for filial duty it was good to know he was still his own man. But next Saturday would be a problem, she and Eveline having agreed to take part in a small, peaceful demonstration after the meeting, outside a hall where an MP had arranged to speak. She could hardly back out. They would probably parade around in front for about an hour or two unless moved on, which the police seldom put themselves out to do so long as it remained orderly.

She drew in a deep, determined breath. 'I have to be somewhere tremendously important. Could we make it later, say six thirty?'

There was her father to consider – friction remained between them. They were still not talking to each other, as if he had washed his hands of her. He spoke to Verity, wrote warmly and often to Denzil and Herbert away at their public school, but it was as though she did not exist.

Should he disapprove of anything she did he would make a point of addressing her mother, requesting his displeasure be passed on, speaking as though she were a third person. If he were there when she came into a room, he would go out without so much as glancing her way. It made life at home exceedingly uncomfortable and she was glad he was mostly at his Harley Street practice, his local surgery or at his club.

George's face lit up. 'Six thirty is fine,' he said.

Connie had never been so happy. Was it possible to fall in love so quickly? On the train home she hung upon George's every word as he spoke more fully of his life.

His father having been a senior clerk in a small bank, George had generously been taken on in a position of junior clerk. When his father had died after a sudden stroke, George had continued to work there with the promise of promotion on reaching twenty-one. He was twenty-three now, no longer a junior, his wages having increased, but on this he kept himself and his mother, paid the rent on a small, landlord-owned terraced house and paid a neighbour to keep an eye on his mother while he worked. The woman more or less cared for her full time now, as his mother had grown steadily more frail in health and weak in the head. The savings his father had left she persisted on hoarding, and though it was now accruing a tidy interest, refused to have it touched, insisting it be kept for a rainy day.

All this he told Connie with no hint of bitterness and her admiration for him mounted during their train journey home at the same rate as this wonderful sense of falling in love. She prayed George might be feeling the same towards her though there was no way to find out and all she could do was hope.

Connie had told her previously that she'd met a young man by the name of George Towers. But Eveline's thoughts had still been lingering around the man who to her mind had fled as fast as he could having found her not to be the easy little catch he'd no doubt been expecting. Presumably he felt she was not worthy of any more attention. It was the only explanation she could give for Laurence's months of absence. She felt angry whenever she thought about it.

'George is such a wonderful person,' Connie was saying today as they helped themselves to tea and jam sponge with their meeting coming to a close. 'I only wish we did not have to meet in secret the whole time.'

'In secret?' she echoed. Connie had never mentioned this before.

She had already spoken of the fiasco following her rejection of her prospective fiancé called Simon, from an eminent family and whom her father had set his heart on her marrying, and the uproar when she'd turned down this Simon's proposal. But this newest bit of information was a surprise.

'My father would not approve of George,' she said. 'A bank clerk is not what my father would want for me. So we meet at Paddington Station on Saturdays and on some Sunday afternoons we go for long walks. I tell my father I am meeting a friend for afternoon tea. If he were to find out about George he would forbid me to see him ever again.'

'He's bound to find out sooner or later,' Eveline said.

'I know. And I am dreading it.'

Eveline made a sympathetic sound but her mind was racing from the reappearance of Larry at the meeting today. She wasn't going to tell Connie who would probably think her an idiot but her heart had soared at the sight of him, looking bronzed and handsome from his long and probably expensive vacation.

He had his cousin with him again, no doubt chaperoning her, but as Eveline went to get her tea and cake, while Connie was occupied in conversation with some other women, he'd come over. His cousin was on his arm; he introduced her as Miss Edith Fitzhugh.

Having acknowledged the attractive, somewhat athletic young woman, Eveline had asked politely if he had only just returned to England.

Larry chuckled. 'I've been home for ... must be a month now.'

The news came as a jolt. She was nothing to him, a girl from the East End, not even good enough to be considered. She felt let down, but she had never been anything but proud, proud of where she lived. Her home shone clean as a new pin, nothing about it was shabby, with Dad's shop bringing in a decent living. If it wasn't a patch on what he was used to with his people intheir large country house, their upper-class friends, their society parties, their horses, their hunts and meets, it wasn't her fault.

She was relieved that Connie was still talking to the other women and hadn't seen her discomfort. Then out of the blue he referred to his offer before leaving on vacation to take her to the seaside. 'If you still want to go.'

Her immediate inclination had been to lift her chin and say with a deal of dignity that, no, she was no longer interested. Instead, she heard herself saying, 'Do you still want to?' Aware how foolish it must sound.

'Of course,' he chuckled, his cousin giving a supportive smile. 'How about next Sunday, just

113

you and me?'

Unable to find words, she nodded, hating herself for being so easily swayed, but her heart was already nearly popping out of her chest, it was beating so madly.

'Right,' he'd said. The bright blue eyes seemed to be devouring her and despite herself she felt a shiver of excitement run through her.

'I'll pick you up in the old motor, say outside Liverpool Street Station around nine o'clock?' he was saying. 'Take a spin down to Brighton, show you what the sea looks like.' It sounded patronising but she no longer cared. 'Bring a veil. You could lose your hat, pinned on or not. Gets breezy in an open top.' He seemed to have forgotten his cousin standing by his side.

'There's a rug for your knees already in the motor and I'll provide the grub. Otherwise just bring your ravishing self. See you tomorrow then.'

He and his cousin were gone by the time Connie turned back to her, too eager to tell her about George Towers to notice the glow Eveline was already feeling in her cheeks.

Names were again being put forward by her father. Through her mother, of course; he was still not wholly speaking to her unless it was the occasional sharp reprimand.

'For heaven's sake, Constance,' her mother would say at regular intervals, 'one might be led to think you had every intention to become an old maid. What is the matter with you, child? Don't you want ever to get married?'

Yes, she had every intention but not to one of

their choice. In fact if they knew what her choice was they would die on the spot.

She'd been seeing George for two months now. He was as much inconvenienced as she was, having to arrange and pay extra for his neighbour to come in on a Sunday to be with his mother those two or three hours he was away.

He said that his mother was growing irritated about his being out on the one full day he could spend with her. He said that he hadn't told his mother about her; she assumed that he would remain a single man caring for and giving his sole attention to her for as long as she lived.

'She'll have to know eventually,' Connie said and then remembered that her parents too would one day have to be told.

Until then, these clandestine meetings were beginning to tell on her.

Her father, convinced she was going down with something, felt it of sufficient importance to confront her directly. 'I intend to arrange for a colleague of mine to take a look at you,' he announced. As her father he would never dream to examine her himself.

'There is nothing wrong with me,' she protested. 'I've no need to see any doctor.'

But he was insistent in his usual obdurate manner. 'You've become as thin as a rake. You are not eating and are too pale.'

Capitulating, she allowed herself to be examined but nothing abnormal was found.

'In my opinion,' Dr Chance advised, 'the girl is pining, nothing more. She needs to settle down to marriage. Becoming the loving wife to a kind and considerate husband is all the cure she needs. There comes a time in every young woman's life when she will begin to pine yet has no idea why. Marriage, Mornington, that's the answer.'

This prompted another urgent quest for another well-placed young man whom this time she might consider more favourably. Connie said little, feeling sick at her inability to reveal the true reason for her reluctance.

Telling George had him concerned. 'I'm going to have to speak to your parents. I love you, Connie, with every fibre of my body. I don't want to lose you.'

'You won't lose me,' she affirmed almost savagely. 'Ever. I do love you so much.'

With his arm round her waist as they walked along the bank of a stream in the clear July afternoon, she felt she could have faced anything with him at her side. And when he bent and kissed her long and ardently, she wanted nothing more than to be his wife, for her and him to confront her parents together, this very moment, to stand up to them and fearlessly declare their love for each other.

She drew a determined breath. Being with him was all that mattered.

'I love you so much,' she whispered. He drew her closer to him and she could feel the tension in that embrace, hear his breath sharp and rapid, felt the strength rise in him as she melted against him, ready for him.

Without warning he broke away. 'No, darling! We mustn't.' His tone was harsh yet he sounded confused and sorrowful. 'Time is getting on. You

116

have to be getting back home.'

She knew instantly that he had been afraid to trust his emotions and she too needed to settle those self-same emotions that had arisen so suddenly, so alarmingly.

'Yes, I must,' she said simply.

The walk home wasn't a long one. Neither spoke until he reached the end of the lane where they always parted.

'Look,' he said abruptly, 'I know this is difficult for you, your parents and all that. Your way of life is so different to mine.' He was choosing his words carefully. 'I could never match your standard of money. If we were to marry, things would be so different to what you've been used to. I can't lie to you. What I'm trying to say is that if you feel that difference will cause problems, I'd rather you tell me.'

Connie came to life to interrupt him fiercely. 'I love you, George. I don't care if we don't have a lot of money. I won't ever give you up, no matter what.'

'You mean that.' He was looking steadily into her eyes.

'I mean every word.'

'But you don't want me to meet your parents.'

'Don't you see, my darling?' She wanted to shake him. 'It would ruin everything. I couldn't bear that. My father, for right or wrong, has such plans for me. He wouldn't rest until he saw you off, and I would have to defy him outright to keep you. He's capable of ruining everything for us.'

For a moment George stood without speaking

while she tried to stem the anger and the fear of what could happen.

'We both seem to be in the same boat,' he said slowly at last. 'I can't ask you to meet my mother. She isn't well enough to meet anyone.'

'I'm sorry,' she said, but in a way felt relieved that she wasn't to be asked to go through that harassing ritual just yet.

She was glad to see him perk up a little. 'Anyway,' he said, 'we're not marrying each other's family.'

'Marry?' she echoed weakly. 'You really are asking me to marry you?' He had come out with it with such certainty that it almost took her off her feet. But he was looking steadily at her.

'That's what I said. Connie, I'm asking you to marry me, if you will. I can't offer you what you've been used to, but I've a decent job with every chance of promotion. As much as I love my mother, and though it sounds unkind to say it, I don't think she will live much longer. She is quite ill and hasn't really had any will to live since we lost my father. There are several life-threatening things wrong with her now.'

He hadn't noticed how stunned she was by the lack of protocol in his proposal, assuming she had consented. 'You don't have to say anything right now,' he said, 'but I do want to marry you, Connie, very much.'

'And I want to marry you,' she burst out impulsively.

As he drew her to him with a gasp of joy, she knew she would face her father and declare this man to be the one she intended to marry. She would be honest and open – no lies, no subterfuge, no deception. All that was needed was to judge the right time to announce it. And while she was about it she would reveal her suffragette activities too.

She felt suddenly stronger than she had ever been in her life, and as she and George kissed, their kiss lingering, she knew she would never give him up, no matter what.

Chapter Eight

It was a wonderful August day. She felt so grand sitting beside him in his fine motor which he said was a Rover, she who'd never been in a motor car in her life much less knew the name of any.

Her first sight of the sea took her breath away; the expanse of it, the salt tang of it, the way the wavelets kissed the pebble beach with small hissing sounds, the bathing huts, the bathers. They had lunch in a little café on the promenade and later a cream tea, driving home as the summer sun began to sink, his hand on her knee, she letting it stay there, she felt very much at ease and in charge of things, like a real lady. Sometimes he drove in silence, other times he talked of all they'd done that day.

'I've just had my apartment redecorated,' he said as they drove across London Bridge. He'd told her about his apartment in Chelsea. 'Cost a mint. I think it looks terrific but it would be nice if you could take a peek at it for a minute or two, to tell me what you think. It's not far out of your way and I can take you home immediately afterwards.'

'Oh, I don't know.' The idea made her sink back into her seat. A good girl shouldn't be visiting a young man's apartment without a chaperone.

What would her dad say? She'd half expected him to go off the deep end when she told him

Larry was taking her to Brighton in his motor car. Instead he'd been quite agreeable for his daughter to go off with her wealthy young man, though Mum, querying why he'd stayed out of the country so long, had been a bit wary, cautioning her against getting too carried away. But going to his apartment?

'I think I should go straight home,' she said. 'It is getting late.'

'It'll only take a minute or two, just to say what you think of it, then I'll take you home. Please, come and see it.' He seemed so enthusiastic.

She melted. 'Well, just for a minute then, but only a minute.'

'Fine,' he said, swinging the motor car in the direction of the West End as they came off London Bridge.

His apartment was on the top floor of a three-storey dwelling set behind railings and an ornate gate. It had two gabled windows and a long straight one giving an uncluttered view of the Thames, its flow here as gentle and sedate as the area itself.

'It's lovely,' Eveline sighed, gazing about at the tasteful eau-de-Nil and fawn wallpaper that set off the brown and biscuit-coloured furnishings and furniture. Everywhere were beautiful vases, bowls, small, delicate statuettes, tasteful ashtrays, and lots of cushions which she felt she could have sunk down into for the rest of her life and never know the time passing. She watched as he threw open a window to let in the evening air.

'You like it.' It was a statement rather than a question and as she nodded, he went on like

121

some excitable boy, 'You should have seen it before. I've had absolutely the whole place done and refurnished. Come and look.'

Grabbing her hand he led her from the room into a smaller dining room, then to a bright little hallway to show her the immaculate kitchen. 'I've been in this place eighteen months now. How I lived with the previous decor I don't know.'

Taking her back into the hall he threw open another door. 'This is my bedroom.' As she instinctively held back, he laughed and closed the door again, leading her back into the first room.

'Sorry about that,' he said lightly. 'Look, now you're here, may I make you a cup of coffee or something? I could percolate some. Won't take a minute.'

The only other time she'd ever tasted real coffee had been with him in that café the night of the rally at the Royal Albert Hall and she hadn't been all that impressed with it then. It was all right, but...

He must have seen her expression, for he went on, 'Tea then? Or there's cocoa?'

'I'd enjoy a cup of cocoa,' she said, her dislike of coffee making her reply more spontaneous than she'd intended. She should have declined altogether and mentioned again about getting home. Too late, he was already on his way to the kitchen leaving her standing in the centre of the room.

Seconds later he was back. 'Look, I've run out of cocoa. It'll have to be tea. But I shan't have any. I'll get myself a whisky and soda.'

For a moment he stood looking at her, then

122

cocking his head on one side in a whimsical, questioning gesture, he said, 'Have you ever tasted whisky?'

Eveline shook her head. Beer was what she knew. Mum with her daily half-pint of Guinness and Dad with his evening pint of bitter. There was port and sherry at Christmas time, perhaps gin for the ladies, but only the men that she knew drank whisky. Her favourite was always port and lemonade.

'Then you ought to try it,' he was saying, already pouring his own and setting down a glass ready for her. He turned round to gaze at her. 'On the other hand it could be far too strong for you.'

That was a relief, he was being considerate, but he followed it up with an enthusiastic, 'I'll tell you what, I'll make you up a whisky cocktail. It's sweet and maybe more to your taste.'

'I don't think...' she began, but he was already grabbing bottles and pouring a drop from each into a silver cocktail shaker, dropping in other bits of ingredients and shaking the container vigorously, pouring the colourful contents into a different glass to his, one with a wide mouth.

'Here,' he said, holding it out to her. 'Taste this. You'll like it.'

She did. It had a flavoured syrupy taste, sweet and hardly any kick as people said, though she didn't quite know what kick would feel like except that she had seen some who'd knocked back a strongish drink choke and laugh.

'Another?' Larry asked.

'I don't think I should.'

'It won't hurt you. As you can see, it's well watered down.'

Yes, it was nice, and as he said, harmless. She nodded and had him refill her glass, enjoying the smooth liquid.

'No point standing,' he said. Grabbing the shaker and his own bottle of whisky he dropped down on to the brown and beige sofa with its myriad of small fawn cushions. 'You'll find your legs aching before long. Here.'

He patted the place beside him and for some reason she didn't decline, dropping down beside him with a little giggle. The cocktail was very more-ish and she let him give her a third refill. Then she really would have to be getting along home. But those cushions looked so comfortable and she sank back in them just to test their comfort as she downed her third refill. It was just like drinking very sweet, fresh orange juice, though not quite, there was such a lovely flavour to it.

Larry drove her home through the dark streets and she had no idea how long it took. It had been a marvellous evening. Larry had made love to her, for the first time ever, and she'd found it not a bit alarming, wondering why she had made so much fuss about their earlier kisses and cuddles becoming too serious. Not that she remembered much about it except that it was lovely.

The motor car had come to a stop. She looked out to see that they were right outside the door of her dad's shop, all in darkness, the glow from the gas lamp on the corner making it seem even more dark and deserted. Upstairs a light glowed in one of the windows. Dad was up. Dad was waiting for her. The knowledge brought her senses partly flooding back through the maze in her head. She sat up from her half reclining position.

'Oh, dear God! I must go. He'll kill me.'

'Who?'

'My dad.'

Larry laid an arm about her shoulders. 'Now wait, darling. You need to give yourself a few minutes. How are you feeling?'

'I don't know, a bit dizzy like.'

'Then just wait a minute.' He leaned forward to open the small compartment set in the dashboard and drew out a small paper bag.

'Look, suck one of these.' Something round and slightly powdery was popped into her mouth and she tasted its peppermint flavour. 'Helps clean the breath,' he said. 'Then I will help you to your door – to steady you.'

He was out of the car and was helping her out, she sucking furiously, knowing now that her dad might very well smell on her breath what she'd been drinking, that he might realise it had been potent, then became aware too of what she had done under its influence. But she couldn't blame Larry. It was her fault. And it had been nice...

Larry had his arm about her waist. He was knocking on the side door by the shop. 'You'll be all right,' he whispered as the sound of footsteps could be heard coming down the stairs. 'Just leave this to me.'

The door opened. Her father stood there, his moustache bristling; the only visible sign of anger was his moustache completely concealing his mouth, but the eyes reflected that anger.

'What in the name of–'

'I'm sorry, Mr Fenton.' Larry spoke fast. 'I am Laurence Jones-Fairbrook. We've never met, and I'm sorry it's in these circumstances, but your daughter had a small accident, slipped down an embankment at Brighton where we spent the afternoon. She's not hurt but was badly shaken, and terrified of course, thinking she might be killed. She had to rest quite a long time, which is why we are so late home and she is still not quite herself. I brought her straight back the moment she seemed able to be moved. I have to admit I'm a bit shaken myself, thinking too that she was going to be badly hurt or even killed. I had to give her a small glass of brandy to help her recover. She hasn't wanted to eat anything, but I gave her some peppermints on the way home. I think she ought to go straight to bed, don't you, Mr Fenton?'

Eveline was near to giving way to tears. How could Larry be so gallant and so brave? Dad could have taken a swipe at him yet he had faced him with this story. So quick-witted to have thought it up. She wanted to hug him for defending her so, but Dad had reached out and was pulling her indoors. At least he wasn't bellowing. His tone was heavy but not angry.

'Thanks, Mr ... er, Mr...'

'Laurence. Larry.'

'Yes, well, thanks fer looking after 'er. She'll be orright now.'

'She should go straight to bed.'

'I know what ter do wiv 'er, Mr Laurence.' Dad

had never been good with names

'Larry. Larry Jones-Fairbrook.'

'Yeah, I know, the one she's said she met. Well, thanks again.'

He was obviously ill at ease, unused to moneyed people. Eveline, her head swimming as she stood slightly behind him, held on to the wall of the narrow hallway for support. Larry glanced past her father and looked straight at her.

'I'll see you next Saturday, after the–' He stopped himself in time, obviously recalling her parents' ignorance of her suffragette interests.

'If that's all right with you, Mr Fenton? I promise I shall look after her.' He regarded Mr Fenton who returned his regard in silence. He nodded.

'I'll say goodnight then. Sorry about the accident. It wasn't steep, just grassy. She was walking too near the edge, I tried to stop her...'

'Yeah, so you said. Well, thanks again, Mr Jones. Ev, say good-night.' She opened her mouth but the door closed before she could utter the word.

All week she had felt strangely torn between a sort of odd elation and churning misgivings wondering what he must think of her for allowing to happen what no decent girl should. Yet it hadn't entirely been of her own free will. She should never have had those cocktails.

They sat in his lounge this Saturday evening. Coming here straight from her meeting, she had not eaten, so he'd taken her to a nearby restaurant and they'd sat gazing over at the river all calm and placid on this golden evening. Now they were in his flat, he with an arm round her.

But as she snuggled closer to him on the sofa, a gramophone record playing 'I Wonder Who's Kissing Her Now,' very softly, his arms came about her, his lips as she responded moving slowly and gently from hers to her neck, then to her throat, and she forgot to wonder what Connie might have thought. This was a declaration of his love, a commitment such as she could only ever have imagined until now. She was his and he was hers.

As she sighed with this joy of that realisation he began carefully to lift her in his arms. Automatically her hands went about his neck as he carried her through to his bedroom. This was so different to last Sunday. That had happened on the spur of the moment and she'd been a bit drunk. This was gentler, sweeter, more purposeful, the start of a love that would continue for the rest of their lives. Into her head crept the words Mrs Laurence Jones-Fairbrook.

She felt herself being lowered on to his bed. Kneeling beside her he slowly removed her blouse, skirt, corset, the rest of her underclothing, while she lay with eyes closed, enjoying the sensation. She only opened her eyes as she felt his bare flesh against hers, sending a little shock through her that turned instantly to arousal.

He'd not spoken at all, neither as he took her, gently at first but rising to a climax, ignoring her little cry at the small pain it caused, nor as he finally left her. Not one word of love, but she knew he loved her, and she loved him.

Lying quietly and contentedly, her head cradled on his arm, her eyes closed, her mind wove her future. She had to be the luckiest girl alive; this time her lips silently formed those words, Mrs Laurence Jones-Fairbook. It sounded so wonderful that a delicious little shiver passed through her.

'Are you all right?' he asked, turning his head to look at her.

As she nodded, he got up abruptly and went out to the bathroom. Lying where he'd left her, she was surprised to see him return fully dressed.

'You'd best get yourself dressed,' he said evenly, moving away from the door towards the lounge. Wondering at his tone, she too got up and began dressing, feverishly, somewhat confused by the abrupt finality of what had been such wonderful moments.

'I'll mix us a drink,' she heard him call from the lounge. She had expected him to come and cuddle her to him again, but it was as if nothing had happened at all.

It came to her that he hadn't kissed her except for that once but it could have been that making love made it awkward to kiss. She couldn't rightly remember now if they had kissed that first time, but maybe it was how it always happened between men and women.

As she came, uncertain and strangely shy, into the room he was lounging back on the sofa, smoking one of his fragrant cigarettes, a glass of whisky in his hand. Seeing her, he patted the sofa for her to sit beside him, handing her a delicate glass of pale wine from the coffee table in front of them.

'Are you feeling all right?' he asked.

'I think so,' she said uncertainly, her voice sounding very small, everything now feeling somewhat unreal. There seemed little to talk about now, and the sense of ease had utterly flown.

'Good,' he said sharply and after a short silence, added, 'You'd better drink up, then I'll take you home. Don't want to be out too late, do you?'

'No,' she said inadequately, taking a much-needed sip of wine.

'So I'll see you next Saturday afternoon, then?'

She put the half-empty glass back on the coffee table. 'I have to go to my meeting first. I'll see you afterwards, in the evening.'

It was his turn to sit up. 'No, I want you to myself. We can have the whole afternoon together, here. You're so sweet, so ravishing, I could teach you so much about making love, that one can make love more than just the once.'

She felt a little shocked. Was he expecting to spend the whole afternoon and evening making love to her? That didn't seem possible and not quite right and it made her feel ever so slightly uneasy.

'Larry, I do have to go to my meeting.'

'Blast your meeting! You don't *have* to do anything. Why do you want to bother with them?'

She stared at him. Why had he suddenly become so domineering?

'It means a lot to me. It's important that I attend as many meetings as I can so as to–'

'Rather than be here with me?' he interrupted fiercely. 'You can forget all that suffragette business. I want you with me. We both enjoyed this afternoon. Surely you like what we did as much as I do?'

This was a side of him she didn't know. She knew he wasn't all that interested in the suffragette cause, had only gone there to please his cousin when she was in town, but now he was coming over all high-handed about her going. What was the matter with him?

'So you can forget all that stuff,' he was saying. 'Or don't you love me?'

'Oh, Larry, of course I do.' Her love for him had overflowed this afternoon. It was overflowing all afresh now. 'But this is important to me too,' she persisted.

'More important than me.'

'No, of course not.'

'Then forget about them. I want you here next Saturday afternoon.' He was looking at her most oddly. 'I want you. You're good for me.'

She felt a wave of anger pass through her. 'I don't *belong* to you, just because...' She got no further.

'Letting me make love to you rather commits you to me a bit, don't you think?'

Eveline sat away from him. 'I'm a suffragette first and foremost,' she said haughtily. She wasn't having him tell her what to do even though, as he'd said, making love had its commitments. Commitment was a word she had wanted to hear, but not the way he was saying it. For a moment it made her doubtful about what they'd done together, but seconds later she had dismissed the thought.

'I've made a lot of friends there,' she hurried on

131

in an effort to make him see how she felt. 'All of them brave in what we're fighting for. I can't let them all down by giving it all up. You must understand.'

'I don't think I need to understand anything,' he said quietly.

She was upset and disappointed. Connie was courting a young man and she hadn't been expected to give up her meetings. She got to her feet.

'I think I should go, Larry. Are you going to take me home?' For a moment he looked so annoyed that she thought he would tell her to find her own way. But no man would let a woman be out alone after dark.

'I'll get your hat and coat,' he said tersely. 'I think it best I don't take you to your door. The end of your street suit?'

She nodded wordlessly, unable to fathom this sudden change in him.

The drive home was strained but by the time they neared her home he was his old self again.

'I'm sorry I behaved so heavy-handedly,' he said as they came to a stop halfway down Finnis Street. 'I had no right. You go off to your meetings. I know they're important to you. I'll see you next week, afterwards, and we'll have something to eat.'

Deeply grateful she leaned towards him, their farewell kiss lingering. He still wanted to see her, despite their row. A small tiff was all it had been, but it was over now and might have made their love, their commitment to each other, all the more binding. She was sure of it.

She would try to do all she could to keep it that way, even though she could never give up her suffragette activities, not now. It was her one fear now – that it could tear them apart.

She would tread a careful path, give herself to him whenever he wanted her, learn not to press him with questions when he failed to turn up as often as she wanted and play down the suffragette cause as much as possible. She couldn't lose him. He was far too precious.

She found herself looking forward so much to being with him next Saturday that it was like an ache, but in the middle of the week a letter came for her saying that he would be with his parents and wasn't sure when he'd be back, a few weeks maybe. Short and terse though the letter was, she took heart as it ended, 'Sorry about this but am counting the days until I see you again. Still loving and wanting you. Larry.'

She was disappointed of course, but at least she felt reassured at being told that he was in love with her.

Try as she might, she couldn't stop her head filling with thoughts of the day when Larry would finally propose to her. But of course that day was in the future. Things like that couldn't be rushed.

It was also far too early at this stage to start broadcasting it to her parents, who'd only scoff and ask who she thought she was thinking some toff like him would ask her to marry him. But they didn't know Larry. She couldn't wait for the day she would flash a huge and sparkling engagement ring before their eyes. Then let them scoff!

Life was too wonderful for words.

Chapter Nine

Connie was looking at her with such a deeply shocked expression as they came away from their Saturday's meeting that Eveline wished she'd never embarked on such a personal confession.

She had opened her heart to Connie because if she didn't confide in someone soon, she'd fall apart. Now she wished she'd kept quiet. After all, it wasn't the sort of thing a young lady should be confessing to, even to her closest friend. But having begun, there was need to justify it.

'He wrote that he loved me and the last time we were together I was sure he did. Then he said he had to see his family for a few weeks. That was in August and I've not heard a thing from him since. It's as if he doesn't care, but I know he does love me.'

'Has he said so to your face?' Connie probed cautiously. 'Have you ever confronted him with it directly?'

'I didn't dare. He might have thought I was trying to push him.'

'But he should have declared himself after ... you know what I mean. After you and he...'

Connie was having trouble getting the words out and was looking decidedly embarrassed. Eveline squirmed, needing to get off that particular subject now.

'He did tell me to give up the suffragettes so I

could give more time to him. Why would he say that if he didn't love me? We had an argument about it. And now I've not seen him for four weeks. I do love him, Connie, but I can't give up everything I've come to believe in. And now he's gone off and I don't know where I stand with him at all.'

'Then what are you going to do?' Her tone was cold and impartial as if she wasn't that interested in the reply.

'He did apologise after,' Eveline rushed on. 'So I think he knows how I feel about it.'

Connie had taken a deep breath, a hint that it was Eveline's problem and she wanted to have done with it. 'George would never ask me to do that. He believes every woman should be allowed the vote. It's comforting to know how he feels. It makes me feel safe.'

So that was it, she had opened her heart to Connie and had received no comfort or advice. All she'd done was to look cheap. She vowed to say nothing else to Connie about her and Larry.

More and more she was being drawn into militant forays. On the Tuesday several women at the George Street meeting had planned a demonstration outside a local hall where a Member of Parliament was speaking. She and Connie had automatically been included. It would be in the evening and still light.

'We intend to make this a notable event,' they were told. 'You've both been on a previous demonstration so you will be there, won't you?'

Eveline looked at Connie as if to say, what do

135

you think? Connie regarded the ten or so women and nodded her agreement without hesitation.

With their chairwoman consulting HQ, it was quickly organised in a proper manner. 'We cannot have our ladies going about causing havoc willy-nilly. It raises all sorts of complications. We must make sure it is all approved and the name of the WSPU not besmirched.'

It gets besmirched whatever we do, Eveline thought facetiously.

'I do hope we're doing the right thing,' Connie said. 'If we were to get arrested, the police will inform our parents. My father will never forgive me.'

But Eveline was feeling rebellious. Still there was no sign of Larry; she was hurt and angry. He could at least have written again. Was it a case of out of sight, out of mind, because he was having such a good time wherever he was abroad? But he had written that once to say he loved her – what if something had stopped him writing? What if he'd fallen ill, or worse? How would she know? On the other hand, what if he'd found someone else? Surely he would have had the decency to write and tell her? All these questions were making her confused and miserable.

'I don't care!' she said to Connie, lifting her chin in a gesture of defiance. 'You can do what you like, Connie, but I'm going!'

It would be exciting, would take her mind off him. She turned her thoughts to herself and others parading in a tight circle outside the meeting hall, holding placards and chanting as loud as they could while the eminent Member of Parliament was inside giving his speech.

136

Of course they would move on as soon as the police told them to. They had been cautioned by headquarters not to cause any undue disruption or to obstruct the police in their duty. There'd be none of the arrests that Connie feared.

Eveline's heart was racing. Her stomach was curling as if someone in there was folding dough. It was just after eight o'clock. In the hall the MP was rising to make his speech.

Quietly the dozen women, their placards held low, their green, white and purple sashes hidden under their coats on this rather unseasonably chilly evening, gathered at the end of the road.

People passing looked at them; some who recognised them for what they were slowed their step, anticipating a spectacle, maybe a scuffle if the police came down on them, otherwise all was quiet. The women formed up in twos and began marching purposefully down the road, in the gutter in the accepted manner so that passing traffic wouldn't be disrupted and pedestrians not obliged to step aside and look on them with disfavour, to stop outside the imposing portico of the meeting hall.

With the speed of magicians producing a rabbit out of a hat, a dozen placards appeared, then sashes were whipped out and quickly donned, their wearers careful not to dislodge their large hats.

Eveline's little pastry cooks ceased folding their dough and her heart calmed; her nervousness was replaced by a feeling of triumph and worth. She glanced at Connie as they began their chanting: *'Votes for women! Enfranchisement is our right!'* Connie's pretty face was set, her lips tight, her eyes focused front.

Ten minutes into the protest, a person came through the portico, waving them off.

'No good you lot marching about out here – no one can hear you.'

'Then why are you out here?' one of the demonstrators called back.

'Because we won't have you disturbing the peace. You're making a spectacle of yourselves.' He glanced at the gathering spectators, their day's work over, pausing to watch this little diversion on their way home, then turned his gaze on the marchers. 'Go on home where you belong and cook your men's tea, as all decent women should be doing.'

'Is that a fact?' came a cry from the last woman in the line. 'I'll tell you what we should be doing. If you can't hear us, then this might help.'

There came a sudden crash and a shattering of glass.

No one had seen her pick up a loose cobblestone and aim it, but in seconds it became infectious. Whatever came to hand was being thrown against the tall windows of the meeting hall, none of it planned. What had been intended as a sedate and controlled protest had suddenly got out of hand.

Excited by physical action, Eveline too began hunting around for a suitable missile and saw Connie doing the same.

People were coming to the door. The doorman swept out a hand to prevent anyone running out into the fray. He reached into his pocket and drew out a whistle, blowing a protracted series of short, piercing blasts without stopping. They shrilled down the street and into every other street around. Within moments policemen were on the scene, police whistles between their lips summoning extra assistance.

Eveline felt her arms pinioned to her sides. Connie too had been apprehended, two constables on either side of her. She was screaming. Eveline wanted to scream but somehow felt such dismay that her throat had dried up. In her mind she saw her father glaring at her, pointing her to the door, telling her never to return. What would happen to her? The vision flashed through her head, the fact that she was about to be carted off to prison not entering into it at all.

Five women had escaped, but seven were being held as a police wagon rattled into the street from around a corner to come to a stop in readiness to accommodate the apprehended. The entire meeting was lined up outside the hall, the MP along with them. He had a self-satisfied look on his face that showed no sympathy for suffragettes. With people like that in parliament, how could they ever win?

'We must stand fast,' Bessie McLeod, a middle-aged widow of some standing who'd been their leader, told them as they were borne away, sitting facing each other in the police wagon. 'We must uphold our cause and make them proud of us, those who have gone before us.'

It was like a speech, all drama and style. Connie smiled across at Eveline who smiled back, though neither felt in the mood for smiles. Eveline was thinking of her father and she knew that Connie was thinking of hers. But the woman had more to say.

'We must all of us go on hunger strike the instant we are sentenced. They will have to let us out or see us die!'

Whether or not she was let out that very same day, she would be taken to court and her parents informed under the usual police procedure – all because one in their group had resorted to violence. Eveline knew she should have bolted at the first sign of trouble but, caught in the excitement, she hadn't. That earlier curling in her stomach had now become a bunched knot with no prospect of unravelling itself in the foreseeable future.

It was still there when they finally filed into court, each refusing to pay her fine, hearing the sentence of one month in Holloway. Most seemed proud of the fact that they were going to prison – it provided an advertisement for their cause. Eveline wished she felt as calm, but all she could think was that she would lose her job over this and as an ex-prisoner would have no prospect of another. What about the repercussions at home?

The ride, all of them cooped up in the van, seemed to take ages. Entering through the huge gates set in a high wall screening the castle-like edifice from the road, they got out to be escorted into the frowning, grey building.

Inside it was dim, cold, stark, a place of bolts and bars, doors that clanged hollowly and voices that echoed, all pressing down on her as she filed into a bare room along with the others.

140

Seeing her comrades, their heads up, defiance clearly written on every face, she knew that same defiance was written on hers too. Gone for good was that old sense of adventure she remembered on first joining these women, the vague uncertainty she'd once had. From out of the blue came at last a sense of purpose, a need to see this thing through to the end when this growing army of courageous women would triumph for the good of all women. It would happen. All that was needed was to stand fast; and this was why she was here.

Yet bitterness was pounding in her chest like a fist. Her and Connie's parents had been notified of their arrest according to police procedure. Connie's father had hastened to court and when Connie had spoken out refusing to pay her fine, he'd stepped forward, a tall, lean and dignified figure, to say that he was paying his daughter's fine. Eveline had watched her finally leave, protesting, unable to meet the eyes of those resolved to go to prison for their beliefs. She had actually felt sorry for Connie, a girl openly betrayed before her comrades in arms, and by her own father.

She had feared her own father might have presented himself on her behalf and was relieved when he didn't. So why was she so bitter? It had been the message he had sent back with the constable who'd informed him of his daughter's arrest: that a taste of hardship in prison would do her good, cure her of all that nonsense and bring her to her senses.

She felt she could never forgive him for that, nor Mum for not having the will for once to dissuade him. Perhaps she'd even agreed with him.

141

This very thought helped get her through the very humiliating process of having to strip before hard-faced wardresses whose cold eyes seemed to her to take in every contour of her nakedness.

From out of bitterness defiance was beginning to grow. If her parents felt this way about her, then she would endure this incarceration with all the dignity and forbearance she could muster.

Slowly pride began to blot out all else as she was made to put on the dark green prison dress with its white arrows marking her out as a convict. She was a suffragette. She would show the world that she could take the bad times as much as the good.

Head up, she followed the wardress to the cell where she was required to remain for thirty days. It wasn't all that long a time and now that she knew where she stood with her family, it felt as though a weight had been lifted from her. Why had she been so worried about them finding out?

Almost with a sense of relief she sat down on the narrow, hard bed with its two scratchy blankets and thin pillow as the door slammed, the key rattling and grating in the lock. With a clinical eye she gazed around the cell measuring just five feet by seven in which she would spend the next month, noting the bucket that was to be her toilet, the tiny, cracked washbasin, then glancing up at the glimmer of daylight filtering through the high-set five bars.

Without warning loneliness flowed over her like a small tide; a little of that brave resolve began to crumble, its veneer thinner than she'd thought, and she felt tears begin to prick the edge of her eyelids. Detecting weakening resolve, she took in a deep breath, straightened her back. Gone the previous sense of adventure. She knew now, being a suffragette was serious business.

She was not going to cry. She was not alone. She could hear voices coming spasmodically from other cells, but not communicating, since prisoners were forbidden to speak to one another. The resolve returned, leaving a feeling of strength she'd never have believed she could possess. She would not fail her friends.

She'd been told there'd be no visitors or letters for the first four weeks, which meant no contact with the outside the whole time she'd be in here. This was just as well – she wouldn't have to face censure from her parents or frustration from Larry, who she tried not to admit to herself that she was already missing. There'd be plenty of time ahead to think of him. Confined to a cell twenty-three hours a day with half an hour in chapel and half an hour silent exercise in the yard, she'd be given knitting and sewing and a book on housekeeping to pass the time. She'd be all right.

'It isn't forever!' she called out loudly, as much so the others would hear her as to convince herself that everything passes.

'Quiet!' a woman's voice bellowed through the door.

Down the line of cells a women started defiantly to sing. In no time at all the other inmates had joined in. Eveline heard a cell door open, the sound of a sharp slap and a small cry followed by a fiercely whispered warning whose words she couldn't catch. The singing stopped.

Suddenly another voice rang out. 'Ladies – we

go on hunger strike!'

'Be silent!' thundered a wardress. 'Any more calling out and you'll get no supper.'

To which came the retort: 'Good!'

After that all went quiet, leaving her to her thoughts, to which was now added this new one. How long did refusal to eat take before it became unbearable? One thing was certain: she'd find out soon enough.

Connie had never felt so mortified. Sitting beside her father in his fine Austin York landaulette, she remained stubbornly silent. Nor had he spoken one word to her. His lips remained compressed into a thin line above his trim beard, his distinguished countenance was inscrutable. His back stiff as a ramrod, he stared straight ahead during the entire journey home.

William, his chauffeur, looked equally uncomfortable, his posture taut where at other times he'd be quite relaxed at the wheel. Though she could see only his back through the glass partition, she felt she had his sympathy but it would have been more than his job was worth to air an opinion.

Reaching home, he swung the huge motor car smoothly into the drive to glide to a stop. Connie sat very still as he got out and smartly opened the door for her father, then came round to her side to help her down with a gentle hand. She watched him get back into his driving seat and the car moved off to the garage and stables at the back of the house. Her father passed her without speaking or looking at her, mounting the few steps to the front door immediately opened to him by Bentick who had no doubt been waiting for the moment the car appeared, aware of the mood in which his employer had left home earlier.

Connie followed at a distance and only when she had stepped inside, handing her coat and hat to Agnes, standing meek and unobtrusive behind their butler, did her father address her in his deep, measured voice. 'I wish to see you in my study, Constance, immediately you have made yourself presentable.'

It was in a state of defiance that she entered at his response to her polite tap on the study door. She was not going to defend her suffragette activities. She felt almost relieved that he was at last aware of it, that she wouldn't have to suffer the embarrassment of telling him herself. She stood before him, tall and straight-backed, her head up, her expression calm.

'I will ask you once and once only,' he began. 'Why've you felt the need to lie to me all this time regarding this foolish and dangerous frivolity?'

Connie stared over his head at the window behind him. The drapes were not yet drawn; the sinking sun threw shafts of light through the heavy lace curtains that broke them up sufficiently not to dazzle her eyes.

'You would have forbidden it. And it's not frivolity. It's–'

His interruption remained steady. 'It is dangerous and I do forbid it.'

'I'm afraid it's too late, Father.' She too kept her voice steady. She was not going to allow herself to be ruffled. 'I am far too committed to the work of women's suffrage. It's important to us and I won't–'

'Won't!' he echoed, his tone rising the tiniest fraction. 'I am giving you an order, Constance, as a daughter over whom I still have parental control until she is twenty-one, and beyond, so long as she remains under my roof. From now on you will divorce yourself from these people. That is my last word on the subject except to say your deceit grieves me deeply. It will take me a long time to forgive you. I'm disappointed in you, Constance, and that too is going to take you a long time to put right. But for now I want your promise never to see these women again. And if you–'

'I'm sorry,' Connie cut in, sensing one of his lengthy speeches. 'I refuse to promise any such thing.'

She was about to say, 'Do what you like,' but that would be going too far. He was her father. He'd spent time, money and patience in bringing her up correctly as he saw it. She couldn't insult him. On the other hand, she couldn't forgive what he had done today, paying her fine in full view of her friends, all of whom were ready to suffer for their cause. Now he was trying to force her to swear that she would give them up entirely.

'You will swear to me that you will stop this nonsense or you will no longer be welcome in this house. It is up to you.'

Her heart seeming to be turning over, but Connie stood her ground. 'If that's an ultimatum, Father, I will pack my things immediately.'

She saw him blink. She had called his bluff.

'This is ridiculous! Why are you so intent on hurting me, Constance, and upsetting your

146

mother, especially your mother? Devastating enough for her to have you refuse every suitor I have gone to great lengths to secure for you. We gave you choices and yet you threw our good intentions in our faces.'

He got up from behind his desk and began pacing the room, turning every now and again to look towards her.

'Why am I so surprised by this present attitude? What have I done to kindle it? I have given you a good home, a good education, both you and Verity, as fine as that for your brothers where many a father would not have taken such trouble over mere daughters. Yet you repay me by refusing every eligible young man I have introduced you to. And now this.'

Watching him pace, Connie was aware that cracks had begun to show in his armour. She waited and before long was rewarded.

'For your mother's sake I will not ask you to leave this house. But I tell you this, Constance, I am not prepared to see a daughter of mine turn herself into a common criminal. You may attend your lectures or whatever it is you do in London, but at the first sign of misconduct, that privilege will cease and I will go to any length to stop you. Do you understand me?'

She wanted so much to say, 'How will you stop me – lock me in my room, chain me to the bedpost?' But a voice in her head warned against imprudence. Although she didn't nod consent, he seemed willing now to take it as agreed and she breathed a silent sigh of relief as he gave a curt nod for her to take her leave.

Chapter Ten

It took six days refusing food for them to be set free, their sentence abruptly cut. It was a triumph. They emerged to a small celebratory deputation, and each freed prisoner got presented with the now-traditional badge of honour, a white brooch in the shape of the arrows stamped on the prison dresses. Eveline had never felt so proud; she firmly resolved to put her dreadful experiences behind her.

After the third day it had become harder to turn her back on the tray brought into her cell and left beside her on her bed. Prison food had been bland and unappetising: breakfast of porridge, with salt, the Scottish way, and weak tea; dinner overcooked vegetables and some sort of stringy meat with stodgy suet pudding and thin custard to follow and more weak tea; for supper bread, jam and a small piece of often stale cake and cocoa. Yet as the days of not eating continued, even the sight of it had made her mouth water and her stomach twist with a need to be filled. She hadn't felt physically weak, which was a blessing, and knowing that food was being refused to a man, or in their case a woman, gave her the will-power to ignore what became for her an almost succulent aroma as time went on.

'They'll give up, you'll see,' came a whisper as they walked in single line in a circle around the exercise yard. 'But we never will.' And after being reprimanded by a wardress, the speaker, undaunted, went on to hiss, 'They daren't let us die. They'll have to let us out.'

She gathered this was normal. But there'd been talk of more drastic measures beginning to be used. On day four she found out just what they meant, something she'd never wish to go through ever again. Her throat was feeling red raw.

On that fourth day she had become aware of a disturbance different to those she'd grown to recognise with a prisoner's ear, a subtle change to the normal, as if the very air had grown alert.

Moments later had come footsteps, a grating of keys, a cell door being opened and people trooping inside.

The cell door closed, muffling the sound of voices. A cry of protest that grew more urgent was abruptly cut off in a strangled gurgling. Not knowing what was happening, it had sent chills rippling along Eveline's spine.

For a moment there was silence, then someone choking and gagging followed by weeping. The cell door opened. A man said, 'It's done,' to be followed by a loud and reproving female voice.

'Foolish girl! There's nothing to cry about.'

'It's violation!' The words came between broken sobs. 'A violation of my person.'

'Stop bleating!' replied the previous voice. 'If you persist in foolishly starving yourself, you must expect to be dealt with as the doctor sees fit.'

'It's over now.' The man's voice had sounded a little more kindly. 'It's for your own good.'

'And perhaps you'll think twice about refusing

decent food.'

The woman's voice rose to address all those who had been listening in their cells. 'And every one of you will be treated exactly the same way if you persist in this idiotic hunger strike.'

It had dawned on Eveline what had been going on. Forced feeding. They would not be set free just as simply as that. She had tried to calm her heavily beating heart as she had made herself ready to continue the strike and suffer the consequences.

They came the same day soon after she had aimed her dinner at the wardress who had entered to put it in front of her, purely as a reaction to what had happened earlier that morning, and out of sheer anger. The woman had hastily withdrawn, leaving the upturned tin plate on the floor.

Moments later came the purposeful footsteps. Eveline had felt herself stiffen. She couldn't remember feeling fear, just a tautness that seemed to take over her whole body as if she were someone else looking on.

From then on it had been a blur. She remembered four wardresses and a doctor, remembered being pushed down into a chair, ankles secured to the front legs by pieces of cloth, her head held back by someone from behind. She would never forget the awful feeling of that rubber tube being slid down her throat, past the gag inserted to stop her clenching her teeth and into her throat, the evil smell of rubber, and pain as the tube scraped the flesh on its way into the oesophagus. She couldn't taste the substance they'd poured into a funnel attached to the tube, but the sensation of it running directly into her stomach cause her to heave. More pain ensued when the tube was withdrawn far too quickly as she vomited.

How many times it was repeated before she kept it down, she could not remember, maybe twice, though it felt more than that. Left sobbing and feeling defiled, unable to believe it was her this was happening to, all she could remember was the nightmare of it.

Thankfully, it hadn't been repeated. Now, after six days, she and the others were free, walking out of the gates in triumph to a warm welcome from waiting colleagues. She had been one of four who had been force-fed. She would never forget it.

To push away the memory, she concentrated her mind on the brooch she'd soon be wearing, the Holloway medal, a badge of honour designed for women who had been to prison for the cause. She would march proudly beside other suffragettes who knew that imprisonment was not a shame to be purged. She would hold her head high while less fortunate suffragettes would look on with awe and even envy. Yet she felt sad – Connie would not have a badge and how would that make her feel? She just hoped Connie would not feel jealous and let it break up their friendship. She'd have to tread carefully when she next saw her – try to play down all she'd gone through. Poor Connie; her father paying her fine, escorting her off like some wayward child. Now that he knew about her, would he stop her coming to meetings? The thought made Eveline sadder than ever.

And how was she going to face her own father? She prepared herself to meet his wrath as she said her goodbyes and made her way homeward.

'So, they let yer out then!' This from her dad.

Other than that, when Eveline entered her parents' corner shop, where they'd been serving a couple of women customers, she was met with a sudden silence. Mum refused to look at her after that first surprised glance. Neither of them had suspected she'd be released from prison so soon, and these were Dad's first words as the first of his two customers left with her goods. But she hadn't expected words of welcome. He'd made that quite clear with his message to the court.

The second customer looked up from paying her bill, her elderly eyes curious, but seeing the set faces around her, she had hurriedly stuffed her few purchases into her shopping bag and hobbled out, eager to escape this icy fog that had descended over a previously cheerful atmosphere.

Eveline stood still as her father came round the end of the counter, lifting the flap to let himself out. Brushing past without a glance at her, he went to the door and turned the sign to CLOSED. Leaving it unlocked, he stood with his back against its frosted panes and glared full in her face.

'I don't know why yer thought yer should come back 'ere. There ain't no room in my family fer convicts.'

'I'm not a *convict*, Dad.' She knew immediately that this was the wrong tone to use. He lunged forward to stop inches from her.

'What else are yer? They convicted yer. So what else would yer be?'

'It was only because I refused to pay the fine, like we all did.'

'I ain't arguing with yer. All I'm saying is you ain't no daughter of mine. Lying, getting up ter mischief what me and yer mum don't approve of, making a spectacle of yerself and keeping us in the dark all this time. That's what I can't get over, keeping us in the dark.'

For someone who'd just vowed not to talk to her, he was making a lengthy job of it, but Eveline didn't smile. She felt sick. He'd never spoken to her this way before. He'd ranted at her in the past for something she'd done wrong, mostly when she'd been a child, but this low, grating tone, full of hurt, was something she had never had directed at her before. Still, what had she expected? That he'd hold out his arms out to her? She supposed she was getting what she deserved. She'd kept him in the dark and Dad seldom forgave those who lied to him and as a result made him feel small and cheated, even ridiculed. It injured his pride, and it was his pride that spoke now.

'I don't want no more ter do with yer.'

'Leonard!' Whipping off her pinafore, her mother lifted the flap of the counter to let her through. 'That's a bit strong, love.'

He turned on her. 'She ain't no daughter of mine – going off with the likes of them, breaking winders and fighting the police. I don't want no more ter do with 'er. She can get out! She can go!'

'Go where?'

'Ter blazes fer all I care!'

Mum had turned to her, trying to pour oil. 'He don't mean it. He's just upset, and angry. And so am I. I think yer'd best go. Just fer a while. Go and see yer gran. Stay there a few hours. Maybe

153

yer dad'll be calmed down by then.'

'I'll never be calmed down,' came the bellow. 'Not after the disgrace she's brought us. She's lied, made fools of us – made a fool of *me*, going be'ind me back to 'ang about with that lot!'

'She won't any more,' Mum said hopefully. 'Now she knows 'ow you feel about it.' But he wasn't listening.

'Yer know what people call 'em? The Screaming Sisterhood. That's 'ow people look on 'em. And ter find me own daughter's one of 'em. It's brought shame on me! I won't be able ter look people in the eye. I'll tell yer one thing, though, if she comes near me I'll put me 'ands round 'er throat and bloody choke 'er before I see 'er with that lot again.'

Mum looked shocked. He never swore in front of women, even mildly. But she didn't reprimand, seeing how deep this had gone with him. When she turned to Eveline there was no kindness in her eyes, just anger that she had caused him to lose his dignity enough to curse. 'Yer'd best go,' she said quietly. 'Yer only making things worse by staying.'

For a moment Eveline stared from one parent to the other but saw no sign of relenting in either face; her mum was looking only to pacify her husband, not to concede to her daughter.

She felt suddenly isolated, as much alone as in that prison cell. But as in prison there came a need to combat this with all the pride she could muster. She pulled herself upright and, turning from the parents she loved so dearly, went to the shop door and let herself out. Only then did the tears spill over as she turned the corner into

Finnis Street and crossed the road towards the entrance to Gran's letting, mounting the two short flights of cold, stone stairs to lift the black iron knocker set high on the door.

It opened at the very first rap as though Gran had been watching her from the window. She would have been told about the arrest.

Her elderly face was filled with concern. 'I knew the moment I 'eard what you did that you'd be over 'ere before long. They was upset at you being arrested, and I suppose they've told you to pack your bags.'

'Dad just told me to hop it, so I did.'

'And I suppose you expect to go back as soon as he calms down.'

Eveline nodded and Gran heaved a deep sigh. 'Well, you'd best come in. I think you're going to be 'ere a bit longer than you think. Once your dad gets a bee in 'is bonnet it takes a while for it to leave.'

Standing back for Eveline to enter, she closed the door quietly. 'Go on into the kitchen,' she ordered. 'I don't suppose you've 'ad anything to eat yet. I've got some stew, you'd best 'ave some of that. I'll make up the old bed in me spare room for you tonight.'

The old double bed had been there for as long as Eveline could remember even though no one had used it for years.

Feeling better after the substantial stew, although there had been food handed out by the wonderful welcoming committee as she left prison, she bathed as best she could in Gran's old tin bath with three large saucepans of water that took ages to heat. But her clothes, put in a cupboard during those six days in prison, still stank of the place, making her ashamed of them. She should never have stalked out of her home like she had but at least paused long enough to collect a few clean things for herself. She would go early tomorrow and collect them. By that time her parents might have mellowed.

They hadn't. In response to her request her mother wordlessly let her in, not going up the stairs with her but waiting until she came down again with a case filled with all she thought she might need. The door remained held open for her to leave.

Eveline faced her. 'Mum?'

The face was turned abruptly away from her. From the kitchen where her father was shaving his chin, she heard his voice. 'Shut the door, Mother, there's a real blooming draught.'

Eveline took one more look at her mother's averted face and walked out. As she left she looked up at the living-room window. Framed there were the faces of her sister May and her younger brothers, Jimmy and Bobby. Len had already gone off to work before she arrived.

May waved, but she couldn't bring herself to wave back. Perhaps later she'd go and see her married sister Tilly, maybe get some sympathy there though Tilly had no interest in suffragettes at all. Nor did her sister-in-law Marion, Fred's wife, who she recalled had totally agreed with Dad last Christmas that they caused a lot of trouble for nothing.

Another thought came to her: to go and see if

Larry was back in London yet.

It wasn't an easy decision; her journey early next morning felt plagued by misgivings and an odd fear of facing him after what had happened. He had no particular interest in the suffragette cause. What would she say to him?

It seemed to take forever, going to Liverpool Street, taking the tube to Sloane Square, walking for ages along King's Road, finishing up outside Larry's flat in Cheyne Walk. After busy King's Road these quiet side streets felt so peaceful, she could have been miles from London. The Thames at high tide had a clean look to it, glinting in the mid-morning sunshine; no sheen of oil marred its surface, here was none of the clutter of tugboats and lighters and cargo vessels one saw further downstream around the Pool of London. All was calm and peaceful.

She breathed in the fresh tang of the river and felt instantly restored after what had been the most horrific week of her life. Glancing up to see that one of his windows was open, joy and relief flooded through her. He was at home.

Already she could feel his arms enfolding her as she pressed the bell to his flat. She had to wait a minute or so before the door opened and there he was. Seeing her, he looked a little taken aback. 'What are you doing here?'

It was an odd question and for a moment she was lost for words. True, she hadn't seen him for a few weeks, but she suddenly felt like a stranger.

Before she could say anything, he said, 'Well, you'd best come into the hall. You don't look too well.'

As she stepped inside, he asked, 'Have you been ill?'

'No,' she replied in a small voice, feeling inexplicably embarrassed, wishing she hadn't come. 'Something happened to me while you were away.' Almost in one breath she gabbled out what had taken place.

He stood silent for a while, as she remained there in the hallway watching him. He hadn't asked her up to his flat but he must have noticed her glance towards the stairs. He took in a sharp breath.

'Look, I'm sorry, Eveline. I can't ask you up. I've got...' He paused then hurried on. 'I've got visitors.'

'Oh.'

'You don't mind, do you?'

'No.'

'I'll probably see you on Saturday at your meeting, then we can talk.'

'All right.'

She felt thwarted, pushed away. She didn't know what she'd expected but this stiff reception was odd. She might not see him as regularly as she would wish, but when she did, he was always all over her. This was quite different.

'I'm sorry, Eveline, I really can't...'

Someone was coming down the stairs, unseen as yet, but the tread was light and quick. A young, feminine voice called, 'Who is it, darling?'

He turned as if stung. 'Go back up! I'll be there in a minute!'

Instinctively glancing upward, for a fraction of a second Eveline glimpsed just a flutter of long fair hair falling over part of a slender, bare arm and shoulder before their owner hastily withdrew. Not even her face could be seen.

Larry turned back to her with a ready grin. 'My cousin,' he said, then became urgent. 'Look, you must go.' He leaned quickly towards her, planting a light kiss on her cheek. 'I'll try and see you on Saturday.'

Before she could reply, she was ushered out of the door, having it closed on her.

For a moment she stood there, still with the sensation of those fleeting lips on her cheek. Her heart seemed to have forgotten to beat, making her feel faintly sick. His cousin. The one he introduced her to did have fair hair but not as fair as that she had glimpsed. It could have been another cousin, but that word, *darling,* purred this early in the morning, the slender arm, the naked shoulder not even displaying a wrap, and the long flowing hair, suggested a quite different explanation.

Slowly she turned and moved off, her thoughts in turmoil with no real answer, or rather, not one she could bring herself to face.

Last night, worn out by the ordeal of prison, she had slept like a top. Tonight she lay awake into the small hours, sick of heart, one minute telling herself she was being silly reading something sinister into what might have been totally innocent, the next seeing the signs she did not want to acknowledge.

Her pillow wet, she finally fell into a fitful sleep in which she was walking from the prison to warm sunshine and a group of women waiting to welcome her. But among them she could see her parents, their faces stern and unyielding. A rubber tube was sliding into her mouth even though she clenched her teeth, a tube so immense that her mouth became a cavern, then suddenly so narrow as to become an edge, an immeasurably thin, hard edge that seemed to be cutting right through her cheeks. Then abruptly it grew huge again, her mouth opening wider, wider... She could hear Larry's voice calling, 'Ev – wake up! Wake up!' and felt long fair hair waving in her face.

Her eyelids shot open. Gran was standing over her, one hand holding her nightdress tightly to her throat as she shook Eveline's shoulder with the other. 'Girl, you're 'aving a bad dream. I 'eard you call out.'

The reality of the dream had already fled yet she knew that for years to come this same nightmare would be waiting in the wings of the night's unguarded small hours; what had been done to her in prison wouldn't leave her so easily. This she knew as she gazed up at her grandmother.

'I'm sorry,' she said and saw the woman smile understandingly.

Her parents' attitude hadn't changed. These past two weeks Eveline had done her best to bury the hatchet but though some of the initial animosity had faded, Dad was still ignoring her, Mum still maintaining it was better to keep out of his way. 'You'll just have to stay 'ere,' her grandmother said.

Unlike the smaller flats hers at the end of the block had two bedrooms as well as parlour and kitchen. Grandad, when he'd had the shop, let the rooms above it and his family lived here opposite. When he died, Gran had refused a smaller letting, and was able to continue with the larger rent. 'Never could abide being cramped up,' she said despite having one bedroom sitting empty.

Eveline was here now, with her clothes and her trinkets – an apt enough announcement to her parents that as long as Gran didn't mind this was where she would be staying for the foreseeable future. But secretly she missed her family, the hubbub, sharing a bed with her sister May, their sleepy chats, exchanging the day's events. Even after two weeks it still felt strange sleeping alone. The unused bedroom smelled damp and, even with a September sun streaming in, felt cold.

She tried to carry on as normal, going to her Saturday meetings where she was now looked up to by newer recruits since her imprisonment. Last week she had even been asked to give a small talk on her views as a first-time prisoner – a bit nerve-racking but something to be proud of.

One thing spoiling it was Connie's absence these last two meetings. Eveline hoped she hadn't given up, after being shown up before the others in court by her father paying her fine. She had written to Connie but had had no response.

Gran said, 'She needs to feel someone's on her side. She'd probably like to go but you don't know what her people 'ave said to her to stop her. Keep writing. She'd like to know she's still got a friend she can turn to.'

It was nice having Gran to talk to. She would listen and advise where Mum would shrug things off, being too busy looking after her family and the shop. But it was a relief to have the suffragette thing out in the open at last, even though she'd been given the sack for being absent while in prison along with having a police record now, another weight for her father's fallen pride to bear.

She'd found another job, and just as well – her old office manager, Mr Prentice, had started to become a little too handy with his paws, laying them on her shoulders when leaning over to check her figures, letting them linger despite her trying to shrug them off, telling her she was as pretty as she was intelligent and how seldom the two went together, saying he'd help her get promotion – if she was interested, and if she was a good girl ... the rest left unsaid, he would allow himself a meaningful tilt of his balding head. She knew what he was after and being sacked had got her away from him before it led to a nasty situation.

She was still doing office work; it was not so grand as a factory office, just a back room in a small clothing factory. Here she worked as the figures clerk with a girl who typed all the letters. The money wasn't good but Gran took less towards her keep than Mum had. Of course Gran had only herself whereas Mum had a family.

She was far more approachable than Mum and Eveline felt able to open her heart to her on things, telling her all about the forced feeding, at which she saw the downy face tighten. She could never have told Mum about it and certainly never have confided in her things of a more personal nature, such as what was vaguely perplexing her this evening.

Sitting in the parlour, Gran knitting, she was reading a library book, or at least trying to. Her mind kept flitting to Larry who despite his promise had not been in touch with her. Each time she thought of him she felt angry, hurt, let down, yet still she hoped and grew angry with herself for hoping. But how had he laid aside what had gone on between them? She tried hard to convince herself that he must still love her, though she'd never go there uninvited ever again. But her heart was telling her it was all over and her heart was breaking.

At the library earlier, she had bumped into Bert Adams, and although he was good-looking in a robust sort of way, she again upset herself by instantly comparing him with Larry: the rough accent, the stall-bought suit against Larry's smart, expensive clothes and sophisticated, elegant manner. But it wasn't about Bert Adams or Larry that she needed her grandmother's advice but something more personal which was baffling her. She kept telling herself it could be quite trivial and not that she must be ill. Gran would know.

Her grandmother sighed and folding her knitting began putting it in its cloth bag, announcing it was time they both went off to seek their beauty sleep. Eveline quickly closed her book. 'Gran, can I ask you something?'

'Anything, love.'

'It's about me. I'm not sure but I think I could be ill or something.'

Quickly she explained what she would never

have been able to speak to her mother about. Gran's response was immediate and direct.

'Lots of young girls don't see their monthlies regular for the first few years. Some never do all their lives.'

'But mine's always been as regular as clockwork. It started when I was fourteen. That was four years ago and it's always happened practically to the day. This should have happened four days ago, but it hasn't and I'm worried I might be ill.'

'Of course there can be that one time,' Gran said. Eveline saw her looking at her oddly. She caught a hardly discernible shake of the head as though Gran had been thinking of something but had immediately brushed the thought away.

'It's probably shock from what you went through in that prison,' she went on. 'You'll likely see by tomorrow or the next day, I shouldn't wonder. A week's delay now and then ain't overlong. Unless...' There came a small hesitation and that earlier look again touched her face. 'You don't seem to see much of that young man you was going out with. It wouldn't be you and... No.' She recovered with a shake of her head. 'No, it's probably the reaction from being in that prison place.'

But Eveline was ahead of her. Colouring, she turning quickly away, hoping the blush hadn't been noticed. If it had, Gran gave no sign as Eveline leapt up, dropping her book down on the chair seat, her head lowered as if making sure it was properly closed.

'I'd better be off to bed then,' she said brightly, pausing just long enough to plant a brief goodnight peck on her grandmother's cheek.

164

Chapter Eleven

A letter finally arrived from Connie just as Eveline was about to leave for her Saturday afternoon meeting at George Street. It had been sent early that morning, the eleventh of September; with three or four posts daily, mail was guaranteed to reach its destination by lunchtime. Though not as fast, the letter was so short as to be as brief as any telegram.

Sorry not to have replied before, but a lot has happened. I will see you at this afternoon's meeting. Connie.

This formal communication did not even respond to her own news that she was now living with Gran, although the letter had come to Gran's address rather than her parents', so Connie must have taken note of what she'd written.

Intrigued and concerned, Eveline arrived at the meeting ahead of most of the women. She watched one after the other hurry in from of the dreary afternoon, shaking their brollies before entering and going downstairs to the cloakroom to take off their wet outdoor things, but could see no sign of Connie.

She grew ever more anxious, having been one of the first to go down to the cloakroom, hardly lingering to hang up her coat, stack her brolly in the umbrella stand and adjust her hat before coming up to begin her wait; she couldn't have missed her.

She'd peeped into the meeting room earlier. Now it was filling rapidly, the chatter beginning to swell. She turned away, disappointed, to join the others, giving the main door one last glance. Connie was coming slowly and wearily up the short flight of steps from the street, struggling with an umbrella while hanging on to a large and cumbersome travelling bag. Eveline was out of the door and taking hold of the receptacle.

'Connie, what are you doing?' she burst out. 'I've really missed you. Where have you been?'

Connie gave her a wan smile, glad to be relieved of the heavy bag. 'I'll tell you later,' she said as they came into the dry.

'Take off your coat,' Eveline ordered with a need to be in charge with Connie looking so sorrowful and worn out. 'I'll pop it down to the cloakroom with your umbrella and your bag.' She tested its weight. 'My goodness, it's heavy. You go on in.'

Sudden panic spread across Connie's face. 'No, I'll wait here for you.'

'We're late.' She made for the narrow spiral staircase. 'See if you can find chairs together for us. The place won't be full, a wet afternoon like this.'

'I can't. I – I don't want to be left in there on my own.'

Pausing to look at her, Eveline instantly knew why. In there could be some of those who had been in court and who'd witnessed her walking away with a father having arranged to pay her fine, while they, electing not to be defeated, had gone to prison. Even though they understood that one might flout the cold authority of the law but not so easily the well-meaning authority of an over-protective parent, Connie could not face them alone.

'Stay there,' Eveline said briskly. 'I won't be two ticks.'

It was just as well Connie did wait. Instead of the chairs being in rows ready for a speaker so that Connie would have only a view of the backs of those in front of her, they'd been arranged in small circles and she, with shame still etched on her face, would have been in full sight of others. This afternoon, as often happened, they were helping to make small banners – normally the sort of afternoon they both loved, doing something practical for the cause, everyone chatting as they sewed or embroidered, exchanging news and views. Eveline always felt a certain pride, making something with her own hands, but this afternoon Connie was her main concern.

Something serious must have happened to keep her away from what she so loved, but she hadn't reckoned on the shock of what Connie had to tell her after they'd come away from the meeting.

As they went to get tea and cake, supplied by volunteers, she asked Connie what the trouble was. Connie looked quickly around her at those clustering by the refreshment table.

'Not here.'

'Why not? What happened?'

Connie's voice had dropped to a whisper. 'Can we can go somewhere for a cup of tea? Somewhere we can talk in private? It's that I'm not going back home. I need to find a hotel for the time being.'

In a nearby café she told Eveline how her father had been surprisingly more lenient than she'd expected in regard to her suffragette interests, but had nevertheless advised her not to attend any more meetings, which she had felt obliged to honour for the time being, hoping to placate him for a while. But then something came to his notice that to him was far worse than a daughter associating with what he termed demented females.

Her voice threatening to let her down, Connie didn't go into too much detail about her father's wrath but said enough to reveal someone had informed him that she had been seen on the arm of a young man. The young man was, of course, George Towers. The informant, it seemed, couldn't wait to tell her parents and by the power of his formidable presence, her father had wormed the truth from her, forbidding her to see George Towers ever again.

'But I couldn't do that,' she whispered. 'I'm far too in love with George. I can't...' This time she broke down completely and had to stop for quite a while to gain control of her emotions. When she began again, her voice had steadied.

'I think I've told you that George is only a bank clerk. He lives in a rented house with his mother. She's widowed. She is quite a sick woman.'

Connie was stirring her tea, slowly, distractedly, the spoon moving round and round, its metallic clinking against the cup rim blending with all the other sounds of afternoon tea in this cosy little place. So far she'd not taken a single sip.

'He looks after her, so we can't go out very much. We can only meet on Saturday evenings and sometimes Sunday afternoons, and go for small walks. So it is quite ironic we should have been seen together.' She set down the spoon down in the saucer only to pick it up moments later to resume stirring.

'Naturally, knowing my father,' she went on, bitterly sarcastic, 'he set about making enquiries straight away – who George Towers was, where did his people stand in society, did he have a tidy inheritance, certainly enough to support a wife in the style to which she was accustomed, or better, that being in my father's book an income of at least nine or ten thousand a year?'

In a monotone she related that when he'd found George to be a mere bank clerk with no real prospects at all, he had stamped down on her, saying she had allowed herself to be blinded by some young and scheming leech looking only to feather his nest and had allowed herself to sink to the level of a common hussy whose head could be turned by the first attractive face to come her way, with not the slightest consideration for the duty a young woman of her upbringing owed her family. This meant to marry well, become wife to a person of high standing, thus furthering her family's status in society. That was her role as a daughter. It was what her education had been about. Why else educate a woman if not to groom her for marriage to the right man?

She quoted this last part with an acrimony that took away Eveline's breath, her eyes wide and blazing as Eveline had never seen them before, her pretty face contorted with rage and cynicism.

'People like you think women like me sleep on beds of roses. But we are treated as chattels, property, expected to be genteel and obedient. *You* have more freedom than I. It's different for my sister – she is the obedient sort. She cannot wait to find a wealthy husband.'

She was calming a little. 'I told him George wasn't a schemer. I said he was kind and honest and hardworking, but it made no impression at all. He refused to listen. In truth I didn't expect him to, which is why I hid it from him all this time. But George and I love each other. I could never give him up!'

She choked back a hiccuping sob, her anger turning to utter dejection.

Eveline sat in silence watching the tears slide slowly down Connie's cheeks as she spoke of her mother taking her father's side against her, telling her to give up her foolish notion, saying she had been given endless opportunities to find a husband of good standing and secure means yet had chosen to insult them by settling on a nobody and that she must be quite insane.

'I *am* insane,' Connie said vehemently. 'Insanely in love. I told them I would never give George up. They were incensed. Finally my father said that if I persisted with my foolishness, he'd have nothing more to do with me and it would be best I leave. So I did. I shall never go back. Nor will I be allowed to unless I come to my senses, as my father so aptly put it.'

As if to emphasise her decision, Connie

dropped the spoon down into the saucer and picked up her cup, draining the half-cold liquid in several large gulps as if her life depended on it, then slamming the cup back down on to the saucer enough to have cracked it across.

She was weeping openly now, tears falling into the empty cup. 'I don't know what to do. Even after all that's happened, I miss being at home. I've never been on my own before.'

Eveline came to herself with a start. 'First thing in the morning,' she said, now in control, 'you must find George and tell him what's happened.'

She saw Connie look up with near terror in her hazel eyes. 'What if it frightens him off, telling him what I've done, all that worry I'm putting on him? I can't go back home after what's happened.'

'He'll still want you if he's all you say he is.'

'But with his mother to look after, how can I heap this on him too?'

'If he loves you.'

'He does. But I can't burden him with this. Imagine turning up and telling him I've nowhere to live. He'll think I'm asking him to take me in.'

Eveline needed time to think. 'You can't stay in a hotel in this state,' she said. 'Not on your own. Have you got any money?'

She could imagine Connie running off without thinking, hardly a few shillings in her purse. Connie shrugged despondently, dabbing her eyes with a handkerchief, becoming aware that people were looking at her.

'I can draw from my bank account.'

'Tomorrow's Sunday – banks are closed.'

Connie wasn't listening. 'My father gives me an allowance, though I expect that will stop now. I've a few pounds on me and my cheque book, but it's being away from home all on my own that's frightening.'

'You're not on your own. You've got George. Go and see him tomorrow.'

She looked so dejected that Eveline found herself debating all sorts of ways out for her other than being all on her own in a strange hotel. She was aware the WSPU had hostels for young women coming into town from afar, but Connie would still be spending a night alone and in her present state, that was unthinkable.

On a sudden whim she said, 'Look, come back with me. My gran might be able to put you up for the night, then in the morning we can think more clearly. You can share my bed. It's a double.'

She saw Connie become attentive but had she been too hasty with her solution, not stopping to think what Gran might say to her bringing home a stranger and asking for her to be put up as well?

'My Gran lives across the street from my parents. I'm lucky I had her to go to. She's a wonderful person. She understands what the suffragettes go through and what they are fighting for.'

It was said with pride. Gran was as sprightly as she'd been fifteen years ago and exceptionally modern for one of seventy, unlike most people of her age, who dwelled in the past. Even though she loved to tell stories of her past life, she was strong, resourceful, calm in a crisis and ready to face up to anything. Her motto was, 'Don't ever let today's problems get you down, 'cos by next year they'll all be behind you and be replaced by another lot!'

Eveline often felt quite envious that she wasn't more like her, though Mum in moments of annoyance towards her often accused her of being *too much like your blooming grandmother!* Gran being a stubborn old devil, she and Mum had never been able to see eye to eye. She couldn't help smiling, wondering if that was why Gran had taken her under her wing, to show her disapproval of Mum taking her father's side against their child.

Eveline gravely regarded her grandmother as the door opened.

'Gran, this is my friend, Constance Mornington.'

Quickly she explained Connie's predicament while her grandmother regarded the girl as though able to see into her mind. She was like that – she discerned things others failed to.

There was a lot of wisdom behind the way she looked at most things, seldom shocked by this modern world. Where most women of seventy clung to their dark bonnets, she moved with the times; her figure was trim and upright, she'd wear a fashionably large hat and Eveline suspected her of secretly using tinted rinses to temper the grey hair, even occasionally a false piece coyly known as a transformation.

It was good to see someone of her age still caring enough to want to look young. She could have walked alongside any of the older suffragettes, just as brisk, plucky, resolute and unafraid.

Gran had switched her gaze back to her. 'Well,

if your friend is going to stay, you'd best both come in.'

Having sized up the situation, she'd already assumed Connie's stay could be a long one but didn't seem at all put out and again Eveline felt that stir of envy, but one that also held a lot of love.

The young woman had the look of someone utterly lost, of someone spoiled by a sheltered life, now suddenly on her own and totally unable to deal with it.

Victoria Ansell smiled to herself. Trust Eveline to assume responsibility for someone else's problem. With her kind heart she always had been one for strays, so to speak. She'd lost count of the bedraggled cats Eveline as a child had brought to her door, the mangy creature cradled in her clean pinafore.

'Gran, can it have something to eat? It looks starved. Mum won't let me bring it upstairs or into the shop. Just a drop of milk or something?'

She always managed to find food, as with old and young heads together they'd crouch on her kitchen floor to watch the frail creature drink and eat whatever was placed before it. Sometimes it left, having filled itself up, or stayed for a day or two if poorly, being cared for before being sent on its way. No pets were allowed in these dwellings other than a canary or linnet. Sometimes it died, was wrapped in newspaper and consigned to one of the dustbins in the yard that separated one row of Waterlow Buildings from another, Eveline intoning a childish and tearful prayer over its tin grave.

After she turned seventeen there were no more stray cats; her mind became focused on higher things, stray boys mostly, and cats had taken a bit of a back seat. Victoria missed those days. It was nice having her here again, comforting.

She'd got used to living alone, hardly noticed it until Eveline came to stay, making her realise that she *had* been on her own. But eventually the girl would go back home, once her parents forgave her as in time they must, leaving her to feel lonelier than she'd ever been since Herbert died.

She could recall when this letting had been a bustling place; her brood, four girls, three boys, filling these three rooms, the boys in one bed in what was now her back parlour, with a curtain to separate it from where everyone ate. The girls all shared one bedroom, she and Herbert occupied the other, very often with a baby in a cot and the next youngest in the bed with them.

She had been nineteen when she'd had her first child; one by one they'd married and left home. Two sons were dead now, the youngest killed in the Boer War, the other from pneumonia. The third lived in New Zealand with his family – she heard from them once a year. Two girls were also dead, both in childbirth. The grandchildren, with kids of their own, she seldom saw. Life was like that; they go off, one by one, forget. The Ansells had never been all that close-knit, not like some East End families with family parties for every occasion – their sing-songs could be heard most Saturday nights all the way down the street.

Only three of her brood were still living. Her daughter Hilda had moved up north years ago, to

Yorkshire with her husband, and hadn't been down this way for years. She might write occasionally; she usually forgot her mother's birthday but sent a Christmas card. Hilda's three children, also with kids of their own, except the youngest, didn't know her though they knew their paternal grandparents who lived with them. And there was Dora to whose husband, Len, Herbert had handed over the shop, and who lived over the road. But for the little she saw of her, she might as well be living in Yorkshire too.

At least Dora's Tilly, married last year and now expecting, and Fred, married two years ago with a little boy, visited now and again, and for that she should be grateful. But for now she had Eveline all to herself. It was like a breath of fresh air and she'd begun to feel ten years younger.

'Sit yerselves down,' she said to the two girls. 'Tell me what's the matter.'

She waited as both exchanged glances from beneath their enormous hats, the newcomer distinctly embarrassed. What was she embarrassed about? She didn't strike Victoria as being in the family way. When a woman is in that condition it would show at a glance, even in the early stages – by the eyes, a certain glow. But this haunted look had something to do with a man, she was sure. Victoria took a guess. Trouble at home because of it perhaps, and she'd been told to leave. Victoria took stock of her: well dressed, well spoken too, she noticed when the girl had hesitantly returned her greeting, the sort of person you wouldn't be afraid to have staying in your home.

She was on the verge of coming to a conclusion when Eveline began, 'It is all right, isn't it, Gran, putting Connie up? We won't be no trouble sharing my bed? Just for tonight until she gets herself together.'

Just like the cats.

Victoria smiled at the girls. 'For as long as she needs to.'

Why had she said that? Was it the bleak look that at those words had instantly changed to a grateful smile of relief, that pretty face lighting up?

'So long as you don't mind sharing the bed with your friend,' she said to Eveline.

Eveline shook her head. 'I don't mind,' she said readily, the other giving such a smile of acquiescence and relief that Victoria felt her old heart go out to her.

As for herself, she felt a gladness that she'd not experienced in years, now that her home was once more filled with youth and all its exuberance.

Chapter Twelve

'It's all arranged.' Connie's eyes were shining. 'We're to be married in three weeks, the eleventh of December. The banns are being called at St John's this Sunday.'

Impulsively, Eveline flung her arms about her. 'Oh, Connie, I'm ever so pleased for you. You and George deserve every happiness after what you've been through.'

George's mother had passed away quite suddenly at the beginning of October. He'd no doubt loved her, probably remembering a time when she had been young and healthy, but as a sick woman who, Connie said, had been steadily losing her wits this past year, her death had nevertheless released him from the responsibility of caring for her.

When he had proposed to Connie not long afterwards, she had readily accepted but had refused to live anywhere near Perivale.

'Nothing would ever persuade me to live within a hundred miles of my parents after all that has happened.' she told Eveline. 'Besides, my friends are here, those who helped me when I needed it most. Who would I know if I went elsewhere to live?'

Connie had changed little since coming to live in Bethnal Green, still a lady in many ways, not given to making new friends easily. But a liveliness was beginning to seep through that her upbringing had probably tried to smother as being too unladylike. She'd persuaded George to give up his landlord-owned house and come to live nearby. He, like the easy-going man he was, had consented, finding himself a modest room in a nicer part of this area, Cambridge Heath Road not far from Victoria Park.

Being nearer to him had helped her through the trauma of her family's cruel rejection though sometimes Eveline saw moments of pensiveness and guessed she'd never forget what they'd done. George, though, was the best thing that could have happened to Connie.

'I don't want to go too far from here to live,' she'd said. 'George has had a small rise in salary so he has put down three weeks' rent on a fourth-floor flat in Corfield Street, not too expensive but bright and sunny.'

That was the next road to Gran's flat. Parallel to the block in which she lived, Eveline would practically be able to lean out of the back room window and wave across the wide central yard to Connie. But she would miss their time together at Gran's.

She meant to continue living with her grand-mother if she was happy with that. Although her family had come round to her going back home, she liked it here. It did give them more room at home and Gran did seem to like having her around.

'It gives me something to look forward to, you coming 'ome for me to cook a meal for. I didn't realise just how lonely it was 'ere until you came 'ere to live. I do enjoy your company, my dear.'

'It won't be forever though,' Eveline told her. 'One day I'll be married too and having a place of my own.'

A stir of envy had caught her when Connie had told her of George's proposal. She'd heard nothing of Larry since the day he'd closed the door on her. Sometimes her heart would feel so heavy it was as if she had a lump of lead inside her. She tried not to admit it, but she was growing anxious when September and October came and her period hadn't. Now, mid-November had arrived and another period had been missed. Gran was giving her looks.

When nothing happened that first time, she'd really believed it could only be due to her bad experiences in prison. Gran had been ready to believe it too.

When again nothing happened last month, she finally told in more detail what she'd previously been unable to put into words: the two days of forced feeding, the shock of it, the pain not only to her throat but deep inside her chest cavity, the feeling that her eardrums had been ready to burst, her diaphragm burning as though it were on fire, the faintness that had followed, and the sense of having been totally violated.

Seeing the anger and revulsion on her grandmother's normally serene face as she recounted it all, Eveline had again convinced herself that her ordeal had to have left its mark, physically, as it was doing on other women who were at this moment being returned to prison, twice and three times over, to suffer the same ordeal when refusing to eat, their health sometimes being ruined by it.

She'd read in the papers that questions were being asked by some members of parliament, but with the People's Budget considered to be infinitely more important, forced feeding was constantly being pushed to the back.

She continued to take comfort that if some women's health was being affected, perhaps hers too had been. But the real reason for that second missed period was now making itself only too apparent with feelings of sickness in the mornings and her breasts growing tender to the touch, and Gran's concern was beginning to take a different path.

'If you really think there's something gone wrong inside you,' she said in a tone that wasn't as sympathetic as it had once been, 'you'd best see a doctor in case some real damage 'as been done.'

A visit to a doctor was becoming imperative. It confirmed her worst fears; she was pronounced to be three months pregnant. The news had her in tears being held tightly to her grandmother's thin bosom.

'You're going to 'ave to sort this out with that chap you was seeing. He's going to 'ave to do right by you. You don't need to be told what a silly-billy you've been, child.'

Gently she rocked Eveline as though she were indeed a child. 'No need for your mum to know yet. Time enough when you can't hide it any more. That'll be a while yet if you keep your corset laces a bit tightish.'

The new style of healthier corset, said to be kinder to the figure, giving a shape known as the

'S' bend, would hide any bulge quite a bit longer.

'Your mum's already shown you the door so not much she can do over this and no point upsetting 'er at this stage. And you never know, the young man might do the right thing and marry you before you show.'

Eveline had her doubts but said nothing. She'd told no one she'd not seen Larry from that day she'd called on him.

'What if he don't want to do the right thing by me?' she ventured, already visualising him backing out in alarm. On this occasion she'd break her vow, go and see him. Gran was usually right and in desperation she took comfort from that. Perhaps, when he saw her distress, his love might be rekindled. She could only pray it would.

'What if he don't?' she put the question again.

Her grandmother held her at arm's length to look into her eyes. 'If you think that could be the case then I don't think much of him. But there are ways of not ... well, you know ... I mean of not having it. I don't trust them women what set themselves up to 'elp such as them in your straits, but...'

She paused, not wanting to mention the word abortionist. To say it outright would offend her delicate sensibilities, even though her granddaughter had already been indelicate enough to get herself in these straits.

The significant pause brought an immediate flush of humiliation and shame to Eveline's cheeks, more than if it had been said outright. Frantically she shook her head. 'Oh, Gran, I couldn't do anything like that. I couldn't!'

Tears welled afresh in her eyes as once more she took refuge in Gran's arms. She knew that tomorrow she had to see Larry. Where else could she turn? One thing she knew: she couldn't face anything so abhorrent and sordid as subjecting herself to the probing and other unspeakable things she'd heard was done by those women her gran had spoken of – so awful that Gran had even broken off mid-sentence. The thought of rejection by Larry, and having to resort to what Gran was proposing, was making her feel physically sick.

Looking at the two young women, none would ever have believed it was Connie's wedding day. The thought came as Victoria helped the girl into her wedding dress. Every now and again she glanced towards Eveline. Both girls were as subdued as if they were going to a funeral.

If nothing else, Connie should have been excited about her bridal gown, which had a cream alpaca fitted bodice with a chiffon yoke and a front panel to the skirt with a pleated waistband, quite formal in a way except for the trimming of white Honiton lace, which matched her veil. Somehow, formality suited her tall and slender regal stature, befitting her good upbringing. Contrasting with the gleaming white, Eveline's bridesmaid's gown was pale heliotrope chiffon that at least helped to bring some brighter highlights to her quite ordinary dark brown hair and light brown eyes.

Victoria looked from one girl to the other and sadness wrenched at her heart for the both of them. Connie had written to her parents, but must have known it would be futile to invite them to the wedding of their eldest daughter.

The weeks passed. No reply came. She'd become quiet and withdrawn. She'd finally pulled herself together, saying she had made up her mind to cut them out of her life as they had cut her out of theirs. Even so, some of that dejection lingered, even though in two hours' time she would be wed to the man she adored enough to give up her family and her sheltered life, with its comfort and privileges for, to become the wife of a modest bank clerk.

She did have money in her bank account that hadn't been touched. Now that George had had a small promotion, they shouldn't have too many financial worries. In time she'd recover her spirits – indeed she would have to if she wanted her marriage to be happy. But as the years passed with no word from her family ever again, how would it tell on her?

Victoria took a deep breath and glanced across at her granddaughter.

Eveline was gazing out of the parlour window at the dwellings across the road as though the preparations for a bride's marriage going on here had no interest for her. Hers had been a particularly awful trauma, yet she had taken it with a fortitude Victoria always knew was in her.

She felt for the humiliation and fear Eveline must be going through, deserted by that despicable swine, Laurence Jones-Fairbrook – an apt name for an arrogant upper-class loafer who saw no wrong in destroying a young girl's future and happiness. There were no words to describe him. All along she'd felt that something like this might happen, but Eveline wouldn't have listened, being silly enough to expect decency from a man of that sort.

Eveline had cried in her arms later that day. 'He didn't even want to know,' she sobbed. 'You should've seen the way he looked at me, like I'd done it deliberately, like I was something he'd just picked up out of the dirt.'

As she listened, Victoria learned that he had told her, without any compunction, that when he married it would be to someone of his own class; that he hadn't expected her to come back at him with this sort of blackmail and when she'd protested that it wasn't blackmail, he'd even said the baby wasn't his.

Eveline had repeated this to her as if her heart was breaking. 'How could he say such a thing? I thought he loved me.'

Victoria had stroked the thick brown hair and had tried to give words of comfort that wouldn't make it sound as if she thought Eveline a fool to think that sort of man would be in love with a girl like her, that all he'd been after was a bit of excitement, slumming, so to speak.

She had tried to warn her that it was getting almost too late to do something about it, but when Eveline had continued to shy from the notion, all she could say when she spoke of having to resign herself to the pointing fingers she knew she'd have to face, was, 'Not from me. I'll stand by you no matter what.'

Surprisingly the words seemed to strengthen her. She hadn't wept from that day to this. Only once had she referred to him again, to say he'd looked scared when she'd told him. Victoria had given a contemptuous 'Pah!' and said that he was scared for his own skin that it might get back to his family, that she might cite him as the father and cause trouble for him.

'I wouldn't lower myself,' was all Eveline had said with a dignity that pulled at Victoria's heartstrings.

From then on she hadn't mentioned him again. Instead, she threw herself into her suffragette work as if her sanity depended upon it. Almost every evening after work, and every weekend, she was out doing something, no longer as militant with a baby inside her now, not daring to risk arrest. Opting for less confrontational duties, she'd stand at street corners selling copies *of The Suffragette,* oblivious to the cold November fogs despite Victoria's warnings that in her condition she could do harm to herself.

Victoria wondered sometimes if Eveline might even be glad if she did lose the child as she stoically paraded with a sandwich board, waving aside concerns that it could be too heavy, although her knees often got bruised from being banged against the boards. It was as though she was bent on punishing herself for allowing that despicable young swine to take such advantage of her as she smiled placidly at the insults from some male passers-by, the very same smile she gave to encouragement from wives and mothers.

She helped at the local WSPU committee rooms, went fly-posting with her companions, and would get up on a platform, cart or soapbox, speaking to any who might stop to listen, taking care not to incite public disorder in case the law came down on her.

She'd display her Holloway arrow brooch and challenge anyone who jeered to go through what she had; she would even in part describe the ordeal; perhaps it was the greater wrong of being deserted by her child's father which put that other evil in the shade. Victoria admired her courage in standing up to those who called her womanhood into question for making an exhibition of herself. Perhaps the heckling reminded her that she was not a weak woman but one who could face adversity with her head held high and the ability to meet insults and barracking with quiet fortitude and common sense.

Victoria felt proud of her, and supportive, which was more than her parents were at present.

Two days ago Eveline had gone across to their flat. 'I really ought to see a bit more of them,' she'd said. 'We can't go on being at loggerheads.'

'You should tell them about your condition while you're there,' Victoria had told her. 'If you don't soon, they'll start to notice and call you underhanded and that won't 'elp matters.' But Eveline shook her head.

'A few more weeks, then I'll tell them.' Victoria understood, and felt sad. That took courage, even for Eveline.

She came back an hour later, her expression bleak, and Victoria could see she was trying hard not to let her lips tremble. Victoria let her take her time, though she guessed what had happened.

Slowly Eveline's face relaxed but there was a

stubborn dignity in it. 'You were right, Gran, they had to know eventually. It was Mum. She made a remark that I was putting on weight around the middle. I don't know how she could tell because I hardly show at all.'

Victoria had gone to sit beside her as she sank down on the edge of the sofa. Her voice was low, controlled. 'Then she said, "To look at you, some would say you was pregnant. Are you?" I felt really shaken, the way she said it. I just looked at her and said, "Yes." I couldn't help it, it just came out.'

She saw her granddaughter's lips tighten again. 'Dad just exploded. He called me a dirty little bitch, wanted to know who the father was. It made me so angry because at one time he was so pleased I was seeing someone with a few quid to his name. But asking me that question – it was just like the way Larry accused me of it not being his. Gran, I'm *not* that sort!'

Giving Victoria no time to comfort her, she had rushed on.

'I never intended to speak of him ever again, but I really did love him and I really thought he wanted to marry me. I've been a fool. And there was Dad bellowing that he was going to sort him out and give him a thorough bashing and *make* him marry me. I told him not to be so silly. He'd already turned his back on me and I wouldn't lower myself to marry him now if he was the last man on earth. That's when I got up and left.'

As Eveline's lips began to tremble, Victoria had gathered her in her arms and held her tight, murmuring what words of comfort she could think of while the comforting embrace only served to send the girl into racking sobs. But at least it got it out of her. Since then no girl could have been more stoic and dry-eyed than her granddaughter.

Yes, she was proud of her, and Dora and Len had every inch of Victoria's contempt; when they were most needed, their hearts were not large enough to let them stand by their own child. And after what her husband Herbert had done for Len, handing the shop over to him all those years ago. Such gratitude! Not to return a little of the goodness that had been done to them.

At least May had come over to see how her sister was, as did her older sister Tilly with her husband and their new son and her brother Fred with his wife and little boy. To Victoria it was so good to have her home filled with those she loved on these odd occasions, just like in the old days, and in a way it was all thanks to Eveline.

The small wedding reception was held in Eveline's grandmother's large front parlour. Connie could hardly express her gratitude for such kindness when her own people hadn't even replied to her invitations. She hadn't expected them to, and did her best to dismiss them from her mind. This was her day.

She and George had escaped in a shower of confetti and good wishes, running hand in hand before a wintry wind that promised snow before long. People they passed waved at them still in their wedding clothes, called out good wishes to them. Reaching the block in Corfield Street that held their new home, they ran hand in hand up the stone stairs to the fourth floor.

Their flat overlooked an open yard of Allen-bury's chemical factory and beyond to a small park on the other side of Cambridge Heath Road, almost as if they were in the countryside. The lower flats didn't have half this view. She'd fallen in love with it when George had first taken her to see it, knowing that each morning she'd see the sun rise when, as George's wife, she got his breakfast before he went off to work. One day, she dreamed, he would be a bank manager and they'd have a grand house with grand views, but she'd always remember this lovely little letting with its own fine views to the east.

But for now with December's short afternoon left outside, they lay together in the double bed all snug and warm. Their wedding attire was now draped over chair backs and they wore night-clothes that smelled all new. This, their first time together, had begun in shyness as they hastily undressed with their backs to each other, but slowly the shyness was dissipating. George's hands were smoothing away her tenseness, his hands warm on her body that she knew would soon lie naked beneath his love.

Waiting, consumed with strange excitement, she thought momentarily of Eveline, alone in the bed they'd once shared, no man to comfort her, and carrying a child without a father's name. Suddenly, despite her own good fortune, Connie found herself crying against George's shoulder. 'It's that I'm so happy,' she said and, as he responded, she forgot about Eveline.

Chapter Thirteen

A small crowd was gathering as, one after another, passers-by had their attention taken by the young lady on the wooden packing case that served as a rostrum. Encouraged, Eveline's voice lifted higher in her public oration.

Now and again she'd glance down at her companions. On one side of her stood Connie with a placard on which was painted the usual wording, *Votes For Women*. On her other side was Agatha Coleman, small and slender, with pencil and clipboard ready to take the name of any who had a fancy to express sympathy for the women's political cause, who perhaps would even care to join them. This was not always very likely, but one had to try.

Here with approval from the WSPU Headquarters this Saturday afternoon, they'd been told not to speak for long and risk being apprehended by the police for causing an obstruction. Their rivals, the National Union of Women's Suffrage Societies, the NUWSS, were even more against any sort of militancy, deeming street-corner oratory to be counterproductive in inciting riots, maintaining that the suffrage problem should be settled by votes not violence. On this the two factions had reached a political impasse.

Connie smiled back at Eveline from under her wide hat brim, its low crown a lot more modest

191

than the millinery she once wore as the pampered daughter of a wealthy Harley Street specialist.

She and George were faring well enough on his wage but needed to be careful with money all the same. He seemed happy for her to continue her suffragette activities, saying he was all for the women's struggle to be given the vote, but Eveline suspected Connie was still trying to make up for not being with her fellow militants last August. Time had probably softened the edges but Eveline tried not to refer to it in her presence if she could help it.

'Try not to go on too long,' Connie warned, her eyes darting up and down the streets she could see from this corner. She shifted her placard to a more comfortable position. 'In case the police do turn up.'

With this in mind, Eveline turned back to the gathered bystanders, most of them huddled in winter coats and scarves and brave enough to pause in a cold January wind that whipped around the skirts of her own coat. Black, its tent-like shape, rather like a duster coat, helped to hide her distended stomach and with only four months to the birth she gave thanks for winter and the need for extra clothing. Even so, people couldn't help noticing her condition if they looked closely, just as one did now.

She'd hardly opened her mouth to speak when the coarse male voice bellowed from the back of the crowd: 'So where's the ole man then? Can't be much of a man, lettin' you out ter spout the odds in your condition.'

Eveline was back at him immediately. 'My husband is dead, sir.'

To her, Larry was dead; in fact using him felt very satisfying and gave her a sense of getting her own back in some small way.

She became aware of the crowd beginning to shuffle and feared she could lose their attention, as nothing was more designed to make people ill at ease than wearing a sorrowing heart on one's sleeve. If she wasn't quick, they'd disperse, glad to be on their way, away from this disturbing declaration.

A woman's voice floated out from the centre of the throng towards the unfeeling voice. 'Why don't yer shut up, 'er carrying 'is baby, poor luv! Shut up an' let 'er 'ave 'er say, 'fore we all freeze ter death, or else sod orf!'

Attention turned back to her and Eveline let a smile touch her lips.

'I carry my baby in his honour,' she lied, raising her voice to express this pride. 'As does any woman who knows the importance of her role as a wife, a mother, and the mainstay of her family. Why should that role not be recognised and similarly honoured by our government? It is as important to this great British Isle of ours as much as that of any male voter, which incidentally includes the drunkard, the ex-convict and the lunatic! Is every respectable woman then to be considered less than such as these? Can that be right?'

She had come with a prepared speech but this was better. She almost wanted to thank the heckler as she felt many of this small audience

193

starting to sympathise with her; a hush fell, a sort of silent intensity that seemed to move through them. She could feel them slowly coming over to her side, some of the men even, despite one or two stalking off shaking their heads at women who unsexed themselves and interfered in politics. But they didn't matter. They were the sort who would never be convinced if the Lord Himself came down to argue the women's cause.

'Isn't it only right,' Eveline continued, turning her eyes from the departing men, 'that such women be allowed to have a say in this nation's future? Any decent woman carrying a child within her and yet struggling to bring up her family has a right to be included as an asset to this country's great name. And the way this can happen is for every responsible woman who raises her family and often even runs a business to be given the franchise. Give women the vote and watch our nation grow stronger because of it!'

There was no stir from the crowd, but it wasn't a hostile silence, just people listening. Instinct told her this was the time to appeal to them.

'Ladies, you who've kindly paused in your important chore, buying food for your families, you know what I'm talking about. And you, kind gentlemen, you who have spared a moment of your time to hear what I'm saying, you too must know our worth.'

'I'd give my old woman a black eye if she started tryin' ter tell me 'er worth!' a wag called out, but to Eveline's immense relief it brought no answering laughter.

'Any of you,' she hurried on, 'who feel just a

trace of sympathy for what we are trying to do, and that includes changing the law to recognise the right of women not to be knocked about at the hands of their husbands, perhaps you'd add your name to the petition my colleague here has ready.'

She indicated Agatha, standing beside her holding the sheaf of lined notepaper. 'We would be most grateful. We will never stop fighting for the cause – for *your* cause – until the day we die or succeed. Sooner or later it *will* happen – women *will* be given the vote!'

She let her speech die away and there came a thin, somewhat ragged clapping. It was risky to go on too long. The police might be kind and merely move them on their way or they could be awkward and take a delight in making an arrest and it wasn't worth it. Eveline stepped down quickly from her rostrum, as one or two women had come up to put their names on the petition, and surprisingly a couple of men, the rest dispersing.

As the three began gathering up their belongings, an elderly woman came over to Eveline who at her approach stood up from manoeuvring the packing case so that two could take one end each when they left. The woman put a blue-veined hand on her arm, her voice hardly above a whisper.

'Yer not married, are yer, my dear?' As Eveline stared at her, half annoyed, half surprised, she went on, 'I 'eard it in yer voice. Them what's lorst an 'usband don't 'ave that bitterness in their voices like the ones what's been left in the lurch by a bloke. I could 'ear it in yer voice.'

195

'I don't know what you mean,' Eveline snapped, but the woman didn't flinch.

'Them what's widowed,' she went on, 'it's the will of God I s'pose and there ain't nothink yer can do abart it. But them what's been done down by a bloke what's gorn orf elsewhere ter get 'is bit of fun, them's the ones what feel bitter against what's bin done to 'em. Look luv, don't you give 'im the satisfaction. You 'old yer 'ead high and Gawd bless yer. 'Ere, let me sign me name, though I dunno what much good it'll do, an old gel like me, but it all 'elps, don't it?'

Adding her name while Eveline continued to stare, the old lady came to touch her arm again as she passed, her voice low. 'I was like you once.'

That was all. She toddled away, leaving Eveline staring after her wondering what she must have gone through in her day to be branded a fallen woman. Perhaps the shame had been even worse in Queen Victoria's time. Now old, she still remembered.

Eveline felt her throat constrict, partly for the woman's unknown life and partly for her own unknown future. She should have drawn strength from her words. Instead she was in danger of breaking down as she helped to lift the packing case ready to take away with them. With her and Agatha at one end, Connie at the other, it wasn't easy lugging the case back to where they'd got it from, hampered as they were by long skirts, the wind playing with their hats and their suffragette sashes of green, purple and white. Once Connie glanced at her and, seeing the look on her face, tilted her head enquiringly. Eveline forced a smile.

'The cold. It's making my eyes water.'

She hadn't fooled Connie, who knew heartache only too well. Despite being happily married now, her parent's callous treatment of her still hurt and, aware of the cause of Eveline's dejection, she looked away. Eveline was grateful yet she felt angry at herself. All this time and the pain of Larry's rejection hadn't diminished; in fact it seemed to be getting worse as the time to the birth grew shorter. She'd fought not to think of the consequences her condition held for her, but the old woman's words had brought it all back.

Back in Gran's flat she avoided Gran's eyes, knowing how perceptive they were, and, not stopping to take off her outdoor clothes, announced that she needed to change her library books before they closed. She was off again before Gran could say a word to her. At least she would have a fresh book to bury her face in so as to continue to avoid any scrutiny of Gran's. With luck it would also help to take her mind off the old lady's words still revolving around in her head which had provoked this deep shame at being left in her state without a man to give her unborn child his name.

As she hurried off towards the library in Cambridge Heath Road, her heart filled again and again with hatred for Larry until it felt as if it were ready to burst. She no longer felt love for him now, only bitterness that had grown to seep into every part of her, an overwhelming wish to see him suffer all the torments she could think of – fall desperately in love and be rejected as he'd rejected her, have a horrible illness, or an accident, even die.

In the library she ignored novels of love and romance: too close to home. Instead she chose the non-fiction section, looking to something to tax her brain enough to sweep away this awful desolation if only for a while.

A cheery "Ello there!' made her swing round to see a young man coming towards her. He was so nicely dressed that for a moment she didn't recognise him. The broad, good-looking features, free of acne, were split almost across by a grin at her obvious confusion.

'Bert?'

'Yeah, it's me. Didn't know who I was, did yer?'

'No, not at first.'

'Well, you see before you a new man. Not at the butcher's any more.'

'Oh, I'm sorry.' She lowered the book she held, her own troubles laid aside for the present.

'Don't be.' He lifted a careless hand. 'Fed up bein' a bloomin' runabout. Got meself a decent job now, behind the counter down at Goodham's Dairies. Nice job, more money, clean overalls, a bit of respect. Mr Goodham says I'm doing well and could be in fer a rise if I keep it up. Calls me Albert, wants me ter speak better too, me being be'ind a counter, so I'm trying hard to watch me aitches an' all that. But I don't go 'ome spouting me fancy talk. Me mother'd 'ave a fit, thinking I've gone all nancyfied.'

He gave a chuckle. 'So what're you doing 'ere in this section of the library? Or should I say *here?* 'Cos you speak quite nice too.'

Eveline made an effort to smile. 'I was just

looking for something just to take my mind off...'

Her smile faded as she realised what she was about to say. She felt her face crease as she fought to control the emotions it was raising afresh. She saw Bert's grin fall away, replaced by an anxious frown.

Slowly and very gently he asked, 'Is something wrong?'

It was a simple question but said with such concern that she was in danger of bursting into tears. It felt as if she had known him all her life. But in reality he was only a casual acquaintance and she didn't want to start breaking down in front of him. She turned away quickly and fumbled in an effort to replace the book in the space it had left. It no longer seemed to fit the gap and in her desperate fumbling she lost her grip and it fell, landing with the flimsy pages spread out and creased.

'Oh!' She made to bend down, awkward in her tight skirt.

'No, let me!' Bending at the same instant as she, his head caught the wide brim of her hat, tilting it. He shot upright.

'Oh blast! I'm so sorry.'

Frantically adjusting it, she too straightened up to find herself gazing into his deep brown eyes not six inches from hers, aware of the confusion in them. It was as though a switch had been pulled somewhere inside her head. Without any warning she burst into tears, the pent-up misery held back for so long gushing out.

'I – I'm not myself,' she gulped. 'I – I don't know what's got into me.'

She felt a pair of steadying hands take hold of

her arms. 'Something what's upset yer badly, that's what's got inter you.'

He seemed to come to a decision. 'Look, it probably ain't none of my business, but you look fair broken up. Let me buy yer a cuppa tea – it might make yer feel better. There's a workman's caff across the road what make a part decent cuppa.'

She didn't really care except to get out of this place, where people were starting to frown at the sound of weeping disturbing the library's tranquillity. All she could do was make a feeble nod of assent.

With his arm round her shoulders he led her away from the fallen book, her head bowed so that the librarian wouldn't see her tear-dampened face beneath its large, all-concealing hat.

It was dark outside now. She let herself be guided between the traffic moving along the Cambridge Heath Road on its way home from work or to a Saturday evening out. Though badly lit and three-quarters empty, the café was nevertheless brighter and warmer than the darkness outside with its wintry wind. Albert found a table at the far end where in the dingy light few customers would be able to make out her distress.

Leaving her a moment to go to the counter, he came back with two thick brown mugs of steaming sweet tea. 'Get that down yer, and when you feel better, I'll take you 'ome.'

He hadn't asked what the matter was. He merely sat drinking his own tea and gazing about the café. She took a gulp of the hot liquid, which instantly scalded her throat and made her give a small choking cough. Albert looked back to her. 'You orright'?'

'No, I'm not,' she responded tremulously. She hadn't intended for it to come out like that.

'I ... I'm...' she began, trying futilely to keep her voice steady but it wasn't working and the state she was in she knew she was going to tell him why. The words tore themselves from her. 'I'm in terrible trouble, and I don't know what to do.'

Moments later she was pouring her heart out to him, about Larry, her belief they would one day be married, the devastation of finding herself deserted when he'd found out what condition she was in, the things he'd said without any feeling except for his own predicament, that when he married it would be to someone of his own class, the way he put it making her feel lower than the women of the streets touting for business.

'We're not poor,' she sniffled. 'My father's a tradesman. He spoke as if tradesmen were the dregs of society. I wasn't interested in his money. I was in love with him. I thought he was with me. But all he wanted...'

She broke off as her eyes began to fill again. With an effort she drew in a determined breath to control her emotions but kept her head lowered so as not to have to look at him directly.

'All he'd wanted was to use me for his own pleasure. I had no idea that was how he saw me and I'm so ashamed. I know now he was going with another girl or even perhaps courting. And now I'm left in such trouble and I feel so ashamed. I've been a fool. I can never hold my head up again. With no father to give a child his name I dread to think what's going to happen to me, trying to bring it up all alone. And I just don't know what to do.'

It had all come out in one long desperate gabble and now she let her voice die away.

Albert had said nothing. She looked up to see him gazing across the café as if he hadn't listened to a word she'd said. Perhaps he was feeling embarrassed. She'd made a fool of herself. How could she have let herself say all this to a man she'd only met casually? Her thoughts collapsed into turmoil; she wanted to leap up from the table, thank him for the tea and his time and walk off with as much dignity she could muster. She would never want to see him again.

He was frowning, maybe thinking she was trying to appeal to his good nature for a handout – that type of girl! Wishing the ground would open up and swallow her, she pushed her tea away and was about to get to her feet, intending to apologise for taking up his time, when he brought his gaze back to her.

'So, what *are* yer goin' ter do? What about yer family?'

'Them!' she burst out fiercely, angry with herself for having opened her heart to him. 'I don't *know* what I'm going to do. I do know I shall face up to whatever happens. My family might not want to know me but I've got a wonderful grandmother who'll stand by me.'

'Grandmothers don't live forever,' he said softly. It sounded to her utterly insensitive. He was staring down into the cooling liquid in his mug. 'Some day yer could be left ter bring it up all on yer own. But an 'usband, God willin', can look after a wife an' family all 'er life.'

Eveline let out a contemptuous hiss. 'What husband? No man's going to want an unmarried mother for a wife.'

Albert hadn't looked up. 'There's one what might care to.'

'Who?' she challenged, shooting the word at him.

'Me,' he said quietly.

Stunned, unable to take in what he'd just said, Eveline stared at the crown of the bowed head. His bowler hat lay on the table beside him and she found herself regarding the wavy, mousy brown hair, darkened a little by brilliantine in an attempt to straighten its waves. It had a neat centre parting and there was a small pimple on the side of his neck below the right ear. It seemed to absorb all her attention the way people in shock often take in things that bear no relationship to what is happening.

Finding her voice she burst out angrily, 'Please don't make a joke of it.'

He looked up. His eyes looked deadly serious, almost sad. 'I'm not making a joke of anything.'

Confusion swept over Eveline. 'But you can't go round saying things like that to someone you hardly know. You can't do that!'

'What'll yer do otherwise?'

'I don't know. But if you're talking about you marrying me – if that's what you're saying...' Even now she wasn't sure of what she'd heard. She was beginning to feel a fool. 'If that's what you're saying, of course I can't.'

'Why not?'

'Because ... because I don't love you.' Her voice had risen and the few customers were beginning to turn round. Quickly she lowered her tone. 'I don't say I don't like you, but I don't love you.'

'Does that matter?' he asked, his voice shaky as if holding back some sort of emotion.

There came a feeling of panic and words poured from her. 'It matters a lot. Bert ... Albert, if what you're proposing is marriage. If that's so, I do appreciate it. You're a very kind and generous-hearted person and one day you'll make someone a wonderful husband, but you don't love me and you can't expect someone you don't love and who doesn't love... I mean who likes you a lot for what you are but shouldn't be taking advantage of you because she doesn't love you enough, to accept your offer. I'm very grateful to you and it's the kindest thing anyone's ever said to me, but–'

'What makes yer think I don't love yer?' he interrupted.

'But you can't,' she flustered. 'It's silly, coming out of the blue like that.'

'It's common sense. And I've 'ad feelings towards yer for a long time.'

'But you can have your pick of any girl. Why would you want to mess it up for someone who doesn't have feelings for you? It's just not right.'

Even as she spoke, it was becoming more real yet utterly irrational. Here she was being presented with a chance for her child to have a name, yet it still had to be an ill sort of joke. But what if it wasn't? What if he meant it?

He'd been watching the dilemma and indecision in her eyes. Now he stopped her. 'I'm the only rope you can cling to, and I do 'ave feelings for you. You caught me eye a long time ago. I'd look for you coming into the library. I wanted to ask you out but you went off with that posh geezer. I couldn't match up to 'im. But I always hoped you'd turn yer eye towards me. Now I can help.' He was trying hard to improve his speech but failing. 'It's what I would've done if we'd been stepping out together. That's all it is.'

'But I'm going to have someone else's...' She couldn't bring herself to finish, but he gave a small quirky smile.

'I can't see no problems. All I'm asking is would you 'ave me? You could get to love me in time. Yer said yer liked me?'

'I do,' she managed to mumble.

He'd begun to grin, seeming to take that as a positive answer. 'I ain't got much to offer you right now but I ain't that bad-looking and I 'ave got prospects. I'm earning a bit more money now and I'm studying 'ard to be a surveyor. One day I'll pass the exams and be one, have a bit of security to offer you. What d'yer say?'

'I don't know what to say,' she said weakly, almost too frightened to acknowledge that her entire insides were bubbling with immeasurable relief, overwhelming, boundless relief, one minute feeling this had to be an unkind dream and the next minute wanting only to believe him and say yes.

Closing her eyes to the unreal feel of it all, she heard herself whisper that very word and saw him nod. He reached out and took her hand gently in his, and she heard him say that they should name a day not too far off, and by the time her baby was born she'd be a respectable married woman.

'I'll start looking for a lettings for us straight away. Nothing too expensive for the time being but in time we'll find somewhere nicer for us.'

It sounded more like a business deal, leaving her to wonder how this had all come about so suddenly and that she might have done the wrong thing after all. But then he said ever so gently, 'I'll try ter be the kind of 'usband you 'oped you'd get in life.' And suddenly she knew this was what must have been mapped out for her and she must accept it gratefully.

They left the café under the gaze of curious onlookers and walked home along the Bethnal Green Road, side by side, not holding hands, not with his arm about her. This wasn't a courtship, or a love match; this would be a marriage of convenience, so to speak, and although gratitude was all but smothering her, Eveline wondered as they walked on home just what she had let herself in for, preparing to marry a man she didn't love. Liked, but didn't love. It still felt indescribably unreal.

Chapter Fourteen

'You'll be 'aving this in the next couple of days,' Victoria announced. Still a bit shaky and panicky from the slow, dull ache that had come on this morning around her back and her waist. Eveline gazed up from the armchair at her gran.

Not knowing what to do, on her own with Albert at work, she'd gone to her neighbour across the way, the woman immediately volunteering to go and get her grandmother. By the time she'd come back with Gran, the ache had subsided, leaving her feeling guilty at having brought her out.

'I didn't know what to do,' she explained as Gran handed her a strong cup of tea with lots of sugar in it. 'I thought I was starting. I was frightened. I didn't mean to call you out for nothing.'

'You did the right thing, love,' Gran said calmly. 'It ain't nice being on your own when it's your first as well. You ain't started but you could in a couple of days – p'raps even tomorrow.'

The words raised fresh alarm, and her gran eyed her closely. 'I think it might be best for me to stay 'ere for the while. Your Bert won't know what to do if anything happens. Men don't. I'll just go and pick up a few things, me nightclothes and stuff, and be back in a jiff.' She smiled encouragingly as Eveline's face registered fresh terror. 'Your neighbour, what's 'er name?'

'Mrs Martin.'

'Right, what I'll do, I'll ask her to stay with you till I come back. I'll call in and tell 'er. Now drink your tea.'

Gran pressed the cup back into her hands; Eveline watched her go then gazed around her room, trying to forget that she was alone once more.

A Wilmott Street basement, it comprised this room, one bedroom and a kitchen and tiny lavatory. The soot-blackened brickwork of the five-storey blocks opposite reflected no light at all and prevented sunlight from ever reaching her windows. It was a bit brighter now the landlords had replaced the old brown wallpaper with something lighter, but even with flowery pink curtains it was a losing battle with the windows below street level.

It didn't worry Bert, or Albert as she preferred to call him. His home had been a ground-floor letting with the opposite buildings also blocking out much of the sunlight and these winter and early spring months of their marriage had meant the curtains were drawn by the time he got home from work in the evening. It was now May and hardly any brighter; she thought of the sun pouring into her parents' south-facing flat over the shop with its views across the railway. Gran's second-floor flat, being in an end block, got just as much light. It made the lack of it here all the more noticeable. Even if the wedding had been a happier occasion this place would have spoiled it.

It had been a quiet affair, with a few sandwiches at Gran's flat afterwards. The guests consisted of her parents, relieved that she was getting married, Connie and George, Albert's mum, a small woman, broad-faced like her son, and his seventeen-year-old brother Jim as his best man. With so few present the church had felt virtually empty, their voices echoing as if in a cavern. It hadn't mattered. The wedding had been a mere formality anyway.

At Connie's little wedding the church had been even emptier but at least Connie had married for love, not in desperation with no other choice left to her.

It had rained on her own wedding day and blown half a gale as though the weather itself saw the lack of romance in this marriage. She wore a coat, her dad holding an umbrella over her as best he could in the high wind. It had been bad everywhere with floods in France and hurricane winds in England causing severe damage and several deaths.

Albert had arranged a church at short notice. She carried no bouquet, just the small white Bible belonging to Gran. Gran had made a wedding gown from cheap white satin bought in Petticoat Lane, making the thing loose with a high neck and wide sleeves, like a tea gown, disguising the normally pinched-in waist with some lace she had found so that the bride's condition wouldn't be so noticeable.

It had been an odd sort of courtship, with no engagement ring. When he made to kiss her she'd turn her cheek, unable to see him as anything but a friend. Such a short while had passed since the time she hadn't really known him at all, even though he'd been her salvation which she silently thanked him for from the bottom of her heart. It hurt her that she didn't feel love for him, that exciting love a young bride should feel for her husband. Whether it hurt him he had never said and she'd never been able to bring herself to enquire.

He'd said that he'd fancied her for a long time and she felt bad that she hadn't the same feelings for him. Lately she'd begun to grow fond of him but it wasn't the same as love. It could hardly even be called a marriage, since they were sleeping back to back in the double bed. If he turned over she would ease herself carefully to the edge of the bed. He must have noticed because he'd quietly withdraw his arm and she'd be left lying awake thinking how different it would have been with Larry while the tears would trickle from the corners of her eyes to dampen her pillow.

She tried to console herself that, even in a normal marriage, making love wouldn't be recommended for a woman soon to have a baby. But what about once it was born? Surely Albert would expect her in time to honour her marital duties. Kind and gentle though he was, he wasn't made of stone.

Eveline gnawed her lip as she looked about her. In a day or two her so-called happy event would occur. She'd had quite an eventful few months. Marriage, a home of her own, and of course the General Election ending in a dead heat between the Tories and Liberals dashing all hope of a favourable decision on female suffrage. She turned her thoughts to that.

Suffragette determination not to back down had

led to increasing demonstrations, more arrests and growing unease at what was going on inside those prisons with women virtually tortured by forced-feeding. Often they would be released in a state of collapse and utter exhaustion to recover. She knew all about that, though her own experience hadn't been half what some women were enduring, not once but six or seven times, being rearrested to go through it again. Their courage was indomitable.

Just as well her condition hadn't allowed her to attend any of the demonstrations; both Gran and Albert had advised against it. He was however sympathetic towards the suffragettes and said he wouldn't prevent her later as long as it didn't interfere with her looking after the baby, which he knew full well would virtually stop her anyway. Sometimes he acted as if the baby were actually his.

The thought provoked a twinge of bitterness that was now mingled with envy. Connie too was pregnant. She'd come hurrying over to see her in March, full of her good news and glowing.

'Isn't it wonderful,' she'd gushed.

Eveline had hugged her, trying to stem that feeling of envy that in fact had grown in strength as Connie began to glow even more. Somehow it seemed justified, though she knew it was wrong. Connie still had her savings despite her father's allowance having ceased when she'd left home, whereas she and Albert were struggling on his earnings with a baby on the way. Often she wondered if Albert didn't regret his move. She dared not ask him.

Connie had a lovely bright flat, and George was bringing in decent wages while all Albert could afford was this dismal basement. Connie's baby had been conceived in wedlock whereas she'd had to accept charity from a man who was not the baby's father no matter how selfless and good-hearted that offer.

She frowned as the ache around her middle began to make itself felt again, not severe but enough to tell her that Gran could be right, she could go into labour in a day or two. If it happened tomorrow, it would be a day to remember, not just by her but millions.

Tomorrow was the twenty-first of May, the funeral of King Edward. On the fourth of May the King had been reported seriously ill with pneumonia. Two days later he was dead. It had taken everyone's breath away.

It was almost unearthly. An object called Halley's Comet had become visible in the evening sky over London. Seen every seventy or eighty years and regarded as an ill omen in the past, it was now as bright as the brightest star, with a great long, ominous tail. Strange the King should pass away while it was still visible – the coincidence made the flesh creep, as people wondered what other ill could befall the nation.

As she waited for Mrs Martin she wondered whether this comet would affect the birth of her baby. Recollection of old wives' tales that a woman in labour carried her own coffin sent a shudder through her as at the open front door she could hear Gran and Mrs Martin talking, no doubt about her. She didn't want the woman

212

sitting with her, poking around, asking questions.

Mrs Martin was a nice enough person, glad to help whenever needed. She was fortunate to have such a good neighbour but she didn't feel at all like talking until Gran returned. The ache that had frightened her had faded and she now felt a fool, panicking and making such a fuss.

Helena was born three days later, Gran and a local midwife tending her – a painful thirty-six hours which afterwards she could recall only vaguely as she held her daughter to her breast for her first feed.

Albert, coming home from work, had beamed down at the child as if she were his, brushing away the fear Eveline had felt that faced with the reality of his actions he would regret them. But his smile swept away those fears and for the first time she felt she almost loved him.

The procession was huge. Despite being five months' pregnant, with the baby due in October, Connie had made up her mind to be among the fifteen thousand here today. She still hardly showed and by tightening her corsets was able to get into last year's summer dresses, probably because she had grown thinner since leaving home to get married. The dress was white and the green, purple and white sash helped to disguise any telltale bump.

Her hat too was white, the wide brim covered in tulle. She'd bought it with her own money but George's reaction had made her feel guilty and certainly angry. When she told him what she was buying, he'd frowned as if it was his money she was spending. Yet he refused to touch hers.

'It's *your* money, darling, to use as you wish,' he'd once stated with such finality that she knew he'd see himself as less of a man if he couldn't provide on his earnings alone, but that slight frown had annoyed her and in retaliation she'd gone out and bought the hat anyway.

He couldn't say she hadn't been careful with her money. Nor had she ever relied on him to clothe her. She still had an extensive wardrobe. Her father had sent on all her belongings when she left – a declaration if ever there was one that all ties with her family had been broken utterly – but it *was* her money and the fact that George had stressed that it was, generous or not, was like saying that though it was hers it shouldn't be frittered away needlessly. Had the hat been needless? She didn't think so, not when everyone else was dressed so beautifully for this momentous occasion.

She wished Eveline were here today to listen to her grumbles. Eveline would have so enjoyed this great spectacle with its seven hundred banners and forty bands, the green, white and purple sashes of the WSPU blending with the green, white and gold of the Women's Freedom League and all the other different shades and colours.

This procession had been long awaited. Postponed to this Saturday the eighteenth of June due to the King's death, it was the first large-scale public procession for two years, made possible by news of the introduction of the Conciliation Bill, which was still in progress and looking hopeful. So it was with jubilation and hope that the two-

214

mile-long procession marched.

There were women around her whom she knew yet without Eveline she felt oddly lonely. But positioned well behind the huge hunger strikers' banner, she knew that Eveline would have been walking not with her but with those six hundred other prison veterans, wearing her prisoner's brooch, the white, broad arrow brooch glittering bravely on her chest. She felt a stab of envy that Eveline was one of them and she was not. No use blaming her father. She should have defied him that day and demanded the fine he'd paid be returned, or behaved so badly as to have been had up for contempt.

Connie gazed stolidly at the enormous banner just ahead of her bearing the embroidered signatures of eighty women heralded as having 'faced death without flinching' and another emblazoned with the words 'From Prison to Citizenship'.

In the golden light of a fine June evening, a fife band led the prisoners' pageant, its band mistress swinging her silver-mounted staff as competently as any guardsman, and behind that, the prisoners' tableau – two white horses with gold and purple trappings and laurel wreaths drawing a cart with a group of young women in white and a single suffragette in prison apparel. It took the whole of Connie's resolve to push away the knowledge that if she hadn't just had had her baby, Eveline would be there enjoying pride of place among that group.

Similar pageants and tableau were positioned at intervals along the entire length of this visual expression of women's strength: nurses in their uniforms; bicyclists, their machines decorated with flowers; athletes and sportswomen in their sportswear. There were artists with their palettes and brushes hung with flowers and ribbons; university graduates; actresses, the best dressed of all with their rose pink and pale green banner and staves tied with foliage and pink roses. There was the Writers Suffrage League and the Freedom League, the Church League led by a group of clergymen, the younger suffragettes, the Fabians, the Ethical Societies and scores of others. The Men's League, formed in 1907 in support of women's suffrage, brought the biggest surprise to the watching crowds. One contingent was made up of hundreds of sweated labourers who toiled in factories and stuffy workrooms, all wearing or carrying the products of their trade. There were those from far places, such as the Irish Women's Franchise League who, so Connie heard, had travelled all night to be here, and others from as far away as Canada, Australia and America.

Bringing up in the rear was a veritable stream of motor cars brightly decked out with flowers. Coachmen wearing rosettes had picked out the wheels and shafts of their coaches with white roses, the harnesses with purple, green and white.

It was all so well planned. Nothing as splendid had been seen since the 1908 Hyde Park rally and after the solemn funeral of King Edward a few weeks back it was a sight to stir the hearts of those crowds lining the route, which was exactly what it was meant to do, the redoubtable Mrs

Drummond astride a huge charger having raised her whip on the dot of six thirty this evening to begin the procession. Her slow and determined advance along Northumberland Avenue had obliged the mounted policemen to clear the way for her as the forty bands struck up all at once.

To Connie's mind, walking in its midst, it was like a festival, every women in summer dress with her bright sash, banners held high, bands playing, traffic forced to pull to one side for them to pass, yet all she could think of was how she'd have felt with Eveline walking in honour in the prisoners' pageant while she remained just one of these fifteen thousand.

Eveline had had her baby on the twenty-third of May, barely four weeks ago. She had named her Helena.

'I want to be there,' she had said. 'A month will have gone by and I'm sure I'll be all right by then.' But even Albert, an easy-going sort, had been against her going off while nursing a month-old baby. Walking all the way from Northumberland Avenue to the Albert Hall and standing with the WSPU prisoners as a guard of honour, she would never have lasted.

She had popped in to see Eveline before leaving and found her fretful and sulky. 'I'll tell you all about it,' Connie soothed, which seemed to make her even more sullen. But she would go and see her after this was all over, try to cheer her up though it might be best to play down the rousing din and wonderful spectacle if she could contain herself to do so.

Poor Eveline. It was hard not to see her as poor

217

Eveline and as envy melted she realised how much she had to be thankful for.

Albert came home with a look of someone who'd won a small fortune.

'I didn't say nothing before,' he said, taking off his cap and his coat to hang them on the peg behind the living-room door, 'but a few weeks ago I asked for a rise, said I had a kiddy to support now. I never really thought I'd get it, but guess what'? I've been given two bob more.'

Eveline stared at him. Two shillings, to some a drop in the ocean, to her meant a bit of extra food on the table, or a dress for Helena.

'We can put in for a transfer to a nicer letting,' he was saying. 'Means paying a bit more rent but Helena will soon need her own room ter sleep in.'

Eveline smiled. 'Best not be too hasty.' She still couldn't trust luck.

It was hard to believe how life had changed; last autumn she had felt out of her mind with worry, abandoned, disgraced. Now she had a home of her own, a husband, her baby with Albert's name, and soon a bit more cash.

One thing was lacking. She missed the suffragette meetings. But it wasn't possible while still nursing. At regular times her breasts would grow hard, milk seeping from her nipples, and as if by instinct Helena would begin to whimper, then bawl if she wasn't given her feed there and then. How could any mother go off on her own pursuits when so tied down?

Even if she could have left Helena with someone, she couldn't have been away for too long before her breasts began to harden and leak uncomfortably. It would be months before Helena was weaned. She had heard somewhere that it was possible to dry the milk up sooner but she had no idea how. There was no question of asking Mum. She'd be appalled and refuse to talk about it. But Gran might know. She knew most things.

A couple of afternoons a week Eveline would pop across to spend an hour or two with Gran. She loved seeing the baby whereas Mum was always busy down in the shop and didn't seem all that interested in Helena, maybe because of the circumstances of the child's birth. Despite Helena being a pretty baby she didn't seem to touch Mum's heart at all.

This afternoon, after days stuck indoors with Helena demanding to be fed every two or three hours so that Eveline was hardly able to go shopping before having to rush back with her to feed her again, she decided in desperation that it was time to ask Gran's advice.

She was certain that even if she disapproved she'd at least be kind about it and understanding. So she was a bit taken aback when Gran lifted her gaze from smiling down at her six-week-old-great-grandchild she was cuddling on her lap to regard her granddaughter with a critical eye.

'Why would yer want to dry it up this soon?' she enquired.

'I need to attend suffragette meetings again. But like this I can't.'

'Need?' The question had a reproving ring to it. Eveline wilted.

'I feel I ought to,' she modified.

'I see.' Gran looked down at Helena and clucked her tongue at her. 'Have you spoken to your 'usband about it?' she asked, not looking up.

'No, not yet.'

'Why not?'

'Because he might not be too happy about it.'

Gran nodded, her eyes still on the baby. 'If yer think he might not be too 'appy about it, then why've you come to me?'

Eveline knew she was losing. Her voice grew high and urgent. 'That's exactly why we're fighting, to have the same rights as men. Why should I have to ask Bert's permission if I want to do something?'

'Because you're 'is wife and Helena's his child.'

'She's *not* his child...' Eveline broke off, realising what she had said. Gran hadn't lifted her gaze once from little Helena's face surrounded by its knitted white shawl, the baby's round, deep blue eyes staring up at her with wide curiosity.

Silenced for a moment, Eveline fought to gloss over what she had just said. 'I *have* to get back to what I was doing,' she rushed on. 'So many things are happening and before long I'll find myself left out.'

Her grandmother looked up, her tone cynical. 'If that's what you're concerned about, don't worry, they won't forget you. You're too important. You've been in prison for your cause. They need women like you.'

'That's why I must get back into it as soon as possible.'

It was as though her grandmother hadn't heard her. 'But if it's just that you're missing the excitement, you'll 'ave to be patient a bit longer and put your mind to being a good mother.'

Eveline caught the dig. 'Please, Gran, I am a good mother, but I'm a good suffragette too, and it's for her future as well that I have to stand with them in this fight for our equality.' It sounded as if she were standing on some soapbox giving a speech. But Gran was taking it all in her stride.

Looking down again at the baby, who had begun to whimper fretfully, twisting her head instinctively towards the elderly bosom in an eagerness to suckle, Victoria inserted a little finger between the rosebud lips. Like a kitten at a teat Helena immediately fastened on to the ageing finger, starting to suck furiously.

'She wants her feed,' Victoria said.

'She's always wanting her feed,' Eveline said petulantly. 'I can't keep up with her. I can't move out of her sight!'

Gran gave her a sharp glance. 'Don't you like being a mother?'

'Of course I do. She's mine. But I can't be twenty-four hours a day, waiting for her to cry to be fed. I just need to—'

'Trying to dry up your milk too soon could bring a lot of discomfort,' Gran interrupted. 'A lot more'n you imagine.' It sounded as if she had done exactly that in the past herself. 'It could even make you very ill. When it does start to dwindle, that's when you can do something about it.'

'That's the trouble – I don't know how.'

'When the time comes I'll show you.'

'Exactly how long before the time comes?' She

221

hadn't meant to be sharp and she saw her grandmother's eyes give a little flicker. 'We're getting closer every day to getting the vote,' she hurried on, trying hard to modify the urgency in her tone.

Gran's shoulders lifted slightly in a dismissive shrug. 'I don't think it's as close as all that. It ain't going to 'appen overnight.'

'It could.' Eveline turned her eyes to her baby, sucking noisily at the finger. 'We've been trying for so long. It's got to happen at some time. It could come sooner than we think.'

Her grandmother's attitude was frustrating. It was early July. The sun had come out to stay. Suffragettes in their summer dresses were holding rallies and processions, delivering speeches from carts decorated with the suffragette colours, in parks, on street corners, outside pubs and men's clubs, all with growing confidence of the Conciliation Bill getting its second reading on the eleventh and twelfth. A second reading! Everyone was sure it would get a majority vote. It was a huge step towards women's suffrage. And here was Gran pouring cold water on it.

'Can you see politicians,' she was saying, 'what's been against it all these years suddenly agreeing to every suffragette demand without going into endless negotiations? Meself, I don' think so.'

Eveline had to admit to that truth about politicians but this woman's negative approach to what was the most important thing ever irritated her.

'I still think it's going to be soon,' she stubbornly contradicted.

Connie had told her about Mrs Pankhurst's speech inside the Albert Hall on the eighteenth of June, saying that the only word in everyone's thoughts was victory and if the government sought to thwart or postpone that victory, may God help them in the times that were coming. After that, Connie had said how Lord Lytton had spoken of the work the Conciliation Committee was doing, with political developments bringing them closer to their long-awaited triumph. With over seventy-three thousand pounds being raised in donations, Connie had made a great deal of the huge cheers that had met the announcement.

Eveline had been so envious and so upset at not being there when she told of how the procession had turned dull streets into a ribbon of festivity. And when Connie had described the scene inside the Albert Hall, the packed audience swaying like coloured grass before a breeze as Mrs Pankhurst came to the stage, a small, lone, elegant and dignified figure in black, to give her address, Eveline could have cried for having missed it all.

'Just don't go getting your 'opes up too much about politicians,' Gran concluded. 'They change their minds like the weather. Expecting them to do anything quick is like asking for miracles to 'appen.'

Eveline remained silent as Gran went on: 'Anyway, even if you wasn't nursing, someone'll 'ave to give eye to Helena when you're out. Your mum won't, and Albert can't stay at 'ome and lose money to look after her.'

'Some of the organisers,' Eveline said, 'say husbands should give a hand in the housework and bringing up the children so we can attend.'

Gran pulled a face, the creases wrinkling alarmingly, showing her age. 'Codswallop! Don't go asking your Bert to do any such thing. It's one thing to tell others what they must do, it's another to do it themselves – unless they've got staff and can afford a nursemaid.'

Eveline said nothing, now aware that she was going to get none of the advice she'd hoped for.

'You'll 'ave ter speak to your Bert about this, love,' Gran went on. 'He's a good man and should be given respect after what he's done for you. You should be grateful to 'im.'

She was grateful. She left feeling frustrated but at least one thing had come out of it – Gran had said that when the time came she might give eye to the baby. 'So long as you don't come it too often,' had been her parting shot, but the offer was enough to bring a spring to Eveline's step as she wheeled Helena away down the street in the second-hand perambulator Albert had bought.

Chapter Fifteen

Three weeks had gone by and she still hadn't plucked up the courage to speak to Albert about her plans to return to suffragette work.

She had no reason to fear him. He was the kindest person she'd ever known, but if he even frowned his disapproval, could she defy him, maybe hurt him?

She'd certainly not mentioned weaning Helena on to a bottle. With no help from Gran she had spoken to her neighbour, Mrs Martin, who without reservation had told her how she had done it many years ago.

'I 'ad just abart enough of breastfeeding one kid after another,' she said. Now in her fifties, Mrs Martin had given birth to ten children in quick succession with two miscarriages and two stillbirths; out of the ten only five had survived to adulthood and were still living.

'Right tyke, my Arfer. Sometimes I thank Gawd 'e went when 'e did or *I'd* of been the one what would of died! Breastfeedin' 'elps stop yer getting pregnant too often of course. But it fair pulled me ter pieces just the same, with one after another on the breast. Till I learned what ter do, that is. I 'ad me first when I was twenty-one. By the time I was thirty I'd 'ad five, and one miscarriage. But I couldn't keep up with all that breastfeeding.'

With Mrs Martin's help, after three weeks,

weeks of secretly enduring the misery of drying up her milk, Eveline had successfully changed Helena to the bottle, telling Albert that her milk wasn't satisfying the child.

He believed her, but it still didn't give her licence just yet to go off to her suffragette meetings any time she wished. It was only right he should be consulted, but what if he said no?

It was horrid seeing Connie going to her meetings and rallies all with her husband's blessing, so when Connie came over this Saturday afternoon to see if she'd be going along with her to the George Street meeting, she shook her head a little churlishly.

'You know I can't. I've got the baby, and Albert's out.'

He'd had gone with a mate to see Tottenham, his favourite football team, play so she was feeling particularly depressed. She'd thought of seeing Gran or perhaps her own parents but had lacked the incentive, so when Connie tilted her head in mild acceptance of her waspish refusal, she instantly interpreted it as not really caring whether she went or not.

'Perhaps when your baby's born you'll understand,' she said tersely, knowing she was being unfair.

But Connie's smile was amiable. 'I expect I shall very soon have to give up going. I can't attend rallies and such once I really begin to show.'

Despite being seven months Connie hardly showed at all. Eveline remembered how she had been at that stage. Though her figure was now back to its former size with the aid of vicious corseting, it was a pity her freedom couldn't be retrieved as easily. She loved Helena dearly but sometimes, seeing how much she looked like her natural father, she'd think of him and want to weep, almost to the point of regretting how things had turned out. It wasn't the baby's fault she was tied down – it was entirely of her own making. But at this moment she'd have given anything to be able to go along with Connie.

The thought strengthened her resolve to have a real talk with Albert. It went against the grain having to be dependent on him but until women won the right to be on a par with men, if only by being given the vote, she'd have to go cap in hand asking his permission.

She did it on the Saturday after supper, when she found herself provoked into it really, as he was sitting in his wooden armchair reading *The Times* newspaper. He didn't normally read *The Times* but his employer did and with an idea of bettering himself he often glanced at it if it was lying around and even brought it home if discarded.

'There's a bit here,' he said now, 'about that Conciliation Bill your suffragettes have been going on about, went for its second reading in Parliament. It says here it passed its second reading by one 'undred and ten votes.'

Eveline looked up from folding a pile of baby napkins and one or two of his aired shirts together with her chemise and other undergarments ready to put in their respective drawers in the bedroom, her mind suddenly alert.

'That's absolutely wonderful!' she blurted. 'I said we'd win eventually but no one–'

''Old on! You didn't let me finish.'

He began quoting aloud. '"Because widening amendments were unlikely to be permitted, both Churchill and Lloyd George voted against it." It says Lloyd George saw it as undemocratic and Churchill said it was likely to provide an electoral advantage – whatever that means – to the Conservatives. It says 'ere, "a few minutes later the Commons voted by three 'undred and twenty votes to one 'undred and seventy five to refer it to a committee of the whole House, and thereby extinguishing its chances." I take it this means your Conciliation Bill has had its chips cashed in again.'

Looking up, he saw the disillusionment on her face. 'I'm sorry Ev,' he said as if it were his fault. It made her want to burst into tears.

Before she could stop herself, she blurted, 'Albert, I've got to go back to our suffragette work. Everyone's needed. We can't let this happen to us. We're being done down at every turn and it isn't fair after what so many women have been through.'

'You too,' he said simply.

There was no need for him to say any more. The mere mention of her time in prison, short though it had been, brought back everything she had gone through: Larry's desertion, the humiliation, the despair, her family turning against her even though they had accepted her again, that and this wonderful man's unselfish act, all compounded to make her crumple, clapping his nicely aired shirt to her eyes and dampening it again. The next thing she knew, he was out of his chair, the newspaper falling to the floor, and his

228

arms were about her. 'Don't cry, Ev. I didn't mean to upset yer.'

'It's not you,' she sobbed.

'But I did and I shouldn't 'ave. I don't want ter see you all upset. I love you, Ev.'

She clung on to him. 'Me too,' she mumbled between her sobs. 'Oh, Albert, how can I not love you? You've done so much for me. Married me.'

She felt his arms tighten about her, almost squeezing her breath from her. To extricate herself before it did, she pulled back and planted a kiss on his lips: the first time they'd ever kissed like this and it felt so good, his lips so firm against hers, that she felt its sensation ripple through her body. No word was spoken but with a shared need, as he still held her close, they stood up together, moving the few feet to the bedroom.

Together they sank on to the bed beside which Helena lay sleeping in her cot, and there Albert made love to his wife with all the need that had for so long been denied him, Eveline accepting him with gasps of pleasure while little Helena slept on.

Bert turned his head to gaze at his wife. For a while he listened to her regular breathing, studied her face, her lips relaxed, her eyelashes dark, gentle fringes against her cheeks. Contented, she was sleeping like a baby, like her baby, her baby that wasn't his.

He turned his face to gaze up at the ceiling visible in the glow of the street lamp shining down into the basement room through the thin curtains Eveline had made from cheap material when they'd first come to live here.

She'd been so full of excitement making things for the home, going around its two rooms as if it were a mansion. He'd understood her avoiding his attempts to approach her. Give her time, he'd reasoned, it had to be a bit of a trauma marrying someone you're not really in love with, especially after being in love with another man enough to have got pregnant by him. Bit of a comedown for her probably, any port in a storm. But he'd been in love with her for a long time, if only from afar. He should have had sense enough to leap in before that chap had and she might have chosen him. Of course in the circumstances it had been asking too much to expect that to happen in a few days or weeks. But seven months and still she'd pulled away from any tenderness he tried to show. He'd feel his needs rise up and nothing be could do about it other than take her by force, and he wouldn't do that. Seven months of lying beside her, their marriage still unconsummated, had nearly slaughtered him.

Sometimes he'd blame himself for thinking his impetuous offer of marriage might get her to fall in love with him. He'd been mad to expect it to happen. Sometimes he'd blame her for not making an effort to love him – not feeling exactly angry with her, for what woman in her state would have said no to any proposal of marriage, but for not even trying to love him.

Now tonight everything had changed. It felt like he was floating on air. His only concern was would she want to repeat what had just consumed them both like some raging fire or would she wake up tomorrow morning regretting it?

How should he approach her tomorrow morning? Should he behave quite normally as if taking it in his stride? That could make her feel used. If he adopted a pleased expression, said how wonderful it had been, she might think he was seeing himself as having scored a great goal like some triumphant footballer. If he chatted away over breakfast, that might make him seem brash. To keep quiet, say nothing, might make her feel that his interest in her was only reserved for the bedroom. On leaving for work he could give her a more ardent kiss than his usual cheery peck, having all those other times resist the impulse to tell her that he loved her in case he was overstepping the marks she had laid down.

But tonight she'd said she loved him. She'd let him make love to her, returning it with a passion that had startled him, he who'd been in such need himself after all this time of behaving like a lump of cement. To wonder why he'd had to wait until *she* was ready, that was unkind. How could any woman married in her circumstances be expected to accept lovemaking as part of the offer? He'd taken her off guard offering to marry her and hadn't stopped to weigh the consequences. Maybe the offer itself had been unkind, a ring of the patronising about it. But she'd agreed, even if out of desperation because he'd been available when she had been at her most vulnerable. She'd been honest, had said she didn't love him. But tonight she had said she did. It must mean something.

He continued to stare at the ceiling. He had to get some sleep. Night was the worst time to dwell on things; it exaggerated them, robbing them of logic. He would just have to play it by ear come the morning, that was all.

He turned over. The movement disturbed her, a restless arm was flung across his shoulder. He could feel her breath warm on the back of his neck, heard her whisper sleepily, 'I do love you, darling.'

For a moment his heart soared, then sank. She was thinking of that bastard who'd got her pregnant and had then abandoned her. Maybe in her sleep she imagined it to be him lying beside her tonight.

He felt consumed by a hot surge of jealousy, After all he'd done for her. He turned back to face her and saw her eyes were wide open, gazing at him. 'What was that?' he asked stupidly.

She smiled. 'I said I love you.' She lifted a hand to his cheek, caressing it. 'I've you to thank for everything, for being so good to me, being so patient, for being a father to Helena and not once... For everything really. I don't deserve you, my dearest man. I don't ever want anyone but you.'

She moved her face towards him. He knew she wanted him to kiss her, and he did, the kiss lingering, in joy and relief, his hands moving over her body in its summer cotton nightdress. He felt her respond, felt his own movements becoming strong, ready to fulfil her again. Except that Helena stirred, awoke and began whimpering for her bottle. Bert sighed and let his hand fall away from the curve of his wife's body as she rose to attend to the baby's wants.

There would always be another time. He knew that now.

Eveline sat beside Connie, who still lay recovering nearly three weeks after the birth of her baby. It had arrived three weeks early, September instead of October; despite that, it was a difficult birth, a breach, leaving her terribly torn and damaged inside enough for the doctor who'd struggled with her labour hour after hour, despairing as she grew ever weaker, finally to announce that if the child came out alive it could be the only one she'd ever give birth to, that was if she herself pulled through it. Much longer and it would have had to be a Caesarean. In the end the baby come out naturally. A miracle, the doctor said, that the baby was undamaged after all he'd had to do to bring it into the world, and surprisingly lusty, despite it being a girl. A small baby, six pounds four ounces, which had been in her favour, else mother and child might certainly never have survived.

With Connie still too tired to suckle her and unable to make enough milk anyway, it was Gran who came to her aid with a feeding bottle. Ironic, thought Eveline, recalling the discomfort she'd suffered to dry up her own milk for the freedom she so needed. Here was Connie dry as a bone and with no urge to be getting back to suffragette work. It was so unfair.

'You're lucky to still be suckling,' Gran remarked, so far with no idea of what she'd been up to. 'I feel so sorry for any mother who can't feed her baby naturally. Till she's her old self again, poor thing, I'll keep an eye on her and make the little mite's bottle.'

'I can help,' Eveline volunteered guiltily, but was frowned at.

'You've got your own little 'un to see to. Besides, looking after this one will keep me sprightly, give me something to do other than think of meself.'

To Eveline's mind Gran was by far the sprightliest person for her age she had ever seen. In deep gratitude, Connie wanted to name the baby Victoria Rebecca. Gran was flattered.

'But no Victorias. Named after the queen, I was. Never did like the name.' So it became Rebecca Isabel for Connie's own mother despite all.

Three weeks and Connie still remained lethargic, Eveline wondered if she would ever be strong again. Connie wondered too.

'To think,' she sighed, propped up by pillows while Eveline cuddled little Rebecca, her own four-month-old baby gurgling at the foot of the bed. 'You'd not long had Helena before you were in that July demonstration on the twenty-third. I couldn't see myself ever having that kind of stamina.'

'Of course you will,' Eveline tried to cheer her, but Connie's earlier upbringing had been so different from hers.

Where hers were the sort of people who had to pull themselves together and get on with the job, even after childbearing, Connie had been used to things being done for her, staff to wait on her, a family doctor more like a friend and not someone who didn't know her from Adam, tending any who could scrape together the shilling he charged. Connie's father could employ proper nursing care rather than a local midwife. At home Connie would have been waited on hand and foot. She'd chosen a life where she must do her own housework and put up with the lack of help, yet her genteel upbringing still had its effect on her.

She had written to tell her parents of her pregnancy and had received no reply. She had written again to them telling them of the birth and still there had been no response. Eveline felt it was this more than the traumatic birth itself that was causing Connie to feel dispirited and weak but said nothing. Connie hadn't spoken of it, which wasn't good for her, and Eveline felt it best not to mention it.

'I don't think I shall be doing suffragette work for a long, long time,' Connie sighed, regarding Eveline with envy and pride. 'I really don't know how you did that July demonstration after having Helena.'

Eveline too wondered, though she didn't make any comment. Her Mum had frowned on it. 'It's 'er lookout if she makes 'erself ill,' was all she said and had looked at Albert as if he wasn't man enough to stop his wife.

In fact Albert, bless him, had understood how she'd felt and had gone along to support her, leaving Gran in charge of Helena.

'I'm not having you brought 'ome in a state of collapse, and me not there,' he'd said, still battling to speak better, but still often failing. 'The second you look like you've had enough, I'm taking you 'ome, and that's that, whether you like it or not.'

He was working hard studying for his hoped-for surveyor's career though it seemed an uphill task for someone with little education.

Going along that day, amazed at the spectacle that met his eyes, he was surprised to see men in the procession. 'Don't make me feel so much of a fish out of water,' he'd said.

Ironically the procession was held on the very day Asquith announced the temporary burial of the Conciliation Bill, though they hadn't read about it until the following day, the parade itself being confidently held to help urge it forward. Despite the later general disillusionment, for her it had been a wonderful day, she and Albert, Connie and George, together, and it didn't matter that she had felt all in by the end of it.

The demonstration had been well publicised with handbills, circulars, endless meetings, groups out every day chalking the event on every London wall they could find. There'd been twenty thousand women, in two separate processions so as not to block the traffic. Again there'd been forty bands, as well as the WSPU drum-and-fife band, and in Hyde Park forty platforms had been set up. Marchers were asked not to wear large hats and trailing gowns to appear more like soldiers in the ranks, not to break step or wave handkerchiefs. One procession began at Holland Park, along Bayswater Road, entering Hyde Park at Marble Arch. The other, which she and Connie had been in, their husbands walking alongside at a respectable distance, had begun at the Embankment, then continued along Northumberland Avenue, Pall Mall and Piccadilly, to enter at Hyde Park Corner.

Although a huge amount of preparation had gone on, Albert had strongly advised her to miss her George Street meetings where, like everywhere else, volunteers were busy with scissors and sewing machines, paint and paste brushes, hammer and nails, making banners and posters.

'You ain't strong enough yet,' he had said. She hadn't argued. He'd at least agreed on her going on that most important July demonstration later.

Hyde Park had been like August Bank Holiday, a hundred speakers or more, brilliant sunshine, both processions merging around half-past five, the bands playing the 'Marseillaise', flags and pennants flying and thousands of onlookers milling about.

Eveline knew she'd never forget that day in July, having put aside her earlier disappointment at missing the June procession. But she'd had to come away early, fatigue and a need to get back to Helena overcoming her.

Connie had looked all in as well. Despite the smallness of her bump, with only three months to go, pregnancy had begun to tell on her by then. They had both returned home, sad to have left so early, but triumphant, the presence of their men beside them an even greater triumph.

Chapter Sixteen

Since the virtual burial of the Conciliation Bill – other government business took precedence until the summer recess and no mention of it occurred when government returned, for it was clearly shelved – large demonstrations had grown somewhat stale in the eyes of the public.

With Christmas only three weeks away, shopping was more on people's minds. Cold weather didn't lend itself to flamboyant demonstrations and pretty dresses, more to coats, scarves and fur collars. Persistent December winds made banners difficult to keep rigid and flags tended to be ripped loose from their poles; things could turn into a fiasco, not the sort of picture women's suffrage campaigners wanted to paint.

Eveline and Connie had grown closer since the birth of their daughters and with Connie taking ages to recover during November, they had lost some of the impetus for suffragette work. And just as well. Some five hundred women who'd rushed the police outside the House of Commons had been treated exceptionally brutally. A hundred and fifteen women and four men were arrested, though on the following day charges against nearly all of them were withdrawn. So many had suffered injury, even sexual humiliation such as one unscrupulous policeman grabbing hold of a woman's breast in full view of the public, that suffragettes were calling that day Black Friday.

'You could easily have been there,' Connie said to Eveline who'd popped in to see her. 'You've always enjoyed being in the thick of things.'

'I don't know about enjoy,' Eveline said. She was holding Connie's baby, her own seven-month-old rolling happily on the bed in which Connie languished. 'I've never shirked my duties, but–'

Hastily she broke off, realising it must sound as though she was referring to the time Connie's father had paid her fine, saving her from imprisonment. It was still a touchy subject with Connie, one it was best to keep well away from. The last thing she wanted was to hurt her friend's feelings.

'But I do think it was a dreadful business,' she hurried on, annoyed with herself. 'Women manhandled by the police like that, and bad language used as well. I was told of one policeman who actually grabbed a rather elderly woman's breast and said she'd been wanting someone to do that to her for a long time. When she protested, he said he could grip her wherever he liked.'

She began rocking Connie's baby, who had started to whimper. 'Some women complained of having had their clothes and even underwear torn, and some of being picked up bodily and thrown into the crowd. It's said the police had specific orders to manhandle them.'

'I can't believe that's entirely true,' Connie broke in gently. 'Probably a misunderstanding of some sort.'

'A misunderstanding?'

'I'm sure it was. They had drafted police from

the East End, men more accustomed to dealing with all sorts of riff-raff, rough gangs and drunks.'

She spoke quite innocently, gazing at Rebecca who was growing more fractious.

'They were probably unaccustomed to dealing with militants from better areas, no doubt saw them as the kind of women who expect to be rough handled. I'm sure police from West London divisions would never have treated women in that way.'

It was Eveline's turn to feel hurt; Connie's words sounded like a slur on an area in which she had been brought up. Of course it had its share of villains, gang fights and regular rough-ups, but the same could be said of anywhere, even the back streets of West London. It seemed the East was always being named and blamed.

'Here, you nurse her for a while,' she said sharply, handing Connie back her baby and, reaching across the bed, picked up her own child. Rebecca fell quiet immediately as Connie took her to begin making little clucking noises at her.

'Some are against militants going off at a tangent,' she said without looking up. 'Some think that any sort of militancy just now could jeopardise any survival of the Conciliation Bill, especially with another general election next week. The next government could be more in sympathy with us. And it does no good having suffragettes shown harassing members of parliament on their way to the House.'

There had been pictures in the newspapers of women walking beside MPs, accosting them, almost blocking their path, and Eveline had to

240

admit that it wasn't the way to get parliamentary sympathy.

Even so, still burning from the apparent aspersion cast on her East End, she said huffily, 'I wouldn't know. I'd best be off. I've got to make a start on Albert's tea.'

But as Connie nodded, though confused and downhearted she mellowed. 'I'll pop in tomorrow, all right? And you ought to start getting up, moving around a bit more. See you tomorrow.'

To help her better temper along, she leaned over and dropped a kiss on Connie's forehead.

Connie brightened instantly. 'I have been getting up. It's just that I still feel I need my afternoon rest.'

'Of course.' Eveline relented. Connie would never have the resilience of women brought up in the East End.

Still hoping, Connie sent a Christmas card to her family, hardly expecting to receive one back. But to her surprise her sister Verity replied with a brief letter wishing her a good Christmas and hoping she was well. She did not mention George at all but hoped Connie's new baby was doing well, Connie having written about the birth but with no response from her parents.

Verity added that she was getting married in the June to the son of a wealthy businessman to whom she'd been introduced and that both families were pleased. Connie could well imagine Verity bowing to her father's wishes even if she hadn't particularly fancied the young man. Not so her, and look at the pain it had caused her.

241

The lack of response from her parents was needling her more than she cared to admit and in that frame of mind she decided to visit or, more correctly, confront them as soon as Christmas had passed. It preyed on her mind right through Christmas despite enjoying the day she and George shared together; it made her feel the loss of her own people all the more acutely.

Still seething she chose the Tuesday following New Year, trying to ignore the drizzle that might have dampened a less determined spirit. It was time to have it out with them once and for all. Waiting for a better day would have had her letting it go altogether. Leaving George a note which explained where she was going, that she might be late back home, and that he could easily warm up his dinner of stew himself, she wrapped Rebecca up snugly and set off.

Her determination was still so intense when she reached Perivale that the ten-minute walk from the station to her parents' home seemed to fly by; Rebecca felt light in her arms, her umbrella gave no hindrance, only the wet hem of her skirt flicking up mud from the pavement noticeable as she went. But by the time she reached her parents' door she was hot and breathless.

In the shelter of the extensive porch she closed the umbrella and lifted a hand to give the bell pull a tentative jerk, suddenly uncertain. What had she been thinking of, coming here? What did she expect?

Not their butler Bentick but a maid, not Agnes but a strapping, plain-faced girl with mousy hair pulled back from her forehead, opened the door and asked who she was and on being told, appeared bewildered and a little suspicious, obviously unaware that this family had another daughter. Connie felt a wave of resentment pass through her as though her very name had been erased from the face of the earth.

'Tell them I'm here on a visit,' she snapped, and before the confused girl could bid her wait and close the door on her, reached out and with the end of the umbrella gave the door such a push that it was thrust open before the girl could catch it. Next second she was in the hall, the familiar hall that had not changed at all since she'd left.

'Tell Mrs Mornington that her daughter Constance is here,' she demanded and the girl scuttled off up the stairs to her mother's bedroom where although it was nearly eleven she was probably taking her time rising. With little else to do, her mother had no doubt breakfasted in bed.

Hoisting Rebecca further up into her arms, she let the umbrella drip on to the dark-tiled hall floor and waited, ignoring the small puddle it began to form. The well-built maid could wipe it up later.

Her mother appeared at the head of the stairs, hesitated, then as if gathering courage began slowly to descend, her eyes not leaving Connie.

She seemed to gather dignity about her like a cloak as she reached the hall and walked with measured steps towards her visitor. Her cream silk wrap and the paleness of her small face and her rapidly greying fair hair made her look as wispy as a ghost. Connie did not speak or move forwards, compelling her mother to come the whole length of the hall before stopping three feet away from her. Only then did Connie say anything.

'Hello, Mother.'

Her voice seemed to take the woman by surprise. She even almost shrank back, her mouth half opening to speak then closing as she looked towards the hovering housemaid, finally saying, 'Milly, Mr Mornington is in his surgery. Ask him to spare a moment of his time. Tell him his daughter Constance is here. It should not take him from his work for too long.'

For Connie those words were glaringly significant – as good as stating that her stay would be short and certainly unwelcome. She stood very still. She had banked on finding her mother alone, her father at his Harley Street practice, and perhaps her mother a little more sympathetic towards her. But it wasn't to be.

Her mother had not once taken her eyes off her and Connie found her own eyes wavering as if she were the guilty one. At that moment, Rebecca gave a little mewl. She saw the woman's eyes flick towards the child and then return back to her. Connie raised a hand to lift the child's bonnet a little.

'Mother, this is Rebecca, your granddaughter, your first grandchild. I wrote to you after her birth, but I don't know if you got my–'

'Why have you come here?'

The question, sharp and toneless, was like a blow between the eyes.

'Your grandchild. I wanted you to see...'

'You left this house without a word to me.'

'What did you expect me to say to you when you just stood by and said nothing as you watched my father turn me out?'

'Your father gave you a choice. You made that choice. You. No one made it for you.'

'But you didn't even *try* to stop me,' Connie said, biting back sudden tears at the recollection. 'You watched me go and did nothing.'

'I trust your father's decisions in all things.'

'Then you are equally to blame.' She was trying hard not to raise her voice but she wanted to leap at her mother and shake some freedom of choice into her. 'You took his side. You made me feel that you had never loved me. I wrote to you telling you where I was, and later about Rebecca. You never answered – not even a note.'

There was a flicker of uncertainty in her mother's eyes. 'A wife has to stand by her husband's decision in all things.'

'Why? Why can't you have some opinion of your own for once? What's the good of us trying to gain women their freedom to vote when there are women like you who think every man's word is law? You just stood there and watched me leave. What was I supposed to do? Give up the man I loved to marry someone my father picked out for me?

'*Love!*' Her mother came suddenly to life, spat the word at her. 'What sort of love is it that breaks a mother's heart with no thought for those who raised you in comfort and security?'

Her tone hadn't risen at all and that made it all the more painful to hear, all the more conclusive. 'I think you had best leave.'

Connie was about to challenge her when the figure of her father appeared in the hall, having been summoned from his surgery by the maid who now crept past everyone towards the main door.

Tall and commanding, Willoughby Mornington came slowly towards the two women, his eyes trained on Connie. He hadn't spoken and it was almost a sense of self-preservation that made her speak first.

'I've come to introduce you to your grand-daughter,' she said firmly, but he totally ignored the child, his stare not leaving Connie's face.

Laying a hand on his wife's arm, he gently but authoritatively eased her to one side. His deep voice, though quiet and controlled, seemed to fill the hall as he held Connie's gaze.

'And what did you expect to achieve? Forgive-ness for the pain you caused your mother and me? I do not forgive and I think you had better go.'

'Is that all you have to say to me?' she asked, hating the entreaty in her tone.

'What else would I have to say to you?'

'But this is your grandchild!'

'She is the child of a person I no longer know and a man I have no wish to know,' he said slowly.

Connie searched for a retort. There was so much she wanted to say: what a good man George was and how dare he belittle him; that this baby was an innocent in this family rift; that the father she had once loved now declared him-self her enemy. But she could only draw herself up with as much dignity as she could muster and, with a small bow of her head, meant as an insult, retrieve her umbrella and, holding Rebecca tightly, turn to go. He wasn't going to have the satisfaction of ordering her from the house.

She saw him flick his hand towards the hovering maid who, skirting the puddle from the wet umbrella, obediently opened the door as if being controlled by machinery.

Without another glance at the two people she had once called her parents, Connie went out into the gloomy afternoon with its cold, fine drizzle, the door closing behind her with a soft click as soon as she reached the last of the few steps to the drive.

No one had asked how she had arrived or what transport would be taking her to the station. It seemed they didn't care, yet a child was a child and as a doctor her father should surely have some thought to its welfare in such miserable weather. Apparently he didn't. But he could have at least asked his chauffeur William to drive her to the station especially with Rebecca in her arms, and if not in his motor at least in her mother's brougham.

She felt eaten up with fury, her eyes so blocked with tears of anger refusing to be shed that it seemed they would overflow into her lungs. She hurried down the drive without looking back. If they were watching from the window, she wouldn't give them the satisfaction of a backward glance. The sound of running footsteps, however, did make her turn as she reached the low iron gates out of sight of the house.

Verity, slightly out of breath, a coat over her shoulders, was hurrying towards her. Seeing her sister glance fearfully towards the house, Connie stepped back behind the tall hedge that separated the house from the road and waited.

'I had to talk to you,' Verity burst out. 'I couldn't let you go like that.'

She glanced towards the baby. 'She's so beautiful.' When Connie did not acknowledge the compliment, she added almost vehemently, 'It's unkind of them allowing you to walk to the station in this weather. They could at least have telephoned for a taxicab to come and collect you.'

Connie didn't reply. Taxicabs cost money. She wasn't hard up but she and George needed to go carefully with money, with rent to pay and a baby to bring up. Her last frivolity had been the hat she'd bought for that suffragette demonstration last June. Since then, she was beginning to learn that money spent doesn't replenish itself as easily as once she had imagined, nor did she want to see that look on George's face again when she had shown him the hat. True, it had been her money, but once gone, it could not so easily be replaced.

'I'll keep you company to the station,' Verity was saying. 'Let me carry the baby.'

'Her name is Rebecca,' Connie reminded her a little stiffly, conscious that she was unfairly taking out her spite on Verity, but neither of her parents had spoken the child's name. Her father hadn't even glanced at her. That wasn't Verity's fault and she had no cause to be spiteful towards her sister.

In a rush of contrition she handed Rebecca over to her; Rebecca's aunt fumbled with the shawl, not being used to holding babies.

'Can you handle her?' she asked. Verity smiled brightly. She had a pretty smile. No wonder she'd landed a likely young man so quickly. Father would have made sure she did. Had she possessed a face like an old boot, he'd have made sure she would have been found a good match.

'I could carry this one for miles, she is so light,' Verity said in a tone somewhat broody and wistful, making Connie smile for the first time today.

'What is this young man of yours like?' asked Connie as they walked. She saw Verity's face fill with serene happiness.

'He's wonderful,' she sighed, her blue eyes so like her mother's taking on a faraway glow. 'I was so fortunate. Father had no idea I already had a crush on Douglas even before we were introduced.'

She'd first seen Douglas Brent-Harrison, she went on, at a coming-out party and her heart had gone pit-a-pat. She'd hardly been able to speak on being formally introduced, later hardly able to believe it when he had asked if he could have her permission for him to see her again. A few months later when both sets of parents began discussing engagement details for the two young people, her joy had been absolute.

'We are very much in love with each other,' she ended as they entered the station booking hall, her tale having taken up the entire ten-minute walk.

Connie wondered if Verity would have behaved as she herself had if her father had tried to marry her to someone she hadn't cared for. Would she too have gone against his wishes? Not in the way Connie had. She could imagine Verity's tears melting her father's heart and him placating her.

Of course the matter had not arisen – Verity was in love with a man her father approved of, very much so; she was a good, obliging daughter.

Connie couldn't completely condemn him. He had always had his daughters' happiness at heart and would never have forced them to marry men whom they couldn't love. It was just that she had fallen in love with someone he could never approve of. It must have been a blow to him for her go off with a man who was virtually penniless – in his eyes, a fortune hunter. It was today's attitude that she could not forgive; he had averted his gaze, not just from her, but from his own granddaughter. He had no right to blame an innocent child for what he assumed were her mother's shortcomings. For that she could not, would not forgive him, and at this moment she didn't care if he never forgave her. She would never come here again.

'I wish you all the luck in your coming marriage, Verity,' she said as Verity handed back the baby. 'You still seem a little too young to marry.'

Verity took on a look of mild indignation 'I'm old enough!'

'Of course you are,' she relented, too drained by today's events to argue. Verity was happy. That was all that should matter. She turned as she passed through the ticket barrier. Her sister was still standing there.

Seeing her wave, Verity waved back, then turned and went out of the ticket office and out of sight.

Verity had said she'd try and invite her to her wedding though it all depended on their father, but Connie knew that if he objected, Verity would not persist. A good, obedient daughter, she thought for the second time. She didn't set much store by an invitation and she'd have to pardon Verity.

Hoisting Rebecca to a more comfortable position in her arms, she walked along the short platform to the ladies' waiting room to pass the time there until her train came.

Chapter Seventeen

Connie's mind had been on Verity's marriage as she emerged from Bethnal Green Station around one o'clock. Seconds later her thoughts were diverted by the distant clanging of police car bells and a faint whiff of burning hanging in the air. She found herself wondering if it might have anything to do with suffragette activity. Lately some had begun to resort to arson.

She was glad to find it had nothing to do with them. That evening, the third of January 1911, George's newspaper reported that a house in Sidney Street, a quarter of a mile from where she and George lived, in which three suspected anarchists had been under siege in a gun battle with a thousand troops and armed police, had been set ablaze; deliberately or not wasn't clear, but the fire was said to have been caused by the criminals themselves.

Even so, thoughts of suffragette activity worried Connie. If police were resorting to gun battles with suspected criminals, would they begin reacting the same way towards stone-throwing and property-wrecking suffragettes?

She spoke of it to Eveline on the Sunday. Her friend had popped over while George had his after-dinner nap, while Albert was occupied in his bedroom studying to be an engineer.

'Engineer?' she'd queried when Eveline had told

her. 'I thought he was going to be a surveyor.'

'He found it a bit beyond him,' Eveline had said. 'He feels engineering might suit him better.'

'That siege in Sidney Street,' she said now, 'I knew something wasn't right when I came out of the railway station. But if the police have started to arm themselves who knows what might happen should any suffragettes get out of hand? The newspapers said several bystanders were hurt in the battle and two of the anarchists were found dead – only one escaped. But what if they begin to think it quite in order to threaten us with firearms? Someone could get badly hurt.'

Eveline appeared not to be taking it quite as seriously as she should have as she busied herself feeding eight-month-old Helena with bits of the cake she had put on plates to go with their cup of tea.

'I don't think that would happen with us,' she said. 'It was on the orders of the Home Secretary and they *were* foreigners. They wouldn't dare use firearms against women like us.'

'You remember Black Friday?' Connie warned darkly. 'Who's to say they won't come at us armed next time?' But Eveline wasn't at all convinced.

'That'll never happen, not to women,' she said.

Connie felt a shudder go through her and glanced down at Rebecca asleep in her pram. 'I know one thing, we should make sure that we aren't included in any more militant protests. It was all very well when we were single, but we have children now.'

At last Eveline's expression deepened, the portent sinking in. She nodded. 'I expect you're right. Stick to passive roles in future. Let others do the dangerous work.'

They needn't have worried. Spring saw little militant activity other than public meetings and peaceful demonstrations, everyone hanging on for the Conciliation Committee to redraft its bill. Though its prospects were far from clear, it was their best chance and people were optimistic. Nothing must mar its chances.

In May the redrafted bill passed its second reading and everyone felt they had been right not to create waves. Even so, over the next seven weeks, with usual government slowness, the tide kept turning, the bill in favour at one point then out of favour days later and so on, keeping everyone on edge and prompting meetings and processions all over the country, but everyone peaceable, no one daring to rock this boat.

As expected, no invitation to her sister's wedding ever arrived but Verity could have written if only to say that circumstances had prevented it. She'd have understood. Maybe Verity *was* too over the moon with her hundred-and-one arrangements to give much thought to it, but that hurt worse than her parents forbidding any invitation. So much for sisterly love! And if this was the case then she would wash her hands of them all, though she'd said that so many times before. They were still her family and always on her mind.

Verity's wedding on the third of June came and went. Connie tried to think of that Saturday as just another day but it was hard not to feel it. In an effort to put it behind her, she turned to her suffragette work as far as a husband and baby allowed. She and Eveline made up a plan to take turns looking after each other's daughters so that one or other could attend a meeting or a rally without getting too involved or being apprehended by the police.

In early June, they along with thousands of others were informed that in support of the campaign every suffragette society in the country would combine in one great and hopefully final demonstration on the seventeenth, an estimated forty thousand women marching five abreast in a gala of music and floats.

As well as being a national procession, with many in historical costume, it would be international with suffragettes from every country with their own banners and flags and traditional dress as well as women from every part of the British Empire. 'Can you imagine the colour and the spectacle?' Connie said, trying to feel excited.

She desperately needed to put her sister's wedding the previous week behind her but the snub continued to hurt. Hopefully, marching in this huge procession would help take her mind off it.

'With so much support we'll win in the end,' she said to Eveline, determined to concentrate on that.

It was to be called the Women's Coronation Procession, arranged to take place six days prior to the coronation of King George V and Queen Mary. With the entire week already earmarked as one of celebration and festivity by the whole country, this procession would have the largest number of onlookers they could ever wish for.

'It could even become a victory march,' Connie said, following Eveline into her kitchen. 'The way things are going, the Conciliation Bill has to go through. We've had so many setbacks in the past, it just has to.'

'Let's hope so,' Eveline said solemnly. 'What I'd like to know is how we are both going to be there?'

'We've got to be there, both of us.'

Eveline remained glum. 'If we both go, who'll look after Helena and Rebecca?' She so wanted to attend, but how could she expect Connie to do the honours on such a special day? 'We can't ask Albert or George,' she pointed out. 'Both of them are at work on Saturday mornings.'

Connie frowned. 'You mean one of us stay behind?' As Eveline gave a phlegmatic shrug, her frown deepened. 'You don't expect me to stay behind, not on an occasion like this.'

'I never said you,' Eveline said waspishly. 'I suppose it'll have to be me.'

'You can't.'

'What other choice is there?' Her tone was still sharp and Connie fell silent; as the silence grew, Eveline made a great business of wiping around her butler sink for a second time since washing up plates from her midday meal.

It was Connie who finally spoke, miserably and ineffectually. 'We'll have to work something out.'

'What? How?'

Connie reflected for a moment. 'Do you think we could ask your gran to oblige?'

'I don't think it comes into it,' Eveline said, putting aside the damp dishcloth as she surveyed the sink that never really looked any cleaner for all the wiping, the stained digs and cracks in the porcelain indelible from years of wear. 'I don't think my Albert would care for me toddling off the second he's home from work on a Saturday.'

She turned abruptly to Connie. 'Though I expect your George doesn't mind too much even if he had been working all morning and wanting his dinner? But everyone has to be at the starting point before midday to find out where they'll be in the procession and everything. It takes time with forty or more thousand before they march off.'

She began to regret the sharpness of her tongue as she saw a blank look creep across Connie's face. 'What I mean is, our lives have changed. It's impossible to do what we once did.'

Connie's lips became a tight line. 'Nothing is impossible. I'm going to tell George exactly what the situation is. He'll understand. He'll have to.'

'What're you going to say?'

'That I'm a suffragette and I believe in what we are doing and that he will have to make allowances and June the seventeenth will be one of them.'

'What about Rebecca?'

For a moment came a prick of suspicion that Connie might have already taken it that she'd look after her baby for her. But Connie had gone quiet, her small show of defiance seeping away. 'I couldn't ask George to take an hour or two off from work so I can go out. His job's important.'

So it's down to me, came the thought, but she held her tongue. The last thing she wanted was to quarrel with Connie though she felt dangerously close to it, beginning to seethe.

Connie was looking contemplative. 'If we could find someone to look after the two of them. If you could persuade your mother to have Helena, perhaps your gran might be willing to have Rebecca. She has said how she likes having them around her.'

'While we're there with them,' Eveline reminded her.

'But she once said she would be happy to keep an eye on them if we had to be somewhere special. And this is special.'

'No. I know what my mum'll say,' Eveline put in. 'There's going to be forty thousand there – they won't miss one. I can just hear her saying it.'

'If we all believed that, there'd be no procession, no one ready to fight, no chance for enfranchisement for us, ever.'

Connie was right. Anger began to dissipate and, full of determination, she went to see her mother.

Dora Fenton's answer was instant. 'Yer think I've got nothing better to do than give eye to a baby so you can go gallivanting off just as you please? I've got a shop ter run, a liveli'ood ter keep going. Do I ever ask someone ter look after that shop so I can go gallivanting off?'

'But Dad is in the shop.'

'And I 'elp 'im. He can't do it all on 'is own. Yer know he ain't getting no younger. Whyn't you go an' ask your mother-in-law?'

Eveline bit at her lip. As nice as the woman was, how could she ask Albert's mother to look after a child that wasn't her son's?

'You've got May,' she said desperately. 'She helps in the shop.'

For a moment or two Dora was stumped. She knew she was being uncooperative, but Eveline had made her bed so to speak and it wasn't her fault that she could find no affection for this baby conceived out of wedlock. Eveline had imagined she could share a bed with some upper-class toff then expect him to marry her when things went wrong. She didn't realise how lucky she was finding Bert Adams to bale her out. Maybe he was a fool to have done so but a nice fool. She liked Bert Adams – in her estimation the finest man there ever was, stepping in like he had, whether he'd been in love with her or not. As for the baby, she'd feel different if Bert was the legitimate father, but he wasn't and she couldn't bring herself to love it. Almost as if it wasn't her flesh and blood at all.

'All this because you want ter go off enjoying yerself,' she snapped. 'Going off and leaving an 'usband what was good enough to 'elp you out of a sticky situation just when yer needed it.'

She turned away to busy herself flicking imaginary specks of dust off the sideboard with a duster she'd been holding the whole time Eveline had been here. The effort was a totally unnecessary chore; the living room gleamed like a new pin, May having cleaned and tidied this morning.

'You 'ad the baby, not me. And only saved from disgrace because a decent man came along and got you out of a scrape, more fool 'im! Now yer want ter 'ave 'im come 'ome and see to 'is own dinner while you go off out. Not only that, yer looking ter foist yer baby off on someone else. If yer so set on going ter this rally lark, then take 'er with yer. I'm sorry, Ev, I'm busy.'

She waited, her back to Eveline, but no more entreaties came. Eveline wasn't a fool – she knew when she was defeated. Proud too. Dora heard her go carefully down the stairs with the baby in her arms. Only then did she turn round, duster in hand, and go to the window to watch her daughter's departure.

Eveline didn't appear immediately, no doubt settling the child into her pram. When she did appear, wheeling the pram off, her pace was sharp, her head high and defiant. But that wasn't her lookout. Eveline asked for all she got.

No doubt she'd pester her gran and get her way. Dora felt anger surge through her. Mum had always been a thorn in her side ever since Dad had generously handed the shop over to Len Junior, even though he was only a son-in-law, knowing he couldn't manage it any more.

When Dad died, Mum began to see fit to poke her nose in concerning the shop, keeping tabs on how was it doing and all that, as if it was still hers. But it wasn't hers. It was Len's. She'd been left everything else and she wasn't hard up. Dad had made a good living in his time even if he had got the gambling bug worse as he got older.

She, Dora, had let Mum know that truth in no uncertain terms, fend or please. They'd not spoken for years after that, and had only recently come round to a grudging reunion, usually at Christmastime. Now Mum was interfering again, taking Eveline's side over the baby.

She turned away as her daughter turned the corner, and putting the duster aside went downstairs into the shop to lend a hand.

The place was busy. On Saturday it was half-day closing, and everyone wanted to get a last few items in before lunchtime. There was only Len there, May having gone out on one of her rare afternoons with a friend who was out of work at the moment. May worked hard; she deserved time to herself.

Len looked up as Dora entered. 'What did she want?' he asked.

'Nothing much,' Dora answered as she prepared to serve the next customer, one in a line of several waiting. He was worked off his feet.

Connie's request was proving more successful with Eveline's gran. Victoria Ansell held the sweet child in sheer joy at having a baby on her lap.

'I've never known such a pretty baby,' she cooed, then let out a contrite little laugh. 'I shouldn't really be saying that, should I? Eveline might feel jealous. In actual fact you've both got lovely-looking little babies.'

She glanced down at Rebecca and began uttering senseless prattle that seemed to delight the child, who responded with little gurgling sounds of her own.

'She enjoys good conversation,' Victoria said, looking up. 'So when d'you want me to 'ave her?'

'On Saturday,' Connie said diffidently. 'I know it's short notice.'

'How much notice does an old lady need when

261

it comes to having a little one all to 'erself for a few hours?'

'I just thought... I only thought you might be able to...'

'Be able?' Victoria smiled understandingly. 'I know I'm seventy – or thereabouts,' she granted with a laugh, 'but not yet in me dotage. I've got all me faculties and can look after a titchy one like this. When a baby starts getting on its feet, that's when it takes young people with energy enough to run after them. But like this she'll be no trouble to me.'

'I'm so glad,' Connie breathed. 'I didn't want to impose on you.'

Victoria grew serious as a sudden thought struck her. 'What does your 'usband say about you going off? 'Ave you arranged with 'im about 'aving to look after 'imself, you 'aving to leave before he gets 'ome from work?'

'I thought I'd ask you about the baby before I told him.'

'And break the news to 'im?'

'Yes, I suppose so.'

'Hmm...' Victoria handed the baby back to its mother. 'Then I think you should ask 'im today. And I mean *ask* him, not tell him. He's the one what goes to work to keep you all.'

As Connie stiffened she hurried on. 'I'm not against women trying to obtain the vote. I'm all for that. But a man's still responsible for his family's welfare, and always will be. Unless, if and when you do get the vote, you think you can start wearing the trousers too, which of course won't ever 'appen, no matter what. Two bosses in the family would end up ruining it.'

Seeing Connie's face begin to fall, she gave her a placatory smile. 'Don't mind me. You go along, settle it with your 'usband. If he says yes, I'll be 'appy enough to give eye to this sweet little one for a few hours.'

With a grateful young mother bent on her cause, Victoria found herself eagerly looking forward to Saturday with just a tinge of anxiety that she was still up to the task. But of course she was. She'd brought up seven children *and* helped out in that busy little shop; she'd been glad to see the back of it in the end, but she hadn't forgotten how to care for a mere baby.

That was until not ten minutes after Connie had left and Eveline came knocking on her door. What could she say? What would her grand-daughter think if she refused to look after her own great-grandchild after promising to look after the child of a comparative outsider?

Yes, she sighed, she'd be glad to and it was shabby of Dora to refuse to do one little favour. 'Why couldn't she?' she asked.

Eveline's neck went thin and stretched. 'I took it she feels she doesn't owe a duty to a kiddie she still sees as illegitimate,' came the stiff reply.

Victoria frowned. 'I can see I'm going to 'ave a word with that woman eventually,' she said angrily. Immediately Eveline began invoking excuses for her mother.

'She's not against the baby. It's me. She'll never forgive me.'

'Then it's about time she learned to, and stopped taking it out on an innocent infant.'

After Eveline left, gratefully relieved, Victoria was left wondering just what she had let herself in for. Having told her that she too must *ask* not tell her husband what she'd planned to do, she found herself almost wishing both men would refuse to be put out, saving her the worry about coping with not one but two babies on Saturday. But she knew they wouldn't refuse. Men these days were becoming far too soft.

'He said yes!' Connie excited as if she'd been given the moon. 'He even said he'd try to be there to see me pass. He's always been for women's suffrage.'

Sitting in Connie's top-floor flat with the summer sunshine streaming in, Eveline felt a wave of jealousy, not only because of this lovely flat but also because her own husband had not been half so forthcoming.

Having finally got her way after a bit of strained atmosphere, she had hurried over this Wednesday morning to tell Connie her good news only to find George had practically urged Connie to attend. She felt that if Gran had not consented to look after Rebecca, he'd even have taken it on. But Rebecca was his baby whereas Helena was nothing to Albert and despite seeming to dote on her no one could be certain what went through his mind sometimes.

She sipped her tea and glanced about Connie's bright and tidy flat. There was no incentive to keep hers as nice. She'd tried but it never looked any better for it, everything being so shabby. But one day when Albert finally got the engineering job he was hoping so much to achieve, they'd have a nice large place and she would take great pleasure showing it off to Connie. That was if George hadn't become an assistant bank manager by then with an even larger house to show for it.

Still, she had to be glad of small mercies. What if Albert had flatly said no? How could she have faced Connie? But it had still been touch and go.

'I do know what women are trying to do,' he'd said negatively. 'But you're a married woman now and we've got a baby to think of.'

'But what we're doing is so very important,' she'd argued. 'It's what nearly every woman in the country is striving for and one day we *will* achieve our goal. Everyone is needed. I can't just drop it all because I'm married.'

There had been a look on Albert's face that made her realise what she'd said. But for him she would not be married, condemned as a slut, her child born without a father.

Filled with contrition she'd rushed into his arms saying she didn't mean it the way it had sounded and could he ever forgive her, her rush crumpling the paper he'd been reading.

'Nothing to forgive,' he'd said, enfolding her in his arms. 'I married you 'cos I love you, Ev. But I just 'ope you know what you're doing with this suffragette thing, that's all.'

She did know what she was doing. So did Connie. They had come to believe that nothing would stop them in their fight, not marriage, not children, although they shouldn't ever be neglected because of it. What they were doing was for those who came after them. It was what she believed,

believed to the core of her being.

She said all this to Connie who replied, 'I know what you're trying to say, and it is true, all of it. But did he actually agree to your going on the procession?'

Eveline nodded uncertainly. 'I think he did. At least he didn't say no. He just cuddled me and said he hoped I knew what I was doing.'

It had been his way of consenting; on the day he wished her good luck before going off to work. Dressed in her summer best, it was hard to express how happy she felt, the sun shining, the air warm, but not too warm, Gran in charge of both children, bless her, youthful eyes sparkling in that elderly face, not a bit apprehensive at having two babies in her care for the next few hours.

'I ain't that past it yet as I can't look after two tiny tots,' she'd said. 'Different if they was running about. I'm not as young as I can get up any speed to run after 'em, but no, they'll be fine with me at the age they are.'

Overwhelmed with gratitude, Eveline gave her a huge, affectionate hug, at the same time aware of a surge of bitterness. It should be her mother she was hugging in gratitude.

Chapter Eighteen

Eveline looked apologetically at Connie as they assembled ready for the procession. 'I'm sorry. They expect it. I can't get out of it.'

She had practically been commanded to be in the prisoners' pageant. Refusal would have been seen as a slight to what the women had gone through for their beliefs. She couldn't say no.

Closely watching Connie's reaction, she still regretted that business with her in court, allowing her father get her off going to prison. If she hadn't submitted so meekly to his paying her fine, they'd both be marching side by side in a place of honour today.

'I'm sorry, Connie, I have to. You don't mind, do you?'

She was surprised to see Connie smile at her, apparently not at all put out. But why should she be when her George was coming to see her pass?

Eveline had hoped Albert might come along after work too, but he'd said he had some studying to do if he hoped ever to be an engineer earning a decent wage. Although he was right, of course, it still irked.

Connie's husband had said he would try to get off work and watch out for her despite the procession being well on its way by then. Eveline couldn't help taking comfort that he'd have to find her among forty thousand women, which didn't seem likely; this was to be the biggest demonstration yet, with all the display and colour of earlier processions.

Connie did look splendid though. She'd splashed out, spending her own money on a new outfit, this time with George's blessings, his wages at the bank having improved with a small promotion. Beside her in her one and only Sunday best white dress, Eveline felt old-fashioned.

In a way she was glad not to be with her in the procession where she would feel a little dowdy beside her. With the 1911 summer fashions changing almost too fast to keep up with, dresses and skirts had become suddenly tube-like although there were still plenty of last year's wide skirts and flared hemlines to be seen. Hair was lower than last year, more puffed out about the ears, swept softly back to a loose roll at the nape of the neck. This she could achieve at no expense, her abundance of brown hair lending itself to the style, but the rest...

She could do nothing about shoes either. Toes were becoming more pointed; while those with money could keep up with changing fashions, she must carry on wearing the old rounded-toed sort.

She felt guilty at feeling somewhat glad when Connie said that her savings weren't stretching all that well towards new clothes. Disowned by her family, with no father to put his hand in his pocket for her, the girl who'd once had everything was now having to watch the pennies despite George's promotion. Wrong perhaps to think this way and Eveline wasn't crowing; in fact she had to admire Connie's resourcefulness in turning her hand to making her own skirts.

She'd bought a little second-hand sewing machine, and with dress patterns from the haberdasher's had started to make the simple skirts and blouses as near to the new style as best she could, saving herself quite a bit. She said she'd make a skirt for Eveline so long as she provided the material, stitched the hems and sewed on the buttons or hooks and eyes.

'Pity I can't make hats,' she said, even though huge, hard-to-balance millinery was giving way to flatter styles with upswept brims, plainer toques in white, cream or beige straw, decorated with a dark feather or two, or black straw with white feathers. Eveline had bought one cheap in beige straw from Petticoat Lane Market, which she'd decorated herself with a darker band and a fan of brown feathers. But it couldn't compare with the fine hat Connie had bought from a departmental store in Oxford Street – still risking her dwindling savings trying to keep up with fashion.

Leaving Connie in order to take her position in the prisoners' pageant, her white arrow badge proclaiming her right, she followed the marshal who'd come to conduct her to her place. How any marshal or steward could find anyone in this milling throng and get them into their positions, with the pavement already clogged with spectators even though the procession would not start until five-thirty, was nothing short of remarkable.

'Look out for me when we get to the Albert Hall,' called Eveline as she left and saw Connie's half-nod; Connie was already craning her neck to see if she could catch sight of her George.

There would be no such prospect of Albert turning up to watch her in her place of honour. The prisoners' pageant was the best yet, seven hundred women, one hundred and forty rows, each row five abreast, all of them in white, holding lances from whose spears pennons fluttered. At their centre there was a huge tableaux of women in loose white gowns and haloes of flowers. Drawn by two white horses, the platform towered above the onlookers, women also clad in white standing with their lances about an even taller platform on which sat other women, and crowning it all on yet another platform a single young woman sitting beneath a canopy of white roses and green garlands, a young girl at her feet.

Once they moved off, people would gasp to see it, realising that every one in those hundred and forty lines had at one time or another endured a harsh and humiliating incarceration for her cause.

There were dozens of other floats just as impressive, women from all over the Empire, even from the United States, all carrying colourful national emblems, many in national dress and as many tableaux as in previous marches. Eveline had never felt so proud of having once been a prisoner, having shared what every one of these seven hundred had endured.

With sunshine pouring down from a brilliant blue sky, the air warm and balmy as though bestowing blessings on the whole affair, it could have been even more wonderful if Albert had been here to see her. He'd obviously considered his studies far more important than watching her pass in this five-mile-long column of women with one thought in mind – to gain the right to vote alongside men who saw them as inferior. And yet, though men made up seventy-five per cent of the crowds watching today, not one had so far lifted voice or fist against this demonstration. By the look of them they seemed overwhelmed by it.

Eveline felt proud, but it was mixed with feelings of bitterness that Connie's husband would keep his promise and even if he were unable to find her in this forty-thousand-strong demonstration, he'd have at least bothered to come.

She knew she shouldn't begrudge Albert studying. He so wanted to improve his life and it was all for his little family, seeing that he included Helena as his own. She tried hard to think of all he'd done for her, marrying her and giving little Helena his name, and knew that she should be grateful. But if only, just for this one day, he'd said he'd be here. Just this one day. If only she could now see his broad face smiling at her from the crowd.

Waiting for the signal to begin as the sun moved across the sky, her eyes searched and searched those who'd clambered on to the parapet along the length of the Embankment or clung to the arms of lamp-posts for a better view. Thousands had thronged to London for the King's Coronation and were in holiday mood ready to enjoy this spectacular procession too, prior to the other one five days from now with its royal golden coach and its colourful troops and its massed bands. But today Eveline's eyes sought only one face in this sea of faces.

Five-thirty came, the procession began to move and still no sign of him. Nor did she expect any now. With an effort she resigned herself that he wouldn't be coming, but it didn't help the heavy weight in her chest.

Going through Trafalgar Square she saw a wondrous sight – people had clambered up on to the four stone lions guarding Nelson's column; they stood on the verges of the fountains, on tops of drays and taxicabs and motor cars.

Hordes filled the stands built especially for the Coronation. Energetic young men clung to the top of signposts or perched precariously along the top of billboards. With the endless procession snaking slowly out of sight along Northumberland Street, the tail end still waited to move off along the Embankment whilst its head with 'General' Drummond leading, Charlotte Marsh as colour-bearer just behind her, and Joan Annan-Bryce, niece of the British Ambassador in Washington, as Joan of Arc in armour and riding a white horse, was well down Piccadilly.

Giving up on Albert, Eveline concentrated her mind on the long walk ahead. Only once did she glance sideways, to her left, not knowing what precisely had prompted her to look in that direction. Afterwards she thought it had to be some sort of sixth sense or that he had willed her. Years later she would call it uncanny. But there he was. She saw him instantly, as plain as if he stood entirely alone. Clinging to a lamp-post, his foot on its tall plinth to steady himself, one arm about the iron post, he was leaning out like some cherub from a frieze and he was waving his boater fit to break an arm.

She could see his mouth opening and closing as he yelled, though over all the cheering he would never have been heard. Eveline's heart leaped from the iron band that had enclosed it and, without thinking, she threw up a hand and waved back with all her might.

'Have a care as to where you are!' the older women walking beside her admonished sharply, but Eveline was so happy that she gave another, this time tentative, wave, amazed that he had actually picked her out. But then he must have known where to look, because on the odd occasion she had talked about the honoured prisoners' pageant. Had she been with Connie he'd never have found her. So prominent was this section of the parade that he couldn't have missed it. Even from here he looked so proud of her.

The girl on her other side switched her eyes briefly in the direction where Eveline had waved, then back to her and grinned. 'Lovely,' was all she said, but it spoke volumes of what Eveline's heart was feeling.

From then on the entire evening went as though in a haze. She didn't see him again. Nigh fifty thousand women filing into the Albert Hall didn't allow finding anyone and if she hadn't known roughly where Connie would be, she wouldn't ever have found her either.

Connie looked despondent as they came away at the end of it all, thoroughly worn out by all the excitement and the speeches, the colour and the pageantry.

'I didn't catch the tiniest glimpse of George,' she moaned. 'I know he was there. He promised he would be.' There was a tiny ring of doubt in her voice but Eveline hardly noticed.

'I saw my Albert!' she blurted out excitedly.

This time she saw a startled, disbelieving look. 'You were probably mistaken. You said he had to study. It couldn't have been him.'

'It was. He was hanging on to a lamp-post as we turned into Piccadilly. I saw him over the heads of everyone lining the route. He looked straight at me. He waved and I waved back.'

'It was probably someone waving to someone else.'

'I know what I saw.'

'It must have been someone who looked like him.'

'I know him enough to know it was him!' Eveline shot back petulantly.

Connie went silent and no more was said as Eveline continued to pout. She wasn't at all sorry about her outburst. Connie had made up her mind not to believe her just because she hadn't seen George. She recalled the doubt in Connie's tone when she'd said he'd promised to be there. What if he had changed his mind? Had that been in Connie's thoughts? Perhaps she was taking it out on her, saying it wasn't Albert she'd seen.

Trouble with Connie, she always wanted to be right, always the top brick on the chimney just because she'd once been the pampered daughter of a well-off father. Well, those days had passed. Connie had suffered a big comedown since then and she was blowed if she wanted to have Connie

274

lording it over her. It *was* Albert she'd seen. It didn't matter that she'd not seen him again. But it *had* been him, she was sure of it. Now Connie had put doubts into her mind. In a way she almost hoped George had changed his mind but she kept that thought to herself, speaking only when necessary as they caught the tube home and then the bus from Liverpool Street.

George Towers quietly allowed his wife to blow off steam until the right moment when he could defend himself without her getting upset all over again.

Connie was justified, he supposed. She had been so sure of his being there to see her and was blaming him for failing her, not pausing to wonder at the cause. Once her hurt feelings had spent themselves he'd be able to explain his inability to get away from the bank to watch her pass in that demonstration today.

She was having these bouts of temper more frequently lately, brief though they were. He felt they stemmed from her need for another child that at the same time vied with a fear of childbirth after all she'd gone through in having Rebecca and being told her life could be in jeopardy if she had another. She didn't seem to realise that he was content with just their one child rather than have her put at risk. But sometimes it could be harrowing.

Biding his time he finally he saw her shoulders sag and she sank down on a chair, spent by her outburst. Now he could explain.

'I wanted to be there to see you off, Connie,' he

said gently. 'I tried my best, but there was this crisis at the bank – a serious discrepancy – it had to be solved.'

Hurriedly he told her of a mistake at one of the tills, which had meant every one of the staff was compelled to stay until it was cleared up and the money balanced.

'I didn't dare to leave, darling. I could have lost my job if I'd walked out. I would have been there if I could. You have to believe that, my love.'

'I know that now,' she pouted. 'But I didn't then.'

'There was no way to let you know.'

'I looked and looked for you.'

Her tone was one of anguish, her eyes beginning to glisten. 'All I knew was that you said you would leave work early. When Eveline told me her own husband was there, how do you think I felt? I was so upset that I actually told her she must have been mistaken.'

'I wanted to be there for the start, my sweet. In fact I rushed off the moment I was able to get away, but everyone had gone. I was too late.'

She looked at him. 'Why didn't you say that just now?'

'How could I with you so overwrought? You gave me no chance to say anything and the last thing I wanted to do was upset you even more. Maybe I should have told them at the bank to sort it out themselves and leave.'

For a moment she stared, tears of sudden contrition trembling on her eyelids. As she lowered her eyes, they spilled over to trickle down her cheeks. 'And lose your job. Oh, George, I'm so sorry. I blamed you and it wasn't your fault. But how was I to know?'

'Well, it's all right now, my sweet,' he said softly, holding out a hand to compel her to come to him to be forgiven, which she did readily enough.

'And I apologise too.'

'No,' she cried as he drew her to him. 'Please, darling, it's been all my fault.'

But even a cuddle hadn't quite consoled her. Blaming herself she set about almost sullenly preparing a simple supper of cheese on toast, washed down with a mug of Fry's cocoa drink.

By the time they went to bed she was recovered enough to let him make love to her though she remained so rigid, insisting he use protection – those thick rubbers that destroyed all sensation and deadened any pleasure of spontaneity – that all the joy of lovemaking went out of it for him.

He couldn't help it; his turn to feel sullen arrived as he turned over to sleep, in fact he found himself blaming her for this lack of fulfillment within him. Since the birth of Rebecca it was happening more and more and sometimes it seemed to him that their marriage wasn't always as happy as she often proclaimed it to be.

Eager to confirm it was Albert she'd seen waving, Eveline was determined to ask him the second she came in. But that disconcerting feeling that Connie must have been right and she'd been mistaken was immediately confirmed on finding him absorbed in one of his engineering manuals.

'Been busy I see,' she said, taking off her hat and jacket.

He looked up from the dining table where he was sitting and smiled. 'Got through quite a bit of work,' he replied unhurriedly. 'Considering.'

'Considering what?'

'That I've brought in supper fer us ready for you to come 'ome to.'

The smell of hot saveloys brought a twinge of hunger but she felt too confused to yield to it. Had she actually waved to someone who'd merely looked like him? The man had even waved back, and she had told Connie it had been Albert she'd seen. Or was Albert really just teasing her?

'So you didn't have any intention of being there?' she countered.

He'd gone back to reading his manual, his reply casual. 'With all this revision I've 'ad to do? What do you think?'

He lifted his eyes to her and smiled playfully. He had to be teasing. She refused to return the smile, turning instead to look out of the window.

An unseen glow of a summer sunset was touching the top of the tenements opposite. If only she could live up there, she would see right across London, see every sunset there was to be seen, every glorious colour, have that setting sun shining in her eyes, her home all bright from it. But no, they lived in this miserable, dingy, basement letting, already dark despite the glorious sunset, so that Albert needed the gaslight on to see what he was reading.

But wasn't this dingy basement letting the sole purpose of all this studying so that one day he'd earn decent enough money to afford a transfer to a lighter and more pleasant letting? Why was she being so petty when he was only thinking of her? What did it matter if he couldn't be there to see her go by?

'What's in the oven?' she queried. Without turning back she knew by the tone of his voice that he was into his manual again.

'Saveloy and pease pudd'n,' he said. 'Got it from the butchers – been keeping it warm for when yer got 'ome.'

She knew she should be grateful. Men usually saw providing supper as women's work but he never seemed to think of it that way. He would even make himself a simple meal, a fry-up or a couple of rounds of cheese on toast if she were out at a suffragette meeting. But that he could find time to interrupt his studies to go out to the butcher's, yet not come and see her, spoiled her gratitude, especially knowing that she'd been so nasty to Connie who had been right all the time.

In silence she ate her supper, the usually succulent fare like chaff in her mouth, but she chewed stubbornly.

'You look about done in,' he said as he lifted his mug of cocoa to his lips. He was smiling across the table at her. What did he have to smile about? Surely he could see she was still upset. She didn't reply.

'It was a long procession,' he said, putting his mug down to dig into his pease pudding, keeping his eyes lowered.

'How would you know?' she challenged.

'They said it was five miles long. Ain't easy ter find anyone yer know in a procession that big.'

She almost said, Well, that wouldn't have concerned you, would it? but instead she went on eating stolidly and in silence.

'You looked nice though.'

Eveline looked up, startled. 'How do you know what I looked like?'

'Because I saw you.'

'You can't have. You wasn't home from work to see me when I left.'

'But you did look nice. In fact you looked ravishing. Second from the left in a row of five, about – let me see – I'd say about sixteen or seventeen rows back from that big float full of women in white. You was 'olding your lance just like a real trooper ready to do battle with anyone in that crowd.'

Suddenly the penny dropped. 'You were there!'

Albert's grin seemed to stretch from ear to ear. He put down his knife and fork. 'Of course I was there. I waved at you and you waved back at me.'

In an instant, Eveline was out of her chair, knife and fork clattering to the floor, throwing herself at him and almost toppling him from his chair, the mug of cocoa wobbling precariously as his arm caught it in his effort to stop them both toppling over. 'You've been having me on all this time,' she cried out and he laughed as he held her to him.

'I didn't go on to the Albert Hall,' he whispered between kisses. 'I'd of never of found you in that crowd. So I came 'ome and got some supper for you instead. Thought you might be 'ungry time you got back.'

'Oh, I love you so much, Albert,' she whispered as he kissed her again. 'So very, very much.'

That night they made love and slept soundly in each other's arms, not disturbed by or disturbing little Helena in her cot beside the bed.

In the morning, Eveline thought how unkind she'd been to Connie. She would pop over and see her, be nice to her, be sympathetic if George hadn't gone after all.

Connie had begun to complain somewhat about him lately – niggardly things, maybe to do with her wanting everything just so, more than he did, though it seemed to Eveline that he tried to do his best.

Then she would go and pay Gran a quick visit. Gran had been so good, taking both children off their hands yesterday, saying they'd both been real little ducks in her care and it would be a pleasure to have them any time. She needed to endorse her gratitude yet again to Gran for all her help yesterday. Then she'd have to hurry home and get Sunday dinner, being that Mum and Dad had invited her and Albert round for tea in the evening.

Mum was making a bit more of fuss of little Helena lately but it was a pity that Gran and not she was the one to offer to have her when needed.

She thought now of herself and Albert and last night. They made love so much more often now, natural-like, without those horribly restrictive, protective sheaths. Her one desire was to give Albert a child of his own. In fact she was willing to have as many as he wished, except that there was no sign of anything as yet.

It was so strange that intimacy on only two

occasions with that despicable Laurence Jones-Fairbrook had got her pregnant so easily, yet nearly twelve months married to Albert had produced nothing.

True, it had been only lately that they'd started making love, yet they did so frequently these days, so why hadn't anything happened yet? It was cruelly ironic, almost as if she were being punished for what she'd done in the past.

Maybe it was her wanting so much to provide him with a family of his own, wanting it too much and being too tense, trying too hard. Perhaps it was that.

Chapter Nineteen

Dora Fenton sat glaring across her kitchen table at her mother blowing her nose into an already wet handkerchief with her first cold of the winter.

'For the life of me I don't know why yer let 'er take advantage of yer like that.'

'I like doing it,' Victoria said, glowering back at her. 'If I didn't, I'd soon say so. You should know me by now.'

'I know you orright. Always 'as ter be the one what's right! Well, you ain't right, doing all this for 'er all the time. Not only 'er, but that friend of 'ers as well. They've got a cheek expecting you ter look after two kids, at your age.'

'My age don't come into it,' Victoria snorted. 'I'm still strong and 'ealthy.'

'Yer look it, I must say!' came the retort as Victoria sneezed yet again into her handkerchief.

'I'm over the worst,' she brazened sharply. 'And young Eveline's been a brick, coming over to 'elp me out while I was really queer.'

It was said pointedly. Eveline did not take advantage of her. It was she herself who had offered to have the little ones in the first place, feeling that Eveline and her friend were both doing an excellent and needy job for the suffragette movement.

Far from taking advantage Eveline did her best to compensate, often popping over to see her

283

while she'd been really down with her cold; she ran her grandmother's errands and got her medicine, and had regularly tidied around the flat. Even Connie tried to make up for *putting on her*, as Dora called it, often bringing a little thank-you gift for looking after Rebecca – a few chocolates or a bottle of Guinness, her favourite tipple, even a couple of dainty handkerchiefs on one occasion.

Dora, her own daughter, hadn't come nigh or by while she'd been down with this blessed cold, much less thought to bring over some groceries from the shop.

'I wish I had the time to get over,' she'd told Eveline, her excuse being the fault of the busy shop. Victoria couldn't recall when last Dora had *had the time* to set foot in her flat.

'And they're getting' older,' Dora was reminding her. 'How are yer going ter be able ter run around after 'em when they find their feet? Yer may think yer active now but you ain't getting any younger.'

'I know that,' Victoria reminded her. 'But while I can–'

'It might've been orright in the summer,' Dora interrupted. 'But this time of year old people tend ter go down with colds and flu and all sort of things much more often than young people. They should know that.'

'I know that too, Dora. But I'm not that crabbed up yet. I'm still able.'

'You look it!' Dora said sarcastically. 'Your nose all red and sore from blowing. Yer look a real picture of 'ealth, I must say!'

'I'm fine now. I'm over the worst.' With no help

from you, came the thought. 'It'll soon go now.'

'And you could give it to the little 'uns.'

Victoria frowned. That was true, but Eveline and Connie had had the common sense not to attend their suffragette meeting while she'd been down with this cold. Instead Eveline had been popping in to see that she had everything she needed.

Dora had seen her frown deepen and quickly changed the subject.

'I take it you're coming to us fer Christmas Day? I expect you'll be over that cold by then. Christmas is a good three weeks away yet.'

Still rattled, Victoria gave a curt nod at this invitation, as offhand as she could have expected from Dora, a duty, not extended out of any great love. Maybe, as Dora said, she did tend to always want to be in the right, but Dora had no idea she was of the same ilk, had inherited the same streak of stubbornness, though Victoria hoped she wasn't so unforgiving as Dora and could at least see and sympathise with another person's point of view.

But yes, she'd go over to Dora and Len's for Christmas Day, if not quite with a good heart. She'd much rather have stayed in her own flat, all nice and comfortable in front of the fire and not have to make small talk or fear that a chance word could make them both fall out again. Still, it was best to keep the peace and she would try her hardest to be pleasant if Dora got all sharp and nasty over something or other.

Eveline felt concerned for Gran. That cold had lasted right through Christmas and into January.

As with many elderly people, something so trivial could easily turn to pneumonia and Gran had come very near to it.

It was February now and she still seemed under the weather. The last thing Eveline dared was ask her to have the children while she and Connie swanned off to meetings. She and Connie had gone back to taking over the care of each other's children while one went off. It was her turn to go but she'd let Connie go so she could pop over and see how Gran was and if she needed any errands done, taking both children with her, now Gran was no longer infectious.

'I'm a lot better now,' she was told. 'You don't have to feel you've got to come over. I'm not an invalid.'

'I like coming here,' Eveline said. 'You do like seeing Helena, don't you?'

'Of course I do. Now you've come to mention it, I'm quite well enough to take charge of her again when you go off to your meetings.'

But Eveline couldn't have that. She did miss her help and longed for the day when she and Connie would be able to go to their meetings together every Saturday as regularly as they used to, but it seemed those days were over.

There'd not been any more glorious processions since the summer. In fact autumn had been something of a damp squib, after everyone had been so full of optimism as well, the WSPU even cooperating for a while with the NUWSS in their insistence on non-violent demonstrations.

It hadn't lasted. When Prime Minister Asquith had made a surprise disclosure in November that the government intended to introduce a Reform Bill – in other words a Franchise Bill – that would not include women but give more men the vote, the WSPU immediately returned to their old militant tactics. Everyone knew Asquith's disclosure was designed to undermine the Conciliation Committee. Despite caution from Mrs Fawcett of the NUWSS, Mrs Pankhurst of the WSPU declared it open warfare.

Every suffragette, she said, must show by whatever means greater determination to convince government to change its mind. So had begun a spate of shop-window-breaking with its resultant arrests, Mrs Emmeline Pankhurst herself advocating acts of violence that included arson and even the planting of bomb material.

It was a dilemma for Eveline and Connie. Despite feeling obligated to do their bit, they now had their children to think of. If either of them went to prison, how would their children cope?

'I agree with Mrs Fawcett,' Connie said as she and Eveline guided the prams between early-evening shoppers in Bethnal Green Road, huddled into their collars and scarves against a chilly February wind. It was already dark at six o'clock; hissing acetylene lamps threw an eerie glow between the rows of market stalls.

Eveline stopped fingering a petticoat she'd have loved to buy but couldn't afford. They had come out to buy groceries and meat for the weekend, not to gawp at more frivolous things. She shot Connie a look. 'Mrs Fawcett? How can you? How far has she got with all her peaceful tactics and arguments? At least our union makes people sit up and take notice.'

'And turns all of them against us,' Connie retorted. 'Just as Mrs Pankhurst says. "If the public are pleased with what we're doing, it means we're not being effective." I think she's wrong. Breaking windows and setting fire to public places is turning the government against the very aims we're all trying to achieve. I still think the NUWSS is right not to make scenes.'

'That's being disloyal,' Eveline said, deftly manoeuvring her pram through a veritable barrier of shoppers.

Connie followed closely with hers. 'It's merely being practical.'

Eveline stopped by the pork butcher's that wafted an appetising aroma of pork dripping and boiled pigs' trotters. 'Then why don't you leave and join them instead?' she snapped. 'I'm going in here for a bit of pork for Sunday.'

'I'll come in with you,' Connie said after a short pause. They left the prams outside, then chose what they wanted, Eveline unable to help noticing that Connie's selection was a nice piece of loin whereas all her money stretched to was a bit of belly of pork which she would bone out at home and roll into something resembling a Sunday joint.

She had more things to think about than suffragettes right now. They had been striving since before the turn of the century. It was now 1912 and it sometimes felt women might never be given the vote, but she couldn't worry about that at the moment.

On Monday Albert was going for an interview

with a small engineering firm. He'd been studying so hard all this time and she was sure he'd get the job. It wasn't like these large companies that take only apprentices straight from school. The advertisement had spoken of training and at twenty-two Albert should be just what they were looking for. She could hardly wait for Monday to come.

He came in out of the snow, his broad face wreathed in a huge grin. He bent and planted a kiss on Helena's little face as she sat on the shabby sofa playing with a rag doll. Two years old in three months' time, Helena lifted a tiny hand and grabbed his nose.

'Honk-honk, Daddeee!' she chuckled in delight as he let her continue to pull at his nose.

'That's right – 'onk, 'onk goes the old 'ooter,' Albert chuckled back. 'And this hooter's frozen stiff,' he added, straightening up to look at Eveline as he took off his jacket, scarf and cloth cap to toss them on to an upright chair. 'It's blooming cold out there. Freezing brass monkeys!'

Eveline stood upright and tense, soupspoon in one hand, saucepan in the other, ready to dish up the stew that would warm his body famished by the cold.

'How did it go?' she asked. 'Did they like you? Did you get the job?'

'As far as I know,' he said. 'Said I was what they were looking for.'

'So you got it then.' Impatience was consuming her. 'What did they say exactly? Did they say you could start? Did they say when you could?'

This was wonderful news after all that hard

289

work, all the years of studying, yet he was holding back, having a game with her, tormenting her, holding out to the last minute before she lost her temper with him.

She noticed he'd gone suddenly very serious, his expression turning to one of concern. Without answering he came and sat at the table. She automatically began ladling the stew on to a deep plate while he tore into smaller pieces the bread she had put out for him to dip into the liquid. He was being exasperating.

'Well?' she prompted as he put the first morsel into his mouth.

'Well.' He swallowed the piece and then stopped eating. 'Well, there is a snag.'

Couldn't she have bet her life on it? Nothing ever came easy in this life, certainly not for people like them who worked so hard for a better life for themselves.

'What snag?' she queried.

'Well,' he said again. 'They seemed impressed with me, said I was bright and that they'd have no trouble taking me on as a trainee, a pupil. They thought I'd do well.'

'And?' she prompted again as he paused.

'And... I'll have to be trained of course and you have to pay for the training. It's quite usual,' he hurried on before she could say anything, 'At nearly twenty-two I'm too old to be an apprentice, but they'll train me and it's customary to pay for the training. After all–'

'How much?' she cut in.

His hesitation should have warned her. 'It's just under fifty guineas a year,' he said finally, adding quickly, 'But it may only be for a year if I put myself to it.'

'Fifty guineas?' she exploded. 'Where are you going to find fifty guineas?'

'I've been saving hard.'

'Not enough for that amount. You'll have to save for a lifetime to get that much together. And what about wages?'

She'd never felt so disappointed. She'd had such high hopes for him and he was bright. He'd worked so hard. He didn't deserve this sort of blow. No wonder he'd taken a time to tell her. It always came down to money, didn't it? Work and study as hard as he might, he would never realise his dream. People like him never did; they were trapped, as all poor people were. No chance of borrowing that much, not even from a backstreet moneylender who, despite knowing he would squeeze them dry, had more sense than lend that kind of money to the likes of Albert with no collateral to be seized.

There were her parents, business people, but as business people they knew he could never pay it back. She thought of Connie, who had savings. But they were her savings and she could never ask her to dip into them. She had her pride, and how could she put Connie into the embarrassing situation of having to refuse? They were stuck in their rut and that was that.

'I'm so sorry for him,' she told Gran when she went round to see how she was.

She hadn't meant to say anything, but the conversation had got round to how Albert's studies were coming along, and it had just come out.

'He's worked so hard, night and day, his nose never out of his books.'

Dismally she stirred the tea Gran had put in front of her, her spoon going incessantly round and round, her voice full of bitterness. 'If he'd been well off he could have gone to college in the evenings and studied properly. But no, people like us are stuck in a hole, no climbing out when no one ever throws you a rope. What chance has he got of bettering himself?'

She thought of Connie's husband, who had followed his father into the bank, his father having pulled strings for him. No matter that he'd started there in a humble capacity, he was there and on his way up. He and Connie would keep going up while she and Albert would stay right where they were, forever and ever!

Gran's voice broke through her thoughts. 'How much did you say it was going to cost?'

'Fifty guineas a year,' she answered absently, defeat and acrimony dulling her reply. 'And if it goes over another year, another fifty guineas.'

'And what about wages?'

'Oh, he'd get a wage, but what's the point? We haven't got the money. Even if we could borrow from a bank, it'd have to be paid back. No, it's just pie in the sky. He was so sure he'd be a mechanical engineer one day. Well, that's all over now.'

Gran stirred her own tea in silence. After a while she said slowly, 'And say if he *could* borrow it?' Despite her despondency, Eveline almost burst out laughing.

'Where from? Banks wouldn't even look at us.

Not even moneylenders would for that kind of loan, us with not one scrap of security to pledge against it. So what's the point of talking about borrowing? We've not even got anything worthwhile pawning for that kind of money.'

She thought she had never felt so bitter, not even when that Larry had abandoned her.

''Ave you talked to your mum about this?' Gran was asking.

Eveline came to herself. 'What?'

'I said 'ave you spoken to your mum about it?'

'I wouldn't humble myself, because I know what she'd say,' she replied with as much dignity as she could muster. 'Fifty guineas isn't a few pence, and you just can't go asking your family to lend that kind of money.'

'And what if you asked me?'

Eveline looked up sharply and blinked, feeling she must have misheard. But her grandmother was still speaking, and speaking very quickly.

'What if I lent it to you? You don't 'ave to pay me back in any certain time and I wouldn't ask for interest, which is what a bank or other lenders would do so that you'd never finish paying. They know what they're about, them people. With me, you could just pay me back bit by bit.'

When Eveline found her voice it was sharp with incredulity. 'I can't take your money, Gran!' Surely she couldn't have that amount around her, not even lying idle in savings.

'Why not? What use 'ave I got for money at my age, so long as I've got enough to get by on?'

'But it's your money.' Eveline fought to push away that sudden prick of eagerness to snatch up the offer that was vying with utter disbelief, hating this almost insidious desire that had crept in. 'I can't take your money.'

'Borrow,' Gran reminded her, smiling.

'Not that either.'

'Why not?'

'Because it's your money. I can't ever even borrow that kind of money off you. No, Gran, I wouldn't!'

Her grandmother gave a little chuckle, the creasing of her face giving it a younger look rather than adding to her age.

'Good Lord, child! I've just said what good is it to me at my time of life just so long as I've enough to see me comfortable? It's been sitting there doing nothing, just reaping interest, ever since your grandfather died, doing no good to no one. But now it can.'

'But it's what you expect to pass on to ... I mean, when you...' She hesitated, fearing to say the word. 'You know what I mean.'

Gran's smile told her that she understood exactly what she meant and her expression grew cunning. 'And 'ow do you know I'm not planning to leave a decent portion of what I've got to you anyway?'

'But...'

'All I'm doing is seeing that you and your 'usband – who's the nicest, most upright man I know – can benefit from it now, not when I've popped me clogs. Waiting until then ain't going to do you two any good at this very moment, is it? And it's this very moment what matters, not ten years from now or, God willing, twenty years.

294

I don't intend to go all that quick!'

Her chuckle was full of amusement, but Eveline could only stare in silence, her thoughts in turmoil. Seeing it, Victoria grew serious. She put out a hand across the kitchen table and laid it on one of her granddaughter's now lying tense and curled on its baize surface.

'You take my offer, gel. It'll do my 'eart good to see it put to some use. But one thing I want you to promise me – don't say anything to your mother about this, or to anyone. What they don't know won't grieve them. In fact there ain't no need to say anything about your Bert paying for 'is training. Just let them think he's got 'imself another job. I'd 'ave *given* it to you both quite readily, but giving causes embarrassment. To my mind lending's much kinder.'

Eveline's eyes were filling with tears. 'I just don't know what to say.'

'Just make sure he don't give up 'alfway through this training thing. It'd grieve me to see that happen and money wasted.'

'Oh, Gran, he won't!' she cried fervently, still unable to believe this was happening. Tears were trickling down her cheeks. 'It's always been his dream and he's worked so hard, too hard to ever let you down.'

'I know. I just thought I'd mention it.'

'But I don't know how long it'll take to pay it all back.'

'I told you, it don't matter. In time I 'ope he's earning a good enough wage for it to be no problem. It ain't like he'll be an apprentice what earns next to nothing. All I want is to see me favourite and nicest grandchild do well in life. You deserve it. You've 'ad enough 'ard knocks. He deserves it as well, after what he did for you. And I trust him.'

'He will, Gran.' She felt her grandmother's hand tighten on hers.

Somehow, trying to say thank-you seemed inappropriate, the words so trite that they would seem diminished in the uttering. The immensity of her gratitude was beyond words and her grateful hug felt just as insubstantial as she leaped up, Gran patting her shoulder as she clung to her.

'Now go and tell him he can pay for this training of 'is.' She gave Eveline a gentle little push. 'Off you go now. I'll sort it all out for you.'

Chapter Twenty

Fourteen months Albert had been with Smarts Ltd, his dream of becoming a qualified mechanical engineer realised. It had been a struggle trying to keep the family on his small wage during his training with Eveline bent on repaying Gran's generous loan, even though she insisted it wasn't necessary.

'But it *is* necessary,' Eveline stressed firmly. 'We've got you to thank for it and Albert can't show his gratitude enough.'

'That's all the thanks I need.'

'No, Gran. What you did was save his life. But for you, this would never have happened. He's got his dream. And all thanks to you.'

'Well, he worked hard for it too. And there's no need to pay it back.'

'But we're going to, every last penny, and as quick as we can. It's the least we can do to show our deep gratitude.'

But it wasn't easy. Paying back would take years, bit by bit, week by week watching the debt grow less by such a tiny amount despite Gran's refusal to consider interest. Sometimes Eveline felt it was a rope round her neck – a self-inflicted form of slow strangulation.

Her dream of a better flat had quickly faded as she viewed the small wage Albert had brought home whilst training.

He'd hand most of it to her for housekeeping and towards repaying the loan, keeping so little for himself that her heart bled for him. He'd even spoken of giving up cigarettes, his only pleasure, and she couldn't even remember when he'd last gone to a pub. Then there was Helena to feed and clothe. She was growing so fast it was hard to keep up with her. It had all cost money and sometimes she'd felt sick with worry.

But now, April 1913, Albert's training was behind him, though he intended to go on studying and become even better.

That Saturday after a week working as a proper engineer he came home, storming into the kitchen like some triumphant knight having floored his quarry, to empty his entire pay packet on the table as she turned round to greet him, his dinner all ready for him.

'Two pounds, five shilling and sixpence!' he blurted. *'Two pounds, five and six!'* That's only for starters. The more I study the better it'll get. I feel like bloody landed gentry! What'll we do with it?'

'Put some of it away,' she said promptly, her thoughts already flying to a nice flat in a few months' time. 'For a rainy day,' she said as an excuse.

He stared at her then laughed. 'There ain't going ter be no more rainy days from now on.'

'We've still got to pay back Gran's loan. We can give her a bit more now. It's only right.'

'Yes, it is,' he agreed, ceasing to laugh, but then brightened. 'But we'll still 'ave enough to live a lot better than we've done in the past. I can 'ave a beer when I want and not worry about spending on fags. I might even be able to afford a decent suit, not that second 'and stuff we've 'ad to get off stalls. And our Helena can 'ave nice dresses from proper shops.'

She loved the way he said *our* Helena as if she were his own child. It wrung her heart that she'd still not fallen pregnant yet. But there was still time. Helena was coming up to three; her birthday was next month and they had been scrimping to get her a cheap little toy for her birthday. Now they could buy something nice. Just so long as when another child was born, the affection he'd had for Helena wouldn't fade in preference for a child of his own loins.

'And you,' he went on, his round, brown eyes shining. 'You can 'ave a lot more nice things.' Since leaving his job behind a counter his speech had roughened again, but she didn't care.

'I'm happy with what I've got,' she said, but her mind was on putting away a bit each week towards the rent of a nicer flat, her heart's desire.

Albert grimaced. 'I've 'ated seeing yer scrimping and scraping ter look decent. Now yer can buy something really nice for yerself.'

Eveline laughed in sheer pleasure, viewing the coins spread across the kitchen table. Yes, a dress, new hat, another pair of stockings, a few bits of underclothing, she'd start putting a bit away each week from the better housekeeping, dividing it between three tins – one for clothing for herself and Helena, one to paying back the rest of Gran's generous loan and one towards the day they'd move into a new flat as good and nicely kept as

Connie's. She would try not to let the feeling of superiority it would give her show, though it was already creeping in, as close and loving towards Connie as she was.

Connie stood in the centre of the as-yet empty Finnis Street flat.

'Eveline, I'm thrilled to bits for you.'

It was said with genuine pleasure that made all sense of superiority melt into humility. 'It's not as nice as yours,' she said quickly. 'I'd have liked it to have been higher and have all the views you've got.'

A third-floor flat. There hadn't been a lot of choice really, since few were willing to exchange to a basement; it could have meant waiting months for a transfer. This flat had come up suddenly, its elderly tenant having died. It had been the only one on offer and Eveline had felt she couldn't wait much longer, so eager was she to get out of her dingy old letting.

Excitement clutched at her every time she glanced around at this new place. In the next block to his mother and brother, Albert had said. 'I can keep an eye on 'er. With me brother courting, out most evenings, I can pop in there any time.'

With Wilmott Street separated from Finnis Street by the school, he'd never had time before to chase over there, with his studies meaning him wasting time walking even that small distance. Now he was happy, so long as he didn't start spending all his time with his mother, Eveline thought, perhaps a little unkindly.

Connie was saying, 'Except that you won't have so many flights of stairs to climb as I,' and for the first time Eveline realised the difficulty one had with a small child and a pushchair or pram.

She thought of the three flights she must now climb. In her basement flat all she'd had to do was ease Helena's pram down the eight shallow steps, often leaving it outside the door. Here there'd now be three flights to struggle with. How much worse was it then for Connie? Along with lots of mothers she had solved the problem by carrying the child up first, leaving her secure in her highchair while she'd go back down for the lightened vehicle.

'Still, she is getting older,' Connie said. 'Eventually I won't need to go through that chore.'

Often several empty perambulators would be left unattended inside the entrance, getting in other people's way. At times it caused quite a few angry words among tenants.

'Maybe one day,' she went on, 'George will get another promotion and you never know, we might even be able to find ourselves a nice little house.'

As she left, Connie's thoughts strayed to the fine house her parents owned, with staff, and a motor car driven by a chauffeur. She thought often about them, comparing their lifestyle with her own. What if she hadn't met George? Her life would now be rather like theirs, with a lovely home and servants. She would never have known hardship or the misery of her separation from them; her father would still dote on her no doubt, and on his granddaughter. But she wouldn't have

301

had Rebecca. She might have had a son, or not have had any children. She wouldn't have known the joy of loving George, and to even think of Rebecca never having been born made her go cold. One small thing, such as meeting a stranger on a train, changes so much in life.

Wheeling Rebecca along the street past Eveline's grandmother's block, turning into Three Colt Lane and then into her own street, she thought the whole time of her family and bitterness settled in her breast at all the small hurts that had occurred since Father had told her to leave.

She'd had a letter from her sister Verity earlier this year, the first in over a year. 'I do wish Father would try to forgive you,' she had included, even now after all this time ignorant of the pain those few words had caused.

Married now, Verity and her husband had a fine house, but it seemed money did not always bring happiness. Last year she had given birth to a stillborn son. She herself had been terribly ill. But not one word of it had reached Connie until this year, and it was hurtful; her own mother had decided not to convey the sad news to her. Verity's eventual letter had said Father had been filled with grief at losing his first grandson, having looked forward to being a grandfather! She had almost torn her sister's letter to pieces in anger. How could he not acknowledge that he was already a grandfather? How could he spurn a little child, his own granddaughter?

She had written back to Verity in case she had wondered why she hadn't sent her condolences at the time, saying how sorry she was about her loss, that she'd had no idea and to please keep in touch, but so far there had been no reply. Out of a sense of duty she had also written to Mother, again receiving no reply. Remembering Mother's previous cold welcome she had kept away. But so many times her parents' faces floated through her head, together with those of Verity and her younger brothers, causing such pain as to bring her to tears – tears which she would wipe swiftly away in suppressed fury before turning her mind to other things.

Apart from her little family's needs, *other things* meant concentrating on suffragette news. Despite all efforts, all the promises and negotiations, they were as far away from women's suffrage as ever. It was so disheartening at times and sometimes it felt that even their leaders who strove so hard to keep everyone's spirits up were losing heart.

It showed in the dissension between the different unions, especially between the WSPU, who still claimed that strong-arm tactics constituted the only argument men understood, and the NUWSS, who still insisted gentler negotiation with parliament was the only way. She still wondered if they weren't right.

'I'm not at all happy with the way our union carries on,' she said to Eveline. 'All this violence hasn't brought us any nearer to getting the vote. I do wonder if I shouldn't have gone over to the NUWSS.'

'They've got no further than us for all their peaceful means,' snapped Eveline.

She could snap at times. Connie had put it down to frustration living in that horrid little basement of hers and hoped she might now become more relaxed in her new flat. 'The government just cocks a snook at them,' Eveline continued. 'At least we make them sit up and take notice.'

'By cutting telephone wires?' Connie reminded her as they drank coffee in Eveline's new kitchen. 'Smashing windows, burning empty houses, throwing acid on golf courses. It merely turns the public against us, makes parliament even more determined not to give in to us.'

'One day we *will* achieve our goal, you'll see,' Eveline repeated for the umpteenth time, as if that was argument enough. It always irked Connie.

'How can we when all they see is our apparent irrational behaviour? We are seen as incapable of dignified argument. All we seem to be achieving is to make fools of ourselves.'

'Such fools as they still put in prison and force-feed as soon as they go on hunger strike! Such fools that they're so scared of any being hailed as martyrs, they're now releasing them as they weaken and as they recover take them back into custody to start the whole thing all over again. It's brutal. Only those who've been through it know just how brutal.'

That always hit home; it evoked the memory of Connie's father leading her away, in front of all those willing to go to prison for their beliefs. She'd fall silent, as ever putting an abrupt end to the argument.

It happened this Sunday morning as she and Eveline walked in the warm sunshine with their girls in Victoria Park. This time, remembering how she'd let her father control her, yet when she'd rebelled he'd turned her out, her fingers tightened around little Rebecca's hand, so tight that the toddler, nearly two and three-quarter years old now, protested, 'Oh, Mummy, hurting me!'

'I'm sorry, darling,' she burst out instantly and, for her own peace of mind, turned her thoughts to what Eveline had been saying.

She still felt she was right. Peaceful negotiations had to be the more sensible way. But she was learning to keep her opinions to herself with Eveline so set on militancy although with a child to look after, Eveline didn't dare join in the violence, risking being sent to prison again.

Though there'd been no more grand processions since last summer, there'd been plenty of action, some of it quite amusing. A group of women in Manchester had locked Labour Party delegates in their conference hall, others had disrupted party members' speeches with catcalls. Some was not so funny – arson attacks, stone-throwing; in February Emmeline Pankhurst admitted responsibility for setting a bomb at Lloyd George's villa at Walton Heath golf course. The thing had exploded only twenty minutes before workmen were due to arrive. Guerrilla warfare, she was calling it. Connie could only see it as irresponsible.

There'd been counter-violence from the public: women were spat on, rough-handled, their clothing torn. Connie wanted none of it. Not any more. She'd attend her benign little meeting in George Street, hand out leaflets, sell suffragette news-sheets and even speak on street corners, but not resort to violence.

It was hopeless trying to air her views to Eveline, and perhaps it was just as well that they had their families to think about now, keeping them away from the more aggressive side to these campaigns.

But she did realise how deep Eveline's feelings went over this Cat and Mouse Act, as it was being called, when hunger strikers released from prison to recover their strength for a few days were taken back into custody with no remission of sentence. She'd felt more or less the same way over a recent episode when one of their foremost activists, Miss Dudley-Cambourne, a middle-aged spinster, recently released from prison while on hunger strike, came to speak to them. The woman had looked so pale and weak, having pushed herself to attend the meeting, and had been hailed a hero. She was rearrested even as she left that meeting, having to be helped gently down the steps to the street by a fellow member.

Connie remembered how appalled and sickened she'd felt seeing her conducted away, a small figure held up between two burly policemen, hardly able to stand much less walk at their pace.

She'd cringed to think of that poor woman again going through that ordeal, knowing the brave woman would never give in; an indomitable spirit burned in that frail body. Although the ordeal would stop short of ending her life – the last thing the authorities wanted was to be vilified by the press – it could cause irrevocable harm for the rest of her days, even shorten them.

Of course Connie felt as strongly about these cat and mouse tactics as anyone, but to her secret shame could only guess what it must be like while Eveline, having had a taste, had never forgotten it and to this day remained touched by it. But she did miss those spectacular marches. She told Eveline so as they walked their daughters to Victoria Park that first Sunday in June.

'I still think it was the only way to really impress the government.'

'I don't!' Eveline said. 'We're no further on than we ever were, still pleading to be taken seriously, still taken for silly women making trouble.'

Connie wanted to snap back that violence wasn't helping either, but held her tongue for the sake of friendship and walked on silently beside her.

With no response from Connie to her comment, Eveline lifted her gaze to the tranquil blue sky, her thoughts turning to how well she felt with the world lately. She'd found a new status – her nice flat, a few bits of new furniture instead of shabby second-hand stuff. Admittedly they were having to pay weekly for it so it wasn't exactly theirs but it felt like it. She now had sunlight pouring into her new home, making her feel she could breathe at last.

She'd invited Mum and Dad; Mum had looked around approvingly, and had even played with Helena, as any good grandmother should, if only for a moment or two.

Most of all she felt more on a par with Connie; the old jealousies were now dying away. She looked at their two toddlers a little way ahead, holding hands and laughing at whatever two-to-three-year-olds laugh about. They'd become such close companions they could easily have been sisters, both of them with fair hair though Helena's was the darker by a shade or two.

Eveline lifted her chin proudly, pleased to note that her daughter was just as nicely dressed these days as Connie's, her strong little legs peeping out from beneath the pale blue frock, her pretty face framed by a frilled bonnet bought from a proper shop rather than from a second-hand stall.

She too could now dress as well as Connie, as far as money allowed. Her well-fitting brown tweed skirt and fully lined Japsilk blouse with its pleated yoke and high neck and turn-back cuffs may not have been from the best shop in the world, but one could ape the wealthy well enough these days. The blouse had cost six shillings and nine pence and the tweed skirt ten shillings. They were for Sunday best only or when she and Connie took their children for an airing in the park. A bit extravagant on Albert's wages maybe, but worth it.

She'd not told him how much it had cost. He'd thought she'd got it all off a Petticoat Lane stall and marvelled that she'd found something so nice and apparently so cheap. But a white lie did no harm and she'd seen that he hadn't gone short on good meals, although she herself had done without for a while. And she felt justified in having such a nice outfit that pleased him.

Wednesday evening George looked up from reading the *Evening Standard* to glance across from his armchair to Connie sitting in hers, busily knitting a cardigan for Rebecca. 'I've just been reading that one of your suffragettes tried to kill herself today.'

The click of Connie's knitting needles came to an abrupt stop and she looked sharply up at him. 'What?'

'It says here,' he glanced again at the paragraph and began to quote, '"At today's Derby a young woman ran on to the course and fell under the King's horse Anmer, sustaining an injury to her head and was taken to hospital." They've a picture of it here.'

Connie let her knitting fall on to her lap as he handed the paper to her. Apart from a blurred photo there was little more to read except that the woman's name was quoted as Emily Wilding Davison. It was a dramatic picture, horse and jockey lying on the ground, the woman's curled body nearby. Connie just hoped she hadn't been too hurt.

The rest of the week she glanced through George's newspaper but nothing more was said and she guessed the woman must have recovered. But on the Sunday they learned that Emily Davison had died of a fractured skull without having recovered consciousness.

Apparently she had told no one of her intention, but it was obvious she had meant to do what she did by running straight out in front of an oncoming horse racing towards her at top speed. In her jacket were found two folded WSPU flags. It could only have been an act of martyrdom and Saturday the fourteenth of June was already being set aside for a huge funeral procession for her.

As with every branch across the country, the

one in George Street convened a special meeting. Everyone wanted to represent their branch and Connie and Eveline were no exception. It was important to everyone to show respect to a brave young woman. Though the government saw it as a mere suicide – Emily Davison was reported to have apparently attempted suicide the year before by jumping from a balcony in Holloway prison – to everyone else it was the ultimate sacrifice to bring women's fight for freedom to public attention. To them all it was martyrdom. Her name would live on forever.

With only so many to be chosen from each branch for the cortège, neither Connie nor Eveline were included. Eveline was especially put out and Connie knew why. As an ex-prisoner she'd expected to be picked. That she wasn't made Connie feel not smug but relieved, not having to go through the humiliating experience yet again of being excluded from the prisoners group.

They were told that only those with no family commitments would be there, keeping the numbers down and the cortège sober and unostentatious, for this would be no procession of protest with bands and banners but a solemn farewell to a brave and honorable comrade.

'We can still go and watch it pass,' Connie consoled, feeling sensitive.

She saw Eveline hesitate for a moment then shrug, and was relieved to see her finally nod her agreement.

Chapter Twenty-one

It was a funeral procession as never before seen except perhaps for royalty, the crowds that had come to watch the cortège pass also as large as any there would have been for royalty.

Sometime after two o'clock that Saturday, Eveline and Connie stood among a subdued crowd as the procession came into sight, led by the white figure of Charlotte Marsh carrying a huge gold cross. Silent masses parted as she made her way, men even doffing headwear as the cortège passed along its route to St George's Church in Bloomsbury.

A contingent of ex-hunger strikers walked beside Mrs Pankhurst's empty carriage – with insensitive ill-timing she had been rearrested as she left in deep mourning to join the cortège. With Christabel Pankhurst exiled in France, only Sylvia Pankhurst was left to do honour.

As the hunger strikers passed, Connie saw Eveline's face become tight at not having been included, but it was obvious that only a handful could be selected from all those who'd suffered, not once like her, but many times. The look soon faded as tears filled her eyes at the sight of the coffin, draped with purple velvet embroidered with silver arrows, looking so lonely on its open carriage drawn by four black horses with their black-clad grooms. Beside it women in their white dresses and black sashes, carrying madonna lilies, stood out stark. Some way behind came several carriages and taxicabs holding wreaths and flower tributes from all over the world.

Connie heard a tremulous sigh come from Eveline at the sight of close friends and family walking mournfully behind, faces inscrutable in grief, the dead woman's half-brother Captain Davison with bowed head.

'Oh, the poor things,' she heard Eveline whisper and knew that she thought no more of the honour it would have been to be included there today.

It was a bigger procession than expected with hundreds of women, not all of them in white, carrying madonna lilies or laurel leaves. There was a purple banner with the words of Joan of Arc: FIGHT ON AND GOD WILL GIVE THEE VIC-TORY! Some were in black or purple, some held bright red peonies; later the *Daily News* spoke of crimson being for sacrifice, purple for loyalty and white for purity, which seemed fair comment. But the bands were a surprise. Despite playing solemn and muffled tunes, they were a splash of colour in all this sombreness, a military band in scarlet and yellow and another in scarlet, as well as the red and blue robes of women graduates, their hoods silver and gold or blue and purple.

Following were columns of the Woman's Freedom League, Church Leagues, the Men's Leagues, even representatives of the Gas Workers' and Dockers' Union, the General Labourers' Union, and several other unions.

'I didn't realise how well we were supported or that we were so well thought of,' Eveline said with awe as the cortège moved on out of sight and the crowds began quietly to disperse.

It hadn't all been quiet. A woman not far from where Connie and Eveline stood had rushed out from the crowd shouting, 'Down with votes for women!'

Trying to grab at a banner she'd been apprehended for breach of the peace – ironic when many of those she'd tried to attack had themselves been arrested for the same thing. Another incident they heard later of one man calling out, 'Keep your hats on!' but it seemed few had taken notice of him.

Eveline was quiet with her own thoughts as they left. In an odd way she was almost glad not having been asked to walk with the hunger strikers. In comparison to what she had endured, these women who had faced it time and time again and never flinched were beginning to put her paltry few days of defiance to shame. In fact she rather wanted to forget it. It was a long time ago. And being singled out to walk with them whenever there was a procession was beginning to come between her and Connie.

The next time they asked her to join a prisoners' pageant she would decline. Continuing friendship with Connie was far more important.

There didn't look like being a next time, however. As summer passed and the year progressed it seemed the steam had gone out of the suffrage campaign. No processions had been planned, though in July there had been what was called the Women's Pilgrimage organised by the NUWSS, with large numbers of women following eight routes spread across England, but while many looked to complete an entire route, others joined only for a certain distance before leaving. Some of the old excitement and pageantry had been lacking. Newspapers giving sketchy accounts of it published pictures of women with sun-browned faces, wearing stout walking shoes, sensible clothing and haversacks. Very dull, Eveline thought.

'We couldn't have found the time anyway,' she remarked to Connie in September. It was the tenth, Rebecca's birthday. She was three and Connie had given a little party for her.

Having spread a two-month old copy of the *Women's Weekly* on the table to catch the cake crumbs she was brushing on to it, she'd become engrossed in a Swan & Edgar advert depicting that summer's slimmer style of women's wear: narrow, button-through skirts and jackets with vertical stripes, small bowler-type hats and low-crowned toques, straight blouses with no bust to speak of. A few years ago the full bosom was a feature of womanly pride. Figures were beginning to have no shape at all.

Carefully she folded the magazine over its debris of cake and bread crumbs – very little, with most children around here ready to eat the tablecloth itself, brought up as they were in near poverty with every crumb of food precious. Eveline knew from a life spent around here that to them even the small spread Connie had provided for Rebecca's third birthday was a feast. But apart from scoffing everything in sight, though it consisted of just a few tinned salmon sandwiches, jelly and the small iced cake Connie had made, they'd behaved very well.

Returning to the living room, Connie glanced at her as Eveline began collecting the empty plates. The half-dozen children of neighbours in Connie's block had gone home and Rebecca herself, tired from the party, had been put to bed a little earlier than usual, leaving Helena sitting on the floor playing with Rebecca's birthday present of a tiny cardboard doll's house.

'Lots of them used bicycles,' she said, taking up Eveline's remark about the pilgrimage.

'I expect they needed them,' Eveline said. The plates stacked, she gingerly sipped the tea Connie had poured for them. Connie's tea always came scalding.

'Going for miles and miles – going nowhere really. I can't see the point of it. Not at all like our old processions with their colour and music. Who was going to take that much notice of women traipsing around from one end of the country to the other? There didn't seem any purpose to it.'

It had seemed pointless. Admittedly, thousands of women had taken part in what was supposed to be a walking pilgrimage, but quite a lot had resorted to transport of one kind or another – bicycle, horseback, pony and trap, even the occasional motor car or small van lent to carry their luggage.

'More like an outing than a serious intention to attract the notice of the public or the government,' she scoffed and dismissed it. It was rather like some marvellous firework that had fizzled out. All that hard work they'd done had, it seemed, come to nothing.

Even so, there had been quite a few rallies in Hyde Park as thousands of the pilgrim women converged on London at the end of July. Some of the old verve took hold beneath the summery skies, the crowds that gathered surprisingly cheerful with no hostility whatsoever. Once again bands had played and banners had fluttered as the redoubtable, round-faced Mrs Fawcett addressed the Hyde Park crowds; an aeroplane had even dropped suffragette leaflets on the heads of the spectators, causing a sensation. But it hadn't lasted. With summer fading there were no more rallies and even WSPU activity appeared to be dying down.

Turning her mind from it, Eveline gathered up the tablecloth, stepping over Helena on her way to empty the cloth over the balcony's iron railings. The few crumbs floating on the air would cause no inconvenience to those living below. She came back, folding it absently, although Connie would want to wash it before putting it away, whereas she might have used it a couple of times more before it needed washing.

It had been a good little birthday. She thought of the passing years. In three months another year would be gone. How things had changed since first meeting Connie, a pampered, wealthy young woman and a girl from an entirely different walk of life. Eveline was amazed how Connie had adjusted to her world even to persuading the young man for whom she'd forsaken all to venture this side of London to be with her. The bond between her and Connie was of course their mutual interest in the suffragette movement. But one day they'd win and maybe Connie would sail off into the blue with her George to take up her old life of ease and plenty and forget all about her.

A passing thought but it suddenly made Eveline feel sad.

Connie and George had Christmas with her and Albert, in Eveline's new little flat where even the winter sun came in. She'd invited Albert's mum and his brother Jim, and Gran too, who needed only to walk the few yards from her block to Eveline's and remained sprightly enough for the three flights of stairs.

She'd climb her own two flights several times a week when she went shopping, with no trouble at all though she was in her seventies and fiercely independent. Eveline was so proud of her, still willing to have charge of the children at odd times despite them being energetic three-year-olds.

'They be'ave like little angels with me,' she'd say. 'Little 'uns always do when someone else looks after 'em. It's when they're with their mothers they start to play up. Lord knows why because it's from them that they get the smacks. Don't know for the life of me why. With me they're little angels.'

Even so, Eveline made sure not to put on her too often, she and Connie for the most part going back to looking after each other's daughters when attending the Saturday suffragette meetings unless something special was going on, and that hadn't been all that often this autumn.

It annoyed her that Gran was willing to take on both children for those couple of hours while her mother couldn't offer to have her own grandchild for that short while. It had come to her ears that she had looked after both Tilly's and Fred's children on odd occasions, and it hurt even more that Mum could do that for her brother and sister and not her.

Boxing Day was spent at Mum's, Connie and George happy to cosily spend it on their own. Mum and Dad's house bulged with the whole family. Lenny, now twenty and courting a girl named Flossie, had invited her. May at nineteen also had a boyfriend, though he was with his own family, but she was talking of getting engaged in the New Year. With Eveline's three younger brothers, her married brother and sister, Fred and Tilly, and their family, it was quite a crowd, yet she could never feel at ease here any more.

Mum thought a lot of Albert but there was this invisible wall between Mum and herself that made her feel she'd never really been forgiven. Nothing said, but it was there. Maybe it was all in her mind but the rift seemed to have grown between her and her married brother and sister, Fred and Tilly, who'd so far not come nigh or by to see her new flat.

It was Gran, bless her, to whom she turned, Gran who was in most ways closer than her mother. Also, the fact that Gran had taken Connie under her wing helped a little to compensate Eveline for the frigidity of her mother and she readily accepted Connie's invitation to see in the New Year at her flat, in the hope that her presence would help take Connie's mind off her own family.

Nineteen fourteen came in on an ominous note, though Eveline along with everyone else took very little notice of Lloyd George referring on the first day of the New Year to a build-up of arms in Europe as insanity.

But of far more importance to British suffragettes was the rearrest of Sylvia Pankhurst three days into January under the Cat and Mouse Act. It caused rumblings or, as some put it, squeakings, referring to the Act rather than the suffragettes, the relative calm of last autumn ready to explode into riots of retaliation against it. In fact four days into February came reports of Scottish suffragettes burning down two mansions and later the same month Whitekirk Parish Church in East Lothian.

When Sylvia Pankhurst was again arrested in early March on her way to a demonstration in Trafalgar Square, the suffragettes there rose with renewed vigour. She and Connie were at the Trafalgar Square demonstration and when the news broke of Sylvia Pankhurst's rearrest, they were caught up in the pandemonium that broke out.

'If they think they're going to dishearten us by continually sending her to prison, they're much mistaken,' Connie yelled defiantly as they were pushed about by the packed throng. 'We're going to fight on until we win!'

Eveline had never heard such emphatic words from her. She certainly sounded a different Connie to the one who a few months ago had been championing the moderate NUWSS, but she had

319

to agree with her that the fight had to go on, especially when, a few days later, Mrs Emmeline Pankhurst was once more arrested in Glasgow.

'They're trying to make us leaderless,' Connie said grimly. 'But we'll always have other leaders to take up the sword in their place. They'll never break us, no matter how they try.' Again Eveline had to agree with her.

But when the news came of a Mary Richardson, a thirty-one-year-old journalist, who had entered the National Gallery with a meat cleaver under the noses of the attendants and hacked a masterpiece, the Rokeby Venus by Velazquez, causing irreparable damage, calmly stating as she was marched off by the police that she had tried to destroy the most beautiful woman in mythological history in protest at the government's destruction of Miss Pankhurst, the most beautiful character in modern history, Eveline had a feeling that this was taking militancy too far.

'It's one thing destroying property,' she confided in Connie, without sympathy this time for the woman arrested, 'but wonderful art you can't replace... She must be insane doing a thing like that.'

But it was soon setting off a chain of quite vicious militant deeds: British Museum cabinets smashed; a militant suffragette named Gertrude Mansell attacking Herkomer's portrait of Wellington in the Royal Academy; a bomb thrown at a London church, another destroying Yarmouth pier, and another attack on the Royal Academy damaging John Singer Sargent's portrait of Henry James.

Then in May came a concerted onslaught by a small army of women led by a frail-looking Emmeline Pankhurst in an attempt to break through a thousand-strong police cordon around Buckingham Palace in an effort to deliver a Votes For Women petition to the King following the defeat of an enfranchisement bill. Though more than fifty women were arrested, two thousand petitions with over a million names had so far been presented to Parliament but it seemed nothing was going to sway the members to even consider the women's pleas.

'At this rate I can't see us ever winning,' Connie said, her spirits at last taking a knock. But it seemed women's spirits refused to take any sort of knock as in June suffragettes set fire to yet another church, Wargrave Church in Henley, as well as disrupting services in many London churches.

On the Tuesday after Connie and Eveline attended their George Street meeting, Gran once again taking on the two children for a couple of hours, the police raided the offices of the WSPU and the next day arrested Sylvia Pankhurst for the eighth time whilst on a march.

'But for the children we could so easily have been in that,' Connie said. 'What if we'd been among those arrested, knowing the state we'd have put our daughters in? It doesn't bear thinking about.'

There had been a good many volunteers on Saturday for the march and they'd almost been swayed by the persuasive words from the speaker that day. It was only Eveline saying that they couldn't keep asking Gran to look after the children. With both their husbands at work and no one else to have them, neither wanted to go alone while the other looked after the two.

In the end they decided to wait for a Saturday march, feeling down and thoroughly out of it, annoyed that as mothers they were tied whilst others could do what they liked. Now, of course, it had been a blessing in disguise.

There was some kind of rally being planned for Sunday intended to be peaceful. Eveline spoke to Albert about it on the Friday. 'I never seem to join in anything these days,' she said. 'I really should be there, just for once.'

'What about Helena?' he asked, oddly obstructive.

'It'll be in the evening,' she told him, trying not to show annoyance. 'Helena will be in bed. It's nearly midsummer. The evenings are light. Connie is asking her George if it's all right with him.' Albert's face grew obdurate, his tone sharp, which wasn't like him. 'I don't think you should go.'

'Why not?' she said angrily.

'Things are getting a bit too nasty lately. Protest is one thing but all this bombing and settling fire ter things. You 'ave to think of Helena. If you went off and got yerself arrested, how's she going to cope?'

He was right of course, but it didn't please her being told in this way. She hated arguing with him just to get her own way, he was such a good man, and even after all these years she still felt she owed him a debt of gratitude for what he'd done for her in her darkest moments.

322

Even after all this time, she couldn't ever forget. The last thing she'd want to do would be to hurt him by her selfishness. But nature being what it was she felt sullen, especially when Connie told her the next day that George had given her permission to go.

As things turned out, there was no Hyde Park rally that Sunday. All plans were washed out by the worst thunderstorm in living memory. It raged over London like an Armageddon with several people killed as four inches of rain falling in three hours caused disastrous flooding.

Eveline, never happy with thunderstorms, crouched in a corner as the thunder cracked and roared simultaneously with blinding and continuous flashes of lightning, sheets of rain beating at the window panes threatening to break the glass. She thought of Gran all on her own in her flat but there was no way she could have gone out to keep her company.

After the storm it was obvious that Hyde Park would have been turned into a quagmire by all those feet, similar to the Mud March in 1907 when some thirty thousand women trudged through fog and slush until they'd more resembled mudlarks, their skirts and shoes covered in muck, a laughing stock.

No one wanted a repetition of that humiliation but by the end of the month, anything to do with the suffragette movement was threatening to be eclipsed by events beginning to take place in Europe.

George was one who found his interest pricked

by. it on Monday as he opened his *London & Manchester Daily News* during his brief midday break at his desk.

He'd have preferred to go home to eat, as Bert Adams did, working just around the corner to his. It would be nice to see a bit of Connie at midday to break up his working hours, but it took a good ten minutes by bus to get home from the City and another ten minutes getting back and that only if his bus arrived on time or wasn't too crowded to get on. Returning late would be frowned on; banks were very hot on punctuality and all in all it wasn't worth the anxiety. His father had always said, when he'd first been taken on, 'If you're punctual, no one notices. If you're not, everyone notices. Avoid being noticed for the wrong reasons, lad.'

Settling down to the cheese and pickle sandwich Connie had made for him this morning to be followed by an apple and a cup of tea in the three-quarters of an hour allowed for lunch, he acknowledged a slightly older colleague at the next desk, Mr Bertram – all employees were ad-dressed by their title – who said something about trouble in Europe and opened his own paper.

'Hmm,' he murmured absently across the desks at the headlines: ASSASSINATION OF AUS-TRIAN HEIR TO THRONE.

His eyes wandering to the sub-headings, he read aloud. '"Consort also shot dead. Two attempts with revolver after bomb fails. Warning of a plot disregarded by Archduke Franz Ferdinand".' Always something, isn't there!' he laughed, but George was already reading for himself.

Further down was the account of the assassin, a nineteen-year-old student named as Gavrilo Princip, darting out from the crowd as the Archduke Franz Ferdinand and his Duchess drove through the streets of Sarajevo in Bosnia. It was reported that on their way to the town hall a bomb was thrown but the Archduke had picked it up and thrown it into the road where it had exploded, injuring the occupant of a following car.

He had complained to the Burgermeister that he hadn't come to Sarajevo to have a bomb thrown at him. But on his return from the town hall a shot hit him in the neck, a second shot piercing his wife's stomach as she threw herself across him while trying to protect him, killing her instantly. The Archduke died ten minutes later.

George sighed and turned the page. There always seemed to be some conflict or other going on in that far-flung part of Europe. But page two was unrelenting, reporting that Serbia was said to have been at fault in not providing soldiers to guard the royal route and that if the country were found to be implicated in a plot, Austria could be expected to take strong action against her.

At that point Mr Bertram came over to ask if he fancied a beer in the pub next door before starting work again. It sounded tempting and, nodding agreement, George neatly folded his newspaper, slipped it into a lower drawer, and leaving his tea untouched followed Bertram – titles were dropped once outside – from the bank into the bright sunshine, plucking his bowler hat off the hatstand as he went.

Chapter Twenty-two

George felt worried and exhausted. It had been a day such as he had never known or wanted to know ever again. All the time his job had felt only a hair's breath from being taken from him as he began to flag. Had it gone on much longer he'd have walked out in frustration and really would have been given his notice. The bank manager himself had looked near to breaking point and one wrong word would have sent the unfortunate packing.

What with events in Europe on a knife's edge, the bank rate had suddenly risen to ten per cent. The Stock Exchange closed its doors and long lines of people queued outside the Bank of England, all seeking desperately to exchange bank notes for gold. With dire rumours flying around, more or less every bank had been in uproar, including his, small though it was.

As soon as he walked in through his front door he could see Connie had noticed how weary he looked. 'I should have guessed something like this would happen,' he said after he'd told her of the day he'd had.

She'd put his Saturday tea in front of him as he came to the table but he could only toy with it. 'I should have guessed,' he repeated. 'But like the rest of us blessed British public, I've watched Europe dissolving into anarchy this past month, us thinking we were untouchable, spectators. Yet we *have* been touched by it all. What if it gets worse and my job goes?'

Connie ceased nibbling on a Peek Frean biscuit she'd chosen to eat after her meal to regard him anxiously. 'It won't do that.'

'It could,' he replied as she got up to remove his cold, untouched lamb cutlet. 'What happens in the world will always rebound on us, banks, business, everything. I should have known good things never last.'

He should have seen it coming. He read the newspapers, watched it all building up. He ought to have known it wouldn't go away as one country after another began baring its teeth at its neighbour: the Vienna government demanding Serbia allow Austrian officials to investigate the plot to kill the Austrian heir to the throne; Serbia mobilising its army in retaliation; the Kaiser pledging support of Austria; Vienna declaring war on Serbia, Austria invading; the Czar mobilising; the Kaiser warning that if he did not cease, Germany would mobilise; his warning ignored, asking France for assurance of its intentions seeing that the French president had been on a recent state visit to Russia, then today's news that Germany had declared war on both Russia and France. All this had been happening with bewildering speed while the British Government had been preoccupied with the Irish question, merely offering to mediate in the Austrian crisis which the Kaiser took as British insolence.

Everyone here had thought that it would all blow over. But with the Kaiser declaring war on his cousin, the Czar, it didn't bode well for finance.

Connie was obviously searching her soul to cheer him. 'It's Sunday tomorrow,' she said, rather inadequately he thought. 'Try to make the most of it and rest and not worry, darling.' She came and dropped a kiss on his furrowed brow. 'I'm sure things at work will have calmed down by Monday.'

She was right. Everything had calmed; his branch had got back to normal, thank God. Apart from noting that the government had informed Germany that Britain would stand by its 1839 treaty guaranteeing Belgian neutrality and would protect French coasts, George breathed a sigh of relief that all seemed well and settled himself down to his normal work routine.

It was the third of August and a fine and sunny day.

While people in Britain slept, thousands of German troops had crossed the Belgian border in the early hours of Tuesday morning as a back door into France, defying the Treaty of London and despite the King of Belgium's refusal.

George awoke at seven thirty, got ready for work, and made his way into Bethnal Green station to find it seething with the news of Britain having declared war on Germany. Buying a paper, he reached his bank through cheering crowds, men waving hats in the air, some off to gather at Downing Street, others making for recruiting offices.

With the excitement transferring itself to him, George found the normally calm atmosphere of his bank gripped by as much euphoria as that outside, despite staff trying to do their best to contain themselves. It was hopeless to think of work with people rushing into the bank and out again, telling of crowds gathering outside Buckngham Palace and Downing Street. In the end employees and management alike gave up and George went home looking for calm and reason. What he found was Connie wringing her hands and saying she didn't want him to go to war and fight and maybe be killed.

'Don't worry, darling,' he said, trying not to chuckle. 'I'm not going anywhere. Besides it'll all be over by Christmas. That's what's being said.'

On Monday, six days after war being declared, Albert came home all agitated to say that more than half his workmates had left to join up.

'A dozen of 'em went off this morning ter enlist.' His good intentions to speak well had long faded. 'The factory's 'alf empty and Mr Smart says the place can't keep going with only a third of us there. There's only older blokes left, an' me an' another bloke, Stan Briggs.'

'He'll probably take others on,' Eveline suggested, but he shrugged.

'Where from? Everyone's joining up. Yer can't move in them recruiting offices. I've seen 'em. Stan's talking about going too.'

'Well, good luck to him,' Eveline remarked, but Albert was excited.

'I feel out of it, the only young one left there. I can't 'ave 'im thinking I've got cold feet. Anyway, it'll be over in a month once we've shown Germany it can't just walk into a neutral country and 'get away with it.'

Knowing what he was getting at brought cold fear. The assassination of that Austrian archduke had happened so far from home as to hardly concern her. Despite Albert reading out snippets from the paper about the bothers in Europe, it had still seemed too far away as she went about her chores in her new flat. Now, having him talk excitedly of joining up brought it all home.

The flat still felt new to her despite having been in it for over a year. She took pleasure in keeping it as spick and span as Connie kept hers. She had enough housekeeping now and had even opened a post office savings account, despite the fact that she was still paying off the money she owed to Gran, and she would buy bits and pieces for the home, each new little purchase a joy.

These last few days she'd felt like one suddenly set free as suffragette agitation ceased abruptly on Britain declaring war. The NUWSS promptly suspended all political activity and had begun setting up Red Cross centres and canteens to help Belgium refugees, with advice centres for those whose husbands had volunteered to fight. Their policy had always been a pacifist one whereas the WSPU had always been militant. But even they had laid aside the sword, turning their attention to East London privation caused by men rushing to join up, leaving wives and families to carry on as best they could without a man's support.

They too had begun setting up kitchens to feed the hungry. The East London Federation of Suffragettes, now called the Workers' Federation, had taken over the disused Gunmakers' Arms pub as a clinic and a day nursery for the children of women now forced to go out to work to keep their families.

It made Eveline think: if Albert were to enlist his wages would stop, and he too would be on only a serviceman's pay, she on a pitiful allowance. She felt faintly angry. Let single men enlist but surely his family should come first.

She thought too about Connie. What if George was having the same idea as Albert? That Monday when Albert had gone back to work after his midday dinner she went across to her. She found her excited.

'Have you seen this morning's paper? It says the government is releasing the remaining eleven women left in prison. And they're not going to pursue any others expecting to be rearrested under that beastly Cat and Mouse Act of theirs. Eveline, we've won! We've triumphed!' She ushered her into her living room. 'Pity it had to take Britain going to war for us to achieve our goal. It would have been lovely if we could have done it all on our own.'

She seemed oblivious to the chance of George enlisting and Eveline decided to say nothing about Albert, glad to go home and escape Connie's exuberance. Albert came in soon afterwards, surprising her, his expression growing cautious when she asked why he was back home so early.

'I've been thinking about this recruiting business all morning,' he said, avoiding her searching eyes. 'In the end I decided I couldn't be left out. I left work early and went with Stan to our local recruiting station to–'

He broke off as she gasped, her worst fears realised. The next moment he'd cut through her horrified protests. 'I had to, Ev. I couldn't be the only one not to put me name down. I couldn't 'ave looked the others in the eye.'

She began to stutter another protest, but was again interrupted.

'Look, it's only going ter last a few months, maybe just a few weeks once we've shown Germany we won't put up with 'em cocking a snook at us, walking inter someone else's country what we swore to protect.'

'But you're not a soldier,' Eveline cried, finally getting a word in. 'Let the regulars do the fighting if there is any. It's *their* job, not yours. Albert, didn't you stop to think what you were doing, leaving us here on our own?'

Her heart was beginning to thump, making her feel sick.

'You'll be orright,' he soothed. 'It'll only be for a little while. I'll be 'ome again before yer know it.'

'But what about your job?' She wanted to tell him that even in a small skirmish he could be the one to be killed, but all she could think to say was what about his job. It was like something being acted out in a play.

'They promise to keep our jobs open.' He was even smiling. What did he have to smile about? She hated his obvious excitement.

'Even they know it ain't goin' ter last long. But I've got ter go with the others, don't yer see? I know a soldier's pay ain't much but we've got savings now and I'll be 'ome again before yer know it, and we'll soon save up again.'

'But we still owe Gran.' How could she think of Gran and paying her back when Albert was going away, perhaps walking into danger?

'She did say she wasn't anxious ter 'ave it back that quick,' he said evenly, relaxing before this domestic concern. 'I'm sure she'll stretch a point for a few months. When I'm back, we can pick up where we left off with my firm saying they'll keep me job open for me, fer everyone what's volunteering, and they're good sort, is Smarts. They'll be taking on older blokes, temporary like. Don't worry, Ev, it'll be over in no time. I won't be in any danger.'

He was like a little boy with the promise of an adventurous holiday from school and all the while Eveline's insides were still tight with the fear of what could happen to him, but what could she say? She who'd fought for a cause all these years, attending her branch meetings, walking the streets with a sandwich board, selling copies of *The Suffragette* on street corners, often with rude remarks from male passers-by, going on rallies and marches and protests and putting herself in danger, expecting him to understand, to sacrifice normal family life for her cause, how could she protest now it was his turn to fight against injustice?

She tried to force her heart to stop its sickening thumping. 'I suppose I can't hold you back with everyone else joining up.'

She thought of George Towers. He was the steady sort, worked in a bank, not the type to get all excited and do something silly just on a whim. Connie was lucky to have someone like George. Yet wouldn't every man feel it his duty to fight for his country with this crisis hanging over their heads?

Moments later she was scolding herself for condemning Albert. She should feel proud that he was doing something heroic. Suddenly she felt strong, not happy, but strong. Would Connie feel as strong if George went? Connie who relied on him for everything, who these days seemed to have everything, comparatively speaking? If he did go... She almost felt sorry for her.

'I've been to volunteer,' Bertram Miller whispered across from his desk on the Tuesday. 'First thing this morning before work. Thought I'd never get away in time to get here, so many chaps there, crowds of 'em!'

George looked up from the bank receipts he was counting. 'Have you told Mr Crossman?'

'Not yet,' came the whispered reply.

Mr Arnold Crossman was the bank manager, a man looking earnestly for promotion to manager of a much larger branch and making sure his staff helped by behaving soberly and sensibly at all times and seeing that no mistakes occurred or that any slightest error was put right before it reached the ears of Head Office.

'I'm plucking up courage to tell him,' Bertram went on, still in a whisper, which made George smile – a man willing to fight for his country yet scared out of his wits by his boss.

At the same time he felt a sudden sense of

loneliness. He and Bertram Miller had become good colleagues over the years, sharing a beer or two in a nearby pub and something stronger prior to bank holidays. The rest of the staff, including the assistant manager, consisted of four older men, an office boy, a young lady on the switchboard and several in the typing room. It didn't bear thinking about being the only young man to be left here.

At lunchtime, instead of eating his sandwich, he hurried down to a hastily set-up recruiting place he remembered passing the day before and added his name to a lengthy list, returning to bide his time before conveying his actions to his manager.

When he told Bertram what he'd done, the man leaped up, suddenly a soldier and afraid of no one, to shake his hand, congratulating him and nodding at Crossman who'd poked his face around his open office door at this interruption to the calm of his branch. Obviously Bertram Miller had told him of his deed. And now another of his staff was off. In a way George felt utter relief at not having had to break the news himself.

Eveline opened her door to a distraught Connie who almost fell into her arms.

'Eveline, what am I to do? George is going off to war!' She whimpered as Eveline held her, unsure how to cope with this sudden need for comfort. 'He told me last night and we had the most awful row. He'd gone to the recruiting office yesterday afternoon and signed up. He's been doing so well at the bank. He'll never get promotion now, leaving to go off to fight. And he could be killed. He gave no thought whatsoever that he'll be leaving behind a wife and child. Not even consulting me. How could he?'

Eveline, with her arms round her, patted the heaving shoulders. 'My Albert's signed on too,' she said quietly.

The words brought home all that had been bottled up inside her since Albert's news, something she'd not dared to confront until this moment – fear for his life, how she and Helena would fare without him and the sudden transition from the certainty of a cosy future to no future at all should he die in battle.

Came the realisation that tomorrow he'd be off – no more coming home at midday for his dinner, no more sitting in his armchair opposite hers of an evening, reading his paper. No more making him cups of tea or evening cocoa, agreeing it was time for bed, kissing goodnight, lying next to him and feeling his body warm against hers, the comfort of his arms about her when they made love. No more waking up and shaking him, getting his breakfast, seeing him off to work. No more...

Seconds later she too was sobbing her heart out, her head resting heavily against Connie's.

The British Expeditionary Force had been the first to be sent into Belgium and to stop the enemy reaching France. Everyone felt they would soon turn the Kaiser back from his intent and avidly followed newspaper reports of the bitter struggle being waged for the Belgian town of Mons.

The BEF were mostly seasoned soldiers, and raw recruits like Albert would be trained at home before being sent out, for which Eveline breathed a sigh of relief.

Her relief soon turned, like everyone else's, to disbelief as the news came of heavy British losses, the British Expeditionary Force compelled to pull back before overwhelming enemy numbers. It seemed the German forces had been halted only temporarily. It was disheartening but people at home were convinced the BEF retreat too would be only temporary.

'Consolidating their position afore their big push,' said the seventy-nine-year-old husband of one of Eveline's neighbours, and he should know, as an old soldier and all, a veteran of the Crimean War. 'Wounded in the Battle of Inkerman, y'know. No, that's what they's doin', consolidating their position.'

By the end of August Belgium had been practically overrun, the Germans crossing the Meuse, the French forced to retreat to the Somme, the last barrier before Paris. Alarm spread through England as well as France as bloody battles raged along an ever-shifting line all the way to Alsace in the south. Thoughts of teaching this enemy a lesson dissipating, bleak faces took on resolute looks, determined not to let this unbelievable defeat get them down.

After her first outburst of weakness Connie had rallied amazingly, and Eveline assumed it had been the shock of George enlisting without even telling her. While she had suppressed her own shock, Connie's had come out in a gush. She

337

wondered who'd been the better served.'

'The WSPU have set up a canteen in Cheshire Street for the Belgian refugees coming here, and the poorer families of men who've gone to fight,' Connie told her a few days later. 'I've volunteered to help. I really do need to do something to keep my mind occupied with George gone.'

'What about Rebecca?' Eveline asked immediately.

Connie had set her mind working. The suffragettes, no longer at odds with the government, had already begun to turn their energy to helping it. In fact Mrs Pankhurst had suddenly become a political champion of the very people she'd once opposed, speaking of 'the common scourge!' the WSPU committed to mobilising women to making recruitment speeches, handing out white feathers to young men not yet in uniform, manning canteens, organising jumble sales for the poor left to shift for themselves, and sewing centres where women could knit mittens, scarves and balaclavas for their fighting men – in case the war did go into winter rather than the few months being predicted.

The George Street branch had now closed, many of its members ready to turn their hands to whatever was required of them elsewhere. She could do that too, and like Connie help combat her own fears for Albert's safety if he were sent to the front. But the idea of her and Connie taking turns again to look after each other's daughters didn't appeal that much and she didn't want to start imposing on Gran again.

'I asked them about Rebecca,' Connie said.

'They didn't mind my bringing her so long as she's no bother. I shall give her plenty of things to play with to keep her occupied. She's well behaved.' That was true. 'All that matters is that we do our bit. It's ironic really – a month or so ago we were reaping the government's condemnation, now we have its blessing.'

Connie's laugh as she said it was a deal more brighter than it had been for days. Eveline smiled but her mind was more on the reaction to another child being toted along, the place turned into some sort of nursery. One might be all right, but more than one? 'Couldn't it be dangerous,' she said, 'if there were children running about with hot food being served?

'It isn't only a canteen,' Connie said brightly. 'The workroom is in the back for us to knit or sew. That's what I'm going to do. I'd be no good pouring soup into bowls and cutting up mounds of bread and margarine, and I couldn't bear handling other people's slops and uneaten food.'

Despite her years in the East End much of the fastidiousness of her upbringing still clung to her.

'It will be so nice just chatting about ordinary things rather than about processions and protests,' she went on enthusiastically. 'I'm going along this afternoon. Perhaps we could go together.'

Eveline nodded readily and just hoped they wouldn't object to another little four-year-old being there.

A few evenings later, not long after Prime Minister Asquith had called for another 500,000 men to sign up for the army which would put at least a million men in the field, Eveline opened her door to a firm knock to find Albert standing there.

For a moment she couldn't speak. Seeing him in uniform, grinning, looking self-assured and different, sent her hands to her lips. Then finding her voice in a squeal of delirious joy, she threw herself into his arms.

Managing to get himself into the flat and calming her ecstatic tears, he was able to tell her that some recruits were being allowed to live at home if they were within a certain travelling distance of their unit and that he had managed to wangle himself on the list. 'I'll be getting two shillings a day board and lodging,' he said proudly, 'on top of me one shilling a day.'

Eveline knew how little his army pay was, but hearing it spoken was humiliating after the financially glowing future that had been promised for them. She'd refrained from asking how on earth she and Helena were going to survive on an army wife's allowance when he'd first told her what he had done, and she didn't mention it now, only too glad to have him here.

The last thing she wanted to do was for him to worry about her. Hard enough avoiding him seeing how she felt about the situation in which his eagerness to sign up had left her. While she hated feeling that the blame lay at his feet, it nagged at her.

There was only one thing for it, she'd have to look for a job. She had a skill with figures and could probably get a job easily enough, but what

340

about Helena? She could ask Gran, but Gran wasn't getting any younger even if she still seemed as sprightly as ever. Albert should never have put this burden on her. And yes, she did blame him, but she loved him and having him home, if only for a few hours at night, if only for a short while, was all she could ask at this moment.

Making love that night felt like one of the best things that had ever happened to her, except that come morning it was marred by one thought; what if she conceived now? Albert would not be here – being boarded at home was only a temporary thing – so she would have to manage all alone and with little money to feed her and Helena, much less another mouth. Wouldn't it be just ironic if after all these years not conceiving, when it had been so easy that first time, she should do so now? Sometimes she felt fortune never turned its face to her for long.

Chapter Twenty-three

As she predicted, Albert's presence at home didn't last long, just three weeks, with part of that time spent round his Mum's.

Saying goodbye again was far worse the second time round. She had counted her blessings when Connie's George hadn't yet got leave but she now wondered if Connie hadn't been the more fortunate in not having to go through the intensified pain of saying goodbye a second time.

When he left this time, the loneliness was almost more than she could bear and she sank herself into her canteen work, dishing out the bowls of soup and pieces of bread, mugs of tea and, something the fastidious Connie cringed at doing, gathering up empty bowls and mugs to wash in quickly-greying, often lukewarm water that fast developed an oily yellow scum despite all the soda she put in to combat it.

'I'm sorry,' Connie said time after time, 'I just can't face it. I don't mind what else I do, sweeping, cleaning, ladling out food and helping in any other way in between knitting, but after a while the sight of that awful washing-up water makes me want to heave.'

She could understand that, and made allowances. No one could say Connie didn't pull her weight. She'd go home exhausted at times, running about doing this, doing that, taking on any other chore but washing up. For a gently brought up girl, it was remarkable how she knuckled down to all the hard work as well as keeping an eye on Rebecca at the same time.

Eveline didn't have that trouble. Most of the time Gran looked after Helena. 'I wouldn't hear of 'er being made to sit in a pushchair all that time.'

'She'd be all right there, Gran,' Eveline said. 'It's only for a morning, or an afternoon.'

'Morning or afternoon, nearly five hours is too long to expect a child of four to be cooped up in one place. She needs to run about. She can run about 'ere, love. I can cope. So long as I only 'ave the one to deal with.'

So that was it. Gran wasn't prepared to look after two children any more, and that was only to be expected now Gran was in her mid-seventies. She only hoped Connie wouldn't feel she was being pushed aside, but she was sure she'd understand.

Obviously Connie did. She seemed content enough to have Rebecca by her side. What did upset her was the way this war was going. It upset Eveline too – the whole nation, come to that. But she kept her fears to herself. It wasn't good to go around lamenting.

The Sunday she'd seen Albert off had brought news that the British Expeditonary Force of seventy thousand men, intended to show the Kaiser what was what, had met huge enemy resistance and had been forced to retreat, with civilians in the Belgian town of Mons attending church service caught in crossfire.

A week later the BEF was reported to be suffering heavy casualties but for the moment the enemy, having swept over most of Belgium and across the River Meuse forcing a French retreat, had been halted for which the nation gave silent thanks.

Eveline herself gave thanks that Albert and George were still in this country, both having been put in the same regiment, a government decision to keep brothers, friends, even men of the same neighbourhood or workplace together for the sake of morale.

It was little consolation to Connie. 'I'm so frightened,' she said to Eveline. 'What if they decide to send them to France? From what we hear, our lads there are being slaughtered by the Boche. I've had no letter from George this week. I couldn't bear to think he could already be out there.'

Eveline felt her impatience flare. Albert was in the same danger as George. Connie wasn't the only one to fear for her man's safety – there were thousands of women in the same plight with the same anxieties.

'They won't send them yet,' she said a little irritably, adding with a ring of hope in her tone, 'They have to be trained before they go into battle – all soldiers have to have that. By that time the war could be over.'

But Connie wasn't at all comforted. 'What if our forces are still being beaten back and the war doesn't end soon? I'm so frightened for George.'

'Don't you think I'm frightened for Albert too?'

Aware how sharp that must have sounded, she hastily changed the subject to the increasing lack of food items in the shops. 'Stuff is simply beginning to disappear off the counters. I bet the people with money have started to hoard. They'll make sure they won't go short even if others do.'

It made her think suddenly of Laurence Jones-Fairbrook: no shortages for well-off people like him. Where was he now? Probably married to some daughter of wealthy parents. That's what wealthy people like him did in the end, once the little bit on the side had been forgotten about. She'd been a fool thinking he would ever have married anyone like her from a totally different class to his.

Resolutely she put him from her, turning her mind again to the BEF defeats, of the seventy thousand men many had already been killed. The war, so confidently spoken of as being over in a couple of months, now didn't seem so certain of conclusion. The army was calling for half a million more men. Yesterday her brother Len had answered the call. Mum was devastated, but what could she do? Eveline decided she would pop over this afternoon and try to offer comfort.

'I couldn't stop 'im,' her mother said bleakly, moving away from Eveline's attempt to cuddle her. 'Twenty-one now, he can do what he likes.'

'But he's courting, isn't he?'

For a moment her mother's mind was distracted from her son going off to fight, her hazel eyes taking on a mild look. 'Nice little girl, that Flossie. I suppose that engagement of theirs'll 'ave ter wait even a bit longer now. They've 'ad ter put it off once due ter lack of funds.'

The mild look was again replaced again by concern for Len, leaving Eveline to utter the phrase that was becoming almost tedious, and lately losing its former optimism, that the war had to be over soon.

Then suddenly news was good again. Not just good, heartening – the first decisive battle so far, fought on the banks of the Marne in France with French forces pushing the enemy back to the river Aisne.

PARIS SAVED: GERMANS IN RETREAT, blared the headlines dated the fourteenth of September.

'I said all along they took on more than they could chew,' said her dad, scanning the headlines as belligerently as if he personally were in charge of this successful counter-attack.

Eveline had taken to popping over each Monday around lunchtime when Dad closed up for an hour. She'd have a bite to eat with them, pick up a few groceries Mum let her have for a few pence off, then go home. Though why she hurried away she wasn't sure. There was only herself and Helena to get a meal for.

Popping in on Mondays would help break up the day after a lonely weekend. She would have Sunday dinners there too, once or twice but not too often in case it looked as if she was relying on them all the time. Mum was a little more inclined towards Helena these days and she was more sociable then she'd once been, so long as Eveline didn't make a habit of popping over too often.

There was Connie of course. Bound by a common sense of loneliness with their men no longer here, especially acute in Connie's case with no family willing to console her, they'd become even closer, so she supposed she should count herself lucky. And they had something to do with their time, for which she thanked the suffragettes even though they no longer had need to raise any ruckus. Queen Mary had appealed to women of the Empire to knit socks for the troops, three thousand pairs according to Her Majesty; the old suffragette branches were among the first to organise knitting circles.

Using the room behind the canteen, Eveline was able to have Helena with her now, which she hoped took some of the weight off Gran. The child was able to play on the floor beside her and in safety with the door to the canteen tightly closed. She and Rebecca kept each other company, and a couple of other little ones too. They couldn't go far in this one room and for the most part played at knitting with odd bits of khaki wool.

'Go on like this,' Eveline's father was saying, beaming at the *Daily Express* headlines, 'and it'll be over before we know it. I always said it'd be all over by Christmas.'

'So do a lot of other people,' Eveline laughed, at last able to feel some real optimism. Albert home for Christmas, demobilised and back to work, coming home at regular hours to the meal she'd have on the table for him: it was a lovely and hopeful thought. They might even try again for a baby.

Connie couldn't help thinking of her family at times like these. It still hurt that they had estranged themselves from her.

'You would think they would put our differences aside and let bygones be bygones with all that is happening,' she said to Eveline in October.

German forces had consolidated their position in Belgium. Ghent and Bruges and Ostend had fallen to them. The Belgian government had fled to France. But Connie was more concerned with her own troubles.

'It is all so foolish. I have been married all this time and with a family and there's nothing they can do about it, so why continue with this grudge?'

She'd heard from Verity, who although happily married had had three miscarriages and still no children. Her most recent letter said that Douglas, her husband, had felt obliged to enlist after seeing posters of Lord Kitchener calling for more men to join their country's fight against tyranny.

'With the man pointing straight at everyone imploring Britons to join their country's army,' her letter went on, 'how could I beg Douglas not to? I am devastated without him. He is an officer. I know I should be brave but I really am utterly in fear.'

Her lamentations prompted Connie to reply that if they were to win this war, every man must do his bit for his country, as her own husband was doing. 'Even if he is only in the ranks,' she hastened to add pointedly, suddenly made very strong by Verity's fear.

Verity's letter had also said that their brother, Denzil, at eighteen, had also enlisted instead of going up to Oxford. He too was considered to be potential officer material; the army sorely needed commissioned men.

'If only my mother could have written to tell

me about him,' Connie said bitterly. 'I feel I've no family at all.'

'You've got mine,' said Eveline, trying to comfort.

She had to admit that Eveline's family did treat her almost as one of their own. She had even accepted invitations to Sunday dinner, but it was small compensation for her own parents' attitude towards her. Verity's letter had prompted her to write once again to them, this time to say that George had enlisted, but there'd been no response, embittering her even more.

'I really feel that if my George was sent off to France and I made a widow, they'd still not write,' she told Eveline, her needles working furiously on the khaki socks she was knitting.

The words made her shudder as if they had been prophetic, as in fact they appeared to have been when days later news came from George that his and Albert's unit had indeed been sent to the front, as it was being called.

The anticipated movements of battle having come to a stalemate in early November, both sides were digging in. Newspapers reported trenches and barbed wire, monotony, and mud with the onset of winter, a series of small advances and small retreats getting both sides nowhere.

George's letter, posted from France, sent Connie falling into Eveline's arms grateful for a shoulder to cry on. She was being a baby knowing so many women throughout the country must be feeling the same as her. She was well aware how weak she must seem but it helped to have someone to cling to and not feel she was being condemned for her frailty.

Eveline too had received a letter, from Albert. She said she'd managed to hold her emotion but Connie's crying had finally made her give way to silly tears. This was spoken almost like an accusation. Connie felt some of her strength return as they comforted each other; Eveline was made of stronger stuff than she ever would be for all her resolve now to face up to whatever came.

Christmas was like no other Eveline had ever known, everyone caught by a new fear. Ten days before, several towns on the east coast had been brought right into the war as, looming out of a December dawn mist, three German warships had shelled the east coast towns of Scarborough, West Hartlepool and Whitby. A hundred people had been killed, mostly civilians.

Most viewed it with something like disbelief. Not since the Civil War had any of England's subjects died in hostilities on English soil. Zeppelins too had been seen over England and the likelihood of bombs being dropped on English towns from those slowly gliding shapes filled everyone with foreboding.

There'd been trouble across the country, mobs venting their anger on German shopkeepers and other suspect foreigners, breaking their windows, destroying their goods, threatening their lives until the police had to rescue them. And aliens were being rounded up and taken off to special camps. Even the First Sea Lord, Prince Louis of Battenberg, German by birth and known to be related to the Kaiser, had been forced to resign because of anti-German feeling, even though his son was serving in the Royal Navy.

The Christmas many predicted would see the end of the war wasn't one for celebrations, since so many remained without their men at home. Determined as Eveline was to make the best of things and, judging by Connie's desperate smiles, she was trying hard to do the same, there was an emptiness about this festive season that couldn't be filled, though her being at her parents for Christmas dinner helped a bit.

The entire family squashed into the flat above the shop as if presenting a united front against the times they were now living in. With the dinner-table leaves extended, somehow twelve adults or near adults, five children and a baby in arms, which didn't count, managed to squeeze round it, the younger ones secured between table and wall and all having to eat with elbows well in but with lots of goodwill and give and take.

Dad's corner shop had made certain of a Christmas dinner to beat all Christmas dinners this year, in an effort to show that this war wasn't going to get any of them down. But there were still the missing faces to remind them: her Albert, her brother Len, and Connie's George.

Eveline's sister, Tilly, chewing steadily, said, 'My Stan keeps talking about needing to do 'is bit. He says most of the blokes he worked with 'ave enlisted. I keep telling 'im he's a married man with children.'

She glanced across the table where her husband was talking to their father, then down at her small daughter, protectively holding her baby boy closer. 'If he enlisted and anything 'appens to 'im, they'd be without a dad.'

'I don't think he'd be that rash,' Eveline said, she too eating steadily. 'He's got a family to think of.'

But so had Albert. That hadn't stopped him. Nor George. She felt let down and angry, for herself and for Connie. Without thinking, both of them had volunteered in the initial fever of excitement to see an enemy off. The recruitment stations hadn't stopped to consider if a man had a family or not. But that first flush of excitement had died down and even though duty and patriotism still counted, some well knew the slaughter going on at the front. To Eveline's mind Stan was being a bit inconsiderate even though they were still pushing for recruits.

If he was seeing only the glory of comradeship against a common foe, the news alone from the front should make him stop and think. Albert's letters were dismal, speaking not of glory but of poor food, cold, hard work, and little change of clothing. And he wasn't yet in the fighting line; his job at the moment consisted of loading boxes of ammunition on trucks and mules to be sent on.

Eveline found herself reading more into his letters than he meant her to, fuelling a lurking fear that at any moment his unit could be sent to the trenches. He and George were still together; generals still remained happy for mates and even those from the same street to be so, for the sake of morale.

She would hear the same echo of fear in the letters Connie sometimes read out to her from her

George. Only occasionally now, and getting less and less as each hesitated to confide in the other what they constantly read into those loving, lonely and often achingly soulful letters, each praying this war would finish before their man could be sent forward.

But while there seemed to be stalemate over there, elsewhere there had been encouraging news. Earlier this month the Royal Navy's magnificent victory in the Falklands had meant sinking the German cruisers *Dresden, Scharnhorst, Gneisenau* and *Nürnberg* with, it was said, no British losses. People were still feeding off it come Christmas. Thinking of it, she felt a little more optimistic.

'Time your Stan gets to thinking of joining up, the Germans will have surrendered,' she said to Tilly. 'We've got a great big Empire to call on. What have they got? A few more months and they'll give up, you wait and see.'

It had been a good Christmas after all, despite her constantly missing Albert. Dinner cleared away, the men still at home, too young or too old to enlist, gathered in the kitchen to drink and smoke and discuss the present situation. Children had been put to bed for the afternoon to sleep off their meal, while the women reclined on the chairs Mum had pushed against the wall ready for a bit of fun in the evening. The mats and rugs taken up had left the linoleum clear for a bit of a knees-up later and to hell with the war for a day.

Later they'd made ham sandwiches for tea with shrimps and winkles and crispy celery. Dad had played records on his beloved gramophone to do the two-step to songs like 'Alexander's Ragtime Band' and 'Hullo-Hullo Who's Your Lady Friend', everyone pausing as he rewound the spring, finally going all sentimental with 'Keep the Home Fires Burning' and 'You Made Me Love You', which a friend of his played on his harmonica.

Tiring of it, they'd played cards for pennies and ha'pennies into the evening, the women finally going off to bed while the men got down to some serious betting at pontoon. The war had seemed a long way away.

Now it was January 1915, with still no end to the war in sight despite newspaper accounts of an unofficial truce on Christmas Day by ordinary troops in one corner of the Western Front. British and German soldiers had come out of their trenches to greet each other, exchange food and cigarettes as if giving Christmas presents, even having a game of football, much to the disapproval of the authorities.

The next day they were again firing at each other from their trenches with intent to kill as if Christmas had never been.

'It's horrible when you come to think of it,' Connie said on reading the account. 'How can they start killing again after that?'

But it was the appalling truth that they could, pushed on by generals and their commanding officers.

'War is so senseless and wicked! If women were able to vote and be in charge of things there would be no more wars.'

'If that day ever comes,' Eveline returned with a bitter laugh to which Connie didn't respond.

Chapter Twenty-four

In the coming weeks all Connie could think about was the possibility of George being sent to the front, a bullet making a widow of her.

'You mustn't let yourself keep dwelling on it,' Eveline told her sternly. 'We all feel the same way but we have to be strong. If we're not, we're just letting our men down.'

That was easier said than done. Eveline going about as if Albert could never be in any danger was only hiding her head in the sand as far as she was concerned, though sometimes she wished she could do the same.

Mid-January gave them something else to think about as the war was brought almost to their very doorstep, newspapers reporting that during the night a German Zeppelin had crossed the Norfolk coast and dropped bombs on Great Yarmouth and King's Lynn, killing twenty people and injuring twice that number.

There was a photograph of the devastation: three cottages completely destroyed, a mass of rubble and splintered wood, the homes on either side wrecked and gutted.

'To think of people under that,' Connie whispered when she came over to show the paper to Eveline. 'A small boy and his sister were killed in one of those cottages. What did two little children ever do to the Germans to be killed like that? It's inhuman. I can't bear to think of it.'

For once, Eveline didn't upbraid her for her horrified reaction, causing her to feel suddenly resolute.

'We simply have to win,' she said. 'We have to stop people like that!' The words made her feel a lot better.

It was in March that her worst nightmare became reality. George's letter told her that his and Albert's battalion was being sent forward; she fled to Eveline's, Rebecca in her arms, as though the enemy was at her heels.

'We've got to be strong,' Eveline repeated as Connie sat in her kitchen trying to stop her insides trembling. Eveline was holding her own letter, and although she sounded calm, her fingers kept creasing and uncreasing the folds of his letter until they were razor-thin.

'I'm trying to be,' Connie replied.

In a way she wished it had been Eveline who had come over to her instead of the other way round. Sitting here she felt like a child who had lost its mother in a crowd. But Eveline was her strength, her prop.

'I shall be,' she promised although her voice wavered. 'I shall be strong.'

With Eveline beside her, she would face this. It was Eveline who for years had helped her face so much – her parents' silence, trying to make a new life here in the East End, even helping her becoming a better suffragette than she might have been alone.

'We must throw ourselves into helping our country,' Eveline went on a little dramatically, but she was right. There was much they could do. They were the only ones left to do it, with their men away.

The government had issued an appeal to women to serve their country. Workers were desperately needed in industry, trade, public services, agriculture, and, most importantly, armaments.

None needed telling twice; women flocked to sign on at local labour exchanges, responding to the Register of Women for War Service the government had organised.

Within days Emmeline Pankhurst was rallying every WSPU member and declaring that its members were only too willing to be recruited.

'That's what we'll do,' Eveline said excitedly when they heard. 'It'll be just like old times.'

Leaving canteen work, which had quietened down with dwindling numbers of refugees and women starting to earn money of their own and no longer needing handouts, they went off to the Labour Exchange. Gran, bless her, had offered to have Rebecca while Eveline's mother agreed, somewhat begrudgingly she felt, to relieve her of Helena.

'Though you do know I've got a shop ter manage but I suppose we've all got ter do our bit,' she said. 'I just 'ope it won't be too much for yer gran looking after Connie's little 'un. After all it ain't as if she was 'er blood.'

Typical of her to make everything sound like a chore, but Eveline said nothing except to thank her and hope it wouldn't be for long, adding that every hand was needed to get this war over as quick as possible, which Mum had to agree with.

It was amazing what women were proving to be capable of, doing jobs hitherto seen as men's work: heaving coal, adeptly managing horse-drawn milk and heavy coal carts alike, delivering post, so-called delicate women handling not just light but heavy industrial machinery, alongside men too old to be accepted for military service. Eveline and Connie, accepted for work, now became just two of a fifty-thousand strong female labour force employed in industry alone.

'Anything we can do will be worthwhile,' declared the chairwoman of their local WSPU branch in Hackney. Branches had sprung up everywhere again, this time in aid of government rather than against it.

'At last we are needed,' she'd gone on. 'And Mr Lloyd George has promised that women will receive the same pay as men for war work.'

Having been a comptometer operator and good at figures, a broad scope offered itself to Eveline, while Connie, never having had to work in her life, was skilled at nothing. Feeling she had little choice but to keep together for Connie's sake, the only thing open to two women refusing to be separated was factory work. But with a promise of being given the same wage as men, factory war work had its attraction, even if it did mean long hours from eight in the morning to six in the evening with half an hour for lunch.

'I don't suppose it'll be very clean work either,' Eveline warned. Working on a factory floor would be new to her too, the old biscuit factory having of necessity been a clean place. Besides, she'd been in the office.

She hadn't reckoned on just how dirty munitions work could be. Not just dirty but smelly and noisy and at times hazardous, but this was what they had chosen and there was no going back to the Labour Exchange crying that they'd changed their minds, that they didn't like the work.

With their hair bundled up into mob caps, wearing thick coveralls, they'd been taken to their work bench that first day and shown what to do, a simple and what promised to be a repetitious and boring task of putting shell cases under a machine that made a screw thread. Before the first hour was up their palms were stained from contact with metal, their backs ached, their ears buzzed from the constant racket of machinery.

'We've got to stick at it,' Connie shouted above the noise and with a ring of determination in her voice that surprised Eveline. 'If our boys can endure what they're enduring, then we can endure this. What we're doing must be heaven in comparison to what they must be going through.'

Their husband's letters increasingly told what it was like even though they tried to fill the page with cheerful trivia. The press was far more explicit and who'd want to look that hell in the teeth after what the papers were saying?

'Maybe it won't be for too much longer,' Connie added, clinging to that hopeful phrase that was steadily becoming more and more hackneyed.

Albert sat with his back to the slimy mud wall of the trench, writing to Eveline, his notepad propped on one knee. It wasn't easy to write with rain trickling off the groundsheet draped over his head and shoulders. It seemed he'd never be dry again, would live and die in these wet clothes he wore.

Licking the stub of pencil, he stared at what he had written so far. It wasn't much. What was there to write about? The conditions? Nothing ever dry? The rivulets of rain streaming down the trench walls? The duckboards at the bottom of the trench almost a foot under water these last two months, so that men were starting to get trench foot? He would examine his own feet to see if the damp, dead-looking skin was the start of that miserable condition or just cold, rub them dry as best he could, holding them out to air, but not for long as another bombardment would have him hastily getting back into wet socks and boots.

He'd already spoken in his letters about the poor food. Ration parties would be sent off to bring it, then return with it all bunged in one sack, loose tea leaves and sugar mixed up with everything else. He had made a joke of it in one of his previous letters.

He could never tell her about the constant bombardment, or being moved from one trench to another to relieve others already there. Or about the tension, the fear, the strange moments of either apathy or hilarity that came during a lull. Or of dropping with fatigue, absolutely whacked after twenty-four hours non-stop trench mortars, high-explosive shelling, tripping over bodies or parts of bodies before the medics and stretcher-bearers could do their job. Most of all, he felt unable to mention the strange lack of sorrow for a fallen man under bombardment.

He'd already written about going for weeks without a proper wash or a change of clothes, picking lice out of the ones he was wearing. He couldn't write that again. Nor would he ever write about going through each day dazed by relentless bombing, trying to carry out duties while mind and body became rigid under the scream of enemy shells and the jarring of explosions, or the almost abject gratitude at being relieved by replacements and told his company was being given a day's rest.

All he could do was say that he was well, that he was cheerful, search for some funny little anecdote to tell her, add that he loved her dearly and missed her, longed to be back home with her, hoped she was coping and that little Helena was fine, that he admired what she was doing for the war effort and thought her a real brick to be doing such work and for sticking by him, with her letters always cheerful and full of encouragement and hope.

The problem was, he'd said this or something like it in every letter he had written her so far. She must be getting bored with it. One thing he hoped she realised – his letters might be pitifully repetitious but each one contained his heart.

One thing writing to her did, it helped him forget what was going on all around him, if only for a short while. Licking the pencil again he ended, 'Will write again soon. Can hardly wait for your next letter. Hope it's not too long coming. Our mail is awful. I love and miss you, my dearest.'

He was about to write, 'Your loving Albert,' when a brief barrage of bursting shells had him ducking down into the mud, praying it wouldn't be his turn yet. One shell exploded near enough to collapse part of the trench on top of him to cover him and George, crouching nearby, in mud.

Next thing, a blessed voice was yelling, 'Move, yer lazy buggers! The relief's arrived.' Words like the singing of an angel!

She'd only been able to glance at Albert's letter before she and Connie rushed off to catch their bus to work, but what she had read had heartened her considerably. Now in their lunch break, she could open it to read in more detail.

'He says him and George have been at a rest camp,' she told Connie. 'Their company was sent there and they both made the most of it, eating, sleeping, having a bath, being given clean clothes, and getting deloused like he was some flea-ridden stray dog. I suppose that's a joke. He says George is sitting next to him in the mess tent writing his letter to you.'

'I've not had George's letter yet,' Connie said dismally.

'It'll come, Connie, don't worry.'

She returned her gaze to her letter. 'He says that though they've now been sent back, it's to a support trench, a lot safer, out of harm's way.'

The relief that had flooded over her at that dissolved seconds later as she read on. 'Oh dear, he says it was only temporary and they've been told they'll be sent forward very soon to relieve a battalion at the front line. Oh, Connie...'

Her hand flew to her lips, unable to help herself as the courage she'd been clinging to all these months drained away. 'Oh, Connie, what if...'

She couldn't finish, Connie's face registering the same fear. 'And George will be with him,' Connie whispered.

Eveline didn't reply. Slowly she folded the letter on Albert's closing words, 'I miss you, my darling. Keep well. Your ever loving husband, Albert.'

The next day George's letter came. Connie didn't read it out as she normally did, sharing the impersonal bits, but Eveline guessed from her friend's bleak face that it bore the same news as Albert's letter. All she could do was take Connie's arm in a firm grip as they stood in the noisy factory that smelled of oil and metal shavings.

'They'll come through, I know they will. We have to take heart and carry on.'

They were being given plenty of encouragement to do so with Mrs Pankhurst calling for every woman who had been a suffragette to do her bit. She was also planning a huge peaceful July demonstration to show support for the war effort. It was to be as large as any of the peacetime marches.

They came readily to her call, working themselves to a standstill as a way to ease their fear for their men away fighting and dull the thumping of the heart whenever the mind was allowed an idle moment to turn to all that was happening in France, now being called the Western Front, and also in Gallipoli in the Dardanelles, making the

Zeppelin raids on London seem trivial.

So much was happening in the world: Russia was fighting Germany on what was being called the Eastern Front. The liner *Lusitania* had been sunk off the Irish coast by a German submarine on her return from New York with several hundred Americans among the passengers; fourteen hundred lives were lost. People were again attacking shops owned by those with foreign names, lumping them all together as German. Zeppelin raids were killing British civilians while along the Western Front there was complete stalemate.

Through it all, like everyone else, Eveline and Connie worked on at their tedious jobs trying not to think of what their husbands might be going through, each day dreading the telegram that would turn their fear to grief.

'A suffragette demonstration *will* be a welcome diversion,' Eveline said, though this time she couldn't bring herself to refer to it as being like old times. It wasn't like old times. It wouldn't be like old times ever again.

As the march moved off from the Embankment on Saturday the seventeenth of July, none would have believed it to be July – driving, squally rain fell. Some had their children with them but Gran had kindly volunteered to have the two girls.

Despite the weather, it promised to equal any of those earlier ones; this was the largest since that of 1913, the papers said, with forty thousand women waiting to march off, to be watched by one hundred thousand spectators lining the route between Westminster and Blackfriars.

The WSPU circular apparently sent to all parts of the country had said, '*So grave is our national danger and so terrible the loss of precious lives due to the shortage of munitions, Mr Lloyd George as Minister of Munitions has been asked to receive a deputation and hear women's demand for the right to make munitions and render other war service.*' So it was only to be expected that the response would be immense, both from those wanting to take part and those ready to give their support by coming along in rain and wind to watch the 'Right To Serve' procession pass.

Connie couldn't help it – as ninety bands struck up the 'Marseillaise,' in honour of those fighting in France and the great resistance France herself was putting up and so many of her soldiers being slaughtered and as one the flags were raised, she burst out, 'It *is* just like old times!'

Despite the weather that called for mackintoshes rather than summer clothing, making it a procession of grey and brown and the khaki of the City Territorials, there was no lack of colour from the hundred and twenty-five contingents raising a patriotic red, white and blue to replace the suffragette colours of purple, green and white.

'I think it's every bit as colourful,' Connie remarked excitedly.

With Mrs Pankhurst at its head, the procession moved up through Whitehall, Trafalgar Square, Piccadilly, Park Lane, turning right into Oxford Street, down Regent Street to Piccadilly Circus, down along Northumberland Avenue and back to Victoria Embankment. Waving banners, no longer calling for votes for women, declared instead, SHELLS MADE BY A WIFE MAY SAVE A HUSBAND'S LIFE, and MEN MUST FIGHT AND WOMEN MUST WORK.

As in the past there were pageants, maybe not so colourful as once they'd been but more appropriate to the times – the pageant of the Allies was led by a woman in purple and black carrying a tattered Belgian flag to depict that country's bereaved but unbroken spirit. There were national costumes, flags and banners of every Allied country while bands played their national airs and anthems.

'Look, they've set up tables all the way along, so people can sign up for war work,' Connie pointed out as they marched by.

At every table, shielded by tarpaulins, Eveline could see women actually queuing in atrocious rain and driving wind to add their signatures.

'It really is amazing,' she said. 'Nothing like this ever happened when we marched before.'

But then this was patriotism and her heart swelled as ninety bands struck up in a thunderous National Anthem at the end of it all.

Connie was smiling as they came away. 'I feel as though I have been given a new lease of life. I feel I could face anything now. Isn't being a suffragette just simply wonderful?'

Despite her years living in the East End she had never quite lost the vernacular of her old life.

But she was right, of course. Eveline too felt that special lift, coming away from what had been one of a most successful, perhaps *the* most successful, of all the demonstrations the suffragette movement had ever produced, and this time with the government's blessing. At that moment, it seemed to her that life was very sweet despite the war.

Had it not been for their husbands away fighting, life would have been even sweeter. Factory work was bringing in a good wage, money was no longer a problem for Eveline, and Connie still had her little nest egg, the money she'd left home with, virtually still intact. If only she would put behind her the family that had thrown her out.

'I know, I really must stop thinking about them,' she admitted when Eveline dropped another little hint in December as they left their suffragette meeting.

Clinging to her hat against wet and blustery gusts of wind, Eveline smiled and said no more. Her parents were never far from Connie's mind. She'd talk about them at any given moment, dragging up the past, opening old wounds.

Eveline had learned to endure it for the most part, well aware that it helped her rid herself of some of the bitterness that lay inside her. It was obvious she would never get over the hurt she'd suffered.

'With this war and all, and my brother Denzil now in France, you'd think they could put the past behind them,' she said as they turned for home. 'If I wrote to say that I was as much at fault as they over what happened, they might warm to me again.'

'But you weren't at fault,' Eveline pointed out, unable to keep silent. 'They told you to give George up, and you couldn't do that. What girl in

367

love could?'

'But if I just wrote to say I was? You can't begin to know how it feels to have your parents turn against you.'

Oh, she knew all right! If not as long drawn out as Connie's, there'd been rejection, nastiness, trying to get her parents to see her side of it, her mother scorning an innocent baby as if it had been its fault to have been illegitimate but for Albert's timely and selfless intervention. Yes, she knew about rejection and hostility.

'I think I will write to them,' Connie went on firmly as she bent her head to another vicious gust of wind.

But she hadn't done so. As the days to Christmas crept nearer and Connie made no mention of it again, Eveline guessed that it had to do with fear – so long as she held back from sending her letter, she couldn't be hurt by any adverse response, or lack of any response at all.

Other than that, she had to admire Connie for the way she was facing up to wartime conditions, hindered as she was by the genteel upbringing she'd had.

Factory work had come hard to her but she'd adjusted to it. They both had, coming home these days not so weary as they'd first been after the long hours expected of them.

Their five-year-old girls were now at Wilmott Street School a few hundred yards away, going alternately to Gran's and Eveline's mother-in-law for their dinner hour. Her mother, suddenly declaring that having them after school was too much for Gran at her age, had decided she would collect and give eye to them until they were picked up and taken home. Eveline guessed her mother harboured a bit of jealousy that Albert's mother might take over completely, but at least Mum's move was a step in the right direction.

Connie had found someone to look after them now and again so they could go to the pictures, the flickering screen helping them to unwind from the endless round of work. A couple of evenings a week they'd go round to each other's flat. They always went shopping for food together after work and most Saturdays went window-shopping up West with the children.

Until the weather became too cold Sunday was spent taking the girls to Victoria Park. They took turns cooking Sunday dinner, unless they were asked to Eveline's parents for a Sunday meal. All in all life wasn't too bad.

'What do you think of this?' Connie asked a few days before Christmas, holding out a Christmas card to her parents for Eveline to read.

Wishing them good tidings she'd added that it could be a right time to forget old differences now that they were all in this war together and, Eveline was dismayed to read, saying that she might have been at fault for leaving home as she had done, even asking for forgiveness in the spirit of Christmas.

'You can't send that!' she burst out, handing it back, her hands – all floury from rolling out pastry for a few mince pies – leaving fingerprints on the simple Christmas picture. 'Connie, you can't!'

'It's only a card. It's not like a letter.'

'It's still humbling yourself.'

Connie's lips tightened. 'I'm going to send it,' she said stubbornly.

'It won't make any difference,' Eveline predicted.

But Connie remained obdurate. 'It *has* to end some time.'

She had sent it, but no card came in reply though she had one from her sister Verity, full of good cheer and saying everyone was well. Eveline wondered if the card didn't accentuate the lack of one from Connie's parents but she said nothing.

She was glad to see Connie perk up, the two of them spending their second Christmas of the war with her mum and dad with most of the family, but without Len. Flossie, his fiancée, though with no ring yet, popped in for an hour or so, making his absence all the more felt. That absence left something lacking around the Christmas dinner table this year.

In early January, Connie received another letter from her sister. She came over to Eveline unexpectedly on the Tuesday morning well before they were due to leave together for work. As Eveline opened the door to her she was holding Verity's letter in her hand as though she would crush it out of existence and the look on her face had Eveline reaching out to drag her inside.

'What is it?' she asked as she closed the door, throwing the lobby into winter darkness. Leading her into the gaslit kitchen, she saw Connie's face was chalk-white. Surely anything her parents had to say to her couldn't produce this look of devastation. 'What is it?' she asked again.

'Verity wrote to me,' came a voice so small she could hardly hear it. 'My brother's been killed.'

Chapter Twenty-five

With her arms about the weeping girl in an effort to comfort her, Eveline found herself thinking of her brother Len, how she would be if he were killed.

He too had been sent abroad but was somewhere in a place called Mesopotamia fighting the Turks. His infrequent letters home had spoken of the heat and dust, flies and fearful disease, the latest in December writing of winter rain turning flat ground to a clinging morass.

Eveline pulled herself up sharply. What was she doing thinking all this when Connie was weeping here in her arms?

'It was left to Verity to tell me,' Connie was sobbing. 'They can't even tell me themselves. How can they hate me so much?' Eveline knew whom she was talking about.

'Try not to think about it,' was all she could say, aware how painfully inadequate that must sound.

'I don't know why I'm being so foolish,' Connie hiccuped between sobs. 'I hardly knew my brother. He was always away at public school, like Herbert. My father believed in that. He only came home during the holidays.' She seemed compelled to talk through her tears, words tumbling out as if with a life of their own. 'He should never have signed on. He'd just turned eighteen, ready to go on to university. He'd be alive now if he had. I hardly ever saw him, I mostly remember him as a little boy of six or seven being sent away. He shouldn't have left home so young. I remember him standing with his suitcase, looking small and lost, and all I can see now is this little boy lying dead in a muddy hole... Oh, Eveline, how could they not *tell* me?'

'They might do yet.' Eveline tried to console her. 'They must be in such grief. When they've gathered their thoughts together, I'm sure they'll tell you.'

She continued cuddling her, waiting for weeping to exhaust itself. 'You must write a reply to your sister, and I think you should get in touch with your mum and dad too, to say how devastated you feel. It could be the turning point.'

Connie did so after she'd calmed down but when no reply came, she sank into a sort of depression. Eveline, feeling partly to blame for advising her, had trouble even making her get ready for work. She'd go there at six thirty in the morning with Helena, making Connie's breakfast and having practically to get little Rebecca ready to take to Gran's until it was time for her to go to school at nine. She'd drop Helena off with her own mother then go back to Connie's flat to find her sitting exactly where she'd left her.

After a week of it sympathy turned to irritation. 'For goodness' sake, Connie, pull yourself together!' Her answer was a bleak stare that made her all the more annoyed.

'I know it's terrible losing your brother,' she said, more impatient than stern. 'But there are thousands and thousands who've lost husbands and sons and brothers. I'm sorry, Connie, but I think this is more to do with your parents, than losing your–'

She broke off, knowing she was treading on very shaky ground. But having Connie flare up at her would be better than this bleak, blank stare.

'I have to say it, Connie,' she hurried on. 'Sod 'em! George and Rebecca are far more important and you've got to carry on with your own life or you'll end up going off your head. If your parents were dead you'd have to carry on.'

She hadn't aimed for her words to do the trick, but they had Connie springing up in sudden fury. 'You know nothing of how I feel. You're just an unfeeling, silly bitch! You don't know how it feels. You've lost no one!'

Eveline had never had Connie turn on her like this before, but realising her own words had had the desired effect, she took the abuse without retaliation as the distraught girl fell into her arms in a fit of weeping and choking apology. When it finally abated, Connie was in control of herself again. There was still the pain of having lost her brother and suffering because of her parents' rejection of her efforts at reconciliation, but she was at least coping again.

'You must have thought me a big baby,' she called over to Eveline above the deafening whirr and rumble of machinery two weeks later as, like two automatons, they fitted shell case after shell case into the hungry mouth of their screw-threading machines.

'Not at all,' Eveline shouted back, deftly and

374

swiftly withdrawing her finished casing to drop it clanging on to the growing pile in a box on her right which was waiting to be taken away, and lifting another from the pile on her left to insert into the noisily whirring aperture.

Since her outburst Connie seemed to have grown so much stronger. Even when another letter arrived from her sister two weeks later saying that their father had suffered a mild heart attack, probably brought on by the shock of losing his eldest son, she hadn't broken down or even flinched.

Verity had said that their other brother Herbert had been so upset by Denzil's death that he'd gone straight to the recruiting office and signed on.

'He was seventeen only last week,' Verity wrote. 'But he ignored all Father's efforts to make him either admit his age to the recruiting officer or agree to officer cadet training for when he is old enough. He says that if he interferes he will join the Merchant Navy, which will take him at that age, and you know how our ships are constantly being torpedoed. There's nothing Father can do. Not only that, Herbert has signed on as an ordinary private soldier. I don't understand why he'd want to do that? He must be mad.'

Defiance: the thought came to Eveline as the letter was read out to her. He was still treated as a child, his parents still telling him what to do when his brother, just sixteen months older than he, had been killed in a foreign land. Now he'd rebelled, just as Connie had rebelled against her life being mapped out for her regardless of whether she was happy or not.

'I have to write to my mother again,' Connie said. 'I'm being quite level-headed about it,' she interrupted as Eveline lifted a warning hand. 'She must be feeling utterly beside herself, losing a son, then Herbert joining up and now my father having a heart attack. She must be going through a terrible time. But if she can't bring herself to reply, then at least I've done my duty.'

Eveline suspected she was feeling it more deeply than she admitted. She was surprised when Connie came to show her a letter from her mother.

'I suppose it is a start,' she said coolly, but there was a slight tremble to her voice and Eveline knew why as it was handed to her to read.

It was the worst letter she thought she'd ever read, filled with unjust condemnation of Connie's apparent coldness over the years, her audacity in holding herself aloof after walking out as she had done and thumbing her nose at them when her father had only had her best interests at heart in seeking a worthy match for her. The letter even intimated that her action could have started her father's heart condition, ending by saying he was recovering slowly but not to continue corresponding, for she'd never be forgiven for what she'd done.

'How can any mother write such stuff?' Eveline burst out, a little more understanding of how Connie must feel, but Connie remained cool.

'It doesn't matter,' she said. 'I've done what I set out to do and have at least jarred her into replying. And I can rest, knowing my father is getting better. If I hadn't written and something had happened to him I would never have forgiven myself.'

Summer was creeping on and it seemed the war was as far away as ever from being won. After two years of it, the government was now introducing conscription.

'George should have waited,' Connie complained as they left the factory. 'He would have had two more years at home and Rebecca would have had a real family, rather than as it is now, being pushed from pillar to post while her mother is working.'

Albert could have done the same but there was no point making a fuss over it. 'Well, what's done is done,' Eveline sighed.

But Connie was right about their daughters. After collecting them they'd take them home, to their supper, put them to bed, then settle down for the evening if they'd made no arrangements to go out anywhere, then go to bed themselves ready for the next morning back at the factory. It all meant no family life at all for a child, both girls being deprived of their right to childhood in a proper family.

'Perhaps it's fate,' she went on, trying to be philosophical. 'If Albert and George had waited to be called up now, who's to say they might not walk straight into a German bullet the moment they were sent to France? You know, the wrong place at the wrong time, or something like that.'

Connie gave her a look as if to say she was obviously talking out of her hat, so she sighed and said no more.

She could say her brother Len had turned out to be in either the wrong place at the wrong time or the right place at the right time depending on how one looked at it, news arriving around April of his being wounded, then shipped down river to a Basra hospital. Finally he returned home in June minus a leg. It was terrible but at least he was alive.

'Damned thing went gangrene,' he'd said as he sat in the rickety hospital wheelchair with the family around him, holding Flossie's hand as she fussed over him. 'Nothing they could do except chop it off.'

He said little else about his experiences but there was much in the papers describing such fearful conditions out there as made a person cringe to read – wounded lying untreated in a primitive Basra hospital with hardly any medical supplies – it was a wonder he'd survived at all.

'One of the lucky ones ter tell the truth,' he said when he was finally discharged. 'A couple of weeks after I got this Blighty one, the whole bloody thirty thousand of my lot surrendered ter the Turks. God knows 'ow them poor sods must be faring, knowing that lot. I can only say thanks for this.' He touched his bandaged stump. 'All I can say is it's a bleedin' ill wind what blows no one any good,' he quoted in all sincerity.

Other than that, he refused to be drawn any further on all he must have gone through, but it was there in his eyes even as he laughed off his disability, saying at least he'd never be sent back. Two weeks later he and Flossie became engaged.

Not long after that Connie was in tears again, this time for her sister, whose letter was written in mid-July from her parents' home. Verity's husband had been excellent officer material, a captain, but a high-explosive shell appeared to have little respect for class.

'He was killed that first day of the Somme offensive, the first of July, but she's only now been able to bring herself to tell me.' Connie bit back her tears. 'She must be devastated. She's staying with our parents for the time being.'

'Will you write to her?' Eveline asked. Every time she heard of a death she thought of Albert, thanked God he was still unharmed and prayed he'd remain so. Sometimes it seemed a miracle that he was still unscathed when thousands of men were being killed and wounded, some horrifically.

Connie shook her head to her question. 'I'm not certain. I know how the post works in that house – if they still have a butler, he takes it straight to my father to open. If that's still being done then anything I write to her will be seen by him. There's no way I can correspond with her.'

'Surely he can't do that,' Eveline said, shocked. 'She's a grown woman, married, it's her letter and she's grieving. Surely she needs a kind word, even from you.'

Connie's face tightened. 'You don't know my father,' she said bitterly.

But she did write. 'I didn't really expect a reply,' she said when there was none. 'Not while she's there with them.'

Her face twisted as she looked up suddenly. 'Eveline, whatever shall I do if that happened to George?'

But Eveline had her own mind on Albert. What would she do if anything happened to *him,* despite her prayers?

August and September with the endless to-ing and fro-ing of fighting the length of the Western Front, the daily newspaper reports of casualties – one hundred and twenty-seven thousand in August alone making readers gasp in horror – crept by for Eveline. Each day she dreaded the arrival of a telegram and felt abject gratitude as another day ended uneventfully with the drawing of her curtains on the long twilight of Daylight Saving, introduced in May. Clocks had been brought forward an extra hour in a drive to save hundreds of thousands of tons of coal much needed for industry.

Before they knew it, it was autumn, British Summer Time, as it was now called, come to an end until next year, making the nights draw in with alarming suddenness with the clocks going back overnight.

Their third Christmas of the war was almost upon them. They were at one and the same time heartened by the news of Allied forces breaking the German lines on the Somme and horrified by the November death toll of six hundred and fifty thousand Allies and only five hundred thousand Germans, but with both Albert and George it seemed still leading charmed lives.

Despite the almost nightly hum of Zeppelins, the explosion as a bomb fell, often too close for comfort, the bleak, expressionless faces of those who had probably had that dread telegram from the front, the rising cost of food which was beginning to be in short supply anyway, and the still-continuing stalemate in the trenches, somehow life went on.

There was a change of Prime Minister, Asquith stepping down to give way to Lloyd George, who was voicing his decision to form a new government dedicated to a more vigorous prosecution of the war.

'I hope that means he'll find a way to end it,' Connie said, her tone full of doubt even so. 'The longer it goes on, the more chance there is of George or Albert being ... well, you know.'

With the children they'd gone to the pictures together to see a Buster Keaton film and forget the war for an hour or so. But the moment they emerged, their minds went straight to it again.

'I try not to think about things like that,' Eveline lied brusquely, neatly ending that turn of conversation as she huddled inside her coat against the snow flurries, leaving her legs exposed to the chill.

Fashions had changed, with low necklines and higher hemlines. With more money in their purse, she and Connie could afford fashionable clothes, enjoying displaying slim ankles and the lower half of those shapely calves previously hidden from view.

One who had noticed her calves was their factory inspector, Mr John Hewitt, a young man in his late twenties, single, but who'd been kept out of the army by a perforated eardrum. He told her this after she asked why he was still a civilian. He'd become angry, his narrow face twisting into a dark frown that had her sympathising with him.

'I tried to join up,' he told her as she and Connie sat eating their sandwiches together with the other women at lunchtime. 'I tried to pretend there was nothing wrong with me but they found out. I'm now frightened to even go out in case I'm confronted by some virago of a woman brandishing a white feather in my face. It happens quite frequently, you know. Perhaps people like me should be given a badge saying what's wrong with us.'

It hadn't been a joke, but Eveline had laughed, making his dark look break into a dashing smile. She had been drawn to that smile; it was so seldom one saw a young man smiling these days. She missed Albert's smile, longed for his arms about her, felt empty of love and comfort. It was good to talk to John Hewitt. They talked about ordinary things during the dinner breaks, ignoring the war, he telling her about his life with his mother, his father having died of some chest complaint years ago. His mother had never remarried. He spoke of his upbringing as an only child, of his hobbies, one of which was woodworking; she talked about Albert and their daughter, aware that she now saw Helena as his daughter.

'Did you have a good Christmas?' she asked him when they returned to work after the so-called festive season.

It had been as good as they could possibly make it as they ate their less sumptuous Christmas dinner this year. The singsong afterwards hadn't been half as jolly as last year's, the songs more plaintive: 'If You Were the Only Girl in the World', and 'Take me Back to Dear Old Blighty', before they had settled down for the usual games of cards.

'It was quiet,' he said as he munched his cheese

sandwich. Connie had turned her back on them to talk to her workmates. 'Just me and my mother. We don't mix with many people.'

Reading between his words, Eveline strongly suspected him of being dominated by his mother with never a chance of breaking free.

She suddenly felt sorry for him. He seemed a lonely young man, kept out of the army that would have made him strong and confident and given him pals.

When he asked her if she'd go to the pictures with him, just friendly like, she agreed. With most of the men away fighting, his must be a lonely existence. 'But just the once,' she warned. As a married woman, going to see a film with a man wasn't something she should be doing. 'And don't get the idea there's anything in it, either.'

'Of course not,' he said, to her relief. She would go just this once, no more, just out of kindness really.

She picked an evening when she wasn't seeing Connie, asking her next-door neighbour if she'd come in to keep an eye on Helena for two hours.

'I'm seeing a cousin of mine, going off to France,' she told her, which was quite readily accepted.

It was quite nice sitting beside a man in the darkened cinema. He had bought her a bag of peanuts which they both ate, the cracking of the shells no interruption to the silent film. She'd feared he might put an arm about her but he sat perfectly still beside her engrossed and amused by the antics of Charlie Chaplin. Afterwards he walked her to the bus stop, moving back with a small goodbye wave as she stepped on the bus.

What am I doing, came the thought as she settled down on the seat. Albert was fighting for his country in a foreign land and she was going to the pictures with another man. This had to stop, right now. She got off the bus at the other end determined that there'd be no more outings with him.

She refused his next invitation to a theatre though the refusal served to heighten the emptiness she felt. She longed to be taken out and about by someone. She so longed for Albert to fill that void; the invitation emphasised the loneliness of her life so much that it would be so easy and tempting to accept.

What she'd tried to guard against happened on a February day as she hung up her coat in the women's cubicle. Connie had gone on ahead with a group of others leaving her on her own.

John Hewitt came by just as she was about to follow. He paused at the opening to the factory, the noise already deafening, innocently barring her way, his coat ready to hang up in the men's section.

'I didn't see you there,' he said, hovering before the now-deserted area. 'I'm a bit late this morning. My mother wasn't too well.'

'Oh, I'm sorry,' she said, making to pass him, but he touched her arm, making her hesitate.

'I've been meaning to ask, would you come out with me one night this week?'

She shook her head. 'I told you, John, our going to the pictures was just that one time. I shouldn't have. It could have started up all sorts of problems.' She realised that his hand still lay lightly on her arm. The hand seemed to tremble.

'Eveline, I can't help what I feel about you,' he whispered. 'I feel ... I feel very strange. I feel...'

He was leaning close to her, and with her heart thumping, her throat tight, the lonely emptiness inside began to mount as, hidden by the coats hanging on wall hooks and free-standing racks, she could hear his rapid panting mingling with hers.

Seconds later she returned to her senses with a jolt. With all her strength she gave him a mighty push, sending him staggering into one of the racks, almost knocking it over.

Frantically he steadied it as she shouted her anger at him. Then he was moving away, stammering that he was sorry, he couldn't imagine what had come over him. She stood silent as he hurried from the cloak area.

She was still there when Connie came in a few minutes later to see where she had got to. Seeing her strained expression she asked if she was feeling ill.

'I came over a bit faint,' she answered and had Connie come to look closer at her, studying her face which she felt must be unnaturally flushed.

'You don't look very well.'

'No, I'm all right now,' she said hurriedly. 'Just a passing thing, but I thought I'd better stay here until I felt better.'

'It's this work,' said Connie. 'It's too much. It can get you down. I really pray this war doesn't go on for much longer or we'll all be falling ill. Are you sure you're all right?'

'Yes, of course,' she insisted, glad to see that Connie finally seemed convinced. How could she have been so silly?

Over the coming week she felt deeply ashamed of what she had nearly allowed to happen. It felt unwholesome too, as if she must have seemed no better than a common slut for him to think he could take advantage of her like that.

Now she couldn't look at him without feeling creepy all over. He too appeared ill at ease and avoided her eyes if ever they met. Unable to believe that she could have actually let herself get into such a situation to warrant that sort of attention, she even thought of leaving her job with some excuse or other. But it was he who left. She didn't know where he'd gone, and wondered if he'd perhaps tried again to join up.

Connie remarked after he'd left, 'He was an odd sort of person, don't you think? He was quite friendly at lunchtimes and then without cause he began to behave as though we'd done him some injury. Strange, leaving so suddenly. I wonder why? Did he say anything to you?'

'I suppose he had his reasons,' she said, shrugging. 'But it doesn't matter, does it?'

'No, I suppose not. I'm glad he left. I thought he was a bit odd sometimes, coming over to eat his sandwiches with us women. I sometimes thought you encouraged him a little too much.'

Eveline made no reply to this observation. But the next three weeks were spent in private reflection. She would never have done so but what if she had and she'd fallen pregnant? It didn't bear thinking about. It had happened to her before, and so easily, her recollection of that time being awful, haunted by fear of being marked out, pointed at as a loose woman.

She'd been so fortunate in having had Albert rescue her as he had, a selfless, wonderful man. How could she have considered allowing herself this time, even if only for a split second, to be carried away all because she had felt so lonely? Thousands of women were feeling lonely without their men, but they didn't allow themselves to get into some ridiculous situation behind a pile of coats in some cloakroom. Thinking back, it might almost have been funny if she hadn't been left hating herself for having come near, as she kept seeing it, to betraying the man she loved.

Chapter Twenty-six

So far the lull had lasted some several minutes other than the occasional snap of rifle fire at a head poked briefly above a parapet; opposing trenches ran only tens of yards apart in some places. A lull always felt uncanny on ears deafened by the scream of shells and still ringing from the unbroken violence of explosions that seemed to rip the very air to shreds.

Crouched in the mud at the bottom of the trench, his back against its crumbling wall, Albert glanced across at George. They grinned at each other, teeth gleaming starkly from dirt-encrusted faces, but neither spoke. The last bombardment had been too shattering to resort now to conversation.

Without a word, he laid his rifle to one side and fished into his breast pocket for a packet of cigarettes, flattened and grubby, offering one to Albert. Wordlessly he took it. Lighting up, they drew satisfying lungfuls of the sweet smoke, smoke that helped ease a tense body, unclench the teeth and calm that peculiar twitch to facial muscles that betrayed a man's secret anguish caused more by the excruciating din of shellfire than fear of death itself.

George dug into his pocket again and drew out a grubby notepad and stub of pencil. Opening the book, he bent his head and began writing. It had to be hastily written, the note to his wife. If allowed to finish it he would put it back into the top pocket of his filthy tunic until it could be handed to someone coming along the line to be posted for him.

Albert looked at the others sprawled along the trench's length as far as he could see, which wasn't far. Originally straight, it now wound like a snake, much of the parapet caved in from direct hits and partially dug out again by sappers, other parts just left. It was a mess.

He turned his glance from the body beside him. The man had fallen back from a lump of shrapnel to the side of his head during this last assault. He now lay face up in the mud, eyes staring sightlessly. Albert wanted to close them for him but lacked an effort of will. Instead he lifted his gaze to survey the trench. Men were slumped in various postures, arses and elbows in half a foot of water, uniforms covered in mud and blood that wouldn't dry in this weather, ears and cheeks wrapped around in mufflers or balaclavas against the freezing wet of February, helmets balanced on top. There was little talking.

Others were moving among them, medics, taking away the worst casualties, stretchers negotiating collapsed parapets, the slightly wounded having field dressings applied by mates, given a cigarette and water. Some groaned but for the most part they lay or sat quiet until they too could be helped away which would depend on when the next assault began. The dead, like Lt. Morrison beside him, lay where they'd fallen, some half buried in mud or with just the odd limb protruding from the collapsed part of the trench, men preferring not to notice them. Removing half-buried bodies, much less parts of bodies, wasn't a priority, if they could be removed at all between attacks. The stench of putrefaction was something one never got used to.

The lull was lasting. Grateful for small mercies, Albert used the moments to find his own notepad and pencil. He could at least start a letter to Eveline in what was left of this break in the shelling. Folded in the notepad was her last letter, a few weeks old now, and a scrap of grubby brown paper, reminder of the Christmas parcel she'd sent – a slab of Christmas cake, a packet of boiled sweets, a slab of milk chocolate, a pair of knitted khaki socks and a khaki balaclava which he was now wearing under his helmet. It felt nice and warm too.

George too had received a food parcel, from Connie. They'd scoffed the lot when thankfully at a rest camp and feeling relatively civilised once more, apart from attending a funeral party and visiting the tiny cemetery with its simple wooden crosses where some of the men they had known were buried.

Before writing, he reread Eveline's letter as he had done a dozen times already. She had written to him about her Christmas, and it was like reading about another world. She'd written light-heartedly about an explosion at Allan & Hanbury's chemical factory behind where they lived in Waterlow Buildings.

It went off with such a crash, I dropped a cup and

saucer from our best china set, broke it to smithereens. Soot came down the chimney and covered everything. Then Connie came rushing round to us carrying Rebecca in her arms. I mean, Rebecca's nearly seven years old and she was carrying her like she was a baby. Their faces were black with soot and she said her flat was covered in it. There was no other damage but she was in such a state, absolutely terrified.

Her other news had had him worried out of his life for her, speaking of raids from Zeppelins and now aeroplanes, and of an explosion at the Venesta munitions works not far from the one where she worked, sixty-nine people killed there. She'd said the newspapers reported that it had been heard in Wiltshire. She'd scared him. It could have been the factory she worked in. What if he survived this war, as he was sure he would, having gone through three years of it, only for her to be killed by some explosion where she was working? It was after all a munitions factory. It could happen.

Bending his head, he began to write: 'My dearest darling,' then found his hand shaking – fear for her or because of this last bombardment, he couldn't say.

His efforts to try again with more determination were cut short anyway by a renewed outbreak of shellfire, an officer yelling for them to go over the top to occupy an enemy trench some forty yards away apparently reported to have been evacuated.

With the others Albert scrambled over the subsided rim of his portion of trench, bounded forward, body bent double, gun held ready to fire, ears battered by whiz-bangs and flashes. Someone beside him threw up his arms and fell backwards, sliding into a shell hole of muddy water. He ran on, intent only on reaching the hopefully vacated trench and – please God – safety. It could be called an advance, though where to in the gathering darkness broken only by the flash of whiz-bangs, no one knew.

It was a tidier, deeper trench than theirs but, with the continuous shelling at last letting up, no haven from the incessant rain as they cleared the place of the dead that Jerry had left behind, ugly sights from which most averted their eyes. That done, in pouring rain they stood most of the night and part of the next day, needing sleep and longing for the relief to arrive, while Lewis gunners and snipers fired sporadically at any moving target.

Albert finished his letter two days later after a series of particularly harrowing bombardments; his section was finally relieved and he was left with a field dressing on a wide shrapnel graze on his upper left arm, George with a dent in his helmet which only a second before he had replaced on his head at the moment of one renewed bombardment. Both did indeed seem to be leading charmed lives when ten of their section, including their officer, had lost theirs, and four had been seriously wounded.

'Let's hope,' he ended his letter, 'I last this war out,' but erased the words as too pessimistic, and wrote instead, 'to see you soon, darling.'

Two and a half years of fighting for just a few feet of ground gained only to be lost again; surely it couldn't last much longer, something had to happen eventually, one or the other side having to give in and call a halt to this stupidest of wars – so long as it wasn't his side!

'See you soon, darling,' he'd written. Then in early April after being sent to the rear for several weeks of other work and further training, that prayer was answered.

His arm healed by then, he and George found themselves being given leave quite out of the blue – a week in old England. Armed with the necessary papers, leave pass, certificate, they were hardly able to believe their luck.

It was strange to set foot in England, clean and brushed up. But it wasn't until he set his foot on English soil at Southampton that a peculiar shaking inside him set in again as it had often done after a particularly nasty bombardment, as if his nerves didn't belong to him. It would take all his willpower to control it, and after a while it would stop, but during that week of unbelievable peace he was to feel it several times more, though he said nothing of it to Eveline.

With no advance warning of his coming – he said there'd been no time to send a letter – Eveline felt her face go first chalk-white on opening the door to his knock, then heat up in a enormous surge of joy, throwing herself into his arms, unable to keep from dissolving into uncontrollable tears as she drew him inside their flat and still unable to believe what was happening.

'Where's Helena?' he asked when finally she'd got control of herself.

'At school,' she told him, still breathless from the shock of seeing him. 'She'll be so excited to see her dad.'

'Let's go an' collect 'er,' he said, ignoring her intention of making him a cup of tea straight away. 'We'll 'ave a proper tea and something to eat, all three of us tergether. An' if they won't let 'er out, I'll 'ave something ter say about it!' he added aggressively.

'George is 'ome on leave too,' he told her as they made their way over to the school. It felt so strange, him walking beside her, talking to her as if they'd never been apart. Mentally, she had to pinch herself to be sure she wasn't dreaming.

It was a week of sheer bliss that she refused to let be marred by the thought of his having to go back to France, telling herself that when he did, it would be somewhere set well behind the lines, some training camp or other, drilling new replacements coming out. He and George had done enough.

Eveline felt the week speeding by, hating so much of it being taken in fulfilling family duty when all they wanted was to spend it together.

'We must spend a bit of time with me mum,' Albert said. ''Er with both me and Jim away fighting.' Which was only right when his mother had some time ago willingly taken on the job of seeing Helena to school and fetching her back to look after her until Eveline could pick her up after work. Though her own mum was more inclined towards Helena these days, the shop kept her busy and she was probably glad for someone else to do it.

'We ought to see my parents as well, at least once,' Eveline said. This seemed only fair, what with her brother Len at home trying to cope with his false leg and hoping to marry Flossie come September and May still at home too, twenty-three and apparently unable to settle to any steady boy. Nor could they leave out Gran, who'd done so much for her where her mother had done so little.

His seven days' leave wasn't even a full week with her; his first day had been taken up getting home, and the last day would be spent getting back, so it was really five days. She almost envied Connie not having relatives to visit – they could spend their whole time together.

They did have an evening or two to themselves, one going off to the pictures to hold hands like lovers as they watched a comedy and then a cowboy film on the flickering, silent screen, while his mother gave eye to little Helena. 'You two need ter be on yer own fer a while,' she'd said.

A second evening was the highlight of the week – seats in the gods to see the musical show *Chu Chin Chow* at His Majesty's Theatre that even after a year was still so popular it was hard to get seats at all.

Albert's mother again looking after Helena, they'd gone to join the snaking queue of waiting hopefuls, lining up for ages in the cold drizzle, and were very lucky to get in. The doorman, taking pity on a half-drenched woman with her uniformed husband also looking haggard enough to have recently come from the front, had ever so slightly lifted the hand he was about to bring down, allowing them to duck underneath.

While the rest of the queue had been turned away to try another evening, they'd run up the several flights of stone stairs to the gods to be found a couple of seats, some people even moving along to allow them to sit together.

The changing colour of scenery, the oriental costumes, the wonderful songs, 'The Cobbler's Song' and 'I'm Chu Chin Chow From China', the exciting music, Albert sitting beside her with the box of chocolates they'd bought for the occasion, his warmth against her: it all made for an evening she knew she would never forget.

The only thing that worried her was Albert waking suddenly at night with a shout that made her blood run cold. Asked what was wrong, he'd say, 'Nothing, just a bloody daft dream, go back ter sleep,' so fiercely that she dared not pry further. It was all she could get out of him, but it worried her.

Their last evening was spent with Connie and George, as felt only right. Hurrying back home to bed, with Helena tucked up and sound asleep, they made love so fondly, as they'd done every night, she was sure she'd find herself pregnant in a few weeks' time and prayed it would be so.

Too soon leave was over. She and Connie went together to see them off, the two men the best of pals. Saying goodbye, trying to be brave, biting back the tears, she said her goodbyes with a smile as best she could. All the tears in the world couldn't stop the march of time and she could only pray Albert would remain safe and well and come back soon. Connie, though, was in floods and she wondered if Albert would have sooner seen her in the same state, but she knew he understood that it would have made it harder. She would shed her tears when she got home. There, in private, she would cry her heart out.

Together they waved their menfolk off at Paddington Station, waving frantically as their heads poking from the carriage window got smaller and smaller, the train puffing out of the station to finally disappear from view.

Being together had helped take off some of the sharp pain of saying goodbye, but returning home each felt alone, quiet and thoughtful and sad. In time they'd become used to their loneliness again, be able to laugh as they went off to work, but for the present each kept this reawakened sense of loneliness to herself.

Chapter Twenty-seven

Eveline felt her prayers had been answered. Albert's next letter said he and George had indeed been sent to a training camp for a spell. She missed him dreadfully but she could at last sleep contented, though for how long?

Connie was so full of relief about her husband that Eveline saw tears sparkle in her eyes as she read out that part of her letter. 'Perhaps they'll be there until the war is over,' she sniffed bravely. 'It can't be too long, now that America is in the war.'

The United States President Woodrow Wilson had signed his country's declaration of war while their husbands had been home on leave and it had been a tremendous bit of news then.

'It's such a huge country,' she gabbled on hopefully. 'With so many thousands more men we're bound to win soon. Oh, I do so hope it'll be over before long, before anything awful should happen to George, and your Albert too.'

Her emotions getting the better of her, she finally indulged herself in a little weep, leaving Eveline trying hard to conceal her impatience.

Connie cried far too easily, she thought, but she couldn't condemn her for shedding more tears a month later when Verity's letter came by late post bearing the terrible news that their brother Herbert had died of wounds.

'Both my brothers. Both gone. My parents,

whatever must they be feeling, both of their sons lost to them? Oh, this terrible, terrible war.'

She seemed less concerned for her own sense of loss than for that of her mother and father, and Eveline, not knowing what sort of comfort she was expected to offer, could only think of the oddity of the wealthy in that siblings were probably never close enough to feel a loss the way she'd have felt it had it been one of her brothers. She could be wrong but was it that they were used to separation, sent away as the boys were to public schools at an early age?

She thanked God that Len losing his leg had taken him out of the war, and that her other brother Fred, called up this year, and her sister Tilly's husband, also called up, were both still safe in England.

'I've decided I shall go and visit my parents,' Connie said as she recovered her composure.

'I wouldn't,' Eveline advised. 'You know the reception you got last time. Perhaps you should just write and say how upset you are. If they don't reply, well, at least you wrote.'

Connie had to agree, but after they got home from work, she was back knocking on Eveline's door, this time dry-eyed. She held a telegram. 'It's from Verity. My father had another heart attack after the news of my brother. He died in the early hours of this morning.'

It was said in such a flat tone that Eveline could hardly believe she was speaking of her father. But it was for her mother that Connie seemed most concerned.

'She must be utterly devastated. She was

devoted to him. They had never been apart in all their married life. How will she survive, her sons and now him? I must go to the funeral. I'll get the arrangements from Verity.'

She seemed so calm, so unlike her, that Eveline was worried for her.

'Would you like me to come with you?' she asked. Connie shook her head, her thoughts seeming to be elsewhere, but Eveline persisted. 'What if you get the same sort of reception you've had at other times? You might need someone to be there with you.'

Again she shook her head. 'Verity will be there. She will stay by me.'

'She's closer to your mum than you are and she might not be of any comfort. I really ought to be there with you, Connie.'

This time Connie put up no objection, merely nodding absently.

When Verity's next letter came giving Thursday as the day of the funeral, together with time and place, Eveline hurried over to her mother-in-law to see if she would take care of Helena overnight, hoping Gran might do the same for Connie. To her surprise, Albert's mum without hesitation offered to take both.

'I raised two blooming boisterous boys,' she said firmly. 'If I can't look after two little well-behaved seven-year-old girls fer one night, I'm a blooming monkey's uncle! Of course I'll 'ave 'em.'

'But two's more trouble than one,' Eveline said, relieved even so.

'They don't 'ave ter be. Now don't yer worry,

Ev love, they'll be orright with me. They can both go in Albert's old bed with no trouble.'

She and Connie left early that Thursday morning. Having informed their employers the day before that there was a family bereavement, no questions were asked. Bereavements had become a frequent occurrence with thousands of men being slaughtered daily.

Eveline hadn't anticipated the shock of witnessing a mother and daughter divided. Somehow it seemed far worse than when she had been divided from her own mother over Helena. At least the rift had healed even if Mum would never alter from the cool-natured women she'd always been.

Meeting Verity for the first time she was surprised to see how like Connie she looked, a friendly, likeable, approachable girl with no side to her. Their mother, whom they both took after in looks and carriage, was another matter entirely. She kissed Verity warmly but the sight of Connie had her moving back, cold and distant, almost as though she didn't see her.

Not once throughout the entire funeral service did she speak to her, Connie taking the hint and standing on the far side of the grave among the friends and colleagues of her father as the coffin was slowly lowered.

Eveline could not see whether the woman wept or not for the dense black veil over her gaunt face, but she held herself erect the whole time for which Eveline found herself admiring her. She started to see how she could have held herself so aloof from her daughter for so long.

She felt Connie, standing with an arm through hers, give a small tremble and heard a stifled sob. Immediately she firmed her grip on the arm. The sob ceased abruptly and it was Connie she now found herself admiring. Watching her father being lowered into his grave, not once in his life having offered words of forgiveness much less love, and her mother standing cold and aloof, well away from her, it had to be a terrible ordeal for any girl to endure. But worse would come.

With her arm still through Eveline's, she moved in the wake of her mother and sister, all that were left of her family, towards the smart funeral limousine taking them back to the large and lonely house.

They were three feet from the vehicle when Connie's mother stepped in front of them, barring her daughter's path.

'You have paid your respects to your father,' she said curtly with not a tremble to her tone. 'Now I ask you to go home. It is a pity you could not show your respect to him whilst he was alive.'

Eveline could hardly believe what she'd heard uttered. Connie seemed shocked into silence for a moment or two, but finally found her voice.

'It was he who asked me to leave my home. And it was both he and you who refused to see me again. I had every respect for Father, except...'

'Except that you preferred to go against his wishes.'

'I was in love with George. I couldn't...'

'You chose your life, Constance, chose to throw your father's concern for your future back into his face. Now you seek to ingratiate yourself with me through your poor father's death. Well, Constance, I think not.'

In all this, the woman had held herself rigid and calm. Now suddenly, she seemed to crumple. She lifted her veil to stare into her daughter's face and Eveline saw the fine features twist. The eyes, lit by a gleam of almost insane fury, almost made her step back. But it was the words hissing from that twisted, unforgiving mouth that stunned her.

'Why is your husband still alive when both my sons are dead, my daughter's husband dead, my own husband dead?'

'Mother!' The cry ripped itself from Connie's lips.

'That rogue you call your husband, why should he live when all the men in my family are gone?' Her eyes burned and glittered with animosity. 'Why are you still living – the one person I shall never grieve for?'

Eveline heard Connie gasp, saw her body begin to fail. She caught her before she could slip to the ground, but Connie's mother had already turned on her heel and was getting into the limousine. Verity, helping her, looked back at her sister, her eyes beseeching.

'I'm so sorry,' she whispered quickly over her shoulder. 'I'm so very sorry, Connie.'

Clambering in beside her mother she closed the door, the limousine moving off slowly.

Eveline sat at ease on a wooden packing case, Connie next to her, eating their lunchtime sandwiches.

403

Beside her, Connie had her head buried in a newspaper she'd just bought from a vendor outside the factory gate. She had recovered pretty well from the deaths of her brother and father though she never mentioned them or her mother in any conversation and Eveline felt it best to let sleeping dogs lie.

She ate slowly to make it seem more than it was. A frugal lunch had become a necessity these days with food shortages biting hard – patriotically she'd cut the bread thin, with a sliver of cheese plus a bit of pickle, and a flask of tea; it was hardly filling. Cake was becoming a thing of the past, even home-made cake, with flour in short supply. Indeed, with German submarines attacking merchant ships – more than a hundred sunk last month alone – everything was in short supply. It was even a job to get a pound of potatoes and everywhere shops and stalls had signs proclaiming no this, no that, so that most of her time after work was taken up trying to find provisions, even with the rationing.

With her back against the warm brick wall of the factory, she closed her eyes against the glare of the June sunshine, its heat on her face making her think of seeking shade. But most of her more sensible fellow workers had already taken up what shade there was.

It was so hot. Inside was unbearable but even out here there was little breeze to temper this heatwave: ninety-three degrees, the newspapers were quoting.

Suddenly Connie looked up, pushing the newspaper at her. 'Eveline, look, just there!' She pointed to the colunm she had been reading. 'It says that the Commons have voted by a three hundred and thirty majority to give the vote to married women over thirty. To think, after all this time.'

Eveline took the paper and scanned it. 'Married women over thirty,' she echoed. 'It won't include us. Me twenty-six and you twenty-seven.'

'But we will eventually be able to vote. It's a start. Wonderful news. After all our struggles, it takes a simple war to give the vote to women.'

Simple! Eveline wanted to laugh, but she didn't. Connie could be so giddy at times. Yes, they had struggled, and fought, and suffered, and some had died. They'd endured imprisonment, forced feeding, ridicule, had been ignored, loathed and often viciously handled by men averse to them. Perhaps Connie was right, it had to take a simple thing like countries going to war against each other to achieve what they had been striving for so long to gain.

She looked at the newspaper column again. So few words, as if it was merely a throwaway decision. Last March Asquith, who had always been opposed to women's suffrage, had stated that women should work out their own salvation. And they had, thousands of women doing what had once been men's jobs, working for their country while men were away fighting, and all there was to be seen of it in the papers was this one small column. Well, grand!

She handed the paper back to Connie. 'You can call it a start, but it hasn't been passed yet. It still has to go through a third parliamentary reading.

Goodness knows when that will be.'

The same old routine: an encouraging beginning, then a few months later, the bill thrown out. She would lay no store by it. The proof of the pudding was in the eating.

'It *is* a start,' Connie pouted, for once stubborn, but Eveline couldn't feel that convinced.

'We've had so many starts, all false,' she added as she folded her empty paper bag to save for tomorrow's sandwiches, got up and went back into the shade of the factory floor, stifling though it was, ready for an afternoon's grind at a gaping machine making shell cases.

Even so, the news was mulled over at their Wednesday branch meeting, though with the same sense of not having achieved it by their own campaigning, as if they had been done out of some triumph. In fact after the first flurry of chatter over it, conversation turned to the recent air raids on London, not by Zeppelins but aeroplanes. These proved far more alarming, being swifter and harder to hit; at one time fifteen had been counted in one air raid. Worse, they caused far greater loss of life. One had hit a school, another a railway station, wrecking a train.

'I don't know what things are coming to,' said one member, going on to complain of the government's decision not to install air-raid hooters in factories in case workers used them as an excuse to take time off work. 'It could cause more loss of life and I think it's disgraceful.' Her listeners murmured agreement, any more talk of women's enfranchisement taking second place to the events of the times.

Len married Flossie early in September. It was a quiet wedding, with him on crutches; his new false leg had been rubbing his stump so badly that it had become infected and was still being treated. She hung on to his arm at the altar as if fearing he might fall down. But they were happy, even though after a hot, dry summer it decided to pour with rain on their wedding day.

The church smelled of wet macs and umbrellas left inside the porch as Flossie divested herself of her mac to reveal a somewhat crumpled wedding dress. Afterwards it was almost a sprint to Len's parents' flat for the celebrations, a sign on his dad's shop saying SORRY – CLOSED FOR THE WEDDING OF MY SON.

This time it was the Fentons' flat that smelled of rain-soaked macs and umbrellas hanging on the coat stand in their narrow upstairs passage, but the weather didn't diminish the fun of eating, drinking and singing – jolly old songs: 'Pack Up Your Troubles in Your Old Kitbag', and 'Goodbye-ee, Don't Cry-ee', and especially 'The Bells are Ringing for Me and My Girl', which felt very appropriate to the day.

For a few hours they could all forget, or try to forget, the desperate fields of Flanders, the pictures of the gaping craters of Ypres and the quagmire Passchendaele was becoming, where their fighting men had got bogged down by mud. It was raining there too. Three women who couldn't forget for one minute were Eveline's sister Tilly, her husband having recently been sent out there, and Eveline and Connie, who was more like her sister than Tilly. Their husbands they now knew were already there, training camp having ended many weeks ago.

Eveline wrote a long letter to Albert all about the wedding, hoping it wouldn't be too delayed. She wanted to tell him about his brother Jim, but thought it best not too. Jim's girl had broken it off with him, while he was away somewhere in France. It seemed such a terribly unfair and cruel thing to do, though from the way his mother had described her perhaps he was better off without her. But it was hard to be told that sort of news when a man's away fighting for his country unable to do anything.

The shattered remains of the small town of Ypres seen from a distance resembled a jumble of rotten teeth, but Albert's mind was too blasted to even look at it as he and a team of wet and weary men heaved and pushed and pulled at a field gun bogged down in the mud. It hadn't stopped raining for so long, he couldn't remember when last it hadn't rained.

'Get yer shoulders to it, yer useless buggers! Move it!'

At the hoarse bellow of the corporal, he heaved harder. Out here in the open wasn't good. But most of the trenches had caved in, from shelling and subsidence from incessant rain, some with three feet of water in them, just like the shell holes, just like the one he could see to the left of him, the water it held deep enough to drown a wounded man if he fell into it. No getting out again up those steep, wet chalky sides. Calm the water looked, calm as any country pond, calm and treacherous, benignly reflecting the overcast sky and other toiling figures on the far side of it.

'Adams! Stop gazing around like some bleedin' love-sick woman! Put some bloody weight be'ind it.'

He saw George grin briefly at him, and saw his feet slip in the slimy morass as he heaved, threatening to send him almost flat on his face, his puttees thick with mud. He couldn't see his own boots, ankle-deep in it; one or two of the others were in halfway to their knees. And they were being expected to haul this perishing gun out? Some bloody hopes! What a blooming life!

He saw the aeroplane, heard the rattle of its machine-gun fire and ducked instinctively as it swooped. Something disengaged itself from the plane and he threw himself flat as the bomb hit the ground with a terrific explosion. He caught a glimpse of George describing a strange revolving movement as though dancing in slow motion and knew George had been hit.

Automatically, with the roar of the aeroplane and racket of returning rifle fire from men on the ground seeming a long way off like in a dream, he leaped towards him with some idea of protecting him.

Others had been hit but he didn't see them. Showered by mud and debris, he caught George's arm as he began to slide down into the newly formed crater along with tons of thick mud. All he could see of his friend's right side was a mass of bloody flesh as if he'd been sliced in two, but he still hung on, he himself almost sliding into the hole. If he went in too he'd never get out again and he knew instinctively that George was already dead.

Letting go, he lay face down in the mud, watching as if in a trance as the limp body slid away from him, slipping slowly downwards amid a flow of wet clay and silt. He saw it come to rest at the bottom while the disturbed sides of the crater continued to flow, slowly, inexorably covering the body, a ready-made grave. He realised he was crying as someone got him on his feet and began helping him away.

There were other bodies nearby, but all he could see was George sliding away from him; he might never be found in this forsaken acre of mire men were fighting over. The gun they'd been trying to extricate was nowhere to be seen; that too had gone into the crater.

'I'm so sorry, mate,' someone said. 'So sorry.' But Albert hardly heard him.

Chapter Twenty-eight

Connie's grief was awful to see, not because she hadn't stopped crying but because she hadn't cried at all – two months had gone by since getting the telegram and not a single tear had Eveline seen her shed, this girl who usually wept at the drop of a hat.

These days of war, grief was kept behind locked doors. With so many men being lost every single day, who would dare to insult the grief of others with public tears as if they were the only one bereaved? And so Connie hadn't cried and Eveline felt utterly helpless to comfort her. In fact any attempt at comfort seemed lost on her.

It was like watching someone in a trance to watch her going about her daily life. Even the day the telegram had come, she'd gone to work as usual, the admirable young widow refusing to let her loss get the better of her, but Eveline believed she knew different.

That day she'd waited for Connie at the school gates as usual, having seen Helena into school. As Connie arrived, Eveline noticed how rigid she seemed and when she straightened up from kissing goodbye to Rebecca, her face was stiff as a mask.

She had held out the buff-coloured telegram every family dreaded. 'It came this morning,' she said, her tone steady, while shock spread through

Eveline's system with no need to read the words that began: REGRET TO INFORM YOU...

An instant later, her breath escaping in a heart-felt cry, she had flung her arms about her, but Connie had pulled away to tug her coat straight as though embarrassed that other mothers might have witnessed the gesture.

'We'll be late for work,' she'd said in such a quiet tone that Eveline could hardly believe she'd heard her right. Never had she seen her so calm, Connie who usually resorted to tears at any given moment. It was unnatural.

'You can't go to work,' she'd said, wanting to cry for her. 'I'll stay with you. I'll take the time off. You can't be alone.'

Connie had shaken her head. 'We have to go to work. It's what we have to do.' And that was what she did.

Now Christmas was upon them, their girls on school holiday sitting in Connie's flat, heads together, making paper chains. Connie had said at first that she wasn't having any, but had meekly submitted to Eveline's urging to have some sort of Christmas decoration for Rebecca's sake. After all, the girl did not seem to be missing her dad, having not seen him for over three years except for the few brief days of his leave.

'She still needs to enjoy Christmas, Connie,' she said and saw the slight, careless shrug of Connie's shoulders.

It was upsetting to see her like this. But how would she have behaved if it had been Albert? Where they had once happily exchanged snippets from their husband's letters, she felt it better not to share the bits of news in Albert's letters. Connie never asked after him, which was understandable, but sometimes she would catch Connie giving her a sideways glance that, if she hadn't known her for her sweet nature, she'd have said bore a touch of pettiness. Perhaps it went with bereavement.

It was, of course, asking too much to expect her to perk up because it was Christmas, but she had hoped it might have made a difference. It didn't.

'You go on and enjoy Christmas Day at your parents',' she said when Eveline told her she was naturally invited. 'I'd sooner stay here at home.'

To brood, Eveline thought, but said, 'For Rebecca's sake. She'll have other children to play with and she's almost like Helena's sister. She'll miss her, being here on her own.'

But Connie remained stubborn, and the last thing Eveline wanted was to speak her mind and say she was wallowing too much in her grief, because that's what it seemed like to her.

She went off to her mum's, but without Connie it was a miserable day for her. She was glad to pop in on Boxing Day and, although no laughter abounded there, it made her feel better.

Thick fog hung over the low ground, everything silent as the grave. Albert stood at his post, surreptitiously smoking a cigarette, its glowing tip screened with one hand though, in this fog, who would see it?

Four thirty in the morning, March 1918. He felt he'd been here for all his life. Life! He swore silently. George would never again know life beyond this miserable one – to him this ugly world no longer mattered. After six months he still pined for him. But the war had gone on without him, a job had to be done and there was no time for pining. It was so quiet. Wrapped in fog, it felt as if he too was in a world other than this one – was that what it could be like to be dead?

'What time is it, sir?' he whispered to Captain Thoroughgood. The man looked at his watch.

'Four thirty-five... No, four thirty-nine. Be getting light in an hour.'

'Not in this fog,' Albert whispered.

The words were no sooner out of his mouth than the air split apart. He didn't know it but some six thousand German guns had crashed out together and for five solid hours the bombardment stunned every man along the whole depth of the British defence line. None of the now-decimated troops noticed the sun rising at six o'clock, the fog still as thick as ever. It held another vapour, invisibly mixing with it. It was in Albert's trench before he realised. Still fumbling for his gas mask, he fell to the ground, choking, blindly trying to drag it from its container, already unable to coordinate his movements. Other men found themselves in the same straits while some, having had the presence of mind to get into theirs, were trying to help the less responsive.

Overwhelmed by the great German push, the Allies could only retreat, the next several days seeing every road packed with units and transport in retreat, followed across the old battlefields of the Somme by an unremitting onslaught of shell bursts, machine gun and rifle fire and the flames of burning buildings.

"Ow yer making out, mate?' Albert heard the words but couldn't reply. His throat burned, his chest burned, his eyes burned. He hung between two comrades he couldn't see for the rag binding his eyes, his legs automatically walking, his weight taken off them. He knew he was dying. All he wanted was to be put down by the roadside and left to it. But somehow, after what seemed like days of this Great Retreat, he ended up in a clean hospital bed, nurses bending over him, soothing mixtures being administered. But still his chest burned and he could hardly breathe.

It would soon be Helena's birthday. Eveline was preparing to give her the best little party possible within the confines of grave food shortages that were beginning to bite. Hardly any flour stocks could be had, meat was rationed to twenty ounces a week per person, now butter and margarine were rationed too and few goodies were available. But she meant to do it, somehow. Since being told of her husband's injuries, she'd resolutely saved up her rations so as to give their daughter something to remember her eighth birthday by.

Albert was in a hospital in France and she'd felt almost grateful that he was no longer fighting, but she was worried. They'd said he was ill though not how ill, only that he'd eventually be sent home for good.

At least he'd be out of the war. He'd dictated a letter to a nurse to post on to her, saying not to worry, that he hoped to be able to see again in time and, though his lungs had been affected, he hoped they'd soon heal. But she couldn't help reading between the lines. She only prayed she was reading things wrongly, and told herself that the thing to remember was that he'd be coming home, which had to be encouraging.

One thing, the depressing and devastating news of Allied retreat before massed German forces transferred to the Western Front since the Russian peace treaty had Germany claiming a victory, was over. British forces had consolidated, stopping the enemy in its tracks, ground lost was being regained, but Albert was safe, badly gassed, but safe. She knew what was in store for her in caring for him, but he'd be with her. Poor Connie hadn't had that luck. Come to think of it, Connie's fate had been awful for years, losing her brothers, her father, then her husband. In a way it had made her much stronger, but strangely withdrawn.

She'd grown distant with Eveline since her husband's death, yet Eveline felt she'd done nothing to warrant it. They were drifting apart and it upset her. Nothing she said or did seemed to make any difference. She had made efforts to cling to her but it was Connie who was doing the drifting and who could often be quite sharp with her; Eveline had no way of combating it.

There were times when she'd get to the school gates with Helena to find Connie had already gone on to work, where once she had always waited so they could go together. Sometimes she wanted to cry at what seemed to be happening between them. After all these years so close to each other, it was like being pushed away by a sister.

'I'm going to give Helena a nice party for her birthday,' she said at the end of April. 'You will

416

help me with it, won't you?'

'I wonder you can find food enough for a party,' came the terse reply.

'I've been saving up,' Eveline said.

'That's nice for you,' Connie said and went on feeding the shell cases into the machine that packed them with high explosive.

Eveline too went on with her work. She needed to have it out with her but now wasn't the time. This work was so dangerous that one had to keep one's mind on it. She waited until they had their lunchtime sandwiches, sitting at their benches to eat, too wet and miserable to go outside, the smell of factory oil and grease and metal tainting their food and, with little fresh air to dispel it, making her feel sick.

'What's wrong?' she began, this strange hostility of Connie's finally beginning to wear her down.

'What should be wrong?' Connie countered airily, turning away to unscrew her vacuum flask of tea.

'I don't know. I thought you might know.'

'I'm sure I have no idea what you mean.'

Connie's refined accents were still with her despite all these years in the East End, but she could make them sound quite scathing when she wanted. And that's how they sounded now as if all this was Eveline's fault.

'Why are you being so horrible to me?' she burst out before she could stop herself. It was the worst thing she could have done.

'Horrible!' Connie turned on her, making her start back mentally to see the hostility in her eyes. 'Well, I'm sorry if that is what you think. You haven't lost a husband...'

'Connie – thousands of women have lost husbands, and brothers and sons and fiancés. I know what you're going through.'

'You don't. How can you?'

'Is this what it's about, Connie? You losing your husband when I've not? Well, I'll tell you this. My Albert's desperately ill. He'll be coming home to go straight into hospital and I don't know what's going to happen. I'm in an awful state over it, and not once have you asked me how I feel.'

'At least you have him.'

Before Eveline could reply, she leaped up and hurried off to the loo. Eveline wanted to follow her, but she had already been before having her sandwiches, and she could hardly take up this argument with other girls in there listening to it all. Connie didn't appear again until the hooter sounded the end of the lunchtime, and then she merely got on with her work without saying another word, her eyes stolidly on what she was doing.

Their shift ending, she made for the cloakroom for her hat and coat and handbag before Eveline could take off her coverall, and was away.

Eveline managed to catch the same bus, but had to stand, since the vehicle was crowded with workers. Because she was one of the first to get off at her stop she waited for Connie but in the mass of people alighting saw her walk right by. She let her go, following at a distance, her heart heavy with misery, still going over what Connie had said, still unable to make any sense of this attitude of hers.

Then as she walked, the truth of what she had said at lunchtime, spoken in anger and not fully comprehended until now, dawned on her. She knew what was wrong with Connie. Jealousy. She felt jealous that Albert was alive and George was dead – hard to believe. How could a friend of so many years begrudge her Albert's life? How could she be so mean? Anger added its own weight to her heart. If that was how she felt then their friendship was over.

In a welter of misery she ignored her as they collected their children, then waited until Connie had walked off with her little one. The girl looked back, bewildered not to be walking home with her best friend in all the world; then, taking Helena's hand, Eveline moved off in the other direction.

'I want to get something from the shops first,' she told her confused daughter.

'But you and Auntie Connie always go shopping together.'

'Well, we aren't today,' Eveline returned, roughly tugging the child along, keeping her eyes averted, eyes that were filling with tears, blurring her world: a world which from now on would be without Connie.

It was hard to understand. At school she and Rebecca were always together in the playground, yet going home they were now being separated. Rebecca was her friend. She loved Rebecca. They were seldom apart.

When Granny Adams came to collect her, and Great-Gran Ansell came to collect Rebecca, or when their mums collected them after what they

419

called their early shift, it was nice walking home together and to play awhile whenever Auntie Connie had a cup of tea with Mummy. Now that was all changed. Perhaps she'd been naughty and wasn't being allowed to be with her friend. She couldn't remember being naughty.

'Why can't I be with Becky when we go 'ome?' she asked as again she and Mummy went off to the shops alone.

'Because things have changed. And the word is home, not 'ome. Say it love, *home*.'

'Home,' Helena repeated sullenly. Perhaps this was where she was being naughty, not speaking properly.

Becky, as she was known at school, spoke really nice, but most of the children in school didn't and sometimes they teased the both of them. Becky took it all in her stride, but for her it was hard, especially as Nanny Adams didn't talk posh. It was easier being like her other school chums and at the same time being popular because, knowing how to talk properly when she wanted, she'd take off the way the teachers spoke.

'Do Mrs Butterfield for us,' they'd beg. 'Do Mrs Jarvis, do our pastor, go on, do 'im.' And she would, mimicking their nice accents and their inflections of voice, making everyone laugh. Trouble was that she forgot to speak nicely in front of Mummy until prompted.

'I want you to grow up speaking as good as Rebecca,' she had often said, but lately there was a sort of edge to it. 'You're going to grow up every bit as good as Rebecca, if I have anything to say about it.'

She didn't know why her mother sounded so cross when she said it these days.

Three weeks and Albert was still in France, still in hospital, still to be sent home. She'd written to him twice a week since he'd been hospitalised but his replies had always come via some nurse or other. Of course they would be; he probably still had bandages over his damaged eyes. The trouble was that it made them sound so distant, and to know that someone else was seeing them before she did was not the same.

Yesterday she'd had a most odd letter from Albert: 'I'm a lot better, dear, but I don't think they're sending me home. It's not a Blighty one. I'm as disappointed as you, reading this, but they get the last say I suppose. It'll still take time for my eyes to get properly better. They say a few more weeks and I should be OK. I was lucky. I'm going to badger them to see if I can get them to send me home for a spot of leave before they send me back.'

Send him back! Eveline hardly read his concluding hopes that she and Helena were well. All she could see now were the words 'send me back'. She didn't understand – he'd been wounded. They didn't send men back to fight, did they? If that was what he meant.

She wanted so much to ask what Connie thought he meant, but that was no longer possible. Connie, still in grief, had drawn into herself, had stopped going to the local suffragette branch meetings – such as they were. So little went on there these days that they were more like a

421

women's social club than the vibrant, purposeful gatherings they had once been. A mere shadow of their former glory remained and she too hadn't attended these last two weeks.

She wouldn't admit even to herself how dreadfully she missed Connie, especially today with this letter. She showed it to Mum but got no real comfort from it. 'He knows 'ow ter get round the authorities. He'll be 'ome, don't you worry.'

Gran had been a bit more sympathetic, but again, her heartfelt words, 'I'm sure he'll be all right, love,' weren't as comforting as she intended.

Showing the letter to Albert's mother had the woman dissolving into tears. She'd had a letter from him too, containing much the same wording. 'Oh, I hope they don't send 'im back to the front. This blessed war – they don't care. Men's lives don't mean nothing to them.'

After several letters saying he was getting better by the day came one postmarked from a place she'd never heard of. 'Me and a lot of others ended up on a ship taking arms to Beirut to give eye to the stuff.' His letters now coming from there filled Eveline with relief that it hadn't been the Western Front where men were still being slaughtered by the hour. October saw him still stationed in the Middle East in charge of supplies, safe and well. Eagerly she waited for each letter, full of interest. Then suddenly they stopped coming.

Three weeks later she was tearing open a telegram and reading the callously brief words MISSING IN ACTION BELIEVED KILLED.

How could it be? He'd been so safe. As she shook her head at the telegram boy when he asked if there was any reply, the light of her world went out, the flesh on her face growing cold, feeling like corrugated parchment. Her heart too felt that it had died inside her, leaving her flesh to chill.

'I'm ready for school, Mummy. I've washed, I've done a wee, and I've finished my bread and jam,' came her daughter's voice from a distance and she tore her stricken gaze from the message to look down at the child. She was so pretty – she would grow up to be a beauty, a beauty Albert would never see. Her heart seemed to be crying but tears refused to reach her eyes.

'There won't be no school today, darling,' she said, hearing her voice sound small and shaky. 'Go and play in your bedroom.'

'But Mummy...' Seeing her mother's expression, her protest fell away and she went quietly into her bedroom as she'd been asked, closing the door softly behind her, not really knowing why she was being banished.

Everything felt unreal. Why couldn't she cry? The tears she had so often shed, usually at night at the mere thought of him being killed, when she would have to go on without him, deserted her now it had happened. She just felt numb, empty, unfocused. At the same time she found herself praying desperately that there could be a mistake. Mistakes had happened before, in the heat of battle especially. Not dead, just missing – that meant hope of some sort. A thought kept coming to her: his mother must have had a telegram too. She would be alone with her own desperate hope. She should go there to her.

In this torpid state, as though moving in a dream, she called Helena from her bedroom, helped her into her coat although at eight years old she was quite capable of doing it herself, and put on her own hat and coat. She looked into her handbag to make sure she had her door key, and let herself and her daughter out of her flat, holding Helena's hand going down the stone stairs, then turning towards her mother-in-law's flat.

She could see Wilmott Street School. A small spark of life came back into her. Perhaps it would be better if Helena was there rather than with her. If she did burst into tears, the child would become confused and frightened.

Eveline blinked. How could she be having these ordinary, everyday thoughts after being told of Albert's death, as if nothing had happened, even to the extent of being aware that it was an overcast morning and that she should have had an umbrella because it could rain?

'Would you rather go to school?' she asked.

Helena pursed her lips. 'I'll be in trouble for being late.'

'I'll come with you and explain to your teacher.'

Explain what? That she'd just heard her husband was missing, could be dead?

She didn't think she could face the look on the woman's face. She'd just tell her that Helena hadn't felt well but was better now.

'I'll see Becky if I go into school,' Helena said, brightening.

'Yes,' she answered absently and, crossing the street, made towards the school.

Children were singing their morning hymn in

the main hall set below street level behind the railings as she went through the gate and into the glowering, three-storey building, still gripping Helena's hand.

'Mummy, you're squeezing my hand too tight.'

She loosened her hold. The singing had finished. There came the low mumble of the Lord's Prayer, then the door below her opened to emit a long, double file of children trooping up the wide, stone stairs like little soldiers, passing her to obediently file off to their respective classrooms.

There was Helena's teacher, Miss Fisher, a spinster in her mid-forties. Eveline approached her. 'Helena was feeling a bit sick this morning,' she said, her voice flat and expressionless. 'But she's feeling better now.'

The woman, in high-necked black blouse and black, belted skirt, nodded and gave a tight smile. 'That's quite all right, Mrs Adams.' She looked down at Helena. 'Come along then, child. Don't dawdle, and if you feel sick in class, hold up your hand.'

Helena lifted her face to be kissed by her mother. ''Bye,' she said, and slipped into her class file.

Eveline turned away. She ought to go and see her mother-in-law now. She'd have to tell Mum and Dad too. She didn't want to see Albert's mother, not just yet. The poor women might be in tears and she felt she couldn't cope with that at this moment.

Finnis Street was quiet and empty, with children at school, grown-ups at work. It was beginning to spit with rain which promised to get heavier. She stopped and looked up at the overcast sky, feeling the spits on her face. She just couldn't compre-hend the possibility of never seeing Albert again; it seemed more like a dream she was having.

Directionless, she moved on, crossing the street into Three Colts Lane, turning automatically into Corfield Street. She found herself at Connie's door, though why, she didn't know. Connie would be at work. Even so she rapped with the black knocker, not knowing what else to do now she was here. The door opened. Connie stood there. 'Oh,' she said. 'It's you.'

Standing in the dim of the landing on this dull morning, she replied in a flat, lifeless tone, 'You're not at work.' It was all she could find to say.

'Rebecca had a tummy bilious attack. I couldn't leave her.' Connie's words were stilted and formal, as if talking to a casual caller. 'Is there something you wanted?'

'I...' Eveline hesitated. What did she want? 'I don't know really.'

Something in her tone, a faintness of breath per-haps, the way the words were whispered, made Connie lean forward to look at her. The stiff atti-tude fell away as she saw the expression Eveline felt must be there on her face and she knew instantly.

'Oh, no!' There was such pain in that voice. 'Oh, Eveline, no!'

Gathered into Connie's arms, the cold fear inside her gave way to what had been waiting for release. Sobbing her heart out on her friend's shoulder, she was vaguely aware that Connie too was crying, her own long-held-in grief finally flooding out of her.

426

Chapter Twenty-nine

Friday, almost the end of another working week. A grey morning with granite skies, cold, as cold as she felt since Albert had been reported missing. Grey days exacerbated her loss, sunny ones only mocked it, and the cessation of hostilities five days ago, though not officially announced as yet, was tearing her apart.

With Helena beside her, she made her way towards the school. Connie would meet her at the gates and together they would go on to work. Connie was doing all she could to make up for her strange resentment towards her after losing George. Eveline was glad that their relationship had improved. One thing was different though. Conversation was no longer light-hearted. Sometimes they'd walk in silence though it was the compatible silence of friends both more or less in the same boat.

This morning they worked side by side without talking, mostly due to the continual noise of machinery smothering any attempt to chat. When lunchtime finally arrived and the thundering racket died away, ears would be left buzzing in the unaccustomed quiet.

Nearly eleven o'clock. An hour and a half to lunchtime and Eveline felt hungry. She'd not eaten breakfast. In fact she had no interest in food at all – it was only there to keep her going.

The boom of maroons made the workers jump. Maroons would go off when an air attack was imminent, but today everyone to a man knew what they proclaimed: the war was over. The Armistice had been signed five days ago, but now it was official. Although they had waited all week for this, no one had been sure quite when.

Eveline's first thought was for Helena. She was at school and she'd be unable to get to her. Connie's face told her she was thinking the same thing about her daughter. On this day of all days they weren't together with their children.

There came the shrill sound of a police whistle, once used by them as they bicycled around the streets to warn people to take cover. There also came discordant blasts of Boy Scout bugles. The young boys too would help the police warn the public. But this time they were sounding the All Clear, fit to burst.

From inside the factory an earsplitting cheer had gone up. As the power was switched off and the roar of machinery died, workers dropped what they were doing and began to surge towards the factory entrance, Eveline and Connie being borne along in the rush to get outside and celebrate as a huge body of people streamed towards and through the factory gates.

Outside in the street it was bedlam. It was as if some gigantic school had been let out as people came flooding from nearby factories, shops, houses, dancing, yelling, singing, cheering for all they were worth.

There were some who did not dance and sing. Instead they stood as if rooted to the spot, perhaps with shock, but mostly – it was written on their faces – they remembered the loved ones they'd lost, who wouldn't be celebrating this wonderful day. Eveline and Connie stood holding hands, each looking into the other's eyes that glistened with tears.

For a moment Connie closed hers, her thoughts focused on this terrible year she had endured. How could she have pushed Eveline away as she had? Just when she needed her, she had rejected her, resentful that Eveline's husband remained alive while hers had died. Eveline was still clinging to the hope that Albert might be found alive somewhere, but she must know that after all this time there could be no such hope. Connie felt filled with guilt. How could she have so begrudged Eveline in the past?

She thought of her mother's words – tinged with that same ring of jealousy – that last time she had gone to see her: 'Why is your husband alive and mine dead?' But she'd felt the same towards Eveline, though she had avoided such direct and cruel confrontation. At the memory, guilt bit into her. It had taken Eveline's loss to bring them together and that was very sad.

She looked again into her friend's glistening eyes. 'I'm sorry,' she said awkwardly.

Eveline seemed to know exactly what she meant. 'No need,' she said.

The next moment she found herself being enfolded in her friend's arms.

'We'll come through,' she whispered with returning determination, her face buried against Eveline's shoulder. 'We have to be strong together.'

She heard the answering whisper, 'Yes.' Meanwhile all about them people continued to celebrate a world finally at peace.

The factory had closed at once, as had all the other workplaces. Every street was crammed with people rejoicing, making it difficult to get home. But they needed to. The schools would have closed too and they had to collect their daughters, though Eveline hoped that either her mother-in-law or Gran would have done the honours.

Bethnal Green Road was as crowded as everywhere else so that their bus could hardly get through, finally giving up, leaving passengers to walk, not that anyone cared. They'd been jigging in the aisles anyway, as the whole country came to a standstill to celebrate Victory Day.

The two women had to push their way through people waving flags while others cheered from roofs and windows and up lampposts, bunting appearing from nowhere. Eveline found herself kissed by total strangers, as did Connie. Pubs were already bulging, customers bringing their beer glasses out into the street, and every serviceman in sight found himself being hoisted shoulder-high.

Their own streets were no less crowded. Eveline got to her mother-in-law's flat to find she had both the children there as well as Gran, who was sipping a glass of Guinness. Gran looked frail.

'I 'ad to come in and sit down for a while,' she said. 'Ain't so young as I was and them crowds out there took all the go out of me. But thanks to Mrs Adams, I'm recovering a bit now.'

'Where's Mum and Dad?' Eveline asked.

'Them? I think they shut up shop and went over to find Len and Flossie.' They now had a small flat in Three Colts Lane, very handy to visit. 'Perhaps in a while you and me can go along there.'

'If you want to,' Eveline said. She was beginning to feel down again – so many were celebrating. What were the rest of those with no reason to celebrate feeling, perhaps sitting in their homes, listening to the excitement going on outside, making their loss all the keener?

She was glad Connie was here. The worst thing would be to sit alone.

'Mummy, they're saying the war's over!' Helena said, her voice shrill.

Eveline looked down at her and forced a smile. At eight years old the girl had no idea what exactly this meant to people, each in their individual way. Helena would never have the misfortune to feel deeply affected by it, and just as well. Her world would go on without any painfully sad memories. If Albert never came home, she would only vaguely remember him; she had been too young when he went away to remember him as he really was, and knew him only from photographs. She would live her young life, fall in love, marry, bring up her children and with luck go contentedly into old age never really knowing what it had been like to go through such a terrible war as this one and lose loved ones to it. The war was over. But the memories for her and Connie and so many others like them would linger on to the end of their lives.

'Daddy will be coming home now, won't he?' Helena broke eagerly through her thoughts, destroying all Eveline's hopes of the child remaining untouched.

'I hope so,' was all she could say, a wave of relief passing over her as Rebecca butted in.

'Can we go outside and join in?' Connie smiled across at Eveline.

'Yes, let's do that,' she said with a defiant lift of the chin.

Eveline felt the emotion touch her and she too lifted her face.

'Then we can all go on to Len's place. And you too, Mum,' she added, addressing her mother-in-law. 'It'll do you good to be with other people.' It would do her good too.

By December, things had grown quieter. The war had been won though the official peace agreement had yet to be signed between the Allies and Germany; that country had become so impoverished by war it was starving, the Kaiser had abdicated, socialist revolutionaries were parading its cities, sailors had mutinied, soldiers seizing their command posts. Germany was falling apart.

Britain was in trouble too. Food shortages were common, men released all at once from the forces found themselves unable to find jobs while those who'd worked during the war were demanding higher wages, threatening to strike if they didn't get them.

One thing that had made a difference was the November General Election, in which twice as many voted as in the last election in 1910. Women had at last been granted the vote, but they had to be over thirty, householders or wives of householders or owning property worth five pounds a year. Seventeen female candidates had stood though only one got elected, a Sinn Fein candidate for a Dublin seat, Countess Markievicz, she promptly declining to attend Parliament, saying it was against her principles to take the oath of allegiance to the King.

Compared to the excitement of the Armistice, the granting of women's suffrage was hardly noticed. No triumphal marches, no great speeches, in fact there was even talk of the WSPU disbanding, now that its demands were apparently satisfied.

'How can they be satisfied?' Connie questioned hotly, disappointed and angry. 'If it had been lowered to twenty-one, we'd have been included.'

'I suppose so,' Eveline said without enthusiasm as she got up from the kitchen chair to give Connie a hand in peeling potatoes for her dinner.

She felt little interest in suffragette matters. What had come to dominate both her sleeping and waking mind of late was a vision of a mutilated body buried by mud on some deserted battlefield, a body missed by searchers, perhaps too torn apart to be recognised as a whole among so many other scattered body parts, the unknown remains gathered up to bury with the rest and given only the dignity of a solemn prayer.

She'd tried so many times to put the vision out of her head but it persisted in returning. Now there was Helena asking more and more where was her dad and when would he be coming home.

Was she old enough at eight to have the situation explained to her? Yes, she was, but Eveline hadn't so far been able to find the words, so had fobbed the child off. But soon she'd not be able to fob her off any longer. How did one go about explaining to a child the wages of warfare, what can happen on a battlefield to cause a man to be missing? She still found herself believing that Albert was just missing, not dead. She thought she would always live with that hope, no matter how many years went by.

'But of course,' Connie was saying as Eveline went on peeling the potatoes with pent-up energy. 'It would have meant the chance of more women standing for parliament, and that'd never do!'

'What wouldn't do?' Eveline echoed, dragged back to the present.

Patiently, Connie repeated her previous words, demanding a sensible reply from Eveline. 'We don't qualify anyway,' she managed to say mildly. 'We don't own property.'

'But we both fought as hard as any for the vote and we get nothing out of it! After years of campaigning it took a war to bring it about.'

That was true. The government had been forced to admit to a debt of gratitude owed to women for so readily filling the gap in the workplace left by men going to fight. But it had been a half-hearted gesture, as Connie said.

'I feel betrayed,' she said as, out shopping with no work to go to that day, they paused to watch older women entering a polling booth.

'Little we can do about it,' Eveline said lamely as they moved on.

Both were on short time; the factory where they

worked did not need to produce so many munitions now the war was over. With men returning home, many of the jobs the women had filled in their absence were being given back to them. Unless she and Connie could find other work, their incomes would plummet, leaving them to manage on the pittance paid to war widows. It spelled a frightening future.

Working, they'd come to make the most of a few good things in life: going to the cinema, seeing a show now and again, regular food on the table as far as wartime rations had allowed, dressing nicely. They had followed the fashion for shorter skirts, cut their hair short to curl around their faces when not restricted by the mob caps they wore at the factory. It was all coming to an end.

'Some women might have been enfranchised,' Eveline said as she thought of her dwindling resources. 'But it's not the emancipation Christabel Pankhurst spoke of. We're still being asked to rely on men for most things.'

They had no men, she thought bitterly. They'd soon have little money. As predicted, in early January their jobs went. She felt so let down that it began making her feel under the weather. In fact in the middle of January she began to feel distinctly ill, waking up one morning with vague aches in her joints and a fever.

'I hope I'm not coming down with that Spanish flu,' she told her mother having gone there for the morning after taking Helena to school. 'There's such a lot of it around. The papers are saying it's an epidemic in other parts of the world and thousands of people have already died from it.'

'That's there, not 'ere,' Mum said, placing a cup of tea in front of her.

'But it is here,' Eveline persisted, straightening her back against the vague pain, her head beginning to feel heavy.

'It's been going round for a month or two,' Mum said without much sympathy. 'If you was going ter get it, you'd of got it by now. It's just you, worrying yerself stiff over losing yer job. I told yer, if you're in 'ard straits, me and yer dad'll help you out as far as we can.'

She was a different woman these days. No more, 'You made yer bed so put up with it.' With any hope of Albert coming home finally seeming futile – the subject was no longer mentioned, being too painful – the fact seemed to have brought her that bit closer.

'Being worried doesn't make you feel feverish,' she said. 'Helena went to school this morning saying she didn't feel well either. I'm worried for her.'

'She'll be orright.'

But Eveline arrived back home to find a note through her door from the school asking her to collect her daughter as soon as possible as she had a nasty headache. The news sent her scurrying off to get her.

One look told her that she had a very sick daughter. Taking off her coat, she draped it round the girl's shoulders giving extra warmth although the day wasn't as cold as January could be, and part walked her, part carried her home. By that time she was in a panic, with the heat of the child's body penetrating right through her clothing.

'Mummy,' Helena moaned plaintively several times on the way, 'I feel ever so ill.'

'I know, love,' she said. 'I'm putting you straight to bed.'

Once there, she heated milk and made her drink it sweet with an aspirin. 'Stay in bed, darling, while I go for the doctor.'

The surgery was crowded. The receptionist looked agitated. 'The doctor's ever so busy as you can see. There's not much he can advise except tell you to do what you're already doing, giving her aspirin.'

'What if it's not the flu? What if she's got meningitis or something?'

The receptionist thought a moment. 'Maybe I can get him to come after surgery. That won't be for ages, though.'

'Well, ask him if he can make a visit as soon as he can.'

'You have to pay for visits.'

'Then I'll pay!' Eveline snapped and rushed off, not stopping to think where the money was coming from.

By the time he arrived about midday, having forgone his lunch to deal with the growing number of influenza victims, Helena looked desperately ill. Eveline too was feeling like death as she forced herself to see to the needs of her daughter, her own head feverish and throbbing, the pain behind her eyes almost unbearable, every limb aching to each movement.

'What is it?' she asked.

The doctor looked up from a brief examination. 'She has influenza.' He studied Eveline's flushed face. 'And so have you.'

'So long as I can take care of her.'

'I don't think you'll be able to. By this evening you'll be in bed as well and in need of someone to take care of *you!* Your husband...'

'My husband was reported missing,' she said abruptly. 'In the war.'

'Hmm.' He made no other comment, his expression inscrutable. 'Is there anyone who can come in and take care of you?'

'There's my mother.' She wasn't sure she wanted to ask her. With the shop to look after she'd probably make her feel it was grudgingly done. Gran would come but had lately lost much of her vitality. She couldn't impose on her either.

She'd have to ask Albert's mother. She was taking the loss of her son badly, and though she still had his brother Jim due to come home from the army soon, Eveline guessed that her firstborn would always be dear to her; she would remember not the man but the little boy, a life wasted. But if she was given something to do it might take her mind off things for a while.

If only her own mind could be taken off things for a while. Her voice shook as she said that her mother-in-law lived in the next block to this one.

'If you give me the number of her flat,' the man said, his tone kind, 'I'll call in and inform her.'

An elderly man, he had probably seen many like her whose sons and husbands would not be coming back, women whose faces looked tight and grief-stricken, who were holding their loss inside themselves. His tone remained gentle.

'You need to take plenty of liquids, keep warm

438

and take two aspirin three times a day. That's the best I can do for you. I shall not charge you for this visit,' he added kindly, seeing her so near to tears. 'I am seeing others on my rounds who will probably demand more of my time, so they can pay for this one.'

He gave a brief chuckle at his joke, waving away her thanks. 'I'll see myself out.'

There was a knock on the front door. 'I'll get that,' he said. 'You look after yourself and your daughter.'

It was Connie. Eveline could hear her talking to the doctor, but she was more concerned by Helena's whimpering to be given comfort. Connie came in to find her cuddling the child to her.

'How is she?' were her first words.

'He said it's flu. She has to be kept warm and given aspirin.'

'Didn't he give you any other medicine?'

'What can he give us? There's no real cure. It just has to run its course. He didn't charge me.'

'I should think not!' Connie stopped to regard her friend. 'You look dreadful. He said you've got it as well.'

'Don't come too close, it's terrible catching,' Eveline warned as Connie came forward to put a hand on her forehead.

Connie took no heed. 'Get undressed and into bed beside Helena. I can better deal with the two of you in one room rather than going from one room to the other to see to you both.'

She turned to her own daughter standing by the bedroom door. 'Go home, Becky. Here's the door key.' She threw it across to her, Rebecca catching it expertly. 'There's food in the larder. Find something for your tea. I shall come home as soon as I can.'

'You can't let her go alone,' Eveline protested.

Connie turned back, her chin up. 'She'll be nine years old come this autumn and can look after herself. With her father no longer here, we must do the best we can. Once she understands that, the better she will be.'

She sounded quite suddenly so efficient that had Eveline not felt so ill she'd have been shocked. The loss of her husband had slowly endowed her with a strength Eveline would never have expected of her last year while it was she who felt weakened by her own stupid hope of Albert's return.

Letting her take charge, Eveline got meekly into bed, wondering at this change in Connie that had happened so gradually she'd hardly noticed it until now. Connie had lost so much in her life – two brothers, a father, her husband, and had suffered the refusal of her mother to forgive her over what to Eveline seemed the trivial matter of wanting to marry the man she loved. She'd had to be strong to bear up under all that. But at least she knew there was no bringing George back to life.

For herself, not knowing if Albert was dead or still alive was tearing her apart. As if in limbo she walked alternately on the edge of hope and resignation. But whereas she had a supportive family, Connie had virtually no one now.

Compared to some families, her own had been relatively fortunate. Apart from her loss of Albert no one in the family had been killed in the war – the only casualty, her brother Len, had lost his leg. Of Connie's family there was only herself, the childless Verity, whose own husband had been killed, and their mother left. Mrs Mornington had no relatives either of her own or her late husband's to turn to.

She did have Rebecca, the only one to continue the family line if not its name, but only three remained of the original family of six, or seven counting Verity's husband, eight if only they'd had the good grace to include George. And if her mother still rejected Connie, she'd be virtually reducing that family to two.

Chapter Thirty

Aches and fever took three days to run its course but had left her weak and listless. Connie had proved a real brick. Without hesitation, she'd stayed with Eveline and Helena. Eveline wondered what she'd have done without her. Connie seemed to be there constantly, going home for a few hours to see how Rebecca was, then back she'd come, staying up for two nights, saying that a neighbour was keeping an eye on Rebecca. Whether it was true of not, Eveline was too ill to ask as her own daughter tossed and coughed and moaned beside her.

Helena, perhaps because she was young, was up two days after the fever had gone, though not ready to go back to school for another couple of weeks. Eveline knew it could take the rest of February for her to regain her own strength. While she stayed in bed Connie did the shopping, coming over to prepare light meals. Her own mother hadn't once come to see her.

'I might as well not have a mum,' she complained feebly as she made herself drink the broth Connie had prepared. Her appetite was still poor.

Connie gave her an odd, sad look. 'She couldn't, Eveline.'

'Of course she could! Or has she got flu too?'

'She had to nurse your gran, Eveline.'

The way she said it made Eveline look up

sharply. 'Is Gran ill?'

'She went down with it as well.'

Something in Connie's tone arrested her. She studied her friend's face. 'I didn't know. Why didn't you say?'

'I couldn't while you were so ill.'

'And how is she now? Has she been very bad?'

Connie nodded, then as though finding it an effort, said slowly, 'Yes, Eveline, very bad. She was getting on in years, and...'

'Was?' Eveline broke in, jumping on the past tense.

'Eveline ... it was too much for her. Your gran, she died from it.'

'Died?' Eveline echoed, then came to, blurting, 'No! She can't have!'

It wasn't sinking in. Gran, who always declared nothing got her down not even at her age, who'd looked after Helena all those years, who had stood by Eveline when her own mother had wanted nothing to do with her. 'No, not my gran,' she continued in disbelief.

'It happened so quickly,' Connie went on. 'It took her after only two days. Eveline, I'm so sorry. You were too ill to be told.'

Connie's voice was droning as if trying to redeem the situation, but Eveline wasn't listening, In her weakened state, she buried her face in her pillow and gave herself up to weeping as Connie gently removed the empty bowl from her trembling hand.

First her wonderful and loving Albert; hopes of his being still alive had faded after these three months of nothing. Now her loving and understanding gran. She felt suddenly alone as she wept into her pillow. Connie, standing by, allowed her to give way to her distress.

Gran's funeral took place several days later, a small gathering on a cold and windy winter morning. Eveline wasn't yet fully enough recovered to attend. Len and Flossie too were down with it. So was her sister Tilly's little one as well as her brother Fred's two kids. So many in this area alone had been stricken; people were dying of it every day. The papers were calling it an epidemic, saying that worldwide as many had died from it so far as had been killed in the war, which was frightening when in Britain alone there'd been three million war casualties with one million killed. Eveline could only pray that Len and his wife, and her brother and sister's children, would recover.

Unable to find strength enough to pay her last respects to the woman who had helped her through so many crises, she felt it keenly. She spent the time crying so much that her eyes swelled and her nose got so blocked up that she could hardly swallow the soup, much less the sandwiches, Connie had with left her.

'I should be there,' Eveline told her, sinking back exhausted into her chair after trying to pull herself together.

'You definitely can't go,' Connie said, arranging a blanket around her knees. 'You can't risk a relapse. You've Helena to consider. I'll be there to represent you. I shall be back as soon as I can. I've left Rebecca with a neighbour, so she'll be all right.'

To Eveline's protests she said, 'I've as much to thank your gran for as you. They will understand you not being there. I shall make sure they do.'

In a way, Connie attending in her stead made Eveline cry all the more.

'Don't cry, Mummy,' Helena said, near to tears herself. 'I loved poor Granny Ansell too. I wish they could find Daddy.'

Eveline had finally found courage enough to explain it all to her after Christmas when she had again wished her daddy were there. Helena had taken the explanation in silence and hadn't spoken of him again until she fell ill, in her fever telling him she wanted him here. It had nearly broken Eveline's heart, since she herself had been in no condition to comfort her daughter.

'I can't help crying,' she wept, but Helena's young face was solemn.

'If you keep crying, you'll be ill again like Auntie Connie said. And I don't want you to have to be buried, because then I'd have no one to love me at all without Daddy here with us any more.'

Eveline bit back her tears to stare at the child. In her own misery she hadn't truly realised that Helena felt the loss as keenly as her. Children are naturally resilient, she'd told herself so many times, they didn't understand. But Helena *did* understand and in her own way had suffered too.

She held out her arms and, as Helena rushed into them, held her in a tight, shared embrace of mutual grief. 'Why didn't you say how you felt?'

'I didn't want to upset you, you was upset already,' came the simple reply. 'I didn't want you to see how I miss Daddy and start you off crying again. I don't like seeing you cry, Mummy.'

'My darling, you can cry! We can all cry. You can cry all you want.'

As if some barrier had been broken, Helena gave a great sob, burying her head against her mother. 'Oh, Mummy, I miss my dad so much!' came the choked, muffled words, the two of them sharing their tears of grief.

'I know, I know, darling.'

Eveline buried her face in the fair, wavy hair, suddenly realising how easily she could have lost Helena too. This terrible flu had mostly touched the young, sending them into unconsciousness, never to recover.

'I know,' she crooned again, closing her eyes as she gently rocked her daughter, grateful that the child had been spared to her.

When Connie let herself into the flat she found the two asleep as if thoroughly exhausted, Helena on her mother's lap, her head against her shoulder, Eveline's arms still clasped about her.

It was a wonder to Connie that she too hadn't caught flu, the time she had spent nursing Eveline. February, and Eveline still hadn't properly regained her former strength.

'I'll be all right soon,' she kept saying. Connie knew it was more than just the aftermath of her illness. Eveline's heart was in turmoil over the continuing lack of news about Albert.

She wondered which was worse, losing a husband outright or this continual lingering uncertainty. Eveline was mourning a treasured grandmother, but Connie suspected the uncertainty about Albert to be the main cause of her friend's failure to recover completely.

Her gran's savings hadn't been much. She had wanted all her grandchildren to benefit, and as Eveline said, 'If anyone needs it our Len does.' The loan she'd been struggling to pay back was no longer a problem but that seemed to make Eveline pine after her even more. Connie felt helpless.

She missed the woman too, a wonderful woman, but she had lived a long life. George had barely begun his. Eveline's family had come through both the war and the Spanish flu, whereas she had lost a husband and two brothers to the war, and her father to a heart attack. She hated the thought that came to her but if somehow Albert *was* found to be miraculously alive, what would her own reaction be?

Hastily she put the thought from her and thought of her sister Verity instead. She'd lost her husband. The last time she'd heard from Verity had been a letter a week after Christmas thanking her for her card and saying she said sold her home and was back living with Mother. 'She'd been all alone in that great big house,' she wrote, 'And I was in mine. We're company for each other.'

It set Connie thinking. Now she had time to herself she'd write to Verity. Even as she penned a few words to ask how she was and put in what news she could find to write about, she felt a whole lot better. Perhaps Verity's reply would help to narrow the rift between her and Mother. She waited for her to reply but when none came she knew Verity, now with their mother, would have come under her influence and certainly been turned against her.

She wrote again, yet still nothing happened. In anger, she wrote a scathing letter to her mother instead, saying that she surely didn't warrant this silence. What with her father dead, her husband dead and far more serious conflict having brought the world to its knees, such trivial old scores as theirs ought finally be buried. Still no reply.

'I'm going to have it out with her, once and for all,' she told Eveline. 'You'll be all right without me for a day or two?'

Eveline offered her a smile. 'I can manage. I might take a walk, just to my mum's and back. I can't sit around here forever.' Helena was back at school, she and Rebecca going off together like little sisters.

'Not that I'll buy anything,' Eveline added wryly. 'And I'm not asking her for any handout. I just need to get out. I'm sick of staring at four walls.'

Connie knew all about that, on both counts. Neither of them was in work now and the suffragette meetings they'd once enjoyed had been disbanded, so there was little to do but gaze at the four walls of her own flat.

A war widow's pension didn't stretch to even the cheapest seats at the cinema or any entertainment that cost more than a walk in the park, and window-shopping only made the lack of money more keen. Nine shillings a week pension plus two shillings per child had to cover everything; rent, heating and lighting, food and clothing. She was constantly dipping into what savings she had left. Before long it would all be gone.

Eveline had even less and even though her parents ran their shop, she had too much pride to go cap in hand to them, as she'd just said. 'After all, they're finding it hard too with everyone frightened to spend too much.'

'Yesterday I received notification to say that my rent is going up to seven shillings and sixpence a week.' Connie began busying herself flicking a duster over Eveline's sideboard while the girl looked on listlessly. 'You must have had one as well.' Eveline gave a miserable nod, seeming to be only half listening, but she ploughed on.

'We're beginning to live from hand to mouth. Anyone falling behind with the rent can be evicted and that would be awful. I was thinking, it does seem silly us both paying rent on our separate lettings. If we shared just one flat we would be paying only half rent each. It does seem sensible, don't you think? And we do get on well together. What do you say?'

She saw Eveline look up at her and was encouraged. 'My flat is the larger of the two and has nicer views.' She waited but Eveline had lowered her eyes again.

'I don't know,' she surprised Connie by answering. 'If Albert suddenly came home and I didn't have our...'

Connie couldn't help herself. Her temper suddenly flew as she shot upright from her dusting.

'He's *not* coming home! The sooner you face that truth, Eveline, the easier you'll be able to get on with your life. It's more than five months now – you can't go on forever hoping. It's wrong!'

Eveline seemed too apathetic to be ruffled by

the outburst. 'Some people go on hoping all their lives,' she said quietly, almost as if talking to herself. 'It's what keeps them going. I don't think that makes them wrong.'

Connie had no answer to that. She fell to the dusting again, quite unnecessarily diligent.

She caught a train for Perivale on the Saturday morning, taking Rebecca with her. It hadn't been easy scraping together the child's half-fare as well as her own but she was determined to have her mother see her only grandchild. Rebecca was beautiful with her grandmother's fair, wavy hair, and wide blue eyes set in a heart-shaped face. Who could resist being drawn to her?

Rebecca had a new dress for the occasion, cheap but a very pretty blue, with a short, flared skirt and wide collar. Connie had sacrificed a few shillings of her savings for the occasion. She had got nothing for herself – the money had to last as long as possible.

Sitting in the carriage she felt utterly shabby, recalling how well she had once dressed. What would her mother think, seeing her in this well-used coat, this hat well out of fashion, she who at one time would have thrown out a garment after a month for some newer style?

She had cut her hair some time ago to conform to the modern shorter style but it was glaringly obvious that she'd done it herself. These days she could not afford to throw away money on a professional cut. Fortunately, having wavy hair had helped soften the stark shape produced by unskilled scissors. She'd also shortened her coat herself, as well as her skirt, but it still looked well out of date. Fashions had changed so dramatically since the war that anything bought even a year ago stood out like a sore thumb.

Some women in her situation might not have worried, but she did; the life she'd once known still remained part of her in her heart. It was horrid being poor. It wasn't as if she hadn't tried looking for work to help swell her dwindling savings. There was no work, at least not for unskilled women. Even those mundane jobs were being given to men returning home from the war. You saw them, queues waiting for jobs that called only for a pitiful few.

Eveline, as skilled a comptometer operator as she had once been, found her sort of job filled by men. Professional women, it seemed, were only wanted in a sort of patronising way even though their high qualifications proved them equal to any man.

It was an odd new world springing up from the war with plenty of professional and skilled vacancies, mostly for men of course, yet no unskilled jobs to be had anywhere. Any vacancy got snapped up the instant it appeared, leaving long dole queues of shabbily dressed men without hope, patiently standing in humiliating line for a few days' work while dozens of ex-servicemen with missing limbs or blinded by gas or gravely disfigured trudged the kerbsides begging for pennies to support their families.

What chance did she and Eveline have? After all they'd done during four years of war while the men were away, the government was cleverly laying stress on *Women's Role in the Home* and *Jobs Fit for Heroes.*

'They're making us the scapegoats now,' Connie had said bitterly. 'They might as well be saying that we're trying to take men's jobs away from them. So much for women's enfranchisement!'

At one time Eveline would have agreed whole-heartedly but it seemed she couldn't care less now. Connie gave up. She had other things on her mind as she sat on the Perivale train, to find why Verity hadn't replied to her letters.

Her mother's face when she opened the door to her this bright, cold, March day took her aback. She had expected frigidity, hostility, but the woman's face was like that of a ghost, white and vacant. She didn't even ask what she was doing here, or say that she was unwelcome.

'Hello Mother,' was all Connie could come up with as she gripped Rebecca's hand.

It sounded foolish and inadequate, especially with her mother gazing down at her from the doorstep and making no response.

She made another attempt. 'How are you, Mother? Are you well?'

Of course she wasn't well. She looked anything but. She made no effort to invite her inside but then Connie should have known the reception she would get.

'I really came to see Verity. She didn't reply to my letter and...'

She broke off as her mother appeared to flinch, the faded blue eyes coming alive for a second. Her mother's mouth twisted.

452

'She'd dead, of influenza.' The shocking words, the first ones she had uttered, were blunt and cold, as if they meant nothing to the woman. For a moment Connie wasn't sure she'd heard correctly.

'What're you saying, Mother?' The bleak expression was already making her throat constrict as the truth began to sink in. Her flesh had gone cold. She heard herself whisper, 'When?'

She realised that she must pull herself together. 'Mother, let me come in. Why didn't you write to tell me? Why didn't you let me know?'

Even now she could hardly believe what she'd heard. At the same time other thoughts were racing through her mind, sensible, everyday thoughts – there had not been time to write, it might have happened just a day or two ago, her mother felt too confused and devastated to put her mind to writing and no one else was there to do it for her. Tears began clouding her vision, but still that wraith's face regarded her as if it possessed no life at all, the blue eyes arid.

'Mother, I'm coming in,' she said abruptly, pushing past into the house.

Its silence seemed to wrap itself around her the instant she stepped inside. Stunned as she was by her mother's news, still hardly able to believe it was true, it came to her that it had been her mother, not a maid, who had opened the door. No staff were to be seen. The atmosphere was still and remote, seeming to bear down on her. She turned to her mother, who was quietly closing the main door with almost deliberate respect for this silence.

'When did she...' She couldn't bring herself to say her sister's name or the word that would follow. 'When did it happen? How long ago?'

Her mother was gazing blankly at her. 'Why are you here? What do you want?'

Connie ignored the question. 'How long ago did...' She had to say it. 'How long since Verity was taken?'

'Verity?'

'My sister, your daughter – when did it happen?'

She was coming to terms with reality enough to gain control of herself though it felt as though there was a great hole in her heart. She wanted to take her mother in her arms, her mother still looking lost and blank. 'I think I've been here on my own for weeks, Verity.'

'I'm not Verity, Mother, I'm Constance, your other daughter.'

'Yes, that's right, Constance is dead,' came the vague reply. Connie began slowly to realise that her mother had become slightly unhinged. Alarm gripped her as the woman went on, 'We sent Verity away for upsetting her father.'

'Father died, Mother. A long time ago.'

'He said I must not mention her name. He said she was dead to him. Now Verity is dead too.'

That made more sense but Connie knew it was making none to her mother. Pity flooded through her, pity and fear. Gently she went and put an arm about her shoulders, still holding on to Rebecca with her other hand, and led her, un-resisting, into the sitting room. There she eased her down on to the sofa and sat down beside her, signalling to Rebecca with her eyes to find somewhere else to sit.

'Where are the staff, Mother?' she queried.

'Staff? I didn't need them. They went away. Constance went away too. So did Verity.'

'You said she died, Mother. Of influenza.'

'Yes. There's no one here now. All gone.'

Connie tried to bite back a sob, not making a very good job of it. In this her mother was right. All gone. Her two brothers, her father, and now her sister. No one was left but herself and her mother. She too was beginning to feel a little unhinged.

'Verity!' She raised her voice, shaking her mother's shoulders with both hands to bring her mind back. 'When did she die? When?'

Her mother seemed to rally. She turned to look her in the eye. Her breathing had become fast.

'Not today. Last month... It rained. They took her to the cemetery. I went there too. The servants left but a nice lady lives with me.'

'I had no idea. Mother, why didn't you write?'

She felt as if she were panting for breath, her voice rising, filled with misery and anger. 'You should have let me know. This lady, why couldn't she have written to tell me?'

Her mother looked at her as if bemused. 'She doesn't know you.' The tone had grown soft again, with no sign of distress now, as if all that had happened had passed completely over her head.

The sound of a key being turned in the lock of the main door stopped any reply Connie might have made. The door opened then closed. A woman came into the room. She was middle-aged, wearing a nursing uniform of old-fashioned length and a nurse's cap. Obviously this was the person Connie's mother had spoken of so distractedly.

She stood gazing at Connie in surprise. 'I beg your pardon, I didn't realise Mrs Mornington had a visitor.'

Connie stood up. 'I am Mrs Mornington's daughter.'

'Her daughter? I didn't know she had another daughter.'

Of course she wouldn't. Giving Connie a dismissive nod, she laid her bulky black bag and a small package on the sideboard and came over to her charge who was beginning to wring her hands and mutter to herself. Protectively taking charge, she bent over her.

'I think you should have your rest now, Mrs Mornington. I'll help you upstairs to your bedroom and then make you some lunch.'

She turned to Connie. 'She does get like this when agitated. I expect it is seeing you. Stay if you want, but I doubt it will help. Your mother is far from well in the head. She is due to go into a nursing home shortly.' Connie stared at her.

'A nursing home? You mean an asylum?'

'No, my dear, a nursing home for the mentally sick. She has signed a consent form and is financially able to afford the best of attention and she will be well cared for.'

Connie bit back the grief of having lost her sister to glare at her. 'If my mother is sick in the head as you say, she could not have been in any condition to sign any consent. As her next of kin I should have been consulted.'

The woman inclined her head. 'Yes, but no one had been informed that she had another daughter. She was probably too confused to mention you.'

Connie smothered the blow that statement brought. She tightened her lips to temper it. 'Well, you know now,' she said sharply. 'And I do not agree to it.'

Resentment was bubbling up inside her against her mother who, sick or not, still refused to recognise her existence. It felt as if it was choking her. The woman was looking levelly at her.

'You mean you wish to care for her and nurse her yourself?'

The assumption stopped Connie in her tracks. What did she owe her mother, who'd virtually disowned her, who'd put up no opposition when her daughter was told by her father to leave, who had refused to answer any of her letters except to tell her that she would never be welcome?

She owed Eveline more loyalty than ever she owed her mother. Eveline had befriended her, had stood by her when at her lowest ebb, had remained staunch through thick and thin. To nurse her mother she would have to leave the best friend she'd ever known and come and live here. No, she could never do that.

Interpreting her change of expression, the woman became kind and understanding.

'Your mother could worsen. She is also very frail physically. Even if you came here to care for her, you would need a trained nurse in constant attendance, and that will cost almost as much as her living in a nursing home with every care and

457

attention available. It would be very hard on you.'

She turned and looked at Rebecca still sitting, silent and frightened, on her chair in the far corner of the room.

'And your daughter would be uprooted from her school and her friends and put into an un-natural environment.' She gave a motherly smile as if everything had been settled. 'I think it best your mother receives professional care, don't you?'

Connie became aware that her mother was muttering to herself again. 'All gone, all gone,' she was saying over and over. 'My family all gone.'

Including me, came the bitter thought as Connie nodded consent to the woman's suggestion, a sense of helplessness and isolation beginning slowly to overwhelm her.

She hardly remembered getting home, clinging tightly to a bewildered Rebecca. Unable to face the loneliness of her own flat, she went straight to Eveline and there, pouring out all that had happened, all but collapsed into her arms to be held tightly as she gave in to the pent-up misery she'd been holding back all through her journey.

Chapter Thirty-one

'Perhaps you're right. Perhaps we should think about what you said.'

As Eveline gazed down at the very few coins Connie had tipped out of her purse after buying the few groceries needed to tide her over the weekend, Connie looked up hopefully.

'So you agree it would be the best thing if we did share just one flat?'

'I suppose so.' Eveline didn't seem at all enthusiastic, but then she had lost her enthusiasm for most things these days.

Connie surveyed the few bits she'd bought, a loaf, a quarter-pound of tea, half a pound of margarine, a bottle of milk and a pound of sausages. 'At least you can get help from your parents now and again.'

Eveline hated asking her parents for help. When visiting she'd say she was coping. They too were experiencing hard times, what with most customers buying only the barest essentials and in smaller and smaller quantities. Moreover they needed to help out the rest of their family whenever possible.

Her sister Tilly's husband had never had his old job back after coming out of the forces. His chest persistently played him up after years of cold damp trenches, so he now did odd jobs when he could get them. Len was out of work too. Few cared to employ a man missing a leg when thousands were queuing for the available vacancies. His parents were left to help him and Flossie make ends meet, she with a baby on the way.

Eveline's brother Jimmy was working. May was no longer going with the boyfriend she had found. She helped in the shop and with housework, virtually as a glorified, unpaid assistant, and was rapidly turning into a true spinster.

Of Eveline's other three brothers, Alfred was still at school, while Bobby at seventeen was merely selling newspapers. Only nineteen-year-old Jimmy, who'd been conscripted, but with the war over not sent to fight, had been lucky to get back his old job behind the counter of a small hardware store in Bethnal Green Road. The proprietor saw him as a polite, likeable young man.

At Connie's remark, Eveline pursed her lips. 'I don't want them to think they've got to keep helping me out. The last thing I want is them feeling sorry for me.' She meant to make Gran's bit of money last as long as possible.

By mid-March, she was well recovered from the flu. The epidemic had begun to give way, at least in Britain. Many fewer new cases were being reported; even so, British deaths from influenza were said to have outnumbered births.

Connie knew she should count herself and Rebecca lucky not to have got it, but she was still pining over the loss of her sister and the fact that her mother hadn't even contacted her about it, still considering her banished.

A few days ago she'd gone to the nursing home

where her mother had been admitted last week. But the woman's mind was fast leaving her, and she alternately called Connie Verity and accused her of causing her father's death. She'd not bothered to argue; her mother's physical condition too was rapidly deteriorating.

Connie vowed not to visit again. It cost money to travel all that way and nothing could be gained from doing so. She would be insulted or spurned by a vindictive and feeble-brained woman. Money was too precious to waste.

Eveline counted the coins on the table. 'Two shillings and seven pence ha'penny. All we've got towards next week's rent. God knows what we're going to do in the end.'

'We're not the only ones in difficulties,' Connie tried to console her as she gathered up the precious money and put it back into the purse.

Eveline had given up her flat this week to come here, which had helped the finances to some extent – heaven knows how they'd have fared if they hadn't done so – but it was a drop in the ocean. Rapid price increases, stagnating wage levels and the threat by employers of wage cuts had begun to lead to strikes, bringing the country down even more.

'There are a lot worse off than us. Families are being evicted and left homeless, we've escaped that by doing what we did.'

'I don't care about other people!' Eveline said waspishly. 'We can hardly afford the food we need. Anyway, I don't want to talk about it!'

Connie was worried too. She knew there was

no point asking Eveline to appeal to her parents. The last time she asked, she was pounced on by Eveline, who said it was below her dignity to beg for handouts and she'd rather die.

Only ten days had passed since she'd moved in, and already Connie was seeing a side of her she hadn't observed before, sharp-tempered and moody. It had never been noticeable when they'd both had their own place.

Perhaps it was being thrown together with one living room between them, a shared kitchen and just the two bedrooms, with nowhere to escape the other's presence; maybe it hadn't been such a brilliant idea after all. She had to admit that her own irritation could show at times, no matter how hard she tried to keep control of herself. The only redeeming feature seemed to be that they were saving money.

She fell silent as Eveline bustled about getting a meal ready for their daughters coming home from school. It was best to remain calm when Eveline turned sharp. The worst thing would be to retaliate and have their long friendship break down over a few thoughtless words.

She couldn't blame Eveline. Despite no word of Albert she was still clinging to the thought that he might still be found alive somewhere, her only explanation for his failure to contact her being that he must be suffering from amnesia. She was driving herself silly.

Eveline knocked on the door of her mother-in-law's flat, telling herself she should visit more often than she did; but these days it was a duty she didn't much look forward to.

One reason was that Mrs Adams appeared to have come to terms with the fact that Albert wouldn't be coming home ever again and would shed a tear at the mere mention of his name.

'Him without a grave I can even visit,' she would mutter tearfully. It was no good trying to tell her Albert had to be alive and lost somewhere and one day would come home.

'Not after all this time, Eveline, and it ain't no good me going on tormenting meself. At my age I need to come to terms.' After several bouts of dissension, Eveline had learned to keep her beliefs to herself.

The other reason was her husband's brother Jim, who seemed to be a little too attentive towards her lately. It often felt that he and his mother were in some sort of conspiracy together concerning her.

'He's been ever so lucky,' Mrs Adams said this Wednesday, cutting a slice of cake to go with the tea she'd poured for her daughter-in-law. 'He's a bus driver now, for the London General Omnibus Company, and bringing in a regular wage.'

Handing tea and cake to Eveline, she went on, 'He don't seem to 'ave no regular girlfriend, but when he do eventually get married, he'll be well able ter provide a good 'ome and income. She'll be a fortunate girl whoever she is. You know what it's like struggling along on next ter nothing. So many what's out of work, a woman could do worse than marry my Jim.'

Her eyes trained on Eveline, she added, 'I must say, you and him both get on ever so well

463

together, don't yer?'

Eveline half nodded, concentrating on sipping her tea as she focused her eyes on the slice of cake on her plate, wishing Mrs Adams would drop the subject of Jim.

Before the war she'd not had much to do with him. Since coming back from the forces she'd found him likeable and friendly, but as a brother-in-law, nothing more. Then these last few months he'd become perhaps a little too friendly to her mind, though it could just have been her imagination.

The last girl he'd met had lately transferred her attentions to another and so far he'd not met anyone else. Once or twice when Eveline came here on the occasional Sunday he'd see her to the front door when she left and take her arm in a way that seemed a little too intimate.

Once he'd said he would always be here for her if she ever *needed* anything. The odd emphasis on the word *need* had made her look sharply at him, though the offer could have been entirely innocent. She'd thanked him for his concern, saying she was fine and needed nothing.

It had been a strange moment, but more recently he'd said, 'You must miss our Bert an awful lot. I mean not 'aving a man around to do odd jobs. You know, things that matter.'

He had again laid his hand gently on her arm, seemingly brotherly, yet so much could be read into it and it brought back memories of moments she'd once known with Albert. This made her feel so desperately empty inside. Unthinkable that he could ever take Albert's place, if Albert was truly dead. But he wasn't. She believed that with all her heart and could only feel angry with Jim and his mother for believing otherwise.

Saturday, the twenty-ninth of March was her mother-in-law's fiftieth birthday. It represented quite a milestone when poverty and excessive childbirth often put paid to women at a much earlier age, and Mrs Adams considered herself old. She dressed as fifty-year-old women usually did, in dark clothes, with no frills or fancies or jewellery except for her wedding ring and a jet brooch that had been her mother's. She wore her iron-grey hair scraped back from her face in an old-fashioned, severe bun, and heavy-rimmed spectacles.

'What do I want to celebrate me birthday for at my age?' she said when Eveline suggested she come to her and Connie's flat for a little birthday celebration. Guilty that she didn't visit the woman as often as she should, Eveline intended to sacrifice a little of her housekeeping on a small iced cake she'd asked Connie to make for her.

'And I can't go gallivanting out when I've got Jim's tea to get for 'im when he comes 'ome from work.'

'Let him come too,' Eveline said rashly. 'And Helena would be thrilled to have her grandma here.'

Mrs Adams hardly went outside her door except to do her shopping, certainly not since losing her son whom she still grieved for. It would be the first time she'd even been up to see the flat Eveline now shared with Connie.

She gave way begrudgingly. 'Well, seeing as you're going to a bit of trouble, and Jim'll be with me, we'll come over for an hour or so.'

The tea party was nothing special, money did not stretch to anything special, but between them Eveline and Connie found her a small cheap brooch off a market stall in Petticoat Lane which she appreciated though Eveline doubted she'd ever wear it.

The afternoon proved a success except in one small thing. Halfway through it, Eveline became aware of Jim eyeing her friend a little too much. Oddly she felt a twinge of something like jealousy run through her. But it couldn't be. She liked him but not like that. She realised then that if anything were to develop between Connie and someone else, she could be left on her own. If Connie ever did remarry, would she want Eveline hanging on? And after all, Connie was a widow – she could take up with someone else quite easily, she was extremely pretty, spoke so nicely. She could have her pick.

Yes, it was jealousy, not of Jim, but Connie, and the fact that it could promise to take the pressure off herself didn't seem as comforting as it might. If Connie and Jim were to marry, Connie's money worries would be over. She would never again know the wealth she had once been used to, but she'd be comfortably off, with a handsome husband, a decent income and a nice little flat. However, this was all speculation.

After Jim and his mother had departed, Eveline realised with a jolt that in fact it wasn't all speculation.

'Jim Adams asked me if I would like to go to the cinema with him,' Connie said when they had left. There was a glow to her cheeks.

'Are you going?' Eveline asked, hearing the coldness in her own voice.

Connie looked doubtful. 'There's Rebecca. I can't take her along.'

'I can look after her,' Eveline heard herself say, almost too quickly. 'We live here together in the same flat, why should I not have her for you?'

Why had she offered so readily? She didn't know. All she knew was that if Connie found happiness again, she must be pleased for her. If only she could find happiness herself. That would only be if ... no, when Albert came walking through that door. The thought made her eyes sting and she had to turn quickly away from Connie to busy herself clearing up the remnants of the little birthday tea.

So much for trying to make ends meet! Eveline stared at the little brooch on the lapel of Connie's jacket.

She'd sold almost all the jewellery she once had and Eveline knew the couple of bits she had left. This wasn't one of them.

'Where did you get that from?' she asked suspiciously.

Connie smiled and glanced down at it, sighing. 'To think my jewellery was once gold, silver, real gems, real pearls. This is just something I found on a stall in the Bethnal Green Road. It reminded me of a brooch I once had and I couldn't resist it.'

Eveline's temper flared suddenly. 'You couldn't

resist it! Anyone would think we was rolling in money.'

Connie looked peeved. 'It was cheap, just a few pence.'

'A few pence on a rubbishy bit of jewellery we can't eat, pay the rent with or burn to keep us warm next winter. Connie, have you gone off your rocker or something?'

She knew why she was being so unreasonably sharp. They were starting to rub on each other's nerves even after this short time sharing the one flat, virtually treading on each other's toes. The tiniest squabble between their daughters had it erupting into something far more serious between their mothers. In their own separate flats it wouldn't have mattered if Connie splashed out on some cheap brooch – her money, her lookout. But pooling two pensions to make money go further, each felt in control of both.

'How can we manage if you start buying stuff like that?'

But it wasn't just that. It was this uncertainty about Connie seeing more of Jim. She'd seen him three times in a week since he'd come to tea and very soon Eveline could see only a bleak road for herself.

It was Connie's turn to be angry. Her hazel eyes flared. 'Threepence, that's all it was, the cost of a loaf and a bit of marg!'

'A loaf and a bit of marg, as you casually put it, Connie, would help to see us through a few days.'

She knew she was being heavy-handed. They weren't starving, just needing to eke out what they had on cheaper bits of meat, less expensive

468

provisions and vegetables. They could fill up with plenty of bread and jam – but not if Connie started throwing away money on herself.

'What about when next winter comes? We need enough to buy coal, and that's already gone up in price. We must keep warm.'

Connie compressed her lips. 'For God's sake, Eveline, let's get spring and summer over first.'

'All right, but the cost of everything else is going up too. The time will come when we won't be able to cope, even sharing this place. Why don't you go off and marry Jim Adams, then you can buy whatever you like.'

She didn't know why she said it. Connie was staring at her. When she spoke her voice was low and deliberate. 'That could even happen.'

It was Eveline's turn to stare as Connie went on. 'He and I have been talking along those lines.'

'It's a bit quick, isn't it?'

'He asked if he and I can start thinking of going steady. He too said it might sound a little quick, given we've only just begun seeing each other. But, yes, it does point to a serious union.'

'Marriage,' Eveline said slowly.

'I think so.'

'But what about me?' It came out as a wail. Connie caught her lip between her teeth, almost like an apology.

'Look, Eveline, nothing is settled. We've a long time to go before anything like that happens.' She glanced at the clock, the action heavy with guilt. 'The girls will be home for lunch soon. Let's forget it. I'm sorry about the brooch. I'll make it up to you, Eveline.'

'It doesn't matter,' Eveline said, deflated, and set about laying the table ready for the children to eat the cheese on toast she planned to give them.

Connie began to help, quiet and subdued. Eventually she said, her tone low, 'If you're worried that I'd leave you to cope alone, I'd never let you go short or be on your own. I haven't forgotten how you stood by me when I needed help most and I don't intend to let you down now. If ever Jim and I marry, which will be a long time yet, I know he'll be only too happy for you to come and live with us.'

Eveline felt her back go up. For a while she didn't speak, fearing to sound abrupt.

'I shall be fine,' she said finally, managing not to sound as bleak as she felt. 'I learned a long time ago to cope on my own. I proved to myself then that I could stand on my own two feet and I can do so again.' She was even making her voice sound lively now.

'In fact I think I might take up with the women trying to get the government to bring the age for women's franchise down to twenty-one. I know that the Pankhursts have turned to other things now and we won't ever see the great figureheads we knew, but our cause is the same as ever it was, and besides, I need something to do.'

She knew too that she would eventually have to accept the fact that Albert wasn't coming home, that she needed no man to help her along her future path, but she said nothing of that to Connie.

Chapter Thirty-two

Connie's face was bent over the letter that had arrived addressed to her.

'It's from the nursing home,' she said almost speaking to herself. 'They say my mother is very ill.'

Eveline glanced up from making sure her daughter was ready for school, her hair combed, a clean hankie in her pocket, her woollen stockings pulled up without wrinkles.

'They say she caught a chill and it's turned to pneumonia,' Connie went on. 'They say it's because her whole body is failing.'

She didn't seem all that put out. She shed no tears, nor did she crumple the letter between anguished fingers. Her tone was level, un-emotional. Eveline felt her heart go cold that so much hostility could exist between her and her mother. Connie, who'd always been warm-hearted, had changed a lot this past year, in small things such as trying to keep up with changing fashions. With little money to spare, she'd cut her own hair even shorter, shortened the hemlines of her skirts another inch to keep up with changing styles. Watching her stitching away, Eveline felt sorry for the girl who would once have merely gone out and bought a completely new outfit any time she fancied.

Kissing their daughters off to school, Eveline

asked hopefully, 'Will you be going to see your mother then?' A day or two here on her own would be heaven.

'I'll have to,' Connie answered. She turned beseeching eyes towards Eveline. 'I don't want to take Rebecca with me, not to a sickbed. Would you mind looking after her while I'm away? It'll only be for the day.'

It was going to be a rush for her, and expensive.

'Of course I'll look after her,' she said readily and saw Connie smile her thanks.

Connie sat at her mother's bedside, looking down at the face she had once so loved, that had once been the young and gentle visage of a vulnerable woman, subservient to her husband, hanging on his every command as if he were a demi-god. It made Connie think, sitting there looking at the ravaged features that showed no recognition of her at all now. It had been her father who had turned her mother from her. He had forbidden her to speak her daughter's name until in the end she had believed it was she who had decided to cast her daughter from her. And now she'd become witless, calling Connie Verity, even now not speaking her name as she tossed in delirium, shallowly panting away her last breath.

She died at seven o'clock in the evening, Connie beside her holding her thin, lined hand, though she quite unaware of it. Tears streamed silently down Connie's face as a nurse gently helped her to her feet and guided her from the still body with its small face looking as though she was sleeping quite peacefully.

Someone gave her a cup of tea, and asked if there was anything she wanted. When she shook her head they withdrew to leave her to grieve in private. Sitting in the small bare room, she fished into her bag and drew out a box of matches and a packet of ten cigarettes that she'd bought on the way here; Eveline was not around to reprimand her for squandering a hard-earned couple of pence. She'd smoked two already and found them calming. Now she lit up and drew in a deep breath of the fragrant smoke. This time it didn't make her choke and she felt calm drift over her.

A middle-aged nurse appeared quietly at the door and smiled to see a young woman with a cigarette. Lots of women smoked these days, mostly the better-off sort, using a cigarette as an elegant addition to their appearance. She coughed politely and saw the young woman give a guilty start. True, smoking was not allowed, but this woman had lost her mother. One must stretch the rules a little.

'I have had your mother's belongings put together if you feel up to collecting them,' she said. 'But take your time. There is no hurry.'

With that she went away, leaving Connie to stare at the door she had gently closed behind her.

In her mother's home, Connie sat at the highly polished dining-room table with the family solicitor Mr Goddard Braithwaite sitting opposite her, the surface in front of him spread with papers.

'I trust you will be content to continue with my services following your mother's sad demise,' he said, almost imperiously. 'I have been your father's solicitor for as long as I can remember. I trust you see no reason to change?'

Connie shook her head, wishing he'd get on with his business. Her father had left everything to her mother but she'd never made a will.

'I urged her so many times to do so, but one cannot move a woman grown unbelievably stubborn in her bereavement. It would have made everything so much simpler, but she persisted in maintaining that as she only had one daughter left, everything would go to her, your sister Verity.'

He ignored the wince his client gave. 'I could make no headway in reminding her that she had another daughter. She refused to listen. I really am very, very sorry.'

Connie found her voice. 'No need. I knew my mother well enough.'

'Quite,' said Goddard Braithwaite. 'She was a stubborn woman. Most surprising as she followed your father in every way, though I suppose in that alone she demonstrated an inner strength one might even venture to say.'

'May we get on with it?' Connie reminded him stiffly. She wanted to have done with all this, learn that her mother had most likely given every last penny and stick of furniture to charity, or the nursing home, or even a casual acquaintance, and that Mr Braithwaite was probably trying to let her down as lightly as he could in telling her that she was as much a pauper as ever.

'Quite,' he said again, bending his head to the papers before him and shuffling through them. 'Well, I have to tell you that due to your mother omitting to make a will of any sort, all that she owned, money, all her property and her considerable savings, as well as a good deal of stocks and shares that had been your father's and which came to her on his death and to this day have remained unsurrendered, will pass to her only surviving kin.' He looked up sharply. 'That is you, my dear Mrs Towers.'

For a moment Connie stared at him, unable to speak.

'You are a wealthy woman,' he enlarged, realising that she hadn't quite taken in what he was saying. 'You have property and can take over as soon as the necessary legal details have been finalised.'

Concluding business, he stood up, tidying and stacking documents and putting them into his case. Connie stood up too as he came to extend his hand in farewell. 'If there is anything else you want to know or are unsure about, I am here to help you. As I said, I hope you will continue to honour my firm with your business.'

'I will,' Connie replied, still dazed as she saw him to the door.

'Goodbye, Mrs Towers, and might I once more add my condolences on the death of your mother as well as congratulations on your inheritance.'

Connie inclined her head and stood watching as he got into his car, tapping his chauffeur on the shoulder to drive off. He didn't look back and Connie went back inside the house that was now hers, complete with every last penny her parents had owned.

This beautiful warm April morning Eveline and Connie were going up to the West End together. Connie was hardly able to wait to buy some expensive clothes on the strength of her inheritance, the solicitors having generously advanced her a tidy sum, knowing they'd reap it all back and more.

'I want to look nice when Jim calls for me this evening,' she said excitedly as they made their way by taxi, no expense spared. 'I'm glad he asked me to marry him when he thought me as poor as a church mouse. He's saying he hopes I don't think he is after my money. I told him not to be so ridiculous.' She laughed, clutching at Eveline's arm. 'I can hardly believe that you and I, having been friends for so long, are now going to be sisters-in-law.'

Eveline smiled, said she was happy for them and meant it, but it was hard trying to ignore the heavy weight inside her while Connie, happy as a lark, dragged her from the taxi as they alighted outside Harrods, her first port of call on this shopping trip.

'You try something on too,' she urged as they stood in the splendid dress department surveying the gorgeous new styles draped upon elegant mannequins. 'Have whatever you want. Don't look at the price. I'll pay.'

Even as she obliged, Eveline's heart wasn't in it. In the first place she didn't want to have a dress or anything else bought for her.

In the second place, though they would be related through marriage before long, she had visions of them drifting further and further from the close friendship they'd known. Married to Jim, Connie would go off with her new wealth, probably moving out to her old family home. Connie would live a charmed life from now on while she would spend hers having eventually to face the fact that her own husband would never ever come home.

Once, she and Connie had been united in a common aim and later by the loss of their menfolk. Now they'd begin to see less and less of each other except for the odd visit, the previous Christmas spent with Jim's mother. It proved the old adage – friends usually stick together, families often drift apart.

'I don't want a dress,' she said trying not to sound petulant.

'Oh, you must! I shall feel so guilty if you don't. What about that one there?'

Despite herself the outfit had already caught Eveline's eye though she had tried not to be drawn by it. Draped on a graceful mannequin, it was in a soft beige with flowing lines, the skirt short enough to reveal nearly half the calf; the dress also featured a deep 'V' neckline and a loose waist caught by a pretty brown belt. A flowing, full-length jacket of the same colour as the belt completed the outfit, which was topped by a neat, deep-crowned hat that also matched the belt. Feeling that she shouldn't, Eveline approached and fingered the price tag. The cost made her gasp.

'Heavens, Connie! I can't take that.' For a moment the thought of Connie miles away, with only the occasional, ever more infrequent visit, fled. Seconds later realisation returned that whether Connie visited or not, she'd be alone, with Helena, and no man in her life, no husband for her or father for her daughter.

'I don't want it!' she burst out resolutely, almost savagely.

In the end, if only to take the bewildered look off Connie's face, she was forced to relent. So much for resolution! But it hadn't made her feel any easier in her heart.

Nor did she feel any easier when in the taxi Connie started to talk about sharing a portion of her inheritance with her, refusing to listen to Eveline's profound protests as her voice became quite emotional.

'Did you really believe that after all we've been through together that I'd leave you to struggle along on nothing? After what you did for me when I was desperate? You took me in, Eveline, and gave me a place to live, a new life, new hope when my parents turned me out like a–'

She had broken off, and the rest of the way was spent in silence. The only thing she said during that time was, 'I mean what I say, Eveline.' Then, as if embarrassed, 'I hope we're home in time for the girls to come out of school.'

As the taxicab reached their end of Bethnal Green Road, abuzz with the usual Saturday-afternoon market stalls and jostle of shoppers, Connie, now recovered, leaped up from her seat to stare out of the window.

'Look! There are some of those campaigners for the women's age limit for voting to be lowered. The demand is for it to be twenty-one.'

Eveline could see a line of eight women, keeping to the kerb except to skirt an ex-serviceman begging for his livelihood from a wheeled board; both his legs were missing.

Two of the women held placards proclaiming VOTES FOR WOMEN OF 21. Two other placards said, ON THE SAME TERMS AS MEN.

'Stop, please, driver!' Connie cried to the cabbie. 'We need to get out a moment. Can we leave our packages here?'

A grunt from the man indicated that he would and that they could.

'Not too long,' he growled. 'I got other fares ter pick up.'

'We'll just be a tick, I'll give you extra,' she said, already out of the cab. Eveline was obliged to follow as she ran over to the approaching line. The leader, a woman of about twenty-seven wearing thick lensed glasses, came to a temporary halt.

'We've a new organisation now,' she replied to Connie's questions. 'The old WSPU is dead but we're members of the newly formed NUSEC. The National Union of Societies for Equal Citizenship.'

Eveline thought of the day she'd fallen into step beside Connie. Such a long time ago it seemed. Soon Connie would marry and go away.

'We're in company with the Six Point League,' continued the woman. 'Under Lady Rhondda. Called the Six Point League because it fights for six things – equal guardianship, widow's pensions, equal moral standards, divorce law reform, equal pay, and provision for birth control information for married women, as well as for

479

the right to vote at twenty-one. Many of us feel let down by this enfranchisement being only for women thirty and over. But there are still too few of us ready to fight on.'

'That's how it started,' Connie said, busily negotiating Friday morning shoppers who were getting in her way as she walked alongside the woman. 'Over fifty years ago, I believe, with just a few women, and now we have one in Parliament, Nancy Astor, our first woman to sit in the House of Commons. My friend and I were once suffragettes,' she added with pride.

'Then maybe you might like to come along to one of our meetings in Holborn.'

Connie tilted her head. 'It may be difficult. We're widows. My friend's daughter is nine, nearly ten, and mine will not be ten until September.'

The woman laughed. 'Bring them with you. Young ladies soon grow up ready to be recruited.'

A sudden memory of when young girls of ten in white dresses walked beside their mothers in the great rallies of the past was interrupted by the cab driver calling impatiently, 'You ladies getting back in or what?'

Connie called back, 'We're coming, driver.'

In the taxi completing the last of their ride, Eveline said, 'I don't see it's really worth you joining them. Before long you'll be married and leaving here, you and Jim, to live in that house you inherited. I'll be on my own.'

She saw Connie frown. 'Is that what you think? Oh, Eveline, we'll soon be related and we'll always be friends.'

Eveline fell silent. Connie might have said more,

but the taxi was already pulling up outside their destination. She went on ahead while Connie paid the fare, no doubt with a sizeable tip. Her inheritance would soon return her to her former extravagant life, where money was no object.

She said she intended to share some of that inheritance with her. To Eveline it felt like accepting a handout even though Connie was insisting. But it wasn't money she wanted. It was Albert. If he were here she'd want nothing more no matter how poor they were.

Even now after all this time she clung to the possibility of his being found. Even though she knew by now that it was futile, it was all she had to cling to for the rest of her life. Almost defiantly she come to a decision. She would told up Connie's offer. She had to survive, and money meant survival even if everything else was lent.

Mounting the stone stairs to their flat, she thought she had never felt so lonely as she did at this moment.

On opening the door she saw the envelope lying face up on the mat. Her heart seemed to stop as she read the bold, black printed initials across the top. OHMS. It was addressed to her. Albert! It had to be news of Albert. Feverishly she picked it up and tore open the flap, fingers trembling as she unfolded the single sheet, her eyes refusing to focus on its contents for a moment or two. When they did her whole body went as cold as ice.

As Connie reached her, Eveline swung round on her as if expecting a blow. Connie must have seen her expression for she instantly dropped the parcels she'd been carrying into the tiny hallway and gently but firmly took the page from the palsied fingers, guiding her into the living room.

'Sit down, Eveline,' she said quietly. 'Can I read it?'

'He's dead.' It was all Eveline could say, her voice tiny. 'Albert's dead.' She stared sightlessly into space for a moment or two then with a spasmodic gesture caught hold of Connie's hand. 'Oh, Connie...'

All she knew was darkness as Connie put her arms about her and held her close, stifling her, so that the breath seemed to be being squeezed from her limp body while she fought with the gulping sobs that were tearing themselves from her.

Chapter Thirty-three

For two days she lay in bed. Nothing Connie could do would get her up. This was not at all the Eveline she once knew. Normally a fighter, if she did sometimes fall a little by the wayside, it was never long before she'd bound up ready to challenge whatever had got her down. Left to take charge of Helena, Connie took her into her own room to share Rebecca's bed, got her up for school in the mornings, made her breakfast and saw her off. She told her that her mother was merely a little under the weather and would be well again soon.

'She hasn't got flu again, has she?' Helena asked anxiously, remembering how ill she had been and how it had killed so many.

Connie forced a smile as she buttered the breakfast toast that second day.

'No, that's gone. It won't come back again. She's a little rundown, that's all. She'll be up in a day or two.'

But Helena wasn't satisfied. 'She won't die, will she?'

'Good Lord, no!' replied Connie, shocked.

'My father died though. Mum keeps saying he'll come home one day. But I think that's just wishful thinking.'

She sounded suddenly so wise that Connie wanted to cry for her. 'She's not going to die. She simply needs to be left alone for a while, so you won't go in there, worrying her, will you?'

'Of course not,' Helena said haughtily, her old self again. 'I've got some sense!' she added, sounding like someone twice her age.

So it was left for another day. After the girls had gone off to school on the third morning, Connie went in with a small bowl of porridge. For the most part every item of food she had tried to tempt Eveline with had had to be removed, barely touched.

'You've got to eat something sometime,' she said as Eveline turned her head away at the sight of the food. 'For Helena's sake. She is beginning to get worried and ask questions.'

That stirred her enough to half turn her head towards Connie. 'You mustn't tell her about her father.'

'She already believes him dead,' Connie said calmly, knowing that the very word would cause Eveline to cringe. It did, visibly, but she continued.

'She said yesterday that you were deluding yourself in thinking her father was coming home, so there is nothing to explain to her. Eveline, you must start pulling yourself together. This is not doing you or Helena any good.'

It was hard to say, cruel perhaps, but true. To her relief Eveline nodded. 'I'll try,' she said. She was still the strong-minded Eveline Connie had always known. She would be all right.

Connie was tidying the kitchen, her ear attuned to sounds of Eveline getting up, when the knock came at the door. She smiled to herself. The rent man was early this morning.

Laying aside the damp dishcloth, she went to answer it. Seconds later she was in Eveline's bedroom. Eveline was already dressed, sitting on the edge of her bed, trying to summon up the will to come out of the room.

'There's a young man at the door, asking for you,' Connie said in a strange voice. 'He says he has something urgent to tell you. I asked him in. He's in the living room. Eveline...'

She broke off, unable to bring herself to say any more. Eveline was looking at her, her hitherto dull expression taking on a questioning aspect.

'What does he want? Did he say who he was?'

Why had Connie asked him in? He could be anybody. She was about to tell her to order the man, whoever he was and whatever he wanted, to leave and stop bothering people. But the look on Connie's face stopped her.

'I think you should see him, Eveline.'

Connie went to the door to stand waiting for her, so Eveline got up with a deep sigh and followed her.

At their entrance the man stood up from the settee where he had been sitting, trilby hat in hand. Tall and slim, he wore a mackintosh against the morning rain, open to reveal a good-quality lounge suit. He was fair, grey-eyed and quite handsome but haggard, a man who'd been through a great deal and seen things that would remain with him for the rest of his life. But what did he want here? By the look on Connie's face, he must have told her what this was all about. Why hadn't she said what it was? Why so secretive?

'Yes,' she said, somewhat abruptly.

'You are Mrs Eveline Adams, your husband is Albert Adams?'

'Yes,' she said again, her heart beginning to thump at the mention of Albert's name.

'I think you should sit down, Mrs Adams.'

What now? What more terrible news? 'Who are you?' she demanded.

'Please, sit down.'

What strength she had summoned up fled and she sank down on the armchair opposite him. With Connie coming to stand supportively beside her the man began.

'I'm Captain Fairbrother, taken prisoner in Turkey in nineteen eighteen interned in a Turkish prison camp in Aleppo. When Turkey surrendered to Arabian troops in October of that year, I was in a Turkish hospital where I met your husband.'

Eveline's sharp intake of breath almost choked her, but the man took little notice as he continued.

'Conditions there, if you'll forgive me, were pretty ghastly...'

'You saw my husband?' Eveline broke in, her heart pounding and her head beginning to reel. But before she could ask whether Albert was dead or still alive, he hurried on.

'In the hospital, if you could call it that, we were crammed in together with Turkish wounded. We'd lost our uniforms, couldn't speak the language and when the hospital became threatened by Arab forces it was abandoned by the fleeing Turkish doctors and staff. Conditions had become appalling by the time they arrived. None of them seemed able to speak English, and they

486

assumed we too were Turkish.'

'What about my husband?' Eveline burst out, feeling Connie's hand touch her shoulder. 'You said you saw him.'

'Yes. Your husband had sustained a throat wound and was unable to talk clearly. He was also badly wounded in the right foot. It had apparently gone untreated in the prison camp. The doctors were an incompetent lot and didn't attend to him properly. Gangrene set in and they amputated the foot but he had a blood infection. He was delirious for most of the time.'

So Albert had died of his wounds. Eveline bit her lips to control the tears threatening to engulf her. She couldn't break down in front of this stranger. In front of Connie, yes, but not this man.

'What are you trying to tell me?' she blurted, suddenly angered. She had already been informed that Albert was killed, so why did this man want to come and rub salt into the wound? 'If you've come to tell me my husband's dead, I've already been informed.'

'That's why I'm here. I came as soon as I could to tell you that the last time I saw him, he was alive. I got your husband out of that hospital when there was talk of killing the patients. I found an abandoned truck and got him into it and tried to make for the British lines I hoped would be to the west. We ran out of petrol and I carried him on my back as far as I could. We ended up in some Turkish village where they fed us and looked after us and for weeks he drifted in and out of consciousness and delirium. I too was in a rather sorry state, suffering from dysentery, virtually a bag of bones, so I could go nowhere either. There was no way to get us to a British unit. He was so ill that I dared not try with him. Finally I recovered enough to leave so that I could get in touch with our allies and let them know where I'd left him. That was when I learned that the war was over.'

'And he was alive when you left him?' Connie questioned, Eveline too choked by tears to speak.

He nodded. 'Would you ladies mind if I were to smoke? This has been rather an ordeal for me.'

'Of course,' Connie said boldly. 'Would you mind if I had one?'

He offered the packet and, flicking his lighter, held the flame to her cigarette before lighting his own. Eveline found her voice.

'How can you both be so casual? Is my Albert still alive or not?'

'Yes,' Fairbrother replied slowly. 'His throat had healed enough for him to talk and tell me his name before I left. But by the time I reached help I was all in and couldn't think of the name of the village though I knew the general direction I'd taken. I was hospitalised and left my home address with the commanding officer with a promise to inform me as soon as, and if, your husband was found. Yesterday I received a telephone call to say that he had been found and was able to give his name, rank and serial number, though by then I guessed you had probably already been informed that he must be presumed dead. I came straight here to tell you what I knew. I was too late?'

'She was notified two days ago,' Connie told him.

At those words, something snapped inside Eveline. She bent forward, hands covering her face, and broke down in near hysterics, Connie holding her tight until the weeping eventually subsided enough for her to sit up.

She dimly remembered Fairbrother saying he'd been told that Albert was in an Istanbul hospital, from which he would be taken by hospital ship to Gibraltar to rest there, as was usual, prior to sailing through the possibly rough Bay of Biscay on his way home to England. All of this could take a month or two yet, and she would eventually be told he was alive, but he, Fairbrother, hadn't wanted her to go through the hell of days not knowing until then. She vaguely remembered him taking his leave, saying that he wished her well. She remembered nodding her thanks, her mind only on Albert. Alive, but what if he had a relapse before they could get him home?

She looked up suddenly to find Connie on her own, making a pot of tea.

'I've got to go to him!' Her raised voice so startled Connie that she nearly spilled the boiling water she was pouring into the teapot.

'I've got to go to him,' she repeated. 'I need to be with him.'

Connie put the kettle back on the hob. 'How can you think of sailing all that way alone? He'll be home soon. Then you can be with him.'

'I can't wait that long. That captain said he was still very ill. How must he be feeling? A prison camp and then some vile hospital, his foot amputated, I dread to think what he must be going through. He's all alone out there. We've been parted for so long and I mean to go and be with him there, help him feel better, help him come back home. I have to go, and I intend to.'

'Eveline, dear.' Connie's voice seemed to float towards her. 'You are not making sense. You are too upset by what you've heard to think straight.'

She glared up at Connie. 'I know what I have to do. You'll look after Helena for me while I'm gone?'

'Don't be silly, Eveline. It's a sea voyage. Everyone says the Bay of Biscay can be treacherous. You could be so seasick. You can't put yourself through that. Wait for him to come home.'

Eveline leapt up. 'I can't do that. I know he needs me. If I'm with him he'll get well quicker. I have to be there. You of all people should know how I feel. We've been close friends, you and me, and we both know what it's like to have our husbands taken from us. You've a new husband to look forward to. I thought I had no one. But now mine is alive. He'll be coming home and I'm going out there to make sure he gets my help to do just that.'

Connie looked at her long and hard, further argument on the edge of her tongue. But then she closed her mouth and nodded sombrely.

'You have to do what you feel is right,' she said in a low voice. 'But it is such a long way for a woman to go.'

'A woman?' Eveline echoed. 'Women have been through worse. There were nurses who went out to the front line itself to find and take care of the wounded. There were women volunteers driving ambulances through all that shellfire to get the

490

stricken to hospital tents. There were women who learned to drive buses and, like you and me, who dealt with heavy machinery and handled dangerous explosives. Some lost their lives. Before the war we were suffragettes. I went to prison and defied those who tried to force-feed me. And my ordeal wasn't half that of some. We marched and we fought for the right for women like me to have a say in what we do. And no one can stop me going off to be with my husband to help keep his spirits up and bring him back home. Once I have him home I shall spend every moment of my time nursing him back to health. With what you've offered to do for me he can set up in business. We will begin to live again.'

She finally paused, her tirade exhausted while Connie stood silent, at last convinced that nothing was going to shake her friend from her purpose.

'I'll have Helena while you're away,' she said slowly. 'I'll explain to her what her mother is doing and that she is going to get her daddy back.'

Eveline lifted her chin, tears already drying. 'I must write immediately to say I'll be there waiting for him.'

She looked searchingly at Connie. 'I could never have done this but for your help, insisting on giving me a portion of what you'll inherit. I'm so deeply grateful, Connie.'

It was Connie's turn to look Eveline in the eye. 'How could you ever have thought I wouldn't after all we've been through together? You'd have done the same for me.'

Eveline dropped her gaze and gave a small laugh. 'It's still all due to you that I can afford to do this, and I'm grateful.' Again she lifted her chin. 'I'll have to start packing straight away. I don't want to get to Gibraltar to find I've missed him and he's already on his way home. Talk about ships that pass!' She gave another laugh. 'That mustn't happen, must it?' She suddenly looked so confident and resolute that to Connie it was like seeing a different woman from a few minutes ago and she made towards her, arms outstretched.

Eveline met her halfway, the two standing in the centre of the tiny kitchen in a tight embrace; friends, one soon to be married, one soon to be reunited with the man she'd thought she had lost.

Finally breaking away, Connie glanced at the clock on the wall. 'Good Lord! The girls will be home from school soon, looking for something to eat. We'd better get started on their lunch.'

'Yes, we'd better,' agreed Eveline, straightening her rumpled skirt and searching for an apron to wear.

There was a lot to do – a lot of things to do.

Author's Note

This novel is set against the backdrop of what I've always considered a fascinating period in British History. Many readers will be familiar with the history of the suffragette movement in the UK and may realise I've taken certain liberties with the timing of events. Forgive me, but I wanted to tell Connie and Eveline's story my way – two ordinary girls who find themselves in extraordinary times.

The publishers hope that this book has given you enjoyable reading. Large Print Books are especially designed to be as easy to see and hold as possible. If you wish a complete list of our books please ask at your local library or write directly to:

Magna Large Print Books
Magna House, Long Preston,
Skipton, North Yorkshire.
BD23 4ND

This Large Print Book for the partially sighted, who cannot read normal print, is published under the auspices of

THE ULVERSCROFT FOUNDATION

THE ULVERSCROFT FOUNDATION

... we hope that you have enjoyed this Large Print Book. Please think for a moment about those people who have worse eyesight problems than you ... and are unable to even read or enjoy Large Print, without great difficulty.

You can help them by sending a donation, large or small to:

**The Ulverscroft Foundation,
1, The Green, Bradgate Road,
Anstey, Leicestershire, LE7 7FU,
England.**
or request a copy of our brochure for more details.

The Foundation will use all your help to assist those people who are handicapped by various sight problems and need special attention.

Thank you very much for your help.